Drama Queen

Susan Conley

D1351048

little
black
dress

Copyright © 2008 Susan Conley

The right of Susan Conley to be identified as the Author of
the Work has been asserted by her in accordance with the
Copyright, Designs and Patents Act 1988.

First published in 2008
by LITTLE BLACK DRESS
An imprint of HEADLINE PUBLISHING GROUP

A LITTLE BLACK DRESS paperback

1

Apart from any use permitted under UK copyright law, this publication
may only be reproduced, stored, or transmitted, in any form, or by any
means, with prior permission in writing of the publishers or, in the case
of reprographic production, in accordance with the terms of licences
issued by the Copyright Licensing Agency.

All characters in this publication are fictitious and any resemblance
to real persons, living or dead, is purely coincidental.

ISBN 978 0 7553 4572 4

Typeset in Transit511BT by Avon DataSet Ltd,
Bidford-on-Avon, Warwickshire

Printed and bound in Great Britain by Clays Ltd, St Ives plc

Headline's policy is to use papers that are natural, renewable and
recyclable products and made from wood grown in sustainable forests.
The logging and manufacturing processes are expected to conform to the
environmental regulations of the country of origin.

HEADLINE PUBLISHING GROUP
An Hachette Livre UK Company
338 Euston Road
London NW1 3BH

www.littleblackdressbooks.com
www.headline.co.uk
www.hachettelivre.co.uk

For Fin

LONDON BOROUGH OF NEWHAM	
Bertrams	25/02/2009
	£4.99
NHGS	

Acknowledgements

Many thanks to Claire Baldwin for making this potentially overwhelming process, er, extremely whelming and enjoyable, and to Catherine Cobain for winnowing me out of the slush pile in the first place. And to friends and family, all of whom reacted to news of this book with such pleasure, and peppered me with endless questions about it (which is exactly the right thing to do, by the way): here it is, and I am grateful to you all.

For all that Jane was surrounded by the cream of television's crop, there was no one more important than Courtney Cox Arquette and the envelope which she held, oh so casually, between her well-manicured fingers. All the glittering personae, the relentless buzz of gossip and tattle, the murmurs of deals being made and broken across rows of beautifully groomed 'players' – all despite the 'distraction' from onstage – meant nothing compared to the sound of her own forcibly measured breathing, the thump of her heart against her sternum, the dampness of Darren's palm in hers. Nothing. Nothing but that little white rectangle and the information contained in its pristine folds. Jane sat still and straight, the way she'd practised for the last four months, and lifted her chin another quarter of an inch. Lauren Bacall (sitting three places to Jane's right) had nothing on her and, swathed as she was in Narciso Rodriguez, Jane was as ready as she'd ever be, as ready as—

The announcement had her rising elegantly to her feet, but then a momentary flash of horror – have they actually called my name or someone else's? I think they've called mine – and then the podium, and her voice, her own voice ringing out, confident, cool, echoing in her ears as she delivers her witty and perfectly timed speech, Courtney beaming at her elbow, the faces blurring, the stage lights shining directly into her eyes, the endless flash of the bulbs of the paparazzi as she does what she's been doing in the shower with a bottle of shampoo: she raises it aloft, the Emmy, the Golden One, raises it up on high and smiles gracefully and triumphantly; and then backstage, in the journalists' scrum, standing serenely in close range of the relentlessly popping flashes, regally turning her head this way and that as the photographers and hacks demand her attention by calling out her name: 'Jane!' 'Jane!' 'Jane!' 'Jane!'—

'Jane!' Darren screeched. The Greene Street Bar was crowded and noisy, but it certainly wasn't *that* noisy. He meaningfully arched his eyebrows at Miranda, who slid further down into her seat, out of boredom and the kind of discomfort that only Manhattan can inspire when you're wearing the wrong clothes. She pulled churlishly at the neck of her pullover and recrossed her legs, her cropped trousers riding up a little further than was de rigueur. She scowled around the fashionable SoHo bar, and wished for Wicklow, and Niall.

Miranda's gaze drifted out of the bar's large plate-glass window on to the Manhattan evening, and a small smile replaced the scowl. It had been . . . she surreptitiously counted on her fingers . . . ten months, two weeks, and four days since she'd taken the plunge, in more ways than one.

Right, she thought to herself: she and Niall had known each other through friends, so he wasn't a complete stranger. And sure, they *had* been dating, here in New York, before she'd taken the chance to emigrate. But to have just moved in with him, practically fresh off the plane . . . she shrugged to herself, and wanted to giggle. Not really her style, and Dar and Jane had certainly been shocked, but holistically minded Miranda trusted in fate. Since they'd been literally heading in the same direction, she to work on a big photography contract and Niall moving home from Brooklyn to take up a big visual arts gig . . . well, that was good enough for her.

So, she'd had a professional reason to go to Ireland – but did she have good enough personal reasons to stay?

She sighed, and absentmindedly picked up the outrageously priced cocktail she'd been sipping halfheartedly. What she'd give for a pint of Guinness – a proper pint, which she knew she couldn't really get in New York (never mind the marketing), much less in this infuriatingly posh little place.

Ten months, two weeks and four days without the buzz of Manhattan, without the convenience of a Yellow Cab a mere raised arm away, and without her two best friends from college, both of whom she was sitting with at the moment, and both of whom were engaged in that annoying head-swivelling thing, that up-and-coming 'dahling-let's-have-lunch' types did to ensure that they were seeing in addition to being seen. It was like having drinks with two closed-circuit television cameras.

Sitting with his back to the door was Darren, surely the most highly therapised interior designer in the five boroughs. She took him in, from the top of his thick blond head (of which the cut and colour was breathtakingly reminiscent of Robert Redford in *The Great Gatsby*) down over his lean, six-feet-two-inch frame clad in very low key, but very designer clothes, to the tips of his lethally pointy Kenneth Coles. Top to bottom, he was the sweetest, most thoughtful, overly solicitous gay male friend a girl could have. He had been a constant in her life since college, he and Jane – and lately, far more so than Jane. He'd not only been over to see her twice in the past ten months, two weeks, etc. etc., but over the length of her stay in the last six days had tirelessly helped her find temporary storage for all the stuff she wanted to keep, and had ruthlessly pushed her into selling the stuff that she didn't. She was now the proud owner of a pocketful of cash, and there was definitely enough to splurge on a new lens for herself and a nice big gift token from Pearl Paint for Niall.

And then there was Jane. Miranda's eyes narrowed as she assessed the woman sitting opposite. In contrast to Darren's fairness, Jane was olive-skinned, with jet-black hair and piercing green eyes. Her stunning cheekbones lent sophistication to her heart-shaped face, and were framed by a timeless bob. Her gift of genetic slenderness was enhanced, Miranda knew, by an unflagging four-times-a-week gym habit. This evening's outfit was designer, but unlike Darren, Jane liked the general public to be aware of who she was wearing. Tonight, it was some punky Italian man-of-the-minute, but Miranda couldn't be sure. Who knew, she shrugged. Who cared?

What she did care about, in her heart of hearts, was that Jane had been a totally crap friend for the past ten months, etc. She'd always figured that success would inevitably go to Jane's head, and upon winning the Emmy last year, what little contact the two women had had – chatty, lengthy, descriptive emails from Miranda reciprocated by a terse three-line reply from Jane – had dribbled off into nothing. Even during her short stay, Jane was not returning phone calls or trying very hard to meet up.

On top of it all, Darren was in a state about Jane, over God knew what, and wouldn't stop talking about it. Miranda slouched even further down into the leather club chair. Here she was, in this snooty little bar, supposedly to meet her friends for a quiet drink so they could catch up with each other before Miranda left for Dublin *the next day* – and it turns out to be some feckin' work thing for WCTV and their cooler-than-thou shaggin' attitudes. She leaned forward to complain, just in time to watch Jane rise and bestow air kisses on some overly made-up actressy-type who was clutching an almost imperceptibly small dog.

'Do you see what I mean?' Darren hissed.

'Dar, I don't know what you're talking about. She seems absolutely the same: thin, well-dressed – although I will say she's even more self-absorbed than ever.' Miranda set her glass down on the impossibly tiny table. 'That drink is shite.'

'Oh, good,' Darren muttered absently, his eyes glued to Jane. 'Let's get another round.' He signalled to the gaunt waitress, who was as spindly as her stilettos, and leaned towards Miranda, grabbing her arm. 'Miranda, I have no one else to turn to. You and I are the only people that really know her. I mean, *look* at her!'

They both turned towards the bar, to which Jane had drifted. There was a great burst of applause as Jane simply tossed her platinum card at the bartender, who caught it deftly and waved it in the air for all to see. Jane tossed her head, her gleaming hair shimmering in the candlelight, and smirked triumphantly as she accepted air kisses from everyone.

'She seems fine, for fuck's sake.' Miranda sat back, annoyed. 'I don't see what you're on about.'

'Didn't you see her before, staring out into space, lost to the world? She's brittle. She's edgy. And there's no reason for it.' He drained his cocktail just as the well-heeled waif came over with fresh drinks. 'She was perfectly fine, totally composed, up to a month before the Emmys. And of *course* she would get a bit stressed before such a momentous occasion. The wardrobe issue alone was exhausting. We had a lovely, if low-level tense time, up until the evening of the awards, and when she won' – his eyes filled with tears, and Miranda regretted, really regretted, that she hadn't been there with them both – 'it was extraordinary. Wonderful.' Darren ran his fingers through his thick blond hair. 'But she didn't relax after that. You know she's not exactly relaxed at the best of times, but now she's über-tense. She's been working fourteen-hour days, Saturdays, Sundays! And she's turned down all sorts of offers, big offers, major network stuff, ABC, CBS, Fox – for no good reason – *and* she's become secretive, not answering her phone; I know that she dumps me, nine times out of ten, when I ring her cell phone! If I didn't know better, I'd say she's become a cokehead! She is utterly not herself!' Darren finished dramatically, sweeping his arm around in the air, almost knocking over Miranda's drink. He looked at her expectantly.

Oh, Jesus. 'Maybe it's not such a bad thing.'

'What are you talking about?'

Christ. 'Maybe she needs to, I don't know, crack up a bit. She's not in therapy, she doesn't do anything to cope with the stress that she's routinely under. As we'd say in Ireland, she's practically disappeared up her own hole. Maybe she needs to fall apart so that she can take the time to put herself back together. Is she seeing anybody?'

'No.'

'Are you sure?'

'I'm sure.' Darren's voice was colder than the vodka in his Martini. 'If anyone knows, it's me. I still care about her.'

Miranda sat forward and took his hand. 'I'm sure you two are as close as ever, but she hasn't been the best of friends to me since I left. She never came to visit, she doesn't answer emails . . . in fairness, she wasn't very supportive of the move in the first place. She was, in fact, ruder than even I could imagine her to be. And I'm not too happy about what happened to tonight's plan, I know Jane talked you into this—'

Darren feared confrontation more than he feared ageing and self-assessed taxation combined. 'Honey, honey, please. OK? Let's just have a nice time on your last night! Just, maybe, try to suss her out a bit, tonight, really casual, over our lovely drinks, you know . . .'

Doo do *do* do doo doo *doo* doo doo . . . saved by the bell! Miranda fished her mobile out of her pocket and smiled apologetically at Darren. 'Let me get this – hallo?'

'Do *doo* do do, *doo* do do do do.' Niall finished singing her tango ringtone.

'Heeey.' Miranda sat back and sighed.

'Howya, gorgeous! Miss me? You in a pub?'

'Yes to the first, and emphatically no to the second. Darren is here with me—'

'Good man—'

'He is, he's very good.' She smiled at Darren, who smiled and turned away, pretending not to listen. 'We're at some crap drinks things for Jane's network.'

'Oh. Her. She who can't even answer a bloody email.' Niall's voice took on an uncharacteristic gruffness – the few times he and Jane had met, while he and Miranda were still in NYC, had been fraught with tension. 'I know she's your college mate, and all, but you're too soft in the heart, Miranda.'

Miranda heard the hiss of the boiled kettle, the tinkle of spoon against mug, and longed for a cuppa with her fella, imagined him looking out over the back garden of his Aunt Sile's cottage.

'I know, I know.' Miranda smirked and looked out over a Manhattan suddenly less alienating and grotesque. Who would have guessed? Living in Ireland and with a handsome lover at that. She was soft in the heart. She sighed – certainly she was, and when it came to him . . .

As Miranda's whole demeanour began to glow, Darren became aware of a feeling, a feeling that was moving up his body, painfully, from his toes, through his knees, through his belly, to lodge like a stone in his heart; a feeling he'd never imagined he would experience in relation to one of his most beloved friends, a feeling that was now roaring through his skull like a runaway train.

He was so jealous of Miranda he could scream.

'– not until shagging July, maybe, or August, which seems a stupid time to bring out a book of photos; they may as well wait until autumn, or Christmas, even!'

'They must have their reasons,' Niall soothed. 'Don't worry about it, you'll get loads of work.'

Miranda scowled at the next batch of transparently thin women slinking their way through the door. 'Things seem a bit thin on the ground for photographers these days. But I was going to convert that wee toilet downstairs—'

He could absolutely screeeeeeeam with it, this jealousy. Now, if Dr Spitz were here he would say: 'How do you feel about that, Darren?' Guilty! I feel so *guilty*! My sweetest, most deserving friend, and I am ready to snatch her bald-headed, listening to this fibre-optic billing and cooing! Then Dr Spitz would say: 'But unless you act on it, you have nothing to feel guilty about. Do you want to harm your friend physically?' NO! Of *course* not! I just . . . I just . . . I . . . I don't know. And if he were in his shrink's office, he would, at this point, disassociate himself by staring off at an object, usually the Chagall print that hung over the small sofa, to the right of the client chair; today, he stared into his drink.

'Don't be silly! I'd love to!' Miranda all but sang her approval.

'I wasn't sure with the jet lag and all—'

'Niall, it's lovely, I really want to.'

'Sure, I'll book it tomorrow, then—' A sound approximate to that of an eighteen-wheel lorry slamming into a brick wall came crashing down the line.

'Jesus!' Miranda pulled the phone away from her ear. 'What was that crash? Did the shed fall down?'

'Emmmm . . .'

Oh, shite! thought Miranda. 'It's Shay, isn't it?'

'Now, darlin', it's only temporary—'

'What's he doing? Opening up a used car lot?'

Niall peeked through the curtains and watched his cousin wheel a rickshaw into the converted cowshed. 'Em, no. Not exactly.'

'It's not that I don't like Shay – OK, he gets on my

nerves, but it's mostly because I just want us to have some time to ourselves, in our – in the cottage.'

'Our cottage. It's our home, Miranda.'

'I don't want to go there right now.' Dammit.

'Right. So . . . I miss you, and all.'

'I miss you, too . . .'

As Miranda's sighs flew invisibly across the Atlantic Ocean, Darren calmly breathed in through his nose . . . out through his mouth . . . in through his nose . . . out through his mouth . . . while repeating an affirmation he'd read in *GQ*: 'I wish my friend well in his (her) joy (promotion, pay raise, porn-star girlfriend/boyfriend), and know that I deserve joy all my own.' I wish my friend well, I wish my friend well, Iwishmyfriendwellllllll—

'Sorry, Dar. The time difference is a bit of a pain in the hole.'

'Nooooo problem. Nooooo problem.' I wish my friend well, I wish my friend—

'All right?'

Darren stopped affirming and let his breathing return to normal. 'Fine, fine. So how's loverboy?' Ouch. Too arch?

That was a bitchy . . . 'He's grand. We're going to fly off to Paris when I get back.' So there.

In through the nose . . . *Out* through the mouth. 'Lovely.'

'Yeah.' Miranda gazed off, imagining a canoodle at that café in Rue de Saint André des Arts. 'Except, well, he's got this cousin – remember the tons of cousins that you met when you came over? There's this other one, I forget which aunt or uncle on whose side, this guy Shay, he's been moving all this stuff into Niall's studio, all this theatre rubbish. It's like he's moving in to stay.'

'Is he a producer?'

'He's a *lawyer*,' Miranda sneered. 'Or was. Now he's got pretensions to "theatuh, dahling", or something – he inherited a load of old shite from, wait for it, a relative, and he thinks he's going to set up a theatre in Dublin.' She shook her head. 'Whatever. He'll be gone by the time we get back from Paris.' She smiled. 'I love Paris.'

'You sound really happy.' That ought to gain him back some friendship points.

'I am. Yeah. Really. Wish I had more work going right now, but I'm trying not to worry about it too much. Niall's been a bit blocked as well . . .' Miranda stared into the depths of her Martini. She sighed. 'It'll be grand, we're just getting used to being around each other all the time, too.'

Ah. 'Is that why you didn't take all your stuff with you?'

'Why what?' Miranda sat up, on the defensive.

'Are you having doubts . . . or anything?'

Darren's 'shrink voice' was truly annoying. 'I'm merely being cautious. It's not even a year yet, only ten months, two weeks and four days. And we haven't talked much about the future, or whatever.' Darren had a thought on that, but Miranda was on a roll. 'And I don't want to ship all my stuff without knowing what happens next. That's all. Just being cautious.'

'It sounds like you're talking yourself out of something before it's even begun—'

'Oh, nooo, trouble in paradise?' Jane slid into her seat and crossed her legs.

'Excuse me?' Miranda snapped. Now I'm getting belligerent, she thought. Maybe I should just go.

'I'm assuming that you're talking about Mr Wonderful, since that's all you talk about these days.'

'Unlike you, who only talks about yourself,' Miranda shot back. If she was surprised at herself, it was nothing to the shock that Darren was visibly experiencing. He'd start hyperventilating if it got out of hand. Wimp.

'Very nice, Miranda, and on my special night.' Jane pretended to pout, her eyes slits of aggression.

'I didn't know this soiree was *pour toi*!' Darren leaned towards Jane, practically climbing into her lap. *Ugh,* thought Miranda. I hate it when he starts pretending he can speak French. I hate it when he tries to 'handle' Jane. I want to go . . . home.

'It's a teeny bit contrived, but it's practically the one-year anniversary of The Emmy' – Miranda rolled her eyes – 'and the pitches are coming up day after tomorrow. There should be plenty to celebrate.' Darren toasted her and she returned the gesture, her gaze once more jerking to the door as it swung open.

'So, Miranda. What's it like, being a kept woman?' Jane spun a Marlboro Light over and under the fingers of her right hand, like a magician, just like she used to do in college, when she'd spent an entire weekend perfecting the move.

That was less than twelve years ago, but right now, it felt more like a million. Miranda looked at the woman who had been her coolest friend, cool without being cold, her craziest friend always up for some wild plan whether it was going to The Rainbow Room when they were flat broke and flirting with Midwestern business-men for drinks, or sneaking up the fire escape of the main building on campus to have a midnight picnic. Jane had practically been her role model in her early twenties, brashly negotiating the strange new world of reality away from the highly creative and protective environs of art school; Jane who'd always be available for late-night identity crises; Jane who always managed to be the centre of attention with room for a friend . . . Jane, who was sitting there like a snake ready to strike, spitefully ignoring Miranda, refusing to meet her halfway.

Bitch. This situation was complete rubbish. She was just pondering instigating a healthy row, even though she wasn't sure she was up to it, when her mobile went off again.

'Sorry.' Not. Miranda rose as she answered, her voice infused with pleasure as she pushed her way out of the bar and on to the street.

Jane watched Miranda pace in front of the window, her entire face lit up, her hands gesturing, her head thrown back in laughter. Miranda's long curly red hair and curvy figure was attracting a lot of attention out in the street – even in that dull outfit – and Jane shrugged. Well, regular sex must be agreeing with the kid. Jane didn't have anything against regular sex, far from it, but when the sex was all tangled up in a relationship, that's where she drew the line – had been drawing the line for more than twelve years . . .

And Miranda's conversation! It had become decidedly dull after she'd left the City: cottages and hill-walking and dinner parties and weekends away in the West of Ireland, her terrific, fabulous little expatriate existence, with her charming Irish boyfriend, her fake Irish accent, her photography career, her book deals, her international representation and her herbal remedies and God knew what else, all happy and snug living in some house in some mountains or something, somewhere in *Ire*land. She watched Miranda shove her phone in her pocket, and turn to look in the window. Their gazes met, and Jane was surprised that it was herself who looked away first.

2

Miranda pushed through the crowd at the door, and paused behind Darren. 'Where's the loo?' she asked, craning her neck over the mass of people now wedged at the bar.

'The *bathroom* is through the curtains at the back.' Jane rolled her eyes and shook her head at Darren. Darren responded by smiling at no one in particular.

'Right,' said Miranda, and she began shoving her way through the madly scanning crowd, a crowd that barely glanced at her as she passed. Oh, don't mind me, she thought, just a nobody from nowhere that none of you need. Wankers.

'Loo! Please.' Jane continued to flip the cigarette around her fingers, and longed for the days before the smoking ban.

'She's a bit upset that you haven't been very . . . interested in her new life—'

'Oh, Darren,' Jane huffed. 'How interested do we have to *be*? It's not as if *life* in New York as we know it has come to a complete stop. Did you get those emails? Who has time to read epic accounts of lakes and B&Bs and country pubs? We've both had lives, too. Your business is going from strength to strength. I continue to be one of America's cutting-edge television producers. And if she couldn't come back and support me on the biggest night of *my* life, well . . .'

Ah, bitterness. He couldn't say much about that, could he? He watched as Jane scanned the next group that shoved its way into the increasingly packed bar. 'Are you waiting for somebody?' He was sure she was avoiding eye contact.

'Why do you ask?' she asked brightly. 'Let's get another round.'

The queue – line – for the toilets – bathroom – was inching forward like traffic through Times Square at rush hour. Surrounded by stylish luvvies, Miranda considered leaving, really leaving, not just the queue but the entire scene. She crossed her arms and leaned against the wall. Just leave, Miranda, get Darren's keys, go up to his flat, finish packing ... even though she was well able to pack in no time, given her highly evolved abilities of organisation. Get out and get away and leave Jane to herself, the only person whose company she seemed to enjoy. Bitch!

What a shame, said a tiny voice that was obviously speaking from the sentimental part of her brain. After all these years—

'After all these *years*! Still hanging *on* ...' A stage whisper drifted down the line.

'I *know*! And no promotion in sight ...' Two nasty giggles ensued.

'Why did she *stay*?' A third stirred the pot. Miranda's ears perked up.

'You mean after the *Emmy*? That's so last year.' A disdainful snort. 'I mean, haven't you heard the *rumour*?'

'*No!*' A breathless chorus of curiosity.

The toilets flushed in tandem, drowning out most of the reply. '... thinks she's totally in, but she's so *not*, even if she has been seen with him at Cicero's for lunch *and* at the *SoHo Grand* for ... drinks.'

'Did they get a *room*?' Gasps of gleeful horror.

'Bob's assistant hasn't gotten to *those* receipts yet.'

'*Well* – I don't think doing Bob is going to do any good. *I* hear that her pitches are shaping up to be total garbage.'

Murmurs of agreement. '*Really* trite. So early nineties.'

'Too bad she didn't take that gig at Fox. *If* she really got an offer . . .'

More malicious whispering followed Miranda into her stall, and she tried not to listen any more.

So Darren was right. Something was going on with Jane. And it sounded like everyone else knew it, too.

Miranda threw herself into her seat. She kicked Darren under the table, obviously tearing him out of a mournful reverie. He takes other people far too personally, she thought. But. First things first. When he looked over quizzically, Miranda infinitesimally jerked her head towards Jane, and started making faces.

And got caught. 'Another quaint Irish custom, Ran? Some sort of post "loo" performance?'

Miranda gestured madly for the waitress. 'Let's have one for the ditch! That's a charming bit of Hiberno-semantics there. I've got a million of them. So, Janie – how *is* work?'

Jane arched a ruthlessly plucked brow. So now we're playing nice, are we? she thought. 'Crazy. We've got the go-ahead for five new series, and I've been working on my pitches day and night.'

'Must be pretty tense around the ol' office. All that top-secret planning behind closed doors.' Miranda nonchalantly took a sip from her empty glass.

'Word gets out,' said Jane, taking an equally nonchalant sip from her full drink.

'I'll bet it's competitive, though. Whoo, boy!'

'Of course it is, Miranda. It's *television*.'

'It must be a drag, working all alone. You are working . . . all alone?'

Jane jerked up her chin. This felt like a scene from a sitcom. A plot point exchange that was going to lead to an unpleasant revelation. 'I'm working closely with a colleague.'

'Oh, well, that's nice. To be working with somebody else. Have some give and take.'

'In a manner of speaking.' Her eyes flicked to the door and she smiled broadly, rising to greet the newcomers. Miranda grabbed Darren by the sleeve and started hissing into his ear.

'We don't have much time. Don't ask any questions! Just answer mine! OK?' Darren nodded frantically. 'What is the name of Jane's boss?'

'Boss? I don't know—'

'Did she get an offer from Fox?'

'Yes, I told you, and she turned it—'

'Would you say she's stayed too long at the network?'

'Well, in dog years, it's been centuries, but—'

Miranda pushed Darren back into his chair and smiled brightly at Jane. 'Was that your boss?'

Jane's brows knit. 'Boss? No.'

Miranda knit her brows in return, quizzically. 'What *is* your boss's name, again?'

What the fuck? 'Bob. Why?'

'Oh! I guess I thought I knew that, but I wasn't sure. Is he here?'

'No.' Jane sat up and straightened her jacket. She looked away, out at the street. 'No . . . still at the office, I suppose.'

'I'd love to meet him!' Miranda grinned and kicked Darren again, who responded by nodding energetically.

'I can't imagine why—' Jane leaned back to exchange departing pleasantries with a clutch of eager interns.

'What's with the Spanish Inquisition?' Darren shot at Miranda, desperate to know what the hell was going on.

'I think that Jane's—'

'Yes? That I'm what?'

'Heeeey, Janie! Bet you thought I wasn't going to make it!'

Even though the music was blaring, and the occupancy rate was strained to its outer limits, and not everyone in the bar had proper visibility, Miranda felt the entire room full of people come to a standstill, as if they were waiting for something.

Darren felt it too, and he looked at Miranda for clues. She widened her eyes meaningfully and he shook his head, at sea. She jerked her head towards Jane and got busted again.

'Really, Miranda, you've acquired a nervous twitch in your travels!' Jane trilled. 'Looks like you got your wish – Miranda was just asking after you, Bob.'

'Heeey, faaantastic!' Bob pinched Jane on the cheek, and then patted her on the behind. 'Great to meet you. Faaantastic!'

Miranda almost recoiled from the extended, highly manicured hand that Bob offered. A full head shorter than Jane, he looked about twenty-five, and his hair, spiked by what had to be enough gel to coif a Third World country, sprang up from his skull in erratic chunks. Highlighted as it was in bright yellow, Bob looked as if he'd sprouted daffodils on his head. He wore an outsized, wrinkled suit with an apparent lack of irony, and— Jesus, thought Miranda, he's wearing fuchsia Crocs!

'Nice to meet you. Darren Larson. Jane was telling us how hard she's working.'

'Oh, yeah, Janie loves to talk about how hard she works!'

Jane's smile froze. 'Now, Bob, you know I haven't even had a *minute* to let the cleaning lady into my apartment!' She turned to Darren. 'I don't even get around to opening my mail!' She laughed shrilly, and Darren laughed along, trying to help.

'Busy, busy, busy,' Miranda mumbled, spotting a trio

of women elbowing their way closer to their table. That must be those gossiping cows, she thought. Shite.

'Yes, well, we all can't retire to the countryside. Miranda lives in Ireland,' she explained to Bob.

'Ireland! Excellent! Ireland is so hip! Yeah!' Bob leaned over Miranda, leering. 'You gotta tell me all about it.'

'With her boyfriend,' Jane said sharply. 'In his cottage. It's all so recherché.'

'Ireland is the hottest thing since Prague, baby!' He patted her dismissively on the behind. 'You're so out of touch.'

Hissing giggles filtered through the hubbub, and Jane heard them. She slowly let her gaze pass over the culprits, who, as one, melted back into the crowd. 'Oh, I'm in touch, Bob. As you well know. Drink?'

'Faaantastic!'

Miranda glared at them as they moved towards the bar, a path miraculously cleared as Bob glad-handed his way through, not without keeping the other firmly on the small of Jane's back.

'Well, he seems . . . bubbly,' Darren said lamely.

'Are you sure Jane's not seeing anybody?'

'Positive.'

'But what if the somebody was somebody that she might not want everybody to know she was seeing?'

It took him a minute, but he got the gist. 'No. Stop. She would never – she would *not* – have you heard anything?'

What were they doing, with their heads together like schoolgirls in the playground? Jane reached down and grabbed her handbag, watching the guilt settle on their faces. 'Gotta schmooze, but let's definitely grab a bite after—'

'Jane.' Darren cleared his throat and gestured to her empty chair.

'I don't have time, darling, must work the room—'

'Are you shagging him?' Miranda hissed.

Not for nothing did Miranda get paid the big bucks for being observant. It was only a split second, but Jane froze, and in that split second Miranda saw an emotion cross Jane's face that she hadn't seen since 1996 – fear. It passed so quickly that only someone whose eye was as well-trained as Miranda's could have caught it, but catch it she did, and she reached out to her friend.

Jane shook off Miranda's hand. 'Really, you're barely speaking English these days. I'm sure I don't know what you mean.' She turned to go and both her friends leapt up to block her path. 'Kids, don't make a scene. These are my colleagues.'

'They all know,' whispered Miranda, frantic.

Jane laughed, brightly, loudly. 'You don't know what you're talking about,' she hissed, a smile pasted on her face.

'She does, hon,' babbled Darren. 'She was in the bathroom and she heard—'

'I don't have time for gossip, especially gossip fuelled by three hours of drinking. I have far too much to do. I have to be seen in this room tonight. I have to prepare the pitches for my next hit shows. I'm a mover and shaker, and I must move and shake. So move, Miranda.' She slung her handbag over her shoulder. 'Get out of my way.'

'Jane!' Miranda was shocked. 'Come on! I know how important your career is to you, and I heard some things that could really mess you up politically—'

Jane laughed again, a harsh, impatient sound. 'I'm sure you're a real wheeler-dealer out in the boondocks. You haven't got a clue about the way things run around here.'

'Fine.' Miranda rose. 'I won't be treated like this. I'm sure you think you know what you're doing. Have a nice life.' Grabbing her jacket and shoulder bag, she stormed out of the bar and out of sight.

Shay Gallagher rubbed his hands together, as much from the excitement of getting down to business as from the nip in the air. Late March in the Wicklow mountains at three in the morning wasn't exactly tropical. Late March in the Wicklow mountains, at three in the morning in a cowshed, converted or not, was even less so. He jumped up and down a bit to get the blood rushing back to his extremities, and took stock.

An outsider would have taken one look at the apparent chaos that was spread across the floor, sneaking up the walls, and threatening to burst out of the skylight, and shaken their heads at the impossibility of organising such a disaster area, but Shay knew better. He knew where everything was, and what everything was – but what he was going to do with it all was still somewhat up for grabs.

Several large flats, his scenery backdrops, were scattered around the place, leaning against the walls, each representing a different texture ranging from marble to cheery chintz to a gritty, grimy farmhouse interior. A large freestanding clothes rack was listing to the left, one of its wheels missing from its castor, and a rainbow of costumes, also covering myriad time periods, rocked gently in the breeze that came in through the open door. There were fake masts for a fake ship, fake palm trees bursting with fake coconuts, and fake storefronts emblazoned with fake Victorian signage. A battered rickshaw, sporting only one wheel, tilted drunkenly, its slightly mouldy wicker canopy sagging down to the moth-eaten seat. An American-style cigar-store Indian stood with his arm outstretched, over which were draped a collection of feather boas in a rainbow of colours. Pieces of furniture in varying degrees of disrepair were piled up in the farthest corner of the cowshed/studio, obscuring what had been the section that his cousin Niall had designated as the no-Shay zone. Sorting that out was his goal tonight – or, rather, this morning.

He was just too excited to sleep.

He looked at the mountain of furniture, as intricately and delicately balanced as a troupe of Chinese acrobats, and grinned. It wouldn't do to move the gear too far away from Niall's workspace, as Shay had a notion of appointing his cousin Chief Carpenter of his fledgling theatre company.

So fledgling, in fact, that he still hadn't come up with a name.

'Gallagher's Players!' He tried that one aloud. No, it sounded too much like a brand of cigarettes. Thinking of cigarettes, he lit one up, and blew out the smoke musingly. He contemplated the glowing end of his cigarette and tried to remember if his Uncle Des, in this great load of theatrical possibility that was his legacy to his nephew, had included an ashtray. He thought he remembered seeing an Art Deco one over in that mahogany trunk . . .

The furniture had remained untouched for the past three days. The trunk yielded nothing in the way of ashtrays, Art Deco or otherwise, but did reveal itself to be a treasure trove of hairpieces, most of which were actually in fairly good nick. Shay selected a particularly magisterial magistrate's wig and set it gingerly on his head. He strode purposefully over to the warped and cloudy full-length mirror that was propped up against the rickshaw, and messed about for a bit, striking body-building poses made all the more ridiculous by the incongruity of the grey curls. His scalp was beginning to itch, and as he relieved himself of the heavy toupée, he scratched his head vigorously, his almost shoulder length blond-brown locks cheerfully disarrayed. He was glad he'd let it grow out. It suited him. He admired himself from a few different angles, but then felt a bit of a prat. Anyway, it was a vast improvement over the regulation buzz cut he'd suffered when he was practising law.

And this was as far from the Four Courts as he was likely to get.

He looked at himself in the mirror again and thanked his lucky stars he didn't want to be an actor. Surely his lack of vanity would destine him to a life of mediocrity on the boards – but look at that waistline. He'd lost at least two stone since he'd stopped jockeying at a desk eighty hours a week. Patting his belly, he released his breath. All right, so, a stone and a half. Better than his ex-workmates could say.

He dropped the wig on to the top of a unicycle, and went over to inspect the replica farmhouse stove that was currently stuffed full of playscripts. Couldn't fault old Uncle Des for a shallowness of inquiry – there were scripts from up and down the Irish canon, the complete works of Shakespeare, a collection of American plays, and French texts in their original language. Shay closed his eyes and randomly grabbed four, disposing of the one that appeared to be written in Japanese.

He had to start somewhere. Shay swung himself up on to the only section of Niall's wrap-around work-table that had an inch to spare. Right. *A Midsummer Night's Dream*; *Tartuffe* (in English); *The Playboy of the Western World*. He looked around the room and reckoned he could produce any one of these plays with the bits and pieces he had under this very roof. With the package he'd received from his former firm, he could at least finance the first show until the company got its feet on the ground. *His* company . . . the plays fell to the floor as Shay leaned back and lay down on the table. The deep black of the night sky showed through the skylight, and he allowed himself to really imagine exactly what he wanted, something along the lines of the pleasure he had experienced directing and producing Dram Soc at Trinity, without the outsized egos and dozy mismanagement. He remembered the feelings of elation and despair, the moments of chaos and of command, as though it were yesterday, remembered the euphoria of opening night and the desolation of closing, and remembered, most of all, the feeling of being what he could only describe as family; one big, happy, mad family all pulling together towards a common goal.

Unlike the lot he'd been unfortunate enough to have been born into.

Ah, now. His mum and sisters weren't bad. It was his father who had been a thorn in his side ever since he'd made his big decision to leave the family firm. It was his father who'd been most appalled by Shay's broken engagement (hadn't there been a glimmer of relief in his mother's eyes?) to the assuredly lovely yet indisputably chilly and ambitious Fiona. And it would be his father who would continue, in that special way he had, to combine a cold shoulder with a dose of strong-arming.

He remembered the year they'd done that Gilbert and Sullivan thing, which one was it, *The Pirates of Penzance*? Ah, Jesus, what was that tune? The one about the – he began to hum, tentatively at first, then, as his rich and warm baritone began to gain confidence, he opened up his mouth and let fly:

'Oh, far better to live and die
Under the brave black flag I fly,
Than play a sanctimonious part
That ne'er will suit my pirate's heart—'

As he swung up and off the table, a huge, draped figure caught his attention.

'Hello, there, missus! Give us turn, will ya?' He began to sing with more gusto, and he changed the tempo of the tune to waltz time, his arms wrapped around the statue's stout waist. He managed to avoid tripping over stray fabrics and random props as he elegantly danced his partner around the room, his voice never faltering even in the exertion. *'And it IS, it IS a glorious thiiiiiiiiing—'*

'Would you ever shut up?' Niall could barely see, his eyes still heavy with sleep, or what was left of it. Woken up by Shay's exuberant yodelling, he figured now was as good a time as any – even if it was almost dawn – to see what progress had been made on the mess in his studio. He looked around at the explosion of props, flats, fabrics, and broken-down bits of chairs and tables and only one thought made it through his sleepy mind: Miranda was going to go absolutely fucking spare. He hoped that the tickets to Paris, tickets he'd impulsively purchased before even checking with Miranda, would go some way to making up for this mad mess.

'Sorry, mate. Didn't mean to wake you.' He set down the wooden replica of Queen Victoria and leaned an elbow on the sovereign's huge and unyielding bosom.

'What'd you reckon you're going to do with that bit of rubbish?' Niall crossed over to Shay and poked at Her Majesty with a bare toe.

Shay shook his long brown hair and dust flew into Niall's face. 'What are you like! This is an irreplaceable object! Maybe I'll give you the lend of her, set her up in

the front garden. Or we could take her down the
Docklands, replay her triumphant entry into Dublin Bay
in 1900. Or! No, here, we'll—'

'Stop right there,' Niall commanded. 'The last time
you had a bright idea that I went along with, we ended
up in Pearse Street Garda Station.'

Shay's big, booming laugh almost blew back Niall's
hair. 'No fault of my own, you eejit. If you hadn't
panicked, we would have been sailing that old curragh
out into the Irish Sea.'

'If we hadn't stolen the thing in the first place—'

'Borrowed it, eejit, borrowed—'

'From the bloody Natural History Museum!'

They both howled with laughter, and Shay stretched
his aching muscles, bending almost completely
backwards. 'How did we manage that, I ask you.'

Niall shoved him, but the bastard had incredible
balance; he didn't even sway an inch. 'How did we get
out of it, more like. You could always talk your way out of
anything – after you'd talked somebody into it in the first
place.'

Shay straightened up, and thumped Niall on the
shoulder as he passed. 'Who's the bigger nutter – the one
who leads or the one who follows?'

Niall grunted, then yawned and, lacking anything
better to do, started looking for his toolbox. Talk about
disorganised. Yet another little aspect of the whole
situation that was sure to get up Miranda's nose. She was
a divil for organisation.

Shay started shifting a dusty prop encyclopedia –
hollowed-out wood painted to look like a shelf-ful of
books – to make room for Niall's search. 'C'mere –
thanks a million for letting me stay here a bit. Until I get
a space, and all.'

'No worries. You're a pain in the arse, but it's vaguely
entertaining to have you about the place.' That wasn't a
lie, but then Niall was only speaking for himself.

'I'll be gone in a week or two, or so. I don't want to get in the way of genius out here.'

Niall shrugged. 'Not getting up to much in there at the minute, anyway. A bit stuck for ideas.'

'Ah, well, Mr Big-Time Artist, it happens to the best of ye. Didn't Picasso himself come out with all that blue stuff after he'd let his own cousin move in for a spell?'

'Yeah, I think I read that in Jansen's *History of Art*.'

'Yeah, Picasso's cousin, hanging about for ages, shagging the mistresses.' Niall's eyes narrowed, and Shay backpedalled immediately. 'Joking, joking . . . come on, cuz, wouldn't stamp on yer patch, as it were.'

Niall lifted up the hasp of saw and rubbed a finger along the edge. 'You wouldn't get half the chance.' He turned away, surprised at how angry he felt, and he heard Shay shuffling around behind him. He knew his cousin was only messing, but anything about Miranda hit nerves he didn't even know he had. Falling in love hadn't really been in the plan, but now that he had, he wasn't going to let anything scupper it, not even Shay's boneheaded teasing.

Touchy bugger. 'Sure, you're not still sore about Sheila Doran, are ya?' Shay laughed, then stopped abruptly as Niall shot a scowl over his shoulder. 'Right.'

The silence was less than companionable and, as usual, once Shay had got a healthy taste of his own shoe leather, he couldn't seem to stop himself taking another bite. 'Now that was only about a century ago, and you know she was only a wee slapper, and, sure, we only had that bit of a snog after the dance. Her friend was the one that fancied you anyway – what was her name? Marie What's-it, the one from Kenmare. That was a summer all right, down there in Irish school; you were snogging the best of them, so you were, and old Father What's-it making that list, and weren't you on the top of it, "Most Likely to Get a Girl up the Duff before August"—'

Niall smirked. 'Shut yer gob. Plonker.'

A measure of good will was restored, but Shay's curiosity got the better of him.

'So you and Miranda, you're serious, like?'

Niall arched an eyebrow. 'Yeah. So mind yourself. As if it needed saying.' He straightened up, and Shay got the message.

'Niall, I wouldn't – and I don't think she likes me much, to be fair.'

'Sure, she hardly met ya.'

Shay scratched his head – it was disturbingly tickly, post-hairpiece. 'So . . . she's all right with it, and all?'

Niall hesitated. 'Ah . . . well. It's only temporary, after all. Right?'

Shay squirmed a bit. 'It is. It is.' Neither man looked at the other as they both pretended to be engrossed in their menial tasks, Niall sorting out some screws and Shay brushing a fur coat that was seriously moulting.

'So where did Uncle Des get all this gear? Queen Victoria and the palm trees?' Niall asked, stealing a cigarette from Shay's packet.

Shay moved away, now intent on brushing the matted fur. 'From his cousin Jack What's-it, the one from outside of Kilkee. They had a wee place for the summer trade, a repertory thing. They'd been there for years and built their own sets and such. Dessie kept up the collection, and tried to take it on the road, in some caravan get-up, but he didn't get past Mayo before old Auntie May –'

'Jesus, she was a wagon herself—'

'– made him pack it in. It was stashed in a disused shed until he left it to me.'

Niall opened an eye and watched as Shay succeeded in denuding the coat. 'So – what's the plan?'

Shay's eyes lit up, and he tossed the brush on to a stack of ladies' shoes, and kicked at the pile of fur at his feet. 'Theatre, my friend. Theatrical entertainment. Shakespeare, Sheridan, Jacobean tragedies and French farces! All those costumes are in fairly good nick, they just need a nip and tuck here and there. Countrywide tours and fame and fortune!' He grinned, arms raised, as if to embrace the entire studio. 'All I need are a play, some actors, a producer, some technicians ... and a carpenter, maybe some photos, you know—'

Niall spun around, eyes wide. 'Don't even think about it.'

'Ah, wait till you see! It'll be fantastic! Like an old-time travelling group of players, everyone living out of trunks, babies being born backstage, the smell of the greasepaint—'

'The roar of my girlfriend when she figures out what you're up to!'

Shay beamed. 'Niall, old friend. Leave it with me.'

At nine a.m., two days after her cocktail party in SoHo, Jane was sitting calmly at her desk, her freshly manicured fingers smoothing down the equally freshly printed-out copy of the four pitches she had submitted to the think tank. She reviewed them with confidence: the spin-off of her award-winning show *Sheila and Boo*, called *The Life and Times of the Upper East Side*, a vehicle for two of Sheila's outwardly prim friends, Katie and Bud, who were secretly off-beat and batty. There was a reality-show concept – well, that's what they had asked for – she hated those shows herself, but she thought the idea of trapping a bunch of work-out freaks in a New York Health and Racquet Club was a good idea. The gritty drama concerning a crowd of eco-activists was suitably 'green' and would draw in the aging baby-boomer demographic and her pièce de résistance, the action-slash-romance-slash-family series that followed each character's story line in real time. That, she thought, was a real winner; having studied precedents in which the real-time story lines hadn't worked, she was sure she'd cracked the concept, and it would put WCTV ahead of the game.

Four pitches. Perfect. Three, as a number, was too predictable – five was overkill. Four. Four perfectly conceived ideas, complete with casting and directing suggestions. Not an inch of room for error. Jane folded her hands over the well-written and flawlessly composed pitches, and tried to make herself relax. Everything was riding on this, her entire future with the station, and she began to feel the first flush of confidence she'd felt in weeks. She found herself breathing deeply and steadily, the way that Miranda had always recommended when—

Let's not go there, Jane, she thought, and spun her ergonomically designed office chair away from her desk to face her full-length window. She couldn't pretend to be as in love with Miranda's life as Miranda herself was, could she? Miranda was so out of touch now, and they couldn't talk about the same things any more and, maybe, it was best that they'd come to a parting of the ways, even if it had been so . . . cold. A queasy feeling collected in her belly again, and Jane forced herself to think of something else.

She'd make it up to Miranda, and she'd already begun; she'd sent a dozen emails, hadn't she? Well, two. Spinning back towards her desk, she busily fussed with her already perfectly ordered file. A little voice inside her said that she'd really made a mess of it this time, and that she'd have to go pretty far out of her way to make it up to her friend. How exactly she was supposed to do that when said friend lived three thousand miles away, she'd like to know –

She stood up and started pacing around her office, the heels of her vintage Joan and David's sinking into the plush maroon carpet. As she wandered around the edges of the vast space – well, vast as compared to her tiny studio apartment – she touched the things that she had accumulated over the past five years. The deep-brown leather couch that could comfortably sit five; the glass table that was less a piece of furniture than a graceful sculpture; the matching Art Deco lamps; the cherry tallboy that she'd cunningly adapted to use as a bookcase. Not that she bought any of this stuff herself – please! – but she'd had the good taste to choose it and charge it to her expense account. Executive taste. Exactly.

Out of the corner of her eye, above the half-frosted glass that comprised two walls of her office, she noticed that there was an awful lot of traffic moving past her door this morning. She casually walked over to the far wall and caught three junior writers staring in at her. She cocked her head questioningly, and they blushed and bustled away. Was it her imagination, or did they stop two of the assistants to the managing director from coming her way?

Getting a bit paranoid, Jane, she thought to herself. I guess it's all part of the package, the executive package. I am executive material. She smoothed her hands over her shining hair. I will get that promotion today. I will sell all my pitches and nothing will stop me. *The next phase is about to begin.*

Her stomach rumbled loudly. She should eat something. Going over to the retro Alessi fridge, gunmetal grey and designed with 1950s fittings, she allowed herself a moment's giddy fantasy, imagined calling in her assistant Margot and sending her down to the corner deli for an egg-bacon-and-cheese on a bagel with a double helping of home-fried potatoes. Home fries! She could see the little packets of salt and ketchup just waiting to be torn open and liberally distributed over the deliciously warm spuds. She could taste that first bite of potato and tomato, the tang of the salt, she could practically smell the grease and onions now . . .

'Snap out of it!' She scolded herself aloud, jerked open the refrigerator door, and picked out a low-fat plain yogurt.

She had enough trouble, and comfort food wasn't going to solve anything.

(Just down the street, whispered an insatiable little voice in her mind, just minutes away, beautiful, lovely home fries and a bagel, toasted golden brown and stuffed with two scrambled eggs, a slice of cheddar cheese, and two glorious strips of crunchy bacon −)

Buttoning up her tight-fitting jacket, Jane scolded herself again. Jane! Please! Breakfast food is not the answer! Fresh, new, cutting-edge ideas are the answer! Carbohydrates will not get you a promotion − if the Emmy didn't, do you think home fries will?

Why *didn't* you get that promotion? an insidious little voice prodded her. Hmmm? After all you've done? Especially after you broke the one and only rule you ever wrote for yourself and started sleeping with—

A brisk knock interrupted her guilt trip, and Margot stuck her head around the door.

'Bob just called. They've bumped up the meeting.'

Jane arched a brow. 'To when?'

'Now.'

Her nerves sizzled, but she refused to let them show. 'Good thing I'm more than prepared.' She collected her file from her desk and turned to leave her office. As she breezed past Margot, forcing her to hold the door open, she grinned cockily and said, 'Wish me luck.'

As Jane swept away down the hall, Margot thought: If what I hear is right, you're going to need it.

Jane paused with her hand on the boardroom door. Here we go, she thought. You've done this a thousand, a million times. No one is better at this than you are, Jane. You are the Queen of the story idea. Here we goooooooooo −

She pushed the door open, with authority, and in a split second took in the shapes of the figures in the room, silhouetted against the glaring early morning light bouncing off the long, gleaming table, the way the figures had arranged themselves in order of importance . . . the small number of people who were actually at the meeting . . . and the lack of catering.

Uh oh.

*

Darren pounded up the stairs to Jane's apartment, taking them two and three at a time. A phone call these days from Jane in the early mid-morning was a rarity, and the strangled plea for help – or rather, the order to come over, depending on your point of view – was even more rare. On the way down from his office in the taxi, he wondered if the powers that be at WCTV had rejected all of Jane's concepts? Nothing less than that would ruffle her feathers, and he knew how important this latest round was to her. Although *why* this should be so was still a mystery to him, and in his head he argued with Jane about all those gigs she had turned down. What was her problem? Why hang on if the idiots didn't appreciate her hard work, her *Emmy award-winning* hard work? In the back of his mind, the suspicion that she was fooling around with her boss wouldn't lie down and shut up.

He knocked rather frantically at her door, which flew open in his face.

'It's not exactly an Upper West Side penthouse – no need to bang the door down.' Jane left him in the doorway and threw herself down on the couch.

Lovely, thought Darren. As if I ran all the way down to Tribeca for this sort of attitude.

'I'm— Come in please.'

He shut the door gently behind him, joining Jane on the couch. She was sitting rather stiffly in the centre. Taking one of her hands, a very cold and clammy hand, Darren stroked it, and asked, 'Didn't go well then?'

'That's an understatement!' Jane snatched her hand away and began to pace up and down, as best she could in the tiny space. 'They fired me!'

'Oh my God!' Darren gasped and covered his mouth with his hands. 'Oh, no!'

As Jane threw herself back down on to the couch, Darren sprang up and adopted full caretaker mode. Wishing he had thought to pick up some coffee – or vodka, had he known – he dashed into the bathroom and grabbed a handful of tissues. Reaching into Jane's wardrobe, he pulled out her fluffy robe and some comfy socks.

'Let's get you comfortable and we'll think this thing through. You've had all those other offers. It might not be such a bad thing—'

'It's a *disaster*,' Jane hissed, refusing the robe and tissues. 'I'm officially poison! And I can't take any of those pitches with me, because they let me pitch and *then* they fired me! So it's like they own them now. And I'll have you know that I had already pitched the eco-activists thing to them last year and they loved it and wanted to wait on it, and now they *fire* me?! I need to talk to a lawyer. I swear to God if I see *any* of those shows I conceived up and running I'm going to sue them blind.'

'But what about the *Emmy*?' Darren whispered.

Jane laughed bitterly. 'Well, that just proved that *Sheila and Boo* was no longer cutting edge, and it was giving the young Turks a bad name. And that's more important than my track record, more important than the hours I slaved in that stinking place; twelve hours a day, Darren, including Saturdays and Sundays!'

'I know, doll, I know.'

'What am I going to do?' Jane curled up into a ball and her voice dropped to a stunned whisper. 'I should have taken that gig at Fox, I should at least have called them back at ABC. Fox will never talk to me now, never in a million years.'

'Impossible!' Darren sat down beside her and gave her a hug. 'All you have to do is get them on the phone, and tell them—'

'Tell them what?' Jane snapped. 'How am I supposed to spin this?'

Darren sat back and took a deep breath. Dr Spitz would quite openly imply that he was getting what he deserved, trying to rescue someone who was happy enough to drown. 'I don't know, Jane. I'm only trying to help.'

'I know. I know.'

And thanks, maybe? Darren thought, annoyed. Sorry I'm biting your well-meaning head off?

Jane stared sightlessly at the opposite wall. 'Oh, God. I've never been fired from a TV job in my life. The only time I ever got fired was in a group from Dairy Queen, when the receipts didn't add up. But that was everyone, not just me, and I know who did it, it was that nasty little creep Arthur Watson. I knew he was dipping into the cash when he showed up with that second-hand Corvette, just to impress Mary Anne Miller, and all of us got fired, all because of *him* –'

Darren let Jane rant away, as he pondered what might be the best thing to do. There was no food in the house, not that Jane would eat anything anyway. There wasn't even the makings of a soothing mug of hot cocoa! He absentmindedly patted her hand as she wound down from her tale of teenage outrage, and decided that the best thing to do would be to go over essentials.

'Let's talk about basics, OK?'

Jane nodded, worn out.

'Did they give you an exit package?'

'Yes. And they're also paying me for all the vacation I never used.'

'How much?'

'Since I started? Five years times three weeks a year—'

'That's almost four months!'

'So?' Jane scowled. 'I *hate* taking vacation.'

Darren shook his head. 'It might be worth taking a little break. You could go see—'

'Don't say, "Go see Miranda". She isn't answering my emails.'

'I think she went off to Paris—'

'She blocked me, Darren! She blocked my address! They all bounced back!'

With her boyfriend, he finished to himself. He sat

back, exhausted. This was not exactly the end of the world, was it? There were other jobs out there, for crying out loud. And she isn't *listening* to me. Did all this make him a bad friend? He thought about calling his shrink.

'I can't just show up on her doorstep.'

'You could call her, you know. Ireland is actually part of the first world. It's quite beautiful and modern at the same time. And Miranda really feels bad that you've never come to see her.'

'Maybe I'll get there someday. It just doesn't sound like anywhere I'd like to be.'

Darren rolled his eyes. 'You've never been anywhere but here!' This was as close to shouting as he got, and it felt good. 'You are unbelievable! I'll never forget that you left us early on our tour of Europe; you didn't even make it to *Italy*, for God's sake.'

'Everything is here!' Jane shouted, and as she shouted regularly, it was much more forceful than Darren could ever be. 'Everything I need is here—' She stopped short, stunned, and stared at Darren. 'Was here. It was here. Everything was . . .'

They sat in silence. Crying would help, Darren thought, but no tears were forthcoming. He couldn't remember ever having seen Jane cry.

'It might not be such a bad thing, taking some time for yourself. Go back to some acting workshops. You were such a wonderful actress, I don't know why you stopped. Honey, maybe this is a good thing! Miranda might say that this was the universe telling you—'

'Don't start with the New Age crap, please. Miranda doesn't know as much as she thinks she does.'

'Doesn't she?' Darren sat back and crossed his arms. 'So, are you?'

'Am I what?' Jane felt her muscles tense.

'Are you screwing your boss?'

Jane shot off the couch and went into the toilet, slamming the door behind her, her muffled shouting drifting out to Darren. 'I don't need this shit from you right now! I don't need you and Miranda colluding behind my back, making up stories! This isn't college any more, you know! You're still acting like we're freshmen!'

Darren shook his head as she continued to rant. The lady doth protest too much, he thought, and he distracted himself by reaching for a Gap catalogue. A pile of letters, all bearing the return address of the building's management company, fluttered to the floor. He looked up at her when she finally returned, and waved the letters at her.

'Haven't you even been opening your mail?'

'I've been extremely busy! I told you so the other day! Very, very busy! And for no good reason, obviously!'

'I don't know, doll, these could be important or something.'

'It's none of your business! I asked you over for some moral support, not to nag me to death about acting classes and my landlord and – and – and the universe and the meaning of my life! Jesus!'

When Darren rose up from the couch, his face a blank, Jane knew that she had gone too far. And as always, when she had gone too far, she followed the old adage, 'The best defence is a good offence.'

'Thanks *so* much for coming by.' Her nasty tone soured in her throat. 'I feel *so* much better.'

'I think Miranda's right, as she often is about many things, about all the things that she said about you.' He decided to leave it there and let her stew about that for a while. 'And if you're not very, very careful, Jane, you won't have me to call on in the middle of the day – my very busy, self-employed day – without reasonable explanation, for much longer.' He took a deep breath and found that he wasn't afraid to say what he meant. 'Like Miranda, I won't be treated like this. I'm sure you'll land on your feet.'

He went to the door, and turned slightly towards her. 'You always do.'

The door clicked shut behind him and Jane listened to his footsteps descend the stairs.

Hours later, the light that snuck over her window sills had faded to grey, and Jane lit another cigarette. The room was full of blue smoke and Jane sat, frozen, sometimes thinking, sometimes not. She made plans and tossed them aside, half-formed, and, in between practical matters, came weird feelings that she couldn't quite describe, possibly because she'd never had them before, or hadn't sat still long enough to feel ... well, icky. Or something.

None of this was her fault – it was all Bob's fault, the liar, the bastard, the creep. He must have bragged about their ... thing. Jane wouldn't stoop to use the word relationship. It was just a thing, a secret thing, at least he said he'd keep it secret. Dammit, how could she have trusted him? It *had* to be all his fault – they'd been discreet, for God's sake.

And Mrs Krane! Her drama teacher in high school had told her she had 'something', had made her think she could be an actress, and then all those years of auditioning and getting nothing, even though she was good, she *knew* she was good, better than all those little blonde bitches who were getting all the parts, and then she was stuck, she had to do something, so she had become a producer, a visionary. Thanks for nothing, Mrs Krane! It was all their fault, all of *them*, Jane thought petulantly. It was certainly not her fault ...

This was not a pleasant thought under any circumstances, and Jane tried to distract herself from it by attacking her mail. Using a nail file, she sliced open the most recent letter from the building's management company – and gasped.

5

At the ungodly hour of 4.45 a.m., the alarm clock went off in Niall and Miranda's bedroom. Niall raised himself up on his elbow, and, reaching over Miranda's head, gently shut it off. He looked down at the wild curls streaming over the pillow and shook his head – she'd sleep through an earthquake that had been triggered by a hurricane. The bloody thing had been screeching in her ear for at least five minutes, and there she was, snoring away. There was a time-honoured method for waking her up, however, one that they didn't have nearly enough time for . . . ah, sure, why not.

Niall ran a finger gently down the side of her face, brushing away a stray curl here and there. He nuzzled her neck, softly, breathing in the smell of her skin, warm with sleep. Moving his other arm around her body, he began to stroke her belly, lightly at first, teasingly, now nibbling at her earlobe, and whispering her name. He knew exactly the moment when she woke, could feel her face crease with a smile, but she would insist on playing possum. The hand that stroked her belly worked its way down to the hem of her nightie, stroking the thigh that it had recently covered, tickling the back of her knee as his mouth dropped down to her shoulder, kissing, biting, until she couldn't possibly stand it any more, she'd have to turn towards him and—

'Shite! It's five o'clock!' Miranda squawked, throwing

back the covers, and Niall along with them. 'The taxi will be here in fifteen minutes!' She leapt out of bed, and Niall groaned. She was a mad one for the punctuality.

'He'll wait,' he grumbled. 'It's my bloody cousin, after all.'

There was no reply but the sound of the shower and Miranda's shouts at the (always initially) cold water. He must get that seen to. Niall rubbed his hands over his eyes and dragged himself out of bed. He could use the downstairs shower . . . or he could pack.

He glanced at the bathroom door – he'd better pack. Taking his duffel bag from the end of the bed, he removed the towels he had stuffed into it so that Miranda would think he'd already got his things sorted. He rushed around, throwing socks, underwear, a pair of black jeans, a few pullovers, and a shirt and tie into the bag. Feck, the dress shoes. He dumped everything out and started all over again. Should he bring a dinner jacket? Bloody well right he should, he thought, remembering watching Miranda pack, in that organised way she had, having sorted everything into an outfit per day; he realised that Saturday night's outfit was a particularly little black dress. Right, shoes, jacket, tie, shirt, iron it all at the hotel, jeans, T-shirts, socks, pants – done.

Niall passed Miranda in the doorway, his bag in hand. 'You want to get a move on, missus,' he commented, getting a rather sharp smack on the arse for his pains.

'Unpacked all those towels, did you?' Miranda mumbled to herself. 'My bag is already by the door!' she shouted down the stairs. 'Are you planning on travelling in your underwear?' The silence that flew up the staircase had Miranda fleeing back to the loo, and slamming the door just before her half-naked boyfriend could get his own back.

'Tickets? Passports? Bank cards? Cameras? Metro passes . . .'

Miranda sat calmly sipping her tea, watching Niall go through everything all over again. That's what he got for being so disorganised, she thought, sighing smugly to herself. He's never, ever completely sure that he got everything he needed. Whereas *I*, she thought, have known all along that everything is in order and if only his bloody taxi-driving cousin would turn up, we'd be away.

'Right, it's all in order.' He fell into a chair next to hers, and rubbed a hand down her back.

This was so . . . lovely, thought Miranda, as she leaned over and kissed him loudly on the cheek. I love this. It's just the best. Who could have known, eleven months ago, as she'd grudgingly gone to take some headshots for a theatrical friend, that she'd meet the love of her life? Sitting here, almost eleven months to the day, in the kitchen of the most beautiful, spacious, and perfect house on the eastern coast of Ireland, with the handsomest, most talented, goofiest man on the planet, and me, myself, she thought, a professional photographer whose first book was coming out any minute now. Life was . . . simply, perfectly—

SLAM. The back door hit the kitchen wall, and Shay came bounding in, dragging an enormous bolt of fabric behind him.

'Ah, no, did I wake you? Sorry, sorry,' he said, knocking over a few chairs and coming dangerously close to breaking the sideboard.

Miranda glared at him and rushed to set the antique oak piece of furniture to rights. Niall jumped up as well, and grabbed the back end of the bolt, which was now veering towards the brass plant stand.

'We're off today. Paris, remember?' Niall waggled his eyebrows meaningfully at Shay, and nodded towards Miranda. Shay looked at him blankly and grinned, wagging his eyebrows suggestively back.

'Gotcha, mate. Have a nice one. Or two. If you take

my meaning.' He laughed and nudged Miranda, who smiled back.

Ah, shite, thought Niall.

'It's been great having you, Shay. Good luck with the theatre and everything.' She grabbed up her luggage, and stuck out her other hand.

Shay shook it, and stared at her, puzzled. 'I didn't know you were off for good. Sure, didn't you only just get back?'

It was Miranda's turn to be confused. 'No, we're only going for a week. You're the one—'

'There's himself!' Niall announced, as a horn tooted briskly from the drive. He grabbed the bags in one hand, and Miranda in the other. 'Cheers, bye!'

Shay shut the door behind them, wondering what Miranda was on about, then shrugged. Just as well they were off – he'd been wanting to dye this muslin for days, and now had free run of that big old tub. He'd do a third of the stuff pale blue, a *Midsummer Night's Dream* robin's-egg blue; a third a kind of *Importance of Being Earnest* emerald green; and, warming to this idea, he'd do the last bit a deep, dark, bloody *Macbeth* red. And with any luck he could bring some of the more rickety set pieces out of the damp and warm them up by the fire. Oh! And if he did a quick wash on the costumes that could handle it, he could dry them in the cottage, and have them ready for a seamstress in no time.

He lugged the fabric up the stairs, very nearly dislodging all the photographs that Miranda had hung with care. He heard the tinny ring of a mobile, and checked his jeans pocket. Not his. Niall or yer one must have left their phone behind . . .

Miranda's phone lay forgotten under the sideboard, where it had fallen after Shay had clumsily gone past. It rang and rang and rang, long after Miranda had gone, and when it stopped, it stopped in mid-ring, sounding almost sad and forlorn.

6

W hy was she sleeping sitting up? Why did the chair, the chair in which she was sleeping sitting up, keep vibrating? Why did her head feel like it was going to explode from her eardrums inward? Why was there some old guy snoring into her shoulder?

Oh.

Yeah.

Jane slowly opened her eyes, and stretched out her numb legs. Business class – well, it did rock, but it wasn't exactly all the comforts of home.

Home.

Jane spritzed her face with her Evian atomiser. She looked blankly out the window and thought: home was where you hung your hat, or your Fendi garment bag, as the case may be. And her Fendi garment bag was securely stowed away in the guts of this 747 non-stop to Dublin.

A flight attendant made her busily chipper way down the aisle, passing out shrink-wrapped trays of sugary carbs and browning fruit, and Jane avoided her portion by dragging out the smaller of her carry-on bags and removing her tray table from its upright position. She flipped open her portable, light-up make-up mirror and peered into its warm, familiar glow. Having removed the previous day's face before going to sleep, she was ready to put on a new one, her first face in Ireland. She smoothed her hands down her cheeks and leaned forward, slightly alarmed by the look in her eyes – what was it? It looked familiar . . . tiredness, sure, who could sleep on a six-hour flight? . . . nerves, maybe? A bit of, what was that, it looked like . . . fright?

Oh *shit*.

Maybe in ten years' time, she'd be happy to recognise her sixteen-year-old face in a mirror but, now, today – no way. Nothing a little moisturiser and foundation couldn't erase.

'Tea? Coffee? Tea? Coffee?' Amazing. The woman had surely been up the entire night and, apart from a few fly-away wisps escaping from her chignon, the attendant looked alert and fresh. Jane slapped on some blush.

'Is that coffee brewed? Like in a pot?' Jane asked.

'It is indeed, ma'am. Shall I pour you a cup?' 'Moira' gestured with her pot. Mo-ee-ra, thought Jane. Sounds Spanish.

'It's not Starbucks, is it?' Jane pressed.

Mo-ee-ra's brows knitted slightly in confusion. 'It isn't, no.'

Jane held out her cup, and as the dark brew poured into the tragically tiny container, the scent of it roused her row-mate, a large beefy man of about sixty. Irish, Jane thought, and, taking in the red face, she decided he was a farmer. Weren't they all farmers, except for Miranda's perfect boyfriend-the-artist?

'Jesus, Moira, give us a cuppa that,' the man begged through a yawn. Moy-ra, Jane thought. Huh.

Feeling self-conscious now that her travelling companion was awake, she rushed through the last few moves of her regime, hurriedly brushing on several layers of mascara. Barely presentable, but thirty-one once again, sixteen successfully banished to the early eighties where it belonged.

'What's that you got there?' boomed her fully lucid fellow passenger. Jane tucked her make-up case into the bag. What *was* it about some people, she thought to herself, irritated, that kept them perfectly, blissfully silent for the majority of a trip and then, the minute that the final approach began, they insisted upon making conversation? The Story of Their Life in five minutes or less?

She edged her bag out of the man's sight, and refused to make eye contact as she answered, in a monotone, 'It happens to be an Emmy.' That ought to discourage him. He wouldn't know an Emmy from a—

'One of them award yokes? Go on, give us a look.'

Jane sized him up. She wasn't keen to award this combination of nosiness and pushiness, but was secretly gratified that he knew the statuette for what it was. She carefully extracted the Golden One from the bag, shining away a stray fingerprint with the edge of her in-flight blanket, and reverently placed her on the Irish man's tray table. They looked at it.

'Sure, we get loads of American television over here, and I thought I recognised your pretty face.'

Not bad, thought Jane. In fact, very, very good. Complimentary, diplomatic, probing, and almost successful in covering up for the fact that he thought she was somebody, but wasn't sure who. This was becoming vaguely interesting.

'I'm a producer, actually,' Jane replied smoothly, 'and we haven't gone foreign yet, so I doubt you're familiar with my show. It's a rom-com.' How about that, smartypants, and she sat back smugly.

'Nothing like "boy meets girl" to bring in the numbers,' he murmured equably, and gestured to the Emmy. 'May I?' Jane nodded and he lifted it gently.

'I'd like to thank me ma!' he roared, waking the few remaining slumberers. He twinkled at Jane as he teased her a bit, waving the gold yoke about, watching her eyes dart madly, following its path. He laughed. 'Always wanted to do that.'

'And what do you do?' Jane retrieved her Lady without betraying the jolt of panic she'd felt, and took

her time returning it to the carry-on – the flight
attendants were agog, and sleepy heads were popping up
over the tops of their seats, blearily trying to focus on
what rumour was already spreading: that a Famous
American Actress was in Business, yer one from *Lost*.

'I'm in the business myself – entertainment business.
Theatre. Got a wee place on the Quays. Do you know
Dublin at all? Do you not? On a holiday? Terrible time of
year for it. Bloody rotten, was raining buckets before I
left – but that was February so maybe it's picked up a bit.
Have you family over here? Do you not? Ah, well. Sure
you don't look Irish, in fairness. Have you friends?
Grand, grand. Ireland's a better place altogether if you're
on the arm of a mate. Fella? No? Ah, well. You'll be
knocking them out left, right and centre, so you will.
Might find yerself an Irish husband, so you might.' He
threw back his head and roared, nudging the dazzled,
speechless Jane with a hearty elbow. 'So you're a
producer – I thought you were an actress, you have that
look about you. We'll have to have a chat, talk shop and
the like, once you get settled in and – ah, now, buckle up,
there you go. Did you fill out all them Jaysus forms? Sit
back now.' He paused and sighed.

'Nothing like coming home.'

Jane sat back and turned her face to the window,
clutching her bag to her chest. As the plane banked and
broke through heavy cloud cover, as the engines began
their descendant whine, as the attendants made their last
pleas for fastened seat belts, Jane felt her heart leap, and
she closed her eyes, not wanting anything to be
unfamiliar before she had a chance to get her feet on the
ground.

Gerard, her New BFF, helpfully guided her through the
unfamiliar fluorescence of the generic hallways of
Dublin Airport. After she had assured him that she was
being met – *Why did I lie?* she wondered – he cheerily

waved her into her passport queue and insisted that she come and visit the theatre when she had a minute.

Those annoying forms – she hated forms, she hadn't ever bothered with the IRS until she discovered accountants, and forget about her driver's licence, she'd let it expire – as she hurriedly filled out the papers, and crept forward in the queue, voices and noises swept and crashed over her head, increasing in volume until she thought she'd be crushed. The lack of sleep was beginning to take its toll. The fluorescent lighting began to burn into her retinas, she could feel every inch of her skin tingling with fatigue, she could feel the adrenalin of arrival draining from her muscles, leaving her shivering and woozy. Bags then taxi then bed, she chanted to herself. Bags then taxi then bed. She'd make it, she'd make it to Miranda's, she'd make it and she'd be herself in a matter of hours.

She stumbled a bit as she made her way towards the escalator, and despite the wonkiness, despite the wild unfamiliarity of it all, she began to see the wisdom of this journey: she did need the rest, she did, the stress – the *horror* – of the last several months, oh my God, she needed this break. It was a good decision, it was, even if she'd left her career in the toilet and was going to stay with a friend who probably hated her guts—

'C'mere, Eileen, did you hear? Jennifer Aniston was on our flight!'

'Go 'way, she wasn't!'

'She was!'

'Did you get a goo at her?'

'I didn't – will she be fetching her own bags, do you think?'

'Sure she's people to do that for her, for fuck's sake.'

Nothing like a good transatlantic show-biz rumour to cheer a girl up, and Jane threw back her head and laughed.

7

She wasn't laughing as she watched, yet again, as the battered guitar case make its lonely circuit of the carousel.

This couldn't be happening to her.

As she very calmly dealt with the lost-luggage lady from the airline, her mind screamed, *This can't be happening to me!* As she steadily gave them Miranda's mobile number – no, there wasn't a what? A land line? Not that she knew of – she imagined herself banging her head on the countertop, splattering blood all over this annoyingly awake and *nice* woman. Backing away, quietly expressing her thanks, she felt like John Hurt in *Alien*: her skin was writhing and she was about to spew out a creature of such slime and disgustingness that she would— well, she'd get to the front of the line for the taxis, anyway.

The driver adjusted his rear-view mirror, and asked, 'That's all yer bags then?'

Jane pointedly stared out the window, weary to the bone. 'Yessssssssss,' she growled, and dropped her head back on to the top of the seat.

'All right, so.' The driver shrugged, and peeled out from the kerb.

Closing her eyes, Jane rocked and swayed with the motion of the cab, trying not to think about exactly what was in those lost bags, the amount of money that those garments and shoes and handbags and bits and pieces of high-quality costume jewellery would ultimately cost her to replace, if they didn't find them. How could they lose them? Where could they *go*?

This was why she never went on vacations, *this* was why she'd never returned to Europe, *this* was why she'd have been better off jetting off to the Cayman Islands or somewhere civilised—

'What?' What was *with* these people, couldn't they sit still without having to chew your ear off?

'Where are you goin', missus?' The picture of patience, the driver spoke slowly and clearly, as he downshifted at a traffic light.

'Wicklow,' Jane snapped, and closed her eyes once more.

'Where in Wicklow?'

'Wicklow. The place. Isn't it a place? A town, or something?'

'Wicklow's a bloody county, missus!' The light changed to green, and he pulled the car over on to the shoulder of the busy highway. He turned in his seat and looked at her. This one, he thought, was one of those high-strung American types. New York, he'd guess. Bloody hell.

'Sorry, love, just want to make sure I know where you want to get to.'

Jane's eyes widened in panic. 'Uh, Wicklow, my friend moved to Wicklow to be with her boyfriend. They live in a cottage, she sent me a picture but I don't—' She dumped the contents of her shoulder bag on to the seat beside her and the taxi man leaned over, transfixed. He'd never get that much into a suitcase.

She emptied some of the smaller bags that had been contained in the larger unit, make-up scattering across the floor of the car, nail files tumbling into her lap, scraps of paper fluttering through the air. 'She sent me a postcard – a change of address thing – with a picture she took on the front. She's a photographer. It's all so last minute, this trip, I didn't know until a day ago that I'd – spur of the – of the – moment –' More paper scattered as the Filofax slipped from her shaking fingers and she practically dove head first into her handbag.

The taxi man picked up what looked like a postcard from the passenger seat. 'Miranda? Miranda McMahon?'

'Do you know her?' She was almost hysterical.

'Here ya are, Teach Roisín, Enniskerry, County Wicklow. All right. We're all sorted.' He reached back and patted her knee. 'We're on our way, so.'

Jane looked out the window, at the passing traffic, at the double-decker buses rumbling towards the airport, the cars that looked like any other kind of car you'd see anywhere in America, if smaller, at the pale, sleepy people cycling on their way to work, at the run-of-the-mill evidence that Ireland, for all Miranda's passion, was a pretty run-of-the-mill place. Nothing special about this highway, nothing *magical*, certainly nothing worth leaving New York City for. There seemed to be a lot of grass, but foliage was so suburban. Unimpressed, she leaned her head back and closed her eyes once more.

'Here on holiday?'

Oh, leave me alone! Why don't I just ask him to leave me alone? she thought.

'Yes.'

'Well, you'll be happy enough to see your friends, I reckon.' Definitely New York, he thought. Jaysus, you'd think a bit of a chat would feckin' kill 'em.

Jesus. 'They're . . . I don't know . . . they may not be there.'

'What d'ya mean, they're not there?'

Jane rubbed her temples. 'I tried calling. I think they may be away.' What had Darren said? Paris? Palermo? Pamplona?

'And there's no one to greet you?'

'I don't *know*.' Acid dripped from her voice and she fought the impulse to put her coat over her head.

Well. That shut him up.

Until they came to another complete stop. Jane had no choice but to open her eyes.

The taxi driver turned around in his seat once more, and gestured towards a shop, a convenience store-type place. Jane looked at him blankly. 'Go on, go in there and get yerself a bit of milk, a bit of bread. God knows they've most likely left nothing behind them, so.' He turned off the meter. 'Go on. No hurry.'

Jane stared at him in disbelief, and in that moment, she kind of began to get the whole Irish thing.

The generic highway (a dual carriageway, the M50, to be exact, or so Jackie said) was fairly easy going at that time of day, as they were going against the morning rush. It curved its way past huge office complexes (Jackie called them 'industrial estates' which to Jane sounded like an oxymoron) and they skirted Dublin's city centre to try to save some time and get her into some comfortable clothes and settled behind a nice cuppa (said Jackie). As the steady stream of very small-looking houses (terraces) began to peter out, the roads narrowed and the way was steep. Hard-core shrubbery took over as the houses began to occupy larger pieces of land, and the traffic thinned. Jackie sped down a road no wider than the car itself, and the trees that arched over the roadway blurred into a lush green canopy.

A sudden turn, and the view that opened up had Jane sitting up straight in her seat. Hills stretched down and away to her right, and though the cloud cover was thick and grey, a shaft of sunlight seemed to fall right into the heart of the valley, setting the river that wound its way through it all aglow. A herd of cows wandered up the verge, and a small house perched on the side of the hill on the opposite side of the flowing water.

'If I'm not mistaken . . .' Jackie trailed off, and Jane thought, horrified: this is where Miranda *lives*? In a fucking *storybook*?

It was. Tucking the business card that Jackie had pressed on her into her coat pocket, she carried her two bags and her groceries up to the door. If this was a cottage, she was Elizabeth Taylor: the long, low house went on for days, and there were at least four chimneys. Its rough exterior was a pristine white, and the shutters were painted a bright red. And the roof . . . it was like bunches of sticks or something. Twigs. The windows all sported flower-filled boxes and a wealth of landscaped shrubs marched down the front of the yard; *plus* there were a bunch of standing pots bursting with greenery that, even in the chill weather, were blossoming. She waved to Jackie as he backed down the drive, and didn't have the heart to tell him that she had no idea if there was a spare key hidden anywhere. She guessed she could just prop herself up in the doorway until someone came back from wherever. She leaned against the door, and as her elbow nudged the handle, it flew open, and she fell into the hall.

Are they nuts?! Jane sat up on the flagstones. Going away without even locking the door? They must be out of their *minds*! She got to her feet, grabbing her things, and closed the door behind her.

The place was freezing, an icebox with windows and tables and chairs. Jane poked her head into the first room she saw – a living room kind of thing, with two big cushy red sofas sporting beautifully woven woollen throws casually draped over the backs. They flanked a fireplace, which displayed on its mantel several small wooden figures in various states of dance. The mirror that hung over the mantelpiece reflected the photograph that hung on the opposite wall – one of Miranda's, she guessed.

Feeling like a prowler, Jane crept down the hallway that led off to the left, the silence of the house somehow friendly, but wary as well. Her Centra bag rustled as if reflecting her unease, and she slowly edged the door open.

Oh, for Christ's *sake*. Was this – it had to be – the most perfect kitchen-slash-dining room she'd ever seen. To her left were the practical things, the fridge, the cupboards – all glass-fronted with wooden frames painted a cheery lemon yellow – the enormous stove, you could cook a whole cow in the thing, and the countertop stretched along the far wall, a window over the sink, and various bits of crockery and pots of herbs tumbled down the length of it. Light fell on to the long oak dining table from the skylight above, and another small sculpture was set in the centre, this one carved to look like a miniature woman made out of water. The right-hand wall of the room was a sliding glass door that led on to some kind of greenhouse thing bursting with, but of course, more plant life; the indoor, housebroken type.

Her heels clicking sharply on the flagstone floor, Jane tossed her groceries on to the countertop and leaned up against it. Miranda's photos, beautifully framed yet haphazardly hung, a combination that reeked of charm, lined the other long wall. Disgustingly happy shots of the two of them, Miranda and the Irish guy, moody shots of cliffs and sunlit shots of mountaintops. Jane felt a jolt, like heartburn or something, something acid in her throat; as she looked around this welcoming, homey *home*, its neatness and orderliness set off by occasional explosions of untidiness, she felt . . .

I am so jet-lagged, she thought, and she started unpacking her plastic bag. Delighted at the many name brands she'd recognised – she'd been afraid that all she'd be able to buy was scones covered in butter and jam – she arranged her apples, bananas, yogurts (organic!) and, as a special treat, a brown bread roll kind of thing. Too bad about the coffee, she thought, completely overlooking the huge, gleaming cappuccino machine behind her. Should I have a cup of tea, or should I sleep? she wondered. Impatiently she pushed aside a glass bowl full of herby things, more evidence of Miranda, and noticed what looked like a pitcher that plugged into the wall. She wiggled it a bit and almost knocked it off its holder. It sounded as if it had some water in it. She tentatively flicked the switch on its handle, and waited.

A low rumble told her that it was indeed an electrical object, and the steam that quickly emitted from the spout signalled boiled water. Feeling like Lewis and Clark, she took down a mug from the irritatingly convenient hooks that hung from the bottom of the cupboard and yawned. For about a full minute.

Nope. Must sleep, she thought. Must sleep, even just a little nap, an hour at the most . . .

Stumbling down that long hallway, the first room she came upon was so obviously his and hers that she shut the door and kept going. Almost completely cross-eyed at this stage, she wandered into the next room she found, stripped down to her panties, grabbed a T-shirt off the floor, put it on, and fell into the unmade bed. She wasn't so tired that she didn't wrap herself as tightly as possible in the thick and toasty comforter. Shivering, she closed her eyes, opened them again, barely took in the room at all, closed her eyes and passed out.

In her dream, she stood on a small stage, not very deep but long, and the spotlight shone in her eyes. She couldn't hear an audience at all – was she that bad, had they left the theatre? The dress she was wearing was diaphanous and flowing, and there were flickering torches and music, drumbeats, slow and deep and she felt a hand at the small of her back, a strong, warm hand, and a voice that she couldn't quite understand, a voice that sounded as if it was underwater. The drumbeats increased and the voice became clearer, telling her to 'Jump. Jump. Jump', and then she was standing on the edge of the stage, and there was no audience because the stage was on the edge of an abyss, and the drum beat and beat, and the hand was pushing, pushing, and she heard a thud – was the stage coming apart? – heard the thud again, and then another and then another, in time with the voice urging her to 'Jump. Jump. Jump. Jump. Jump—'

Thump! Thump! Thump! Thump! Jane sat up in bed, horrified. Where am I? she shrieked in her mind— oh, Ireland, Miranda's cottage. Was there an intruder? The noise grew louder, moved further and further down the hallway, closer to where she was lying, and without thinking it through, she leapt from the bed, grabbed what looked like a baseball bat that was resting by the door, and ran screaming out of the room.

Her bloodcurdling shrieks served to send the huge, looming figure into further confusion, causing it to bump its huge donkey-shaped head even more loudly against the walls. Jane lifted her weapon and began hitting the creature around the head and shoulders, screaming incoherently and jumping up and down, trying to knock him senseless.

Shay defended himself as best he could against this screeching harridan wielding a hurley, struggling to remove the papier mâché skull and prevent himself from getting knocked silly by the wooden club.

'For fuck's sake!' he shouted, catching glimpses of the half-naked woman alternately through the nostrils and mouth of the donkey's head. 'Would you ever let me— would you calm down! Calm down!'

He wrenched his head free while simultaneously grabbing the fat end of the hurley, disarming the mad wagon, and avoiding staring at what were two very lovely and long legs.

Jane planted her hands on her hips and demanded, 'What are you doing in my friend's house?'

'What are *you* doing in my cousin's gaff?' he shot back.

'Cousin? Whose cousin?' Had Miranda mentioned a cousin of What's-his-name?

'Niall's cousin. This is his house.'

'This is Miranda's house, his girlfriend, it's hers too,' Jane insisted, moving a bit closer now that she felt the danger had passed.

He didn't look like a crook, more like a . . . pirate. A pirate?! Transatlantic travel quite obviously didn't agree with her. She was hallucinating. But he did look like a pirate, in a way, in a sexy romance-novel kind of way, what with that long blondish-brownish hair and his lanky body; he was a bit on the thin side, maybe, but she could see the well-formed muscles outlined by his pullover . . . maybe the fake parrot he had perching on his shoulder had something to do with the knee-jerk impression as well.

'What's with the parrot?'

Shay ripped the stuffed bird from its perch. 'Oh, that. Just testing out the attachment.' Did the woman not realise she was practically nude? 'Em, looks like it works.'

'So you're Niall's cousin.' Jane wasn't liking his cagey attitude.

'I am. And you still haven't told me who you are.'

'Jane Boyers.' She extended her hand. 'I'm one of Miranda's closest friends.'

Shay's grip was firm, but brief, and Jane began to feel even more suspicious.

'I'd like some proof, if you don't mind.'

The cheek of her! 'You would, would you?'

'I would. You're acting pretty shifty, as far as I'm concerned, and I suspect that you might very well be lying.'

'Shifty?'

Jane jerked up her chin, subconsciously storing away the information that he was a good six inches taller than she was. 'You're not making eye contact, for starters.'

'Well, you're only in your knickers, aren't you? Just trying to preserve your dignity, missus.' Shay's eyes lit up with merriment, and finally met hers and held her gaze. They were a light golden brown, like the eyes of a cat – a very lean, sexy cat.

She'd thought her knees felt a bit chilly. OK, so she'd forgotten to put on her trousers. It could have happened to anyone. With as much dignity as she could muster – and it was quite a lot – Jane marched back into the bedroom and slammed the door.

Having traded the T-shirt for a bulky sweater which she'd grabbed off the back of a chair, Jane crawled back under the covers. The bedside clock read 14.25. What was that – 2.25 in normal, American time. 'I'd better not go back to sleep, I'll never catch up,' she said aloud. 'You have to stay awake or else—' Suddenly she thought better of talking to herself – Bluebeard might be listening at the door. Throwing back the comforter, she crept to the door and put her ear against it. Muffled sounds were coming from the kitchen.

The kitchen. What she wouldn't give for a cup of coffee . . .

Shit. She sank down to the floor, indecisive. She could go back out there and pretend that nothing had happened, that she often ran around half-naked in front of people whom she thought were doing a little breaking and entering . . . Oh, God, what was wrong with her? She felt like her brain was swathed in bubble wrap. She didn't know what to do. She wished she could talk to somebody, somebody she knew . . .

Going back over to the bed, she picked up the mobile phone she'd found on the floor by some chest-of-drawers thing in the dining area. It must be Miranda's, she thought, that must be why there'd been no answer when she'd rung. Punching up the phone-book function, she found Darren's number then hesitated, wondering if he'd even answer, wondering if she hadn't totally blown that friendship, too. That weird thing came over her again, like a stomach-ache accompanied by a soreness in her throat. Did I pick up a bug on the plane? she wondered. If I kind of let him know that I didn't want to be a bitch, good ol' Darren will let me off the hook, and I won't have to stumble through some lame apology. She hit 'call' and jumped back into bed.

Two rings, and the familiar, comforting tones of Darren's voice flew across the Atlantic and into her ear. 'Hey, honey! How's Paris?'

'It's me,' Jane squeaked. 'It's me. Jane.'

A buzz of transatlantic silence. 'Jane? What? But—'

'I'm in Ireland!' She tried for a light, excited tone. 'Jumped on a plane last night! Um, Miranda seems to have left her phone behind. She's in Paris?'

Darren's tone was cool. 'They went for a long weekend, or a week, or something.' He didn't burble on, as Jane had expected. He really is mad at me . . .

'Yeah, um, I – I guess I took you up on that idea you had. The other day.'

The beats of silence were making the unrest in Jane's belly increase exponentially. 'Yes. The other day.'

Dammit. 'Dar, I – I didn't mean to – I know I was kind of short with you—'

Darren stared out his window, down on to the lightening street below. She expects me to do my usual, just charge in and make everything OK . . . which I don't intend to do. Ha! he thought to himself. Say the words, Jane. Go on. Say them.

'Um.' She stalled for time. Shouldn't he be jumping in and saying all the icky feelings-type things he always did? Ugh. 'So, I'm, you know . . . sorry.'

'Thank you for apologising,' Darren said stiffly, while jumping in the air with glee at his own fortitude.

'Well, you're welcome.' What, did he want blood?

There was a beat of silence, into which intruded a light knock at the door. 'Hold on,' Jane said into the phone. 'Yes?' she called out coldly.

Shay entered with a mug in his hand, and made his way over to the bed. He did a double take at the jumper Jane was wearing, causing her to clutch it defensively to her throat. He merely grinned and set the mug on the table.

'I don't drink tea,' she snapped.

'It's coffee. A latte, in fact.' He set the mug down on the nightstand and left the room, closing the door gently behind him.

'Who was *that*?' Darren decided that being frosty wasn't suiting him, and besides, he was dying of curiosity on several fronts.

Jane took a tentative sip of the coffee, and found it to be as good as any she'd get in New York. 'He says he's Niall's cousin. I don't remember Miranda mentioning him.'

'Oh, Shay. He's staying there temporarily, supposedly. I thought he was meant to be gone by now . . . He sounds cute.'

'Sounds cute? You and Miranda were always suckers for a foreign accent.'

'Is he?'

'What?'

'Cute.'

Jane took another swig from the mug. 'I suppose so. If a bit weird.'

'Well, he's a performer.'

'An actor?' God, not an actor.

'No, well, maybe, I don't know. But he wants to start a theatre company.'

'Huh.'

There was another silence, less antagonistic this time around.

'So, what are you doing there?'

'Oh . . .' Jane trailed off, and began to pick at the hem of the sweater. 'I guess I needed a break, and I did want to fix things up with Miranda, and um, the landlord sold my apartment building to Starbucks.'

'The entire building?'

'Yeah. So I had to get out anyway.'

'What about your things?'

'I didn't have that much, I just kind of panicked and put them into storage.'

'But the expense!' Darren was beside himself.

'I didn't know what else to do! I don't really have that much stuff, furniture-wise, and I have the Emmy with me, in my carry-on, luckily, because my bags got lost.'

'Lost?' Darren had to sit down. 'You sound calm enough.'

Jane sighed, and got up to look out the window. She saw Shay in the backyard, hammering away at several flats, either trying to break them up or put them together – it was hard to tell. He leaned over the wood, his jeans strained at what, even from this distance, Jane judged to be a pretty nice ass. She pulled at a loose bit of yarn, and didn't notice that it began to work free of its weave. As she absentmindedly filled Darren in on the flight, the taxi ride, and her trouser-less frenzy with Shay, she was aware that they had re-established equilibrium – it was sure to be this easy with Miranda.

'You must have been mortified.'

'I think I'm coming down with something, like I've got a fever. And my stomach feels a bit off.'

Was she that out of touch? 'Jane! You're embarrassed! You're feeling embarrassed and maybe a bit guilty, perhaps? Take some time while you're away to get in touch with your feelings!'

'Yeah, yeah, yeah,' Jane grumbled.

'So how long are you staying?' All his best friends were gone, and Darren began to feel sorry for himself.

Jane turned away from the window, and flopped down on the bed. 'I don't know. I mean, I have no job, no apartment, no prospects . . . I suppose I'm on a well-deserved vacation –'

Darren felt a jolt of panic. 'So you're staying for what, six months?'

'No way! Are you nuts? I probably can't even replace any of my lovely lost designer things here; it's the middle of nowhere!' In the heat of the moment, she gave a great yank to the bit of yarn she was clutching, and was appalled to see that the sweater had unravelled past her belly. She decided to pretend that she hadn't seen that, and closed her eyes.

'I'm planning on coming out in a month or two, for Miranda's book launch – why not stay around and then maybe we can go off to Italy or something. Plenty of shopping there.'

Jane's throat closed and her eyes began to sting. She really needed more sleep. 'We'll see. That sounds good.' She stared gloomily out the window at the distant mountain and the endless green. 'Although I can't imagine being stuck here until then.'

Something was cooking. Someone – Shay – was cooking, and it smelled like heaven. In her weakened state, Jane pulled on some sweatpants and followed her nose out of the room.

The pirate was working away at the stove, and he turned slightly when he heard Jane come in and put the mug on the countertop.

'Thanks,' she said. 'Good coffee.'

'Not a big fan of tea, myself. Loaded up with it half my life. Hungry?'

Starving, Jane thought. She watched him ravenously

as he awkwardly nudged whatever was in the skillet with a spatula. 'A little. What is it?'

'Rashers. Want a buttie?'

'What, and do I want what?' Who said that the Irish and the Americans shared a common language? It explained Miranda's new lexicon. She went and sat down at the table.

'Ah, wait for it now.' Shay grinned at her and started buttering slices of bread.

'Is that white bread? Do you know how bad that is for you? Full of chemicals and additives and calories and—'

Shay slid a plate in front of her, which held a slice, folded over what looked like an enormous piece of meat. She sniffed at it – smelled like pork? Oh my God!

'I can't eat this! It's all butter and fat and white bread!'

Shay bit into his sandwich and smiled. Jane apprehensively picked up the concoction and very delicately bit into it.

Bliss. Sheer fatty bliss.

They ate in silence, and drank the fresh coffee that Shay had brought over as well.

'This is cholesterol hell.' Jane took another big bite. 'But it's not bad.'

'Not much of a cook myself – that's Niall's deal – but I can do a decent buttie. So. You here for a visit?'

Jane nodded, her mouth full.

'Em . . . a surprise visit, I take it?'

'Something like that.' The last thing she was going to do was tell this crazy stranger her life story. 'I find it hard to believe that Niall and Miranda left the door open if they were going to Paris.'

'I've been around all day. So you must be from New York.'

'Yes.'

'Staying a while? Looks like you're travelling light?'

He was nosy. 'And what makes you say that?' she evaded again.

'Well, for starters, you're wearing my clothes.'

Jane felt hot all over, all over again. Embarrassment. Darren said it was embarrassment.

She hated embarrassment. 'Look, the airline lost my luggage, which is par for the course as I have just lost my job as a producer in television, and I have also just lost my apartment, and I'm now hoping to stay with my friend, one of my oldest friends, for a while until I get myself back together, OK? Is that enough information for you?'

She wasn't going to win any congeniality awards, thought Shay, but then he took in the jet-lagged look about her eyes, and gave her a break. 'Sure, plenty.' He pushed the platter of butties towards her, and she took another before her conscience could talk her out of it. 'It's lovely to see a woman eat.' Jane rolled her eyes. What a patronising comment. 'Especially an American woman. You're all too thin.'

'You've obviously never been a woman in America.'

'Not even in a past life.' Shay snagged the last buttie, and Jane sat back, feeling wonderfully full and drowsy. She laughed.

'Past lives, huh? You and Miranda must get along great.'

Shay grimaced. 'Miranda? She's a stroppy one.'

'Stroppy?'

'You know, like, em, easily needled, bad-tempered—'

'I figured out what "stroppy" means. She's a teddy bear!'

'I reckon I bring out the grizzly in her.'

Jane's eyes narrowed. 'Weren't you supposed to be gone by now, before they came back?'

Shite. 'We're still working that out.'

Ha ha, Jane thought. Your turn on the hot seat. 'That just goes to show how little you know about Miranda. She's pretty territorial, likes her home life to be just so. I mean, she even moved all the way out to Brooklyn for a little peace and quiet.'

'Right, so, gotta get back to work, take care of that jet lag, maybe see you at tea!' And Shay leapt up from the table and swiftly made his way out the back door.

Jane laughed. Gotcha there, Mr Easygoing Pirate. Leaving the plates and mugs in the sink, Jane went off, much lighter in heart, certain she'd evened the score. She rubbed her belly, feeling fuller than she had in years, and refused to feel guilty about it – this was, after all, vacation time. And it was time she started acting like it.

Jane's body jerked and shot up from the mattress. She was late, late for work, she had to pitch her shows, she had to get her nails done – no, she had to get her nails done and *then* pitch her shows, godammit, godammit, godammit—

She was halfway out of the door before she realised where she was.

She was in Ireland, freezing to death.

Jumping back into the bed and burying herself under the comforter until only her nose was showing, she peeped guiltily around the room. What was clear to her now, after a deep night's sleep, was that the room was definitely inhabited. She'd been too wiped out yesterday to notice. Although the clues were few, they were definitely there: the scatter of belongings trailing across the top of the bureau, the suitcases stacked next to the wardrobe, the pile of laundry shoved into the corner. Shivering, she reached a hand out from under the cosy warmth and picked up a pile of books from the nightstand. *The Empty Space* by Peter Brook. *Impro* by Keith Johnstone. Hmmph. Theory. Didn't get you very far unless you got some practice.

Unable to bear the frosty air on her arm, she tucked it back under the covers and lay there, wrapped up like a mummy. How about a little heat, Shay, old pal, she thought. How about a little bit of the old warmth in this stone frigging house! Her nose felt like a block of ice, and she felt a weird twinge in her belly as she thought about the endless steam heat that used to pump into her adorable little studio in Tribeca, the waves of warmth that used to flow unceasingly, so much so that she'd routinely leave the window open, even in the depths of winter. She rubbed her hands over her chest, where she felt a little pang, somehow linked to the peculiar feeling in her gut.

For all she knew, she could be coming down with frostbite.

She lay, immobile, her head turned slightly to the left, looking out the window at the half-blue, half-grey sky. She'd have to get up. She'd have to get up and get out of the bed and get on with things. She'd have to get up and find somewhere else in the house to sleep. She'd have to check in with the airline again, although she'd got the feeling, from the last lady she spoke to, that her bags were gone for good. She'd have to get to a store some- where. Maybe they had malls in this country, like in the suburbs, maybe they had Bloomie's here . . . maybe? Wouldn't it be amazing if they had Bloomie's here and she could just whip out her plastic and buy herself an entire new wardrobe?

There is no Bloomingdale's in Ireland, Jane, she thought. She shivered some more and rolled completely over on to her side. A bird chirped sweetly on the window sill. 'Easy for you to say,' she grumbled. 'Unless you've flown east for the winter, you don't know what you're missing.' I'm going to end up looking like some hippy drop-out artist like Miranda, she thought, all turtlenecks and hiking boots. Why did I come here? She pulled on her hair as if she could yank the answer out of her brain. What in the world possessed me to come here?

The bird abruptly stopped singing and flew away. The silence was utterly deafening. She couldn't hear a thing, nothing but silence, nothing but nothing. It buzzed in her ears until she thought she was going to scream.

OK, Janie, she told herself, caffeine, now, before you crack up. A nice, hot cup of coffee. OK, get up. Go on. Go!'

She shot up from the bed and, hopping around on the stone floor, grabbed the trousers she'd worn on the journey and nabbed a pair of socks from an open drawer. Trying to keep as many square inches of flesh covered as possible, she shimmied into her bra while still wearing Shay's T-shirt, and threw that off once she'd located her blouse. She hopped up and down, trying to encourage her blood to warm, then, giving up, she wrapped herself up in the comforter and ventured out into the hall.

To her right lay unexplored territory. Three doors ranged down towards a spiral staircase: one definitely had the look of a spare bedroom, its matching-blanket-and-curtains vibe giving it a pleasing but impersonal air. A bit quaint, Jane sniffed, but it would have to do. The second door revealed a room so small and narrow that it made Jane think fondly once more of her little bijou apartment on Worth Street – her ex-bijou. It was gone now. Jane slammed the door and opened the last door, finding an office-cum-library set up.

Well. *Someone* had landed on her feet. Jane slammed that door, too. She tried to see what was at the top of the stair, but got distracted by the view out of the window at the end of the hall.

It looked out over the valley, a valley that even in the very early stages of spring, was brilliantly green. Those cows were at it again, wandering around peacefully, and flowers bloomed all over the place. Was that a palm tree?

What was with this place?

Turning her back on the view, Jane trudged towards the bathroom and thought she'd have a good soak. There were bath salts and oils and bubbles all over the place, and she couldn't remember the last time she'd run herself a tub. Certainly not in the time she'd lived in Tribeca – that bathroom had barely been big enough to contain a shower stall.

Selecting musk-scented bubbles, Jane ran the water into the bath, a huge, gleaming affair of white porcelain and clawed feet. Enough with the storybook, already, she thought. She turned the hot tap on full, added a bit of cold, and went out to make the coffee.

A steaming cup of glorious Colombian roast accompanied her back to the bath, almost filled to the rim with delightful bubbles. Hurriedly undressing, Jane set the mug down on the floor, and slid a leg into the water. Shrieking, she leapt away and almost slipped on the bath mat.

The water was completely and utterly ice cold.

She turned on the hot tap, and out gushed water that was so frigid it was practically solid.

'God*dammit*!' she shouted. I *hate* it here!

The door to the studio burst open, and Shay, arms full of robes which he thought might be vaguely Greek, spun around at the sound. Jane strode across the floor to stand in front of him, swathed in what looked like the duvet from his bed.

'Listen, I know that I'm totally inconveniencing you by being here, but the least you could have done was save me some hot water!'

'Did you not put on the immersion?' he asked. Her red nose was quivering, a sight that Shay found to be rather endearing.

'The what?'

'The immersion. To heat up the water.'

'You have to heat up the water?'

'The immersion heats up the water.'

'Why isn't it hot all by itself?'

'You have to turn on the yoke to heat it up.' Shay was beginning to enjoy this.

'The what? A yoke? Like with buckets?'

'Buckets?'

Jane started gesturing madly underneath the comforter. 'A yoke, a thing, over your neck, you hang buckets – do you have to get water from a *well*?'

She looked positively apoplectic. Stop winding her up, Shay, he told himself sternly, fighting back a laugh. 'No, chicken, the immersion's the yoke. Yoke means "thing". You have to turn on the "thing" to heat up the water.'

'Jesus *Christ*.' Jane sat down on a tattered divan and shivered. 'That's *ridiculous*. Water should come out hot if that's what you *want*.'

'You're not in Kansas any more,' Shay said cheerily.

'Excuse me?' She glared at him.

Did she understand nothing? 'That's from your own culture, missus. Dorothy. Kansas. *Wizard of Oz*?' He shook his head and began shaking out the robes, raising a cloud of mothball-scented dust.

'Hmph.' Jane huddled under the duvet. Silence descended and she glanced around the room. It had the look of the property shop from her college theatre, and it made her want to smile. There was enough stuff in here, she guessed, from furniture to costumes, to produce anything in the classical repertory, and she felt a little jump in her pulse as she ran her eye over the costume rack. Getting up, she shuffled over and started flicking through the hangers. She became so engrossed that the comforter fell away, unnoticed.

'D'ya mind picking up that duvet? It's a bit dusty on the floor.'

'The what? Never mind. I figured it out.' She picked up the 'duvet' and folded it up. Turning, she saw that Shay had set aside the robes and was now wearing a Venetian mask. Pulling on a deep red robe, she wandered over to a table stacked with props. Beaten metal candlesticks sat next to a gramophone, which shared the surface with a few duelling swords and an ugly tea set that looked like cabbages. Shay grabbed one of the swords and began waving it around – testing for balance, he thought – showing off, she thought.

'Who are you?' she wondered aloud.

'Well,' began Shay, taking her seriously, 'I'm a director. And a producer. I will be, anyway, thanks to all this gear.' He removed the mask, and she could see the light in his eyes, a light that she recognised. He's got the bug – but does he have the chops?

'What have you done?' she asked casually, as she removed the robe and traded it for a diaphanous gown. Tugging it over her head, she found that it didn't quite fit over her shirt and slacks, but it didn't stop her from going over to the mirror to check herself out.

'Ophelia,' Shay murmured, watching Jane swish a bit, making the drape of the dress swirl around her feet.

'You played Ophelia? That's seriously period.' Jane wished she had long blond hair, and a veil or something.

'No. That's Ophelia's. That's what they find her in, in the stream, drowned for love of Hamlet, and grief for her father.' His voice softened and he picked up a wig and set it on her head.

Jane adjusted the fit, and automatically held out a hand for the caplet of slightly ratty flowers he extended to her. She set it on her head, and neither of them saw the dusty buds, nor the torn veil, nor the ill-fitting garment. Both saw only the image of a tragic young girl, in their minds and in the soft focus of the cloudy glass.

' "There's fennel for you, and columbines – there's rue for you; and here's some for me – we may call it grace o' herbs of Sundays – O, you must wear your rue with a difference. There's a daisy – I would give you some violets, but they wither'd all when my father died – they say he made a good end . . ." ' Lost in the moment, Jane went on and sang, ' "For bonny sweet Robin is all my joy".'

Her voice was youthful and clear, and Shay responded. ' "Thought and affliction, passion, hell itself. She turns to favour and to prettiness." '

Jane opened her mouth and sang a note that descended into a laugh. Embarrassed, she removed the veil and wig and moved away from the mirror. 'Oops. Forgot the rest.' Liar, she thought. You know that speech as well as you know your own name. She tossed the wig aside and began to struggle out of the dress.

Shay batted away her hands, and guided the delicate material over her head. 'That's good. Very good. I thought you said you were a producer?'

'I am,' Jane said defensively, and moved further away. He had been so gentle with her – with the dress, it gave her the shivers. 'I produce TV.'

'But you're an actress,' Shay insisted. 'Surely you couldn't just run the mad scene off the top of your head without some training, not as well as you did just now.'

Jane shrugged. 'I acted a bit in college. Stayed in New York to seek fame and fortune – hardly anybody does that, you know.' She wondered if he'd heard the bitterness in her voice. 'It wasn't my scene. So I got into production instead. I prefer being in control.'

'Ah, well. I got distracted myself from the bright lights. Ended up in law school.' Shay wondered if he sounded as sullen as he felt.

'That explains the inquisitiveness, anyway.' She poked around the flats that were stacked against a wall. 'So, what have you done? Laertes? Ivanov? Jack Clitheroe?'

'Ah, very good. You know your Irish theatre.' He picked up what looked like a heap of rags that turned out to be peasant costumes, and began to separate them as he continued. 'Played a bit in college, in the drama society, always got the youthful parts because of my boyish good looks.' He grinned at her arched brow. 'I see you're thinking I'm still in possession of them. Thought

I'd go to drama school after I got the law degree – just a precaution, mind – but the father had different ideas.'

'Don't tell me – you joined the family firm.'

'Got it in one.' He handed her some of the clothes, which she held away from her at a safe distance. 'Could do with a wash, hey? Da was the executor of the uncle's will, the one who bequeathed me this treasure trove – snuck that clause in at the last minute without his brother knowing, even got a local solicitor to redraw the will. I like to think it was his last act as a doting uncle.'

'It must have made dramatic reading.' Jane was sure that there were fleas in the skirts she was holding.

'My old fella almost keeled over himself.'

Jane shook out a shawl and draped it over her head. In response, Shay pulled on a waistcoat and a pair of knee breeches.

'And now what?' she asked, tying on an apron.

'And now, having wielded the symbolic loy and lowered it on to himself's greying pate – I get to play.' He whooped and grabbed Jane, pulling her into a reel that she took up quickly, with only a few false steps.

'You follow well!' he shouted, whooping again.

Jane stopped the mad dance. 'Trust me, no one has ever said that to me before.' She moved away; the feeling of his hand on her back, his hand in hers, was a little bit disturbing.

Jane did not like being disturbed. 'So what are you going to *do*?'

Shay examined what looked like a parasol, denuded of its cloth. 'Hmmm. Eh? That's the problem. I can do anything. The choice is baffling. I don't know where to start.'

'You start with a property.' Jane crossed her arms and began to pace.

What a bossy little voice she had. 'It needs to be the right property.'

'Shakespeare?'

'Too English.'

'Surely they do Shakespeare here.'

'I wouldn't want that to be my first thing out of the gate. Politically incorrect, as you Yanks would say.'

Jane rolled her eyes. 'What difference does that make?'

'Give yourself a few more days here, you'll cop on. That means—'

'I got it, I got it. So . . . something Irish.'

Shay swung the staff around a bit. 'But that hasn't been done to death.'

'Something new?'

'No. I've no patience for living playwrights. I worked with one once. I'll never do it again.'

'I know what you mean,' Jane agreed. 'Something old with a modern twist?'

'What, you mean the camp version of *The Importance of Being Earnest*, like?'

'It's camp enough as it is.' Jane's brow furrowed as she paced.

'You know your stuff, so you do.' Shay assessed her as she wore tracks into the floor. Here was an idea. He grinned, wide and cheerful. 'C'mere. You can help.'

Jane arched her brows as only she could. 'Help?'

'Produce.'

'This?' She choked back a little laugh.

Shay's big brown eyes narrowed dangerously. 'What "this"?'

'This . . . stuff. These old costumes and broken-down furniture. I don't do theatre,' she replied loftily, her heart doing a little flip that belied her disdain. 'I do big budgets with bankable talent.'

'Not at the minute, you don't.' Stung, Shay threw down the parasol and picked up a box of fabric. 'And you mustn't have been any great shakes at it either, seeing as how you were let go and all.'

Slowly and carefully, Jane removed the shawl and the

apron and returned them to the pile – pile of filthy rags, she thought spitefully, and, picking up the duvet – *comforter!* – she turned to leave.

'Jane—' Ah, Jesus, he'd done it now, hadn't he.

She turned and just looked at him, coldly, blankly, as if the preceding moments hadn't happened. She said nothing, just stood there, waiting.

He wasn't equal to it, but he had to try.

'If you change your mind, you know where I am. I might even have a part for ya.'

She arched a brow, turned, and left.

Jane got out of Jackie's taxi, and he honked smartly as he pulled away from the kerb. A crisp breeze blew in from the park across the street, whatever it was called, and she turned and looked at the huge, greenhouse-esque mall that rose up in front of her. It didn't look promising, but Jane had shopping to do, shopping that for once was less out of habit than out of sheer necessity.

Stephen's Green Shopping Centre was large and airy and, to Jane's practised eye, as predictable as any American mall. Standing in front of the information booth, she glanced up at the ceiling, all glass and metal, and her sensitive nose picked up the slightly sour smell of some kind of baking cheese sandwich, and a whiff of candy, cloying and sharp.

No. No way. The place evoked one too many memories of adolescence, and she strode out to what Jackie had told her would be Grafton Street, the best shopping in Dublin City. The pedestrianised road was teeming with people, even at eleven a.m. Squaring her shoulders, she held her handbag tightly and marched down the street.

Right, OK, Laura Ashley – not her style by a long shot, but a familiar name. Dunnes – no idea. Monsoon – kind of teenybopper trendy. Carl Scarpa – well, in a pinch, she supposed, but footwear wasn't really the priority. Unfamiliar names and methods of window dressing began to swirl around her, with some comic relief thrown in by the hopelessly touristy shops flogging shamrock-laden shirts, beer mugs and underwear. Shit, she thought to herself, standing in front of A Wear, watching young girls finger scanty skirts, I'm going to end up looking like an ageing Tweenie.

She pushed through the meandering crowd, a blaze of colour catching her eye. Buckets of flowers in a riot of colours banked two sides of the street, and one of the vendors caught her looking.

'Flowers, love?' she called out, and Jane actually stopped for a fraction of a second, wondering: when was the last time she'd bought a bouquet of flowers? She'd certainly never received any – a sloppy, sentimental thought that had her glaring at the flower seller and moving on.

Not my style, she thought again. Very little in this country is my style. Big eat-in kitchens and cows on hillsides and palm trees and meat-and-butter sandwiches and, and nasty ex-lawyers who come on all friendly and affable and then go for the jugular. Jerk.

Excuse me, Jane? she heard her good angel whisper in her ear. You were, in fact, an unbelievably big bitch, laughing at his dreams. You did, in fact, start it.

'Oh, leave me alone,' she snapped, scattering a crowd of Spanish-speaking youngsters who had been loitering in her path. Blindly trudging down the street, she suddenly found herself at the end of it and stopped, aghast.

Was that *it*? She clutched the collar of her coat to her throat, and closed her eyes. That couldn't be all there was . . .

She spun on her heel, earning a few dirty looks from the group of old ladies who were trying to cross against the light. Taking a deep breath, she began to retrace her steps, and prayed that Laura Ashley made something, anything, in black –

And then she saw it. Rising up before her, gleaming

white, the sun shining on its pristine glass doors – Jane had caught her first glimpse of Brown Thomas.

Barely breathing, she stumbled around to the front of the store. Reaching almost desperately for the door handle, she found it swinging open before her, and a doorman in full livery smiled at her and tipped his cap.

'Morning, miss,' he said, as he beckoned her inside.

'Thank you,' Jane whispered. 'Thank you so much.' She moved into the store, paused, and took a deep breath.

A heady mixture of perfumes wafted on the air, and Jane could identify at least seventy per cent of them. She looked around, immensely comforted by the familiar logos – Clinique, Clarins, Calvin Klein – and moved slowly through the cosmetics department, fondly stroking the Estée Lauder display, reaching out and touching the Lancôme lipsticks. She almost fell to her knees in gratitude, for this was, without question, her spiritual home.

She wandered towards the back of the ground floor, passing the section devoted to Aveda hair care, and considered grabbing up shampoo and conditioner by the armful, when a half-assembled display caught her eye. Oh, thank God! She wanted to weep with relief. This wonderful and amazing store stocked Diva.

She almost knocked over two very thin, blonde, beige-bedecked orangey women in her rush to get to the products. Even in the present disarray, she saw that she ought to be able to replace everything that she had lost in her luggage. As she searched for her preferred colours, a flurry of cursing drifted up from behind the counter.

Crouched on the floor was a petite, if irate, blonde. She scrabbled through the boxes like a dog looking for a bone, tossing papers aside and scattering the contents of endless cartons all around her. Sections of glowing red Lucite were stacked up against the wall, in danger of toppling over as the woman's frantic activity reached a crescendo.

'Excuse me,' Jane prompted. The fumbling increased. 'Hel*lo*!'

The blonde looked wildly over her shoulder at Jane, and rose, clumsily balanced on a pair of stilettos that Jane would have to track down for herself or die in the attempt.

'Howya.' The woman huffed a stray lock out of her face on an impatient breath. 'Listen, we're not quite open for business, as you can see.'

'Hmmm, yes, I can see that, but I know exactly what I'm looking for.'

The blonde nudged at the mess at her feet with the toe of her shoe. 'Well, that's a sight more than I do, I'm afraid,' she mumbled grumpily. 'Bloody mess of a bunch of slap – they've got some kind of legend or map for the gear and I can't find the feckin' thing, nor can I find the shagging instructions for that yoke there!'

I, thought Jane, know what a yoke is. And, on top of which, 'I know all about this line,' she offered. 'And I know what the "yoke" is supposed to look like.'

'Jesus, you're not some kind of company inspector!' The woman's flushed face went a deep scarlet.

'No,' said Jane, 'I am an avid consumer. And I can, um, help.'

'You sort this out, and you can have my employee discount until I quit.'

Jane came around the back and began arranging the products in sections. 'The entire line is named for various high-profile Hollywood starlets from the twenties to the present,' she said authoritatively. 'The more innocent colours are, for example, Mary Pickford and Shirley Temple. Middle range is Vivien Leigh, Claudette Colbert and Carole Lombard. The most obviously sexy are your Jayne Mansfield, your Rita Hayworth, and, of course, Marilyn.'

'You're a star. Will you start on that monster, and I'll go on with these. Cathleen's my name.'

'Jane Boyers.'

'American?'

'New York.'

'Jesus, I've always meant to go.'

They chatted companionably; Jane constructed the Lucite display efficiently, from memory, explaining to Cathleen that the bits of velvet were pillows for use in the display, and that each purchase was wrapped in a gold ribbon and adorned with a silver feather.

'It's all very posh,' mused Cathleen, her face having lost its furious blush.

'It's delicious,' murmured Jane, stroking a powder puff along her cheek.

'It's certainly top drawer – wouldn't have it in my own kit, work or play. Not that this is my real work. I'm only at this part time.'

'What do you do?' Jane considered a nail varnish from the Clara Bow line.

'Well, I'm trying to get into make-up for theatre and film. I went to business school, did a diploma course in drama, but the placement scheme was useless.' This was not Cathleen's favourite subject at the minute, so she changed to another. 'So, you over on holiday?'

'Umm hmm,' Jane replied, her noncommittal tone putting off Cathleen not one bit.

'Staying with friends?'

'Sort of. They're not around until next week.'

'You must be lonely, on your own.' Cathleen's brow furrowed as she fussed with the Veronica Lake hair gel.

'I know a few people,' Jane replied a bit tersely. Lonely? Please.

'A crowd of us are going out night after next, so come along.'

Jane's hand froze in the act of choosing her Jane Russell Red lipstick. Something bloomed in her chest, a light kind of something that made her turn to Cathleen and smile. How weird. Do people really just ask other people along for a drink? Just like that?

'Go on, give us your number – have you got a mobile?' Cathleen searched the pockets of her smock for a pen.

'I'm, er, using my friend's, until she gets back.'

They entered each other's numbers into their respective phones, and then Jane very patiently walked Cathleen through the wrapping ritual. It's the least I can do, she thought, for a new friend.

'Had a busy day, so.' Jackie shook his head – the back of his car was stuffed full of shopping bags.

'Isn't Brown Thomas fantastic! It's almost exactly like Saks – in fact, it's actually like a combination of Saks and Bloomingdales!' Jane sat back, utterly relaxed for the first time in days. Maybe even months.

'I'll take your word for it.' Jackie downshifted and glanced over at his passenger. She'd finally got the hang of sitting up front with him, and looked miles better than she had the other day. 'You've beaten the jet lag, anyway.'

'I feel great!' And Jane was surprised to find that it was true. She reached back and unearthed a small carrier bag from beneath the impressive pile. 'Are you hungry? I got a bunch of stuff from Marks & Spencer. Isn't their food fantastic?'

'A bit on the fancy side. Yuppie food, like. No offence.'

Jane just laughed, and cracked open a plastic container of grapes. 'Have some, seriously, they're fab.'

'Fab.' Jackie tried out the fruit and the slang. 'Faaaab.'

They rode in silence as the traffic started to build when they neared Bray. Jane looked out the window, far less blindly than before, and began to notice things: the general tidiness of front yards and flower beds, the odd ruin plopped on top of a hill, the glimpses of the sea as the road rose and fell. A few dark clouds skittered across the sky, chasing the sun as it began to set. She sighed, and decided that she felt . . . fantastic.

Apart from the twinge of guilt over Shay.

'You all right out there, on your own?' Jackie took a right towards Roundwood.

What, is this guy like a mind reader? 'Ummm. Well, there's a cousin of my friend's boyfriend staying there. He's a bit of a character.' Jane sank down in her seat guiltily.

Jackie frowned. 'What sort is he?'

'Sort?' Jane frowned in return. 'What do you mean? Like, what does he do?'

Americans! As if a profession explained everything! 'No, no, like, is he sound? He's no madzer, is he?'

Jane's brow cleared and she patted Jackie on the arm. 'He's fine. A bit crazy, but not psychotic.' She grinned. 'And he's kinda cute.'

'Jane.' Jackie stopped at a light and turned in his seat to look her dead in the eye. 'Surely you must know that, unless he's five years old, you're never to call the male of the species "cute".'

'I'll keep that in mind.'

It took three trips for Jane to bring in her shopping, and an hour to put everything away. She felt a bit wistful moving into the spare room, a stupid sort of feeling, as if she'd had any fondness for Shay's bed. Ha! She wouldn't touch that guy with a ten-foot pole. But she would have to make it up to him, somehow. The guilt wouldn't go away, and as Jane had given up guilt for life when she'd turned eighteen, she didn't want to relapse.

And she guessed that a home-cooked meal might do the trick.

'Home-cooked', of course, being a relative term.

She unpacked the food she'd bought with undisguised glee. She'd never seen anything so cunningly packaged, even the little basket of plums had a certain *je ne sais quoi*, covered in its little net, wrapped with its own little handle. Punnet, she read on the label. A punnet of plums. I've purchased a punnet of plums. Delighted with herself, she laughed aloud, and danced around the kitchen putting things away. Sauces, bags of ready-made salad, finely cut asparagus and, as an unusual treat, a block of cheese veined with cranberries. As she spun around in a graceful pirouette, tossing a bag of gourmet, low-fat, cracked-pepper-seasoned pretzels high in the air, she came face to face with a slightly guilty-looking Shay. The pretzels hit the floor with a crunchy thwack.

Oh, good, she thought. Let's make him suffer, shall we?

'Pardon me,' she said icily, and turned her back on him. She heard him shuffle around a bit, and fought back a smile.

She was still steamed, he could tell. It looked like she'd gone shopping – she was wearing a snug and flattering little dress. There were those legs again, he mused, and those high heels! Jesus Christ. He distracted himself for a few moments, admiring Jane's back, but the stiffness of that back, and her cold silence, reminded him that he had a job to do.

'Sorry,' he grumbled, scratching his jaw in embarrassment. For someone who often found himself in exactly the position he was in now, he still hadn't got the hang of apologising.

'For?' Jane started unwrapping the asparagus.

Ah, come on, missus! 'For before. This morning. I was – well, you had been a bit of a – I shouldn't have said – So I'm sorry, right? I mean, I know that you American women get all fired up over your careers, and such—'

Jane slammed the asparagus down on the counter, purely for the effect. 'You really know just the right thing to say, don't you?'

Shay picked up a tea towel and started flogging himself with it, doing a circuit of the kitchen's work island to impress his sincerity upon her. 'I'm begging your forgiveness, milady, and will do a pilgrimage to knock on my knees, complete with self-flagellation in order to win myself back into your good graces—'

'I've already forgiven you,' Jane announced loftily. Shay feel to his knees in exaggerated gratitude. He wrapped his arms around her knees, leaned his head on her belly, and pretended to babble his thanks incoherently.

His hands were warm and large and . . . manly. No way were these hands cute. Playfully, Jane grabbed a handful of his hair, and jerked his head back. They looked into each other's eyes, both slowly becoming aware of their posture, of their hands on each other, of the closeness of their bodies. His arms were wiry and strong and tightened a bit as Jane began to tense up, feeling every muscle in those arms draw her closer, if that were possible. Her breath caught in her throat, and her fingers began to stroke his hair. Those eyes, golden brown and fringed by lashes that were blond at the tips, warmed as he rubbed his chin against her taut stomach. A deep and sinful scent seemed to waft tantalisingly close to his face, infusing his senses, making him want to snuggle into her hip, caress her back, draw her down before him so that they were face to face, mouth to mouth . . .

'Let go.' That sounded a bit intense, Janie, she thought. 'Let me go or you won't get your dinner.'

'The magic words. And it's called tea.' Shay leapt lightly to his feet, and moved back a step. He nervously ran a hand through his hair. Flustered, Jane turned and ripped open a bag of salad.

'What's tea?'

'Your dinner.'

'The fish?'

'No, American dinner equals Irish tea.'

'What*ever*. Here, chop this garlic.'

'Yes, ma'am.'

They worked a while in silence, both having forgotten the earlier tiff, and both wondering if the other had felt that sexual charge. We should keep it light, thought Jane, and she fired up the stove to roast some pine nuts.

'You know your way around a kitchen,' Shay observed.

'I most definitely do not. I'll have you know that I never once used my oven in the six years I lived in Tribeca. I used it to store my accessories. But! I can do four things extremely well.' Jane slanted a glance at him and gave him what he decided was a very sexy little smile. 'I can make a delicious Caesar salad, I make a fantastic fresh fruit and yogurt smoothie, and I can compose an amazing vegetable stir fry using low-fat olive oil.'

'Rabbit food,' he scoffed, and reached up to the wine rack, exposing a rather tight set of abs. He selected a bottle of white and stuck it in the freezer.

'You may as well leave it out, it'll chill right there on the countertop,' Jane grumbled.

'You'll get used to it.' Shay grinned, and rubbed those interesting hands up and down her arms. 'That was only three things you do extremely well.'

Jane moved away, and pointlessly looked into the fridge. 'I make lasagna. Only very rarely, and only on very, very special occasions.'

'That's more like it.' He moved with her, and caught a scent off her hair that was deep and rich and mysterious. 'And what's cause for a very, very special occasion?'

She moved away, flustered again. What did it matter if she flirted with him? She was only passing through, after all . . .

'We'll just have to see.' She smiled again, and started cutting up a lemon.

He watched her wield the knife, precisely slicing the

lemon into evenly sized wedges. A tempting stretch of neck was exposed as she concentrated on her task, and if she didn't have the knife in her hand, and what he suspected were fairly good reflexes, he'd chance a bit of a nuzzle. Down, Shay boy, he thought. They were only having a bit of a flirt. He expelled a breath – it was getting a bit close in there. Too warm over by the stove, that must be it.

Time to shift gears.

'So?'

'Hmmm?' Jane was admiring the glorious and fresh and completely prepared salmon steak.

'So what'd you think?'

'It's lovely – and there's no fat in the sauce at all.' She held up the label.

'Of signing on.'

Jane paused, a wedge of lemon in hand. Unbelievable. 'To what?'

Shay banged his head against the cabinet. 'My company, my theatre company, for fuck's sake, missus!'

'I'm not *married*.'

'I know, it doesn't mean – it's only a – never mind. So?'

'Persistent. An excellent quality in a producer. Is there a pan, or something, for this?'

Shay went on as he hunted up a baking tray. 'I meant it before, before we fell out. You've got experience, you can take care of some bits that I won't be able to do on my own.'

Jane took out some aluminium foil and wrapped up the fish, placing it on the tray that Shay had discovered in the cabinet over the sink. She decided not to start an argument over the idea that the many complicated and arduous tasks that comprised 'production' could ever possibly be termed 'bits'. 'I'm on vacation.'

'Sure, it'll be a busman's holiday, but I – well, I wouldn't say no to the help.'

Sliding the fish into the oven, Jane handed Shay a corkscrew. 'No,' she said amicably, and went over to the table to have a smoke.

That, thought Shay, was not a real 'no'. He could feel it in his bones.

She had to hand it to him – he knew when to back off. Dinner conversation was kept easy and breezy, and if he mentioned his nascent theatre company, he didn't try to sell her on his grand plan. What a crazy idea, she thought as they sipped whiskeys and did a bit of stargazing. She hadn't bothered with theatre for years, and for good reason. Way too much aggravation for too little pay-off. But she couldn't help feeling a bit of the old spark when he started talking about plays, and found herself wondering what would happen if maybe, possibly, she took a little part or something . . . just for fun . . .

'. . . if I can find the time to read through a few of them.'

She was a million miles away. Shay nudged her with his pack of cigarettes and waited until she took one.

'Uh huh.' So he was back on it again, she could see that look in his eye.

'And then, I reckon, I'll make a big splash here, and head off for the States.'

Jane blew out some smoke rings towards the ceiling. 'What, Broadway, your name in lights?'

'You're very cynical.'

'*You're* terribly idealistic.'

'We'd make a great team.' He kicked back and blew some smoke rings at her smoke rings. Every one of them joined together.

'Very persistent.'

'I've heard it's a good quality in a producer.'

Shay topped up their drinks, and Jane looked out at the stars. They'd shut off all the lights in the kitchen, leaving only the candle on the table. She looked away from the inky black sky and considered him in the flickering light. 'You've got a good look, a young Harrison Ford vibe going on – you'd get plenty of commercial work.'

'I want to direct.'

Jane snorted. 'You and everybody else. With either acting or directing, if you don't know anyone in the city, in the channels, you can forget it.'

'Did you give up that easily?' Shay sat back.

'How about we designate that a "no go" zone?' Jane stubbed out her cigarette in irritation.

'No old dreams?' Shay insisted.

'I achieved my dream. I won a prestigious industry award, I was at the top of my game. The network begged to differ.' Jane looked away from his piercing gaze.

'Why not just get another job?'

A thousand reasons flew through Jane's mind in under three seconds, endless options presented themselves in a blur, and she couldn't grab on to a single one and make it stick.

'I don't know!' she snapped. And then added, more quietly, 'I don't know.'

She was a puzzle, all right, and he hated leaving a puzzle unsolved. 'Why did you not go to your family?'

Jane smiled thinly. 'I plead the fifth, counsellor.'

It was Shay's turn to scowl. 'I'm not a counsellor.'

'Could have fooled me. You must have been pretty good. Tenacious, stubborn . . .' She almost said 'convincing'. 'There's a fine line between being a lawyer and being an actor, they say.'

'I'm not an actor.' Shay lit up another cigarette and exhaled furiously.

They stared at each other, combative, in the candlelight.

'Neither am I.' Jane stood. 'Well, that's settled. Think I'll turn in.'

Shay watched her leave, disappear into the dark of

the hall, listened as her heels clicked on the stone floor, and called out, 'Auditions are on Friday!'

'You don't even have a *play*!' Jane shouted, then closed her door with a snap.

He smiled, and downed his whiskey in one go. She was a piece of work, so she was. And if she wasn't careful, if she didn't learn to guard the hunger in her eyes when they talked about theatre, she'd be onside before she knew it.

And if he wasn't careful, he'd go mad for her, head over heels, attitude and all.

D espite the cluster of flowers and the note reading 'Sorry – again' which Shay had left on the kitchen table, Jane avoided his company for the next few days. The odd time she was in the cottage, she'd seen him, through the window, dragging splintery lengths of wood, arms full of tattered costumes, and unsalvageable bits of furniture, to a battered van which had appeared as if from nowhere. Sounds of hammering rang through the evening hours, and declaimed lines of recognisable plays floated into the window of her room late at night, but she wouldn't budge. She had to give him points for determination – but she wasn't going to give him her time.

Oh, but time: Had she ever had so much of it? It reminded her of the last summer of her teens before she got her driving licence. Nothing to do, nothing, but broil in heat and wait for something, anything to happen.

Nothing ever did.

Nothing started to happen until she fled the family home, and got to Manhattan. She laughed to think of her erstwhile colleagues ever finding out exactly how earthbound her roots were. Only Darren and Miranda knew of the unsophisticated beginnings of one J. Boyers. They were the only two people in the world she trusted with her life story, and, despite having thought in the past there'd be a way to spin it to the media, to make her more ... approachable, she'd chosen coolness over congeniality.

It had been slow work, this image-development thing, but it had paid off, and once things had started to happen, it seemed as though they would never stop.

And when they did stop, thought Jane, they sure stopped with a bang. It was time to make the next thing happen!

Except nothing much was happening now, what with avoiding Shay and waiting, nervously, for Miranda to come back from her trip. She'd shopped every day, for hours, and managed to approximate what she considered to be a reasonable wardrobe, but the scary thing was, she was getting a little ... bored. The commando-like manner in which she'd grabbed an hour here, an hour there, on a lunch break or on a weekend, to dash through Bloomie's or Bendel's had been adrenalin-infused affairs that raced against time and trendiness. Wandering around a city centre at such a leisurely pace didn't give her the same kind of buzz.

She did feel a bit buzzy, though, as Jackie dropped her off in Camden Street. When was the last time she'd walked into an unfamiliar bar? When was the last time she'd met people she barely knew? She nervously smoothed her hair back from her face, and took a deep breath. Jane, you know how to work a room. You're a visitor, you're from *New York*, how could you fail?

Fail? Was it a contest? She nervously fumbled through her new handbag for a cigarette. When was the last time you had a new friend? whispered a nasty little voice in the back of her brain. You've had colleagues, not friends, and look at the way you've treated the ones you *do* have, yelling at Darren, being jealous of Miranda –

Jealous? Please. Living in cottages is fine for some, but for me? Flowers left on tables and long, leisurely dinners were one thing, once and while, but all the time? Every day? Jane shuddered in distaste and inhaled briskly on her Marlboro Light. An image of Shay, kneeling on the kitchen floor, arms around her hips, chin resting on her belly, eyes lit up with a smile, flashed through her mind's eye, and Jane inhaled again, as if the smoke could erase it. Nope, none of that either: maybe it was time to turn over a new leaf, time to give abstinence a whirl, time to be a little bit more discerning. Not that she wouldn't mind a bit of flirtation now and then, as she fielded some appreciative looks from a group of lads whose average age looked to be about eighteen. OK, definitely flirtation, but nothing impulsive, nothing . . . big. She'd been burned enough in the past – both the recent past, and the murkier past as well. A flash of that old pain, that old rejection, sputtered across her brain, then, tauntingly, a flash of Shay looking across the table at her in the candlelight sneaked back into her traitorous mind's eye, and she shook her head, driving it away.

She headed up the street Jackie had told her to take. Thank God for Jackie, Jane thought. Cathleen's directions were oblique at best, and mostly consisted of using other pubs as landmarks. 'How about "The corner of Somewhere and Somewhere else"?' Jane griped. 'How about the name of a street, for God's sake!' While she didn't think that 'Head up that road that goes up by the market' was going to be much help, 'The corner place by the stoplights' was at least something to grab on to, and she had to assume that The Bleeding Horse was as noticeable as its name was dismaying.

Ah, 'the corner place'. The road Jane had been striding up curved away in either direction, and in that curve loomed a pleasant-looking pub. Jane paused with her hand on the door, as her heart lurched and dropped simultaneously. If only Darren were here – he could not only keep her company, but also tell her what she was feeling.

OK, Janie, here goes nothing . . .

The dark and stylish interior was not what Jane

expected. The bar, which curved in concert with its geographical location, gleamed in the low light, and while the room was dotted with the poky kinds of tables that Jane expected in a pub, there was a feeling of airiness and lightness that was surprising. The music wasn't too loud, and everyone seemed to be just like her: youngish, modish and, with any luck, in a few hours, drunkish.

She blew out a breath she hadn't realised she was holding, and wandered further in.

'There she is,' Cathleen said. 'Jane!' she called and waved, and Jane smiled, nodding in response, working her way over to where Cathleen and her friend were sitting, in a kind of half-enclosed street space where – thank God – people were smoking.

'Jesus, where'd you get those shoes?' demanded a tall, rangy woman as Jane took a seat on a high stool. Cathleen patted Jane's arm comfortingly, and snapped at the girl, 'Give her a chance to get her breath! And I have a pair of those myself, got them over at that shop at the top of Grafton Street, the one by the children's store.'

'They don't look like that on you, I'm afraid,' laughed the tall woman.

'Leave it, Sinead. So, here's Jane, over from New York. Jane, here's Sinead, it's just the three of us at the moment, but the night is young, and Shinny and I are out on the pull. What'll you have?'

'Uh . . .' Jane looked around at what people were drinking, and panicked. Large glasses full of black liquid seemed to be the norm. 'Can I get a gin and tonic, um, here?'

'Of course you can,' said Sinead briskly. 'We may have one foot in the bog—'

'Shut it, Sinead,' said Cathleen, and Jane, no stranger to confrontation, actually felt her skin quiver in alarm. 'Don't mind her, she's got a chip on her shoulder. Jealousy, plain and simple.'

'And never mind her,' Sinead grinned, 'she's putting on airs since she's started working in BT's.'

'You would have liked to have seen this one putting together that shaggin' make-up yoke.' Cathleen patted Jane on the arm again. 'Saved my life.'

'You saved mine,' insisted Jane, almost forgetting what her own voice sounded like. 'The airline lost all my things,' she said to Sinead.

'Right, so Cathleen said. And you're out in the middle of nowhere in Wicklow, and staying with some actor fella, and you lost your job and all.' Sinead offered Jane a cigarette.

Well, that was *that* in a nutshell. Jane arched an annoyed brow. 'Basically, yes.'

'Seriously, Jane, don't mind her,' said Cathleen, rising to go and organise the drinks. 'Sinead's got a form of social Tourette's Syndrome, she's no superego at all. She's a headcase.'

'Oh, my friend Darren goes to therapy!' Jane said excitedly. This wasn't all that hard, this talking-to-strangers thing. Jane felt another twinge of nerves release itself and disappear. She and Sinead sat in companionable silence until Cathleen returned, masterfully managing two full pints, a glass of ice, and a small bottle. Sinead raised her pint, and proceeded to say something in a language that Jane had to assume was –

'Irish,' explained Cathleen. 'Sinead lectures in our beloved language at Trinity to posh little brats. Explains her disposition.'

Sinead opened her mouth to reply, then thought the better of it. 'So, Jane, you found the place all right?'

'Yeah, I got a ride from somebody—'

Sinead grimaced, and Cathleen nearly choked on her mouthful of Carlsberg.

'Em,' Cathleen began, 'I see we've got to give you a lesson in Irish slang, missus.'

'Well, I know what a "yoke" is,' Jane replied huffily. 'All I said was—'

A wave of laughter out of Sinead cut her off, good humoured and playful, and Jane joined in after the women had thoroughly cautioned her to ask for lifts as opposed to what could be construed as a reference to sex. The conversation soon ranged over a lexicon of slang, first from Dublin's northside, then from its south, a difference contested quite hotly between Cathleen and Sinead. Jane listened and laughed, and relaxed in spite of herself, powerless to do otherwise, as round followed round, a glass never permitted to remain empty for long, and cigarettes were smoked in the semi-out-of-doors.

Jane was laughing at something Cathleen had just said, when she felt both women stiffen slightly. She looked up, and saw that a man had come up to the table: he slouched casually, but self-consciously, running a hand through dark brown hair that was short but slicked back. His button-down shirt was, Jane noticed as she narrowed her eyes, one of those new prints by Paul Smith, and was left casually untucked from his dark brown, moleskin trousers.

'Ronan,' said Cathleen unenthusiastically, 'howya?'

'Super, Cath, super.' His light blue eyes were glued to Jane, and she openly returned his stare. Good-looking, she thought, in a kind of actorish way.

Sinead turned to Jane. 'Our Ro's an actor, just came back from RADA, if you don't mind. The Gaiety School not good enough for him, thank you very much.'

Ronan's accent was yet again different from the others, a kind of lazy drawl that rounded all his vowels and came across slightly nasal. He took his eyes off Jane for the moment. 'How're your first years, Shinny? Still have them doing press-ups when they don't know their verbs?'

'Ah, sure, yer lordship, amn't dey all schmart like yerself, all graduated from Gonzaga, same as ye?' Sinead put on a brogue that even to Jane's ears was exaggerated, and Cathleen hooted with laughter.

'C'mere, Ro, give us some of that good auld Blackrock slang, will ya. We're making sure Jane here doesn't make an eejit of herself.'

Ronan looked deep into her eyes, smiling, yet intense. He dropped down on the banquette next to her. 'She'd be the sexiest eejit on this island if she did.'

Jane impassively sipped from her fourth – fifth? – sixth? – G&T. Raking her eyes down from the top of his slick head, over his open-necked button-down shirt, to his shiny leather oxfords, Jane thought to herself, *Maybe* . . . As he smoothly slid into the seat beside her, brushing her thigh with his own, Jane thought, Ha. Why not?

Cathleen's mobile rang, and she had a brief, shouted conversation before turning to the group. 'Caroline's got a crowd over at Café en Seine, will we go?'

'I hate that poncey place,' Sinead grumbled, while polishing off her drink and grabbing her jacket.

After a flurry of activity and downed drinks, they were out in the lane, slightly tipsy and very boisterous. The slap of cold air was a relief as they headed down the street which Jane had so uncertainly walked up only hours before. As she strolled, distracted by the feeling of the fresh air on her face, the thin edge of Jane's heel caught a snag in the pavement, and Ronan was right there to steady her, whispering in her ear, 'Mind yourself. Wouldn't want you to twist one of those lovely ankles.'

'Yooooooooo're a staaaaaaawrrr,' Jane drawled, perfectly mimicking Ronan's accent, winning a shout of laughter out of Sinead.

'You've met yer match there, Ro,' she laughed, and set a brisk pace for the four of them as they headed down Dawson Street.

12

Café en Seine was heaving – there was no other word for it, and Cathleen had to ring her friend in order to find her. Shoving their way towards the back, Jane was overwhelmed by the number of people who were already out and, by the looks of it, well on their way to having a good time. She checked her watch – was it only eight o'clock? No one in New York would have even thought of dinner by then. And it didn't seem that anyone in Dublin was going to be thinking of dinner at all – unless you counted those little packets of peanuts.

'You're miles away.' Ronan grinned up at her – so he was a little short, so what? thought Jane, as she locked eyes with him. It was only a flirtation, after all.

'I was just thinking of New York,' she said, taking yet another drink from Sinead. She grabbed her arm. 'You've got to let me get the next one!'

Sinead just smiled and shook her head, her eyes narrowing a bit at Ronan, and she went off to have a quick whisper with Cathleen.

'You can buy me a drink, if you like.' Ronan moved closer under the pretext of letting a rowdy hen party get by. He slipped a hand behind Jane to rest on the edge of a huge planter. Jane brushed some palm fronds out of her face, only to have Ronan hold them back.

'There,' he purred. 'That's better. I can see your pretty face now.'

Oh, well, thought Jane. This kind of game is the same no matter what country you're in. 'Just pretty?' She thought about having another cigarette and it made her vaguely sick to her stomach.

'Gorgeous. Totally,' Ronan breathed, and moved in to nuzzle her neck.

Whoa, there! Jane shifted so that he ended up with a mouthful of palm. 'So. You're an actor?' Am I really here, doing this, this banal 'So-you're-an-actor' crap? she wondered. She sighed internally, while smiling brightly at Ronan.

As he began to bang on about his training and his agent and his recent turn as Othello (Jane doubted it) in an end-of-year production in London, Jane went through all the moves on automatic, not sure why she was bothering. She nodded and smiled and asked more questions, wondering at how it really was all the same, the world over, this meeting-someone-in-a-bar scenario. She let her mind wander, contriving to write a scene for *Sheila and Boo* before she remembered that it wasn't her show any more. A wave of something – maybe it was too hot in the bar, maybe she'd had too much to drink, maybe chain smoking at least two packs of cigarettes wasn't such a good idea – had her excusing herself. Even that was flirtatious as she laid a finger over Ronan's attractive but unstoppably nattering mouth and asked for directions to the bathroom.

'She means the loo,' barked Sinead. 'Come along.'

'Hurry back,' Ronan whispered in her ear, lightly kissing it. Jane ran a hand across his arm, and followed Sinead up a set of stairs.

'He's a bit of a chancer, that one,' said Sinead.

'I don't think we covered "chancer",' said Jane, as they both reapplied their make-up at the sink.

'How do you get your lipstick to *do* that?' demanded Sinead, and Jane handed over her lip liner. 'Ah. Right. Chancer? It means he's – well, like, opportunistic. I guess that's the best way to put it.'

Jane stood back and fluffed up her hair. 'Yeah, I figured that out for myself.'

'Well, don't say you weren't warned,' Sinead said darkly.

'I can handle it,' said Jane, smiling at her reflection in the mirror. The smile didn't reach her eyes. 'And anyway, I'm on vacation.'

'Just don't take a holiday from your good sense.'

An hour later, sprawled across Ronan's lap in yet another bar, Jane had cause to remember Sinead's warning. Sunk into a plush leather couch, with the river and some bridge or other on view through the large plate-glass window, Ronan had his hands firmly planted on her hips, and he was trying to kiss her.

The only thing stopping him was the fact that Jane was talking non-stop.

'What *is* this place? It's very slick. I wasn't expecting anything like this at all. I mean, what do I know about Ireland? This is a lot like New York. I don't like that. I don't *belieeeve* it, but no, nope, no, I don't like that. Huh. I guess Miranda's not really living in the middle of nowhere. No offence.'

Ronan tried to get his lips around hers while she took a breath, but she was off again. 'You know, I think this was a *realllly* good idea after all. But I don't think that last drink was a good idea. I think maybe I still have some jet lag—' She reached over to pick up her drink and almost fell off Ronan's lap. 'Whoopsie daisy!' she bellowed, and drew Cathleen and Sinead's attention. A look passed between them and they edged over to the couch. Ronan grabbed Jane's face, and she struggled to focus on him.

'Oh, hello there.' Jane watched the traffic outside the window begin to tilt.

'Jane, give us a kiss.' Ronan stroked her jaw and Jane shrugged.

'Oh, OK, why not.'

It wasn't very graceful, and Ronan's eagerness outstripped her own. What am I doing, sitting on the lap of this Irishman in Ireland, making out? She laughed, and almost dislocated Ronan's jaw. He started dropping kisses along her cheek, and she yawned – he didn't notice. As he worked his way down her neck, she dropped her head to one side, leaned an elbow on his shoulder, and propped her chin on her hand, staring off dreamily. What would it be like if this was Shay instead of what's-his-name? she wondered. She relaxed and leaned back, absentmindedly batting at Ronan's wandering hands. It would be less cursory, less ... connecting-the-dots. Not that she was above a little bit of kissing in a bar, but she couldn't keep her mind on Ronnie. Ronan! Whoops! She started to laugh, and yawned again, and pushed him away.

'Ah, Jane, you're destroying me,' Ronan muttered. 'Let's get out of here.'

'Ugh, not another bar – pub – bar. No way.'

He ran his hands down her legs. 'Exactly. Let's go back to mine.'

'Your what?' Jane reached for her cigarettes and saw the table sway out of reach.

'My place. Come on, gorgeous, let's leg it.'

'Nooooooo, I don't want to leave my friends –'

'Heeeeeeey, kinky—'

Jane sat back abruptly, and glared at Ronan. 'You know, you remind me of somebody I know back home. And that's not a good thing. Let me up.'

Ronan increased the pressure of his arms around her. 'I said, let me up.'

Sinead loomed over the couch. 'C'mere, Ro, I think I saw your agent going up to some party in the suite—'

Ronan stood up so quickly that Jane slid to the floor. Oh, good, she thought, at least the room's stopped spinning.

But not for long. Cathleen and Sinead hauled her to her feet, grabbed their handbags and coats, and led Jane out into the street.

She let them guide her down the steps as she hummed a bit to herself.

'She's well locked,' grunted Sinead.

'What'll we do? We can't dump her in a cab. She's scuttered.'

'Are you two talking in that language again?' Jane laughed and tried to stand up on her own. They caught her just in time.

'We'd better bring her back to ours,' said Sinead, and hailed a taxi.

'In you get, missus,' said Cathleen cheerfully. 'You won't be happy in the morning.'

'That's not true!' Jane declared as the taxi sped away from the quays. 'I feel *really* happy! You guys are so *nice*! I *never* had such a nice time with total strangers!'

'Same goes. Though I can't say that Ronan's going to go home happy.' Sinead propped Jane further up the seat.

'That Ronan,' Jane scoffed. 'He's a feckin' chancer!' Sinead roared and Jane laughed too. 'A feckin' chancer!'

'So he is,' agreed Sinead. 'Didn't I warn you.'

'You did! He is a chancer. Not like Shay. Shay's not a chancer.'

'Shay?' Sinead crooked a brow at Cathleen. 'No flies on this one.'

'He's the fella at the cottage. Somebody's cousin,' Cathleen informed her.

'He's Miranda's boyfriend's cousin-the-actor, except he says he's not an actor but he is, he's good; he's got it, you can see it, he's got the thing.' She turned and stared intently at Sinead. 'You could be an actress. You could play comedy, character parts.'

'Sure, she couldn't act her way out of a paper bag!' Cathleen laughed.

'She could so. I know. I can tell. You come audition for the play, the one we – he – Shay doesn't have yet, and Cathleen, you can do the make-up and I'll . . .' She trailed off and her head dropped on to her chest.

'All right there, Jane, just close your eyes and relax. You'll be home and dry soon enough.' Cathleen opened the window a crack, and the driver looked at them nervously, in his rear-view mirror.

'Home,' Jane mumbled into her cleavage. 'I don't have a home. I'm homeless! Jobless! I'd be friendless if it wasn't for you guys! You guuuuys!' She hugged both women rather sloppily. 'My stomach feels funny.'

Sinead grabbed Jane's bag and dumped the contents on to the floor of the cab. Jane's wobbling head snapped to attention and she glared at Sinead.

'Surely you don't expect me to vomit into my new Orla Kiely bag!' Closing her eyes, she dropped her head back on to the seat, and passed out.

Jane didn't so much resume consciousness as crawl upwards from a dark and painful pit towards a sliver of light. When she opened her eyes, she re-evaluated the wisdom behind the idea of said consciousness, as the result was an increase in the frequency and force of the throbbing in her skull. Her bleary eyes struggled to focus, and she found herself frightened and disoriented until she saw a piece of paper pinned to her chest, on which was drawn an arrow, in lip liner. She slowly – very slowly – turned her head and saw that a glass of water and – oh, thank God! – a handful of aspirin had been put on the end table next to the couch on which she had apparently slept. She tilted her head near the edge of the table, swept the tablets into her open mouth, and gently tipped the water down her throat. She was prone once more within seconds.

She vaguely remembered the taxi ... well, maybe not. She definitely remembered leaving the bar, or hotel or whatever it was ... yes, she remembered that. She was sure she'd never forget – and here she pulled the covers over her head – dangling off Ronnie's – Ronan's! – lap like a – a – a floozy. 'Floozy' made her laugh, then cringe at the racket.

Slowly edging her legs over the side of the couch, Jane congratulated herself when she achieved partial verticality. Breathing cautiously, she used the coffee table to help her through the last part of the ascent. Barefoot, she padded towards the next bright red arrow, which pointed her in the direction of the kettle and the jar of instant coffee sitting beside it. 'These women rock,' whispered Jane, as she hit the button, and picked up the note that was underneath the coffee mug.

'Make yourself a cuppa,' it read, 'and help yourself to the last of the hot water, if Sinead left you any. Don't worry about anything last night, it was great craic, and I'll give you a bell later. Cheers, Cathleen. P.S. If you're going to ring your taxi man, here's your present address . . .' Scrawled beneath this in the last of the red lip liner was 'YOU'RE A DISGRACE! ☺ XXO S'.

Jane sighed and made herself the strongest cup of instant Nescafé that money could buy. Breathing in its healing fumes, she wandered back into the living room, and poked her head into the doors that led off it, at opposite ends. Cathleen's room was neat as a pin, and Sinead's looked as if she'd had a whirling dervish in to do the cleaning. Not a bad little space, she thought, except for the fact that they're sharing. She looked at the note again. Phibsboro. Wherever that was. She was certainly getting around – too bad she wasn't exactly sure where she'd been most of the time.

Shay tiptoed down the hall, and stood outside the door to Jane's room. He was pretty sure she hadn't come in last night. He'd been up for hours, cleaning out the last of the unsaveable props and costumes, and preparing the photocopied scenes for the day's auditions. He started to lean in and listen at the door and stopped himself.

'You're not her minder,' he muttered. She was a grown woman, she was from New York for Jesus' sake, she could take care of herself. An image of Jane dancing and snogging some IT drone at Renard's or Lillie's flickered unpleasantly into his mind. None of his business.

Except – well, of course – for the fact that she was a

stranger to Ireland and didn't know about declining 'cups of tea' unless, well she was going to, you know. He scratched his head and gave in to the temptation. Leaning against the door, he listened for signs of life.

She was his cousin's girlfriend's friend, for crying out loud! Didn't he have some responsibility to see to her welfare?! He slowly turned the knob, and more slowly still, peeked his head around the door.

Empty. He pushed the door fully open and stood in the middle of the room, hands on hips.

The least she could have done was ring! Off God knew where, and with whom, he'd like to know. She hadn't been in town for over a week, surely she wasn't going off to the pubs on her own! Unbelievable!

He moved over to the window, which overlooked the drive. Nothing, and it was gone nine o'clock. He'd ring her but for the fact that he didn't know Miranda's mobile phone number – 'I've no time for this,' he said aloud, and went to leave the room . . . but the assortment of bits and bobs littering the dresser caught his eye.

He flicked through her passport – there was only one other stamp apart from the one from Dublin airport. He glanced at the picture and laughed – it had to be more than ten years old, and in it Jane sported a streak of hot-pink framing the left side of her face. There was little jewellery about, little that looked well worn at any rate, and the newness of everything on the bureau made Shay feel a little bit sorry for Jane, and all her lost things. He picked up one of the four – four! – bottles of perfume and took a sniff. She'd worn that the other night, at dinner, its smoky scent forever emblazoned on his mind. 24 Faubourg – Hermès. He'd remember that one, all right.

A car door slammed in the drive and he bobbled the bottle before safely putting it back in its place. Jogging out of the room, he closed the door gently and scurried down to the kitchen.

Laboured steps sounded down the hall and Shay stuck his head around the corner.

'Well. You look like you had a night of it.' That's me sounding like the father, he thought, and he cringed.

'There's no need to shout,' Jane croaked.

'Out with friends?' And thank you Ma, for making an appearance. Shay blushed in mortification.

'Hrglmph,' Jane mumbled, staggering for the cappuccino machine.

The least he could do after that embarrassing interrogation was make her a cup of coffee. 'Go on, go to bed. I'll make you a cuppa.'

'Coffee, not tea—'

'I know, I know!'

Jane winced. 'Stop *shouting*!'

She made her way down the hall, and Shay turned to the machine. She looked well enough for someone who'd been out on the razz. He slammed the little cup underneath the brewing espresso and roughly jerked the milk frother around to the mug he was holding. Dumping the coffee into the hot milk, he then strode down the hall, back to her room, and rapped briskly on the door.

'Shay! Please! I'm dying!' Already under the duvet, and with her face cleaned and her teeth brushed, Jane felt almost human again, but for her sensitivity to loud noises.

'Sorry, missus.' Contrite, Shay sat down on the bed and handed her the mug.

'Thanks, but – I think I'd better take a nap.'

She lay back and closed her eyes, and jumped a bit when Shay started massaging her hands.

'Is that some kind of Irish hangover cure?'

He grinned. 'Well, I don't think you'd let me give you a back rub—'

'And you'd be right—'

'But an improvement in blood circulation somewhere on your body won't do you any harm.'

Jane smiled up at him weakly, and he tilted his head, taking in her appearance minus slap and polish. 'You've got a look about you, that film star, from the fifties—'

'Wow, it's been a while since I got that. Natalie Wood.'

Shay gaped. '*Rebel Without a Cause*, yes, exactly. God, I was mad for her; stroppy but soft underneath it all.'

'I can claim half of that description, anyway.' Jane yawned and closed her eyes.

'Ah, now,' Shay said, and he leaned down closer to her, 'I'll bet there's something deep down inside that's all soft and cuddly, that's just begging to be found out.'

'Shay,' Jane whispered and he leaned closer, 'not now, I have a headache.'

'Jane,' Shay whispered back, 'you mightn't later.'

'Go away,' she whispered again, pulling the duvet up over her chin and snuggling down.

'I'm going,' he whispered, wanting to plant a little kiss on her nose. I reckon that'd be a bad idea, he thought, and sprang to his feet. Taking a normal tone, he said, 'I've got people coming for auditions. You—'

Eyes still closed, Jane held up a warning hand.

'Well, we won't disturb you, in any case. But if you change your mind . . .'

The door shut gently behind him, and Jane fell asleep with a smile on her face.

A gentle hum filled Jane's ears, and waking was far less painful than it had been hours ago. The hum was full of life and colour, a kind of chorus of tone that Jane recognised immediately.

Actors preparing, nervously and earnestly, their audition monologues.

She peeked through the curtains, and was surprised to see the queue stretching past her window and down the drive. How he had got all these people to turn up in the middle of the country . . . She was starting to believe that he could pull this off.

Jane yawned and stretched and wondered if there was any heated water left in the immersion. Taking her cold cup of coffee out to the kitchen, she absentmindedly opened the cupboard – press – that concealed the water tank. The little orange light blinked at her merrily, and the tank was wonderfully, blisteringly hot. Shay was really racking up the points today. Jane smirked, and made for the shower.

It was amazing how little time – and how little hot water – it took to resume full human status, and as she finished off a much-deserved but guilt-inducing ham and cheese sandwich, Jane stood in the kitchen window, watching the queue make its torturously slow way towards the studio. She shook her head – just from eyeballing the crowd, it shouldn't be taking this long. Far too many of the usual type – thin, blonde, female – and far too few interesting sorts of characters that would be in line with – well, with what? He doesn't even have a *play*, Jane reminded herself, dumping her plate in the sink. She peered through the window that was set over the countertop, and watched a couple of giggling girls rehearsing. Get 'em in and *out*, Shay, honestly – although if he was hoping to get some inspiration from this bunch, then no wonder it was taking for ever . . .

Shoving her hands into the pockets of her jeans, she idly wandered over to the back door, and laughed as an older couple came into view, shifting their portable seats without taking their eyes off their respective books. Those two are pros, Jane thought, and saw one of the gigglers throwing envious looks their way. And that, missy, is what you get for wearing those ridiculous shoes.

The line shifted imperceptibly, and a very tall, thin, bald man appeared. He stood as still as a statue, the picture of composure, and he, too, was on the receiving end of some curious stares. A little scary, but Jane would bet her bottom dollar that he had all the classical 'second banana' parts down pat. A tall, thin Iago, she mused, or a looming Macduff. Almost against her will, she went out the back door and hiked down the grass.

'Excuse me, but there's a queue, right?' A blandly beautiful girl – alco-pop commercials, Jane thought dismissively – reached out an arm to block Jane's way. Withering her with a look, Jane said nothing and walked into the room.

Shay was on his feet, practically jumping up and down as he tried to get his point across. 'Don't be nervous,' he entreated, and the girl he was leaping in front of shrank back with fright. 'What I'm after is a kind of joy that's not like, you know, plain happiness, but like, this –' And he jumped up and down again. The girl clutched her photocopies and looked as if she might cry.

'Exuberance,' called Jane, leaning back against the far wall. Shay looked up, and nodded at her, pointing. The girl turned and looked at Jane, as if desperate to be saved from the crazy man.

'Exuberance,' Shay sighed, and went back behind the table he'd set up. As the girl went through her paces again, this time 'exuberantly', Shay madly began making notes. Why, why, why?! Jane shouted in her head. The girl needs about three years more training before she'll even be ready for spear carrying. She edged up along the side of the room, barely noticing that most of the rubbish was gone from the place, and that what was there was neatly composed and piled up against the east wall.

Shay was still scribbling madly long after the girl had finished. Jane nodded to her, and the girl practically ran out of the room.

'Thanks, Deirdre, I'll— Oh. She's gone, then?' Shay looked around a bit wildly.

'What in the world could you have been writing?' Jane angled her head to look.

'I had to do something – she could barely speak if she

thought I was "staring" at her.' Shay ran his fingers through his hair and it stood up wildly.

Jane resisted an incredibly strong urge to smooth it down and smooth away the stress that was etched on his face. 'She needs more training. And you need some water, or something.'

Shay groaned. 'No time. Did you not see how many people were out there?' He looked caught between dismay and triumph, and Jane gave up.

'All right, I'll help with this.' She cut him off before he could speak. 'Just for the next few hours, and only out of the kindness of my heart. I'll get the next victim.'

A stout young man took his place, in front of the table. Jane sat next to Shay, picked up a pen, and felt something like home flow through her body. She smiled and said, 'Go ahead, Jason, whenever you're ready.'

The usual tedium of auditioning was broken up by flashes of brilliance and sheer horror. Shay and Jane took turns reading scenes with a few of the more promising actors, and as Jane watched Shay work, she became even more convinced that he should be on the other side of the table. His range was impressive, and he managed to take on some physical characterisations with every turn, despite the lack of preparation. He's a natural, she thought, and so uncomfortable being tough on the lost causes. Thank God for me, she mused, as she gently cut off another hopeless case. Shay's tendency was to give even *more* time to performers who really should be investigating other career options. She sighed, and massaged the small of her back.

At least her hangover was cured.

She stuck her head out the door. The older couple with the portable stools looked at her hopefully.

'Would we ever be able to come in together?' asked the woman.

'Yeah, sure, come on in,' said Jane, far more easy

going than she would have been in New York, and took their headshots.

'Is that an American accent I hear?' queried the man as he folded up his seat and followed behind.

'It is.' Jane smiled. 'East coast. New York.'

'Hmmm ... not born and bred, surely. Thought I heard a bit of the Midwest in there somewhere,' said the woman.

Jane said nothing, just arched a brow.

'Well done, missus, that's us out,' grumbled the man.

'If you keep it between us, I might have mercy on you. And good ear, by the way.'

Shay looked up from the mess of papers in front of him as Jane handed him the photographs. 'Marie and Martin O'Connor. They wanted to read together. I thought that would be fine with you.'

'Fine, fine.' He smiled weakly at the couple and indicated that they should begin.

They began.

What pleasure. What joy. Jane grabbed their headshots and ran her eye quickly over their credits. A bit of judicious fabrication would have come in handy here, when she noted that the last time either of them had worked was the late nineties. The ensuing ten years may have caught them in an age slump, as both looked pretty well for what Jane guessed was their early sixties.

Thank Jesus, thought Shay. Talent. Presence. Confidence. Oh, thank you.

As they watched Marie and Martin rip the arse out of a scene from *Who's Afraid of Virginia Woolf?*, Jane moved their pictures to the small pile of 'definites' that had been collected. She smiled at Shay and they nodded to each other almost imperceptibly.

The O'Connors concluded, and Shay beamed at them. 'Grand, grand, really wonderful. Good accents, too', and Jane nodded her agreement. 'All right, so ... I've got a scene here from *The Rivals*. Jane, would you do us a favour and read Lydia? Martin, you're Sir Anthony Absolute, and Marie, you're Mrs Malaprop. There's a bit of a conflict thing going on here; Mrs Malaprop is going on about Lydia's reading novels, it's basic family carry on, you know, so, right.'

Jane looked at the O'Connors, and they shrugged as one.

' "You thought, Miss!" ' Marie infused that first line with a stunning range of bluster. ' "I don't know any business you have to think at all – thought does not become a young woman; the point we would request of you is, that you will promise to forget this fellow – to illiterate him, I say, quite from your memory." '

Jane earnestly and desperately replied. ' "Ah! Madam! Our memories are independent of our wills. It is not so easy to forget . . ." '

The scene sprang to life before his very eyes – Jane sprang to life before his very eyes. She slipped into the role the way she'd slipped into the room, with confidence yet with a certain amount of hesitancy which Shay wondered if she sensed in herself. Within seconds the trio gelled, and Jane blossomed. Shay was enraptured, and impressed as he was with Marie and Martin, he couldn't take his eyes off Jane.

She was bloody wonderful.

'Shay. Shay!' Jane smiled at the O'Connors. 'That good, were we?'

He snapped out of his reverie, and leapt to his feet. 'Bloody great, all of you. I'm thinking of having callbacks in a week's time, will we give you a bell?' The O'Connors nodded happily, and gathered up their belongings.

'Please ask the next person to come in, would you?' asked Jane, as they shook hands all around, and the couple left the studio.

'They're good,' Jane said. 'Really good. They'd be worth choosing a play around.'

'*You're* good,' said Shay. 'You're mad that you don't—'

The door swung back on its hinges dramatically, and in ambled Ronan.

Oh, shit, thought Jane. This country is one small world.

'Jane. Babe. How are you?' Ronan leaned in and kissed her cheek. Shay scowled and grabbed Ronan's headshot out of his hand.

'Right. Ronan Jones-Smyth.' Shay jerked his head to the front of the table. 'Go on, so.'

'And you would be . . .?' Ronan extended a hand.

Ignoring it, Shay sat down. 'I'd be the producer. And the director. You do have a monologue prepared?'

'Totally. I *am* a professional.' Ronan winked at Jane as she, too, took a seat. He launched into a soliloquy from *Hamlet*, and Jane could feel Shay's scowl burning into her skull. She squirmed and tried to pay attention to Ronan's reading. It was polished, it was presentable, it could fool an audience into thinking it had passion . . . except that his technique was clinical, almost coldly calculating . . . cold, but good. Better than any of the men they'd seen today.

Dammit!

Ronan finished and took a moment to return to the present moment. Ponce, thought Shay, watching Ronan shake his body down and rub his hands over his face before he breathed deeply and smiled at them. He was, unfortunately, the only fella who'd been any good all day.

Bloody hell.

'Always takes me a while to get back to myself, if you know what I mean.' Ronan slipped his hands into his pockets and looked at them expectantly, as if waiting for them to prostrate themselves at his feet.

'I've got a scene here from *She Stoops to Conquer*, but we haven't got a girl to read with you—'

'Jane, come on up here!' Ronan extended a hand, again, dramatically. 'Give it a go. I promise not to push you too hard.'

Shay handed her the script, and Jane reluctantly took her place beside Ronan.

'At least, I won't push you hard unless you like it,' Ronan murmured into her ear.

'Begin!' Shay barked.

He tried not to glare as they ran through the early, playful scene between Marlow and Miss Hardcastle, tried not to leap over the table as Ronan made a bit free with his hands, tried not to jump in himself and kick Ronan out the door. He was perfect for the part, it had to be said: high-flown, pretentious, and slightly seedy.

Jane tossed off her last line, and made herself stand there. Ugh, she thought, had she really kissed this . . . wanker?

Shay reluctantly put Ronan's headshot in the 'definites' pile. 'We'll give you a buzz. Callbacks are next week.'

Ronan laughed shortly. 'I'd like to know the property before I commit to anything, I mean, I am a profess—'

'Professional, yes. We have several plays under advisement at the moment, we'll let you know when we've made a decision. All right with you?' Shay rose and moved around the table to tower over the little wanker.

'Totally, totally. Film's a bit slow these days, would love to do a bit of theatre, get my chops up again. Jane, can I have a word? Want to apologise for running off last night.' He winked at Shay and turned for the door.

Busying himself with the collected headshots – fighting off the urge to rip Ronan's to shreds, Shay watched them out of the corner of his eye. Ronan's laughter rang out and Shay ground his teeth. Was he the reason why she hadn't been home? No, he'd said he'd 'run off'. What an eejit. So how well did they know one another? And could he stand working with a pretentious git who might have got further with Jane than he had?

14

It was a hard slog through the last twelve people, and Jane made a precise count of the number of bodies that had crossed their threshold.

'Seventy-five!' she sang out cheerfully. 'And only about fifty per cent need to, er, embark on a different path, I think is the kindest way to put it.'

Shay grunted and tried to put his notes in order.

'Here's the pile of call backs. Only seven, but the "maybes" could be worth another look. You wouldn't need more than ten, anyway. Probably. Who can tell.'

Shay shrugged and mumbled.

'The O'Connors were fantastic. And so was that tall guy . . .' Jane consulted his resumé. 'My-hall O Kee-li-a-gag?'

'Mihal O Kelliagh.'

'Oh, O'Kelly.'

Silence descended again. What was *his* problem? Jane got up and went over to the garment rack, now fixed and no longer listing. He'd divided everything by genre and what was left was in really superb condition. A few nips and tucks here and there and—

'So, Ronan. Friend of yours?'

Jane smirked into a rather lethal-looking corset. So *that* was what was bugging him.

'Ummmm hmmmm.' She turned and held up a pink petticoat. 'Can I borrow this sometime?'

'Met him last night, did you?'

'He knew the people I knew.' Jane smoothed down the frocks and moved over to inspect the set pieces.

Shay crumpled a handful of paper. 'Bit of a posh git.'

'So that means he's stuck up, right? I learned all sorts of new words last night!' Jane laughed brightly and pretended to be lost in memory.

Shay got up and took the ceramic vase Jane was dreamily tossing back and forth between her hands and set it down. 'You want to mind yourself around that one.'

'Ronan? He's a pussycat,' Jane purred, and would have walked out had Shay not grabbed her arm.

'You're a grown woman and I'm sure you'll be telling me to mind my own business, but—'

Jane yanked her arm away. 'No buts. It isn't your business.'

A dark silence descended, and Jane wasn't sure why she was trying to get Shay's goat. She rubbed her hands, remembered him rubbing them, remembered that pooling feeling in her belly, soothing and sexy at the same time. It was easier to keep him at a distance, like this, wound up, annoyed than . . . than?

'So you're welcome, anyway.' Jane sat down at the table and swung her feet up on to it.

It's none of your business, Shay, he said to himself, and sat down beside her. 'You were a great help. Thanks a million.'

'Couldn't have done it without me.' Jane crossed her arms over her chest.

'Bit off a bit more than I could chew,' Shay allowed.

'Yup, and the times when I got up to read with practically everyone—'

'Yes, yes, yes, missus. Yes, thank you, thank you and thank you.'

'Just as long as you're properly grateful.'

Shay leaned towards her, his elbows on his knees. 'You were excellent. In all the parts.'

Jane shrugged, and looked down at her hands. 'I did OK. I didn't like the way I handled Pegeen Mike—'

'No, no,' Shay insisted. 'She's so often played so hard, like, you found her lightness in that scene with Christy.'

'It was OK,' Jane said dismissively. 'You were very good, too. When you read with that blonde—'

'Which one?' Shay groaned.

'The one with those plasticy blue streaks in her hair. You did the scene from *Streetcar*, although why in the world you thought she was up to Blanche, I'll never know.'

'I panicked. She kept jiggling at me.'

'Ah, ha. Anyway, you were very good, really, I think you should—'

'Can't do it. I get terrible stage fright.'

Jane shook her head. 'We all do; it's part of the package.'

'There, you said "we". You do think of yourself as an—'

'Nope. That's all behind me.'

Shay sat back, and Jane looked away.

'So thanks, anyway.' Shay looked around the room, and heaved a sigh. 'That was hard work.'

'It's as hard from behind the table as it is in front of it.'

Shay slapped his hands on his thighs. 'Now for a "property", as your dear friend Ronan called it.' Shay looked at her searchingly, and Jane decided to tell him the truth about—

SLAM! Jane jerked and her chair fell backwards as Shay launched to his feet.

Miranda stood in the doorway, a thundercloud about to burst. 'What are you still doing here?' she demanded.

Miranda's back. Jane's mouth went dry. She popped her head up from behind the table. 'Uh. Hi!' She felt her smile wobble under Miranda's furious stare.

Miranda's jaw dropped. 'What are *you* doing here?'

Shay and Jane froze until, finally, Miranda stormed back to the house.

'Uh oh,' groaned Jane.

'You can say that again,' sighed Shay. 'We're in for a bollocking.'

Shay and Jane huddled together on one side of the dining-room table, with Niall opposite.

'She going to stay in there all night?' joked Shay.

Niall glared at him. 'You were meant to be on your way out by now, not holding bloody auditions.'

Shay squirmed. 'Sorry, mate, lost track of the time—'

'And you! When did you get here?' Niall rounded on Jane.

She gulped. 'Uh, the day you left.'

Niall ran agitated fingers through his curly black hair. 'What possessed you to come all the way to Ireland? Seeing as you and Miranda fell out before she left New York?'

'I had my reasons. They're not that important right now, are they? Not when Miranda's off sulking in your bedroom.'

You had to admire her nerve, thought Shay.

'And besides,' she continued, 'you're as much, if not more, to blame than either of us, seeing as you *lied* to Miranda about Shay's intentions.'

'All right, all right!' Niall grumbled.

'Do you make a habit of lying to Miranda? Some boyfriend, some *partner*, as she prefers to call you, although after this I have to wonder—'

Niall got to his feet angrily. 'I said all right!'

'Come on, lads,' Shay intervened. 'We've got to band together or we're all out on our tots.'

Niall went and got down a bottle of whiskey and three glasses. Sitting down again, he poured out three measures.

'Good luck,' he said, and they all toasted. 'We'll need it.'

They downed their shots, and Niall poured again.

Shay offered around his cigarettes. Niall sat with his head in his hands. Jane guiltily put Miranda's mobile on the table. Niall did a double take.

Jane shrugged. 'It was here on the floor. I've been, uh, using it. A bit.'

'Right.' Fortified by the Jameson's, Shay decided it was time to take action. 'If it's me she doesn't like, I'll clear out, go find a hostel or something—'

'How are you going to produce a play from a bunk bed?' Jane shook her head impatiently. 'There's plenty of room in this place, cottage or not, and I don't understand why we all can't just manage like this for a while. And Miranda's not exactly unsociable, so what's the problem?'

Niall shrugged. 'She just wants us to have the place to ourselves. We both do. We haven't had much time together until now, what with her travelling around the country on the photography job, and the big commission I had to finish . . . we want to be alone, is all.'

'So why did you let him pitch up in the first place?' Jane demanded.

'You've got the hang of it – did you hear that? "Pitch up"! Well done!' Shay beamed at her, and was treated to glares from both Jane and Niall.

'So?' Jane insisted.

'He's family, right?' Niall got up and paced. 'So, I come from a big family. So we've had . . . guests every now and again. So we've had people in and out for the last few months. The mother and father came out for a week, the cousins from Kerry – Shay, the Mad Murrays, they were down for . . . a while, and the sisters had to call in to get a goo at Miranda, and then there was that crowd down from Sligo . . .' Both Jane and Shay stared at him in amazement, causing his catalogue to run down. He leaned dejectedly against a wall. 'It's my aunt's gaff, how can I say no?'

'So if you don't feel like you can lay down the law,

then Miranda must feel even less able.' Jane shook her head. Poor kid. Flew off to be with Mr Wonderful and got the whole Wonderful family.

'You Americans, you just don't have the same feelings for the kin.' Shay shook his head condescendingly.

'No, we don't. *We* know when it's time to pat "the kin" on their heads and shove them out the door! And while we're on the subject . . .' Both Jane and Niall turned on Shay. 'You knew what the score was, you *knew* that you were outstaying your welcome, and you didn't leave!'

'I told you it wasn't cool, Shay—' Niall began.

'You bloody well didn't. "Ah, sure, it's grand to have you about the place!" "No worries, Shay, mate, just get yourself sorted when you can!" Never once did you come right out and say, "Time to go, Shay, time to scarper!" '

'You took advantage of the both of them,' said Jane primly, satisfied to have the upper hand.

Until she saw both Niall and Shay turn on her.

'Miranda didn't look very happy to see *you*,' accused Shay.

'Well, she wouldn't be, seeing as our Jane here has been dead rotten to her since she left last year,' explained Niall bitingly.

'I . . . was busy . . . I was . . . you should have seen those emails she sent, 22K clogging up my mailbox! She was very rude to me, too!'

Glares all around, and then nervous silence as they heard the bedroom door open. Niall sat down hurriedly, and Jane fought the compulsion to grab Shay's hand.

The front door slammed closed. Niall looked at Shay and Jane, alarmed, and then ran down the hall and out the door as well.

Shay blew out an anxious breath. 'Christ.'

Jane rolled her tense shoulders. 'You said it. She's not normally this sulky. Do you think they're having problems, or something?'

'You're her mate, you'd know better than I.' Shay shrugged.

'You've been living here for a month, who would know better than you!' Jane retorted. She grabbed the bottle of whiskey and topped up their glasses. 'It's not like her to be this dramatic.'

'Well, if there was a script to hand, at least we'd know what happens next.' Shay got up and peered out the window worriedly.

He missed the gleam in Jane's eye, but couldn't overlook the hand grabbing his jumper and pulling him back down in his seat.

'Hand me that pen. I've got an idea.'

Miranda yanked a little too vigorously on the weeds that were sprouting around her lavender bushes. She consulted the book that was open beside her, and tried to match the line drawing on the page with the actual living plants. She sat back on her heels and sighed.

This bad humour didn't really suit her. She knew it, but she had to admit she was getting some perverse pleasure out of making Jane and Shay squirm. Especially Jane, who had gotten used to Miranda always either giving in to keep the peace, or working hard to make sure that their friendship remained intact. Ha! thought Miranda. Waiting for me to break down and patch things up, hey? Well, you're in for a long wait, missy.

But talk about perverse . . . what the hell was Jane *doing* here? What in the world could have compelled her to leave her little cocoon of a stupidly small flat and outrageously busy career to land up in Wicklow? I don't need this, not on top of not knowing what to do about staying in Ireland, on top of not feeling like the cottage is really my home . . . She sighed. After all the complaining she'd done about Jane's not coming to visit, here she was, and all Miranda wanted was for her to beat it.

And Shay! Miranda starting yanking weeds with renewed energy. Nice to see Mr Sociable, Mr Affable taken down a peg. Although that hangdog, woebegone look on his face was starting to get on Miranda's nerves – starting to make her feel guilty.

She sat crosslegged on the ground, and ran her fingers over the decorative stones she'd laid around the border of the strip of garden she'd tilled underneath the kitchen window. And then there was Niall ... She'd stomped down the drive last night, and taken a left to head towards the lakes, regardless of the time and the fact that the sun was going to sink like a stone any minute. She'd heard the sound of running behind her and hoped it was going to be Niall, telling her it was all right, that he'd ordered those two to leave, that they'd finally have the place to themselves ...

'Miranda – come on back.' He ran in front of her and jogged backwards as she continued down the road. 'Come on back, we'll make dinner.'

Miranda kept walking. 'I'm not hungry.' She shook off the hand he'd placed on her arm.

'It's getting dark, come on.' Niall fell into step beside her, and she stopped and sat on the wall.

They sat in silence as a few maniacal Wicklow drivers sped by.

'Darlin'. I'll tell Shay to go.'

Miranda looked off into the woods opposite. 'That's what you said the last time.'

'He needed a place to stay.' Niall's tone was extremely rational. 'He stayed out of your way – out of our way. He's almost finished, over half that gear is gone—'

'That's what you said three weeks ago.' Miranda was calm. 'And two weeks ago, and last week. You kept saying he was going to leave, and – and he didn't. He had no intention of leaving. Did you even ask him?'

'I couldn't just turf him out,' Niall muttered.

'We've been over this before.' Miranda took a deep

breath, afraid she was going to cry. 'I know that it's not my house—'

'Miranda—'

'And I know we keep going over and over this, and you keep saying it's my house, too . . . but when it comes down to it, I haven't got any say in who stays or who goes.' And I feel like your family are more important than I am, she thought – but was too afraid to say so.

'He'll be gone, I swear—'

Miranda got up and started walking back to the house. She stopped when Niall didn't follow, and turned back to him. 'If we can't figure this out, I . . . don't know what to do next.' Her eyes filled with tears when Niall just sat there, looking at her.

She turned and went back into the house.

They hadn't spoken since. Jane and Shay had disappeared into the studio before breakfast, and Niall had joined them when Miranda went into her new darkroom. When she'd heard them come back in at lunch, she'd gone out into the garden, alone.

The sun ducked behind a cloud and Miranda tried to get interested in the weeds again. What if we can't work this out? Is it over? They'd had such a lovely time in Paris, it had felt like it had in the beginning, the two of them, together, alone, loving each other, being in love . . . If they couldn't handle a small thing like this, how were they going to move forward? Grabbing a tall, tough-looking ragweed plant, she yanked with both hands and, grunting, fell over.

She didn't hear the kitchen window open, slowly.

Jane turned to Shay and Niall and nodded. Niall clutched a piece of paper in his hands, his eyes glued to it anxiously as she gestured for him to begin.

' "Right, you two, we need to talk," ' Niall said loudly, woodenly. Jane rolled her eyes, and Shay whispered, 'Act natural, mate.'

Miranda crept closer to the side of the house.

' "Niall, listen, I know Miranda better than either of you, she'll snap out of it," ' Jane replied, breezily, snottily – *typically*, thought Miranda.

' "We don't need to hear anything more out of you, miss," ' barked Niall, warming to the lines Jane and Shay had written out. ' "Showing up here without even a warning." '

' "Absolutely right, mate," ' chipped in Shay cheekily. ' "She's got less right to be here than anyone." '

' "Not so fast, pal. You and that junk better be outta here by sundown!" ' Niall shot back. Why does he sound like Clint Eastwood all of sudden? wondered Miranda, and inside Jane rolled her eyes at Niall. Niall coughed, self-conscious, and resumed in a tone more like his own. ' "Tonight. Uh, leave tonight." '

' "And me?" ' Jane asked, her voice beginning to wobble. ' "Where will I go? I don't know a soul!" '

Miranda squinted suspiciously up at the window. *Jane – crying?* She raised herself into a squat, and edged up the side of the wall.

' "I wouldn't want to do *anything* to come between you and Miranda – she loves you so much!" ' Jane stuck out her tongue and shivered in disgust – that had been one of Shay's lines.

' "Young people in love deserve time to be alone as they explore their commitment and grow as a couple," ' agreed Shay, glaring at Jane. She grinned, having written *that* to pay him back for her last line.

Nobody saw the top of a curly red head peeking through the window.

' "It's about time you two saw the light," ' said Niall, cringing. ' "And if we don't see the back of yees—" ' He threw down the paper in disgust. 'Listen. If Miranda's not happy, then off you go. It's up to her, and I won't get in the way of anything she decides. She's more important to me than either of you, no offence, like, but that's that.'

Jane threw up her hands, and Shay silently

applauded his cousin. All three jumped when the back door opened suddenly.

'Shay, put the kettle on.' Going over to Niall, Miranda looked up at him and stroked a hand down his face. 'Let's sort this out.'

Jane turned with Shay and they gave each other the thumbs up out of Miranda's sight. 'Told you it would work,' Jane hissed.

'A flawless act of devious genius,' he whispered back. 'Went off without a hitch—'

'Jane? Would you mind picking that script up off the floor?' Miranda smiled at her thinly.

Well, thought Jane, it was a smile, at least – and it would have to be enough to be getting on with.

15

Miranda waved to a passing motorist, and then lightly jumped over the wall that ran alongside the Dublin road. Picking her way carefully down the grassy slope, she paused when she got to the small stone circle that sat about halfway down the rise. She breathed deeply . . . spring was definitely in the air; after the false one they'd had at the end of February, with all the daffodils and crocuses springing up all over the place, they'd had their hopes dashed by a blustery and grim March. Running her hands over the silky grass, checking for dampness, Miranda sat and leaned back against one of the stones. Looking down into the valley, at the late morning sun sparkling over the lough, she smiled and closed her eyes. The wind teased her curly hair out of the clip she'd secured it with, and she unzipped the neck of her anorak an inch or two.

Sweating with exertion, hair alternately plastering to and flying in her face, Jane struggled over the limestone wall and all but rolled down the hill to join Miranda. Her short suede jacket did the bare minimum in the way of wind-breaking, and the closest thing she had to a pair of walking shoes – a pair of patent leather Nine West ankle boots – were pinching at the heels. Struggling to catch her breath, she dropped down on the ground, only just missing a little pile of sheep poo.

'My God,' she huffed, 'these hills—'

'That was nothing,' said Miranda, leaning forward with her elbows on her knees.

That was nothing, Jane mimicked in her mind.

My Gaaaaawd, Miranda smirked to herself. A four-day-a-week gym habit and a little hill is too much for her.

They sighed in concert. Where do I begin? thought Jane.

Is she ever going to get on with it? thought Miranda.

'Sorry.' Jane shook her hair out of her eyes again, and wondered if she was allowed to smoke in a place like this.

'For?' Miranda kept her eyes glued on the ripples of the lake.

'What do you mean, *for*?' Jane massaged the back of her right heel.

'For showing up here, unwelcome? For blowing me off when I was in Manhattan? For being such a – a snot about my moving here? For being such a crap friend for the last year, maybe even longer?' She hated the way Jane made everybody else do her work for her.

'What – even longer? You kept inviting me! Every single email: "Oh please come and see it, you'll love it, please come!" and so I came and, and—'

'Don't you dare try to make this my fault!'

They both stared stubbornly down at the lake. Miranda watched a breeze tease the long grass that surrounded her, making it flatten and flutter, and as the wind moved down the hill, it made the lake ripple and roll in response.

'Did you see that?' Jane whispered.

'Yeah.' Miranda turned and was surprised to see joy on Jane's face. This from a woman for whom Central Park was too rural?

'I guess I can see why you like it here.' Miranda said nothing, and Jane stumbled on. 'All the nature stuff, and the plants and everything. You were always into—

remember all those plants you had in the window of your dorm room? I forgot about that. Always running around with aloe vera for burns and mint for tea. I forgot.' Jane laughed.

'Remember the time you tried to make daiquiris with my tomatoes?'

'A Bloody Mary is an alcoholic drink that requires toma—'

'Tomato *juice*! With vodka! Not with crushed ice and rum!'

They both shuddered, and shrieked with laughter.

'That night scarred me for life,' moaned Miranda.

'Darren's worse. He can't even look at gazpacho without getting dry heaves.'

'He rang yesterday . . . looking for a body count, I reckon.'

Jane rolled her eyes. 'Considering he's the only one of us in therapy, you'd think he'd have learned to mind his own business.'

'Then I've got no excuse asking you what the hell is going on.'

Jane shifted over and leaned against the stone, her back to Miranda. 'Where do I begin?' she sighed dramatically. 'Well, I got fired.'

Miranda gasped, a balm to Jane's spirit. But not for long. 'So you lost your job – because you were shagging your boss?'

'Don't be so middle class,' Jane scoffed. 'That kind of thing doesn't matter any more. Who cares? Everybody's "shagging" everybody else – work is the only place to meet prospective partners. What do you suggest? The Internet? Personal ads? Please.'

Miranda shifted so that she could see Jane's face. 'Were you in love with him?'

'Miranda, don't ever change. Of course I wasn't!'

'But you called him your partner—'

'*Miranda*, please!'

'You said "partner"!'

'When did you get so pushy? I should have said "fuck buddy", OK? We clear on that?'

Miranda threw up her hands. 'If it's so middle class, why was everybody at that bar all over it when—'

Jane closed her eyes and breathed in the cool air. 'The Bob thing was just a convenient . . . chink in the armour. It's politics! Nothing gives the underlings greater joy than to be able to feel one up on the overlings! They all wanted me to tank, just to see me tank. They wanted me to take the fall.'

'Jealous?'

'Oh, yeah.' Jane realised that she'd rather violently torn fistfuls of grass from the mud. She guiltily laid the jagged blades down on the ground, and wiped her hands on Miranda's anorak.

'Be my guest.' They looked at each other, Miranda expectantly, Jane sheepish. 'So?' Miranda urged.

'So . . . take your pick. Jealous of the Emmy? Sure. Sexism? Possibly – and not just from the men, if you don't mind. Ageism? Oh, yeah—'

'What! You're only young!'

'Not in television.'

'It's not your fault that a bunch of post-adolescent wannabees got their noses out of joint! And don't you dare think that winning that Emmy wasn't worth it!'

Jane looked down at the ground. 'I . . . I was kinda pissed that you didn't come. To the ceremony.'

Miranda looked away at the lake. 'I was upset that you hadn't bothered to visit me here.'

The wind blew gently down the hill again, and in its wake a flock of sparrows seemed to leap, rather than fly, through the air. Miranda leaned back against the stone, and Jane moved closer until their shoulders touched.

'So I guess I'm sorry,' Jane choked out.

Miranda shook her head. 'Well, don't break a rib.'

'Come on, Miranda! For me, this is operatic!'

They both laughed, and Miranda squeezed Jane's hand. 'I accept your apology. I'm sorry too.'

'OK, then let's get over it.'

'OK. Come on, we'll go down to the water.'

Miranda rose and started striding down the hill. Leaning heavily on the rock, Jane pulled herself up and began to pick her way down the grass cautiously. A brace of hardy daffodils gently nodded as she made her way to the shore, where Miranda was already collecting stones to add to her garden's border.

'So what's up with you and Niall?' Jane asked.

Miranda threw a stone as far as she could. She watched the ripples until they reached her feet before she answered. 'Nothing and everything. I don't know. It's a really important relationship to me – maybe the most important, ever. And I know that he feels the same way. He says he does . . . but I'm just nervous about my work permit, and about not working much, and about the stupid, bloody, shagging house.' She threw a fistful of rocks into the water, sending a flock of drakes into a spiralling frenzy. 'I've never been this involved before, either. I kind of feel like I don't know what to do, I don't know what comes next.'

'Can't help you there, "mate",' Jane laughed shortly.

They walked around the lake in silence, the only sounds the lapping of the water, the wind, and the cows lowing in the distance. Miranda resumed her rock collecting, and Jane allowed herself more introspection than usual.

It got to be too much.

'It's so quiet!' Jane crossed her arms in discomfort. 'IT'S SO QUIET!' she shouted, reagitating the recently relaxed drakes.

'I love it,' Miranda said simply. She looked at Jane. 'You seem to be getting on well enough, making friends, running auditions.'

'I said I'd just help him that one day, and I'm sticking by it.'

Miranda snorted. 'Why don't you just take a part? You were always so good, I'll never understand—'

'NO,' Jane shouted again, loudly enough to silence the cows. 'NOOOOOOOOO!'

'But why not?' Miranda stopped, and blocked Jane's path. They looked at each other for a long minute, before Jane shoved her way forward.

'I don't know.' Her barely audible reply shouted louder than that 'no', thought Miranda. What was going on here?

'Well, who could blame you? Shay's just an accident waiting to happen.'

'He's all right,' mumbled Jane.

'He's like an overgrown, spazzy Labrador or something, bouncing all over the gaff . . . I don't know, I can't see him as a producer—'

Jane spun sharply around. 'He's got a vision at least. He's got passion. He's pretty stubborn, and that's half the battle. I don't see why you guys can't just let him use the stupid place for a while. I mean, so what? He'll be so busy you won't even know he's there, and from what I can tell, he'd be crazy not to give it a shot since he's got all that stuff, and the talent, too.' Then she stalked off down the path.

Hee hee! thought Miranda. Are you falling for that big goofball, missus? Wait till I tell Niall.

Shay passed by the kitchen window on his way into the cottage, and saw Niall and Miranda canoodling at the sink. Well, there you are, he thought, and gave himself another virtual pat on the back. Oh, and one for Jane, of course. He'd seen her storm into the house earlier, her face like a thundercloud, and decided that slipping a script under her door would probably be a bad idea.

He let himself in loudly – he didn't want to embarrass the lovebirds.

Miranda sprang back from Niall. 'Hey! There you are!'

Unused to being on the receiving end of a big, beaming smile from Miranda, Shay automatically looked behind him.

'Are you around for dinner tonight? Niall's got this massive chicken he was going to roast.'

'Em,' Shay looked over his shoulder once more, just in case. 'Wouldn't want to get in the way—'

Miranda stamped on Niall's toe. 'Ow – I – no worries. I got this massive bird.'

Shay looked from the beaming Miranda to the grimacing Niall, and shrugged. 'Sure thing. Got a bit of work to do—'

'Go right ahead! We'll call you when it's ready!' Miranda's smile upgraded to blinding, and she started pulling dishes out of the cupboard.

Shay carefully made his way out of the kitchen, feeling as if he'd got enough good will from herself to last him a lifetime.

Shifting the pile of headshots and notes from one arm to the other, he nudged open the door of the front lounge – and was met with a roomful of smoke.

'Close the door! Close the door! They'll kill me! Dammit! I had the stinking rotten thing going fine and then all the smoke started backing up or something.'

Shay slammed the door, opened a window, and was kneeling beside Jane before she'd even stopped swearing. 'You're all right, hang on, hang on—'

Taking the poker, he dragged out the newspaper that he'd stuffed up the chimney against the draught. Dropping it down on to the smoking turf, it burst into flames and the smoke began to draw properly.

Jane rubbed at her stinging eyes. 'What rocket scientist stuffed the chimney full of paper?'

'Em, don't know.' Shay wiped his hands on his work trousers. 'Want a cuppa?'

'No thanks.' Jane stood, at a loose end. Should she stay? She wanted the fire – she was freezing. She'd also wanted to sit somewhere besides the guest room – hanging out on her bed all day felt too childish. Was he going to try to make conversation? Or try, again, to get her involved in his stupid play?

Shay plopped down on one of the couches, and spread out all his papers. 'Late in the season for a fire.'

Jane sat defiantly on the opposite couch. 'It's arctic in this house.'

'You'll get used to it . . .' Shay trailed off as he sorted through the actors' pictures. Engrossed, he fell silent and became absorbed in the work.

Don't mind me, thought Jane huffily. She stared into the now blazing fire and huffed out a little breath. Fine. Let's just be quiet, shall we?

She leaned back and tried to concentrate on the orange and blue flames. She'd searched the room for logs and only out of desperation had piled those brown bricks into the grate. They smelled like dirt, and since they were stored in a kind of log-holder thing, she'd assumed they were flammable. Now that the flames were under control, the hearth gave off a pleasant, earthy scent – it made her think of dark nights and rain.

Sighing loudly, she laid her head back against the sofa and dragged a lap blanket over herself. Shifting herself noisily, she plumped up a throw pillow and propped it up behind her head. Shifting again, the pillow fell over the back of the couch. As she rose, the blanket dropped on to the low table on which Shay was working, and scattered some of his papers.

'Sorry.' Jane stooped to pick them up.

'Hmmm?' Shay looked up, distracted.

'Your papers.' Jane waved them in his face. 'They fell.'

'Oh. All right.' Shay looked back down at his list of figures.

'It was my fault.' She pointedly laid them down.

'All right, so,' Shay mumbled.

'I apologise.' Jane thrust her chin into the air. I am making a career out of contrition.

'What?' Shay looked up at her blankly.

'I'm sorry. I said I was sorry. I didn't mean to disturb you.' She went over to the hearth and knocked over the fire irons. They clattered loudly on to the slate floor.

'You weren't until now,' Shay muttered, dropping his head into his hand.

'Sorry.'

'All right!'

Jane poked at the bricks, and threw on a few more. Sparks shot up the chimney with a loud hiss. Shay sighed noisily.

'I can leave you alone if you'd prefer.' Jane rose and stood expectantly at the fireplace.

'You needn't – I'm just going over figures, and it's wrecking my head.'

'Ooh, budgets! Let's see!' Jane practically leapt over to his side.

'It's the little bits and bobs that come back to bite you on the arse,' Shay grumbled, and shoved a sheaf of notes over to Jane.

'Absolutely right. I'll never forget, my first budget was a music video for an ageing hair band making their comeback – if I'd only thought to get sponsorship from Vidal Sassoon, we wouldn't have lost thousands in gel and hairspray.'

'I don't have thousands to lose, like. I can't even pay anybody up front.' Shay leaned back against the couch as Jane leaned forward.

'No one expects to get paid at this level. Sad, but true – and necessary,' Jane murmured, as she ran the pencil she'd snatched up down the first column of numbers.

Shay watched her mutter, and nod, and shake her head, the light of the fire dancing in her eyes, eyes that were lost in the focus of what she was doing.

For someone who didn't want to be bothered, she was getting fairly bothered.

'OK, listen, you're going to take a bath on the rights. You've got no choice. But you haven't set aside nearly enough for the lighting rig. What's the point of producing something no one's going to be able to see?'

'Most theatres have their own gear.'

'Well, it couldn't hurt to add in a few rentals.'

'I could borrow some from my old college.' Shay scratched his head with his pencil. Was What's-his-thing still there?

'Good idea, but bear with me as I pencil in a few dollars – euros – whatever – OK? Right here, only in pencil, erases in a heartbeat . . .' Jane patiently wrote down a number that seemed reasonable. 'You did a good job on the expendables, but I think you need to look at your publicity budget. You know, photos and such.'

'Em . . .'

'And you've got nobody down for carpentry either.' Jane scowled at the figures, and Shay shifted uneasily.

'Hey, you guys!' Miranda bounded into the room and grinned brightly at the sight of them, shoulder to shoulder in front of the roaring fire. 'Dinner's almost ready. Want a drink?' She bustled over to the grate and dragged the fireguard across the hearth. 'Oh, working on the show? That's exciting!'

Miranda danced out of the room leaving utter confusion and sneaking suspicion in her wake.

16

Shay shrugged and rose. 'She's a right moody one, isn't she?' He held out a hand to Jane.

She reached up without thinking and let him pull her to her feet . . . effortlessly, and with a little ripple of bicep that peeked out from beneath the sleeve of his Monty Python T-shirt. She stared at the logo, a swirl of flying pigs and scrolling typography, and thought of the terrible crush she used to have on both John Cleese and Michael Palin, remembered that when she was twelve she'd vowed that she'd never kiss a boy who couldn't do the entire Dead Parrot sketch from start to finish. She sneaked a peek up at Shay's face. He was smiling down at her, friendly yet watchful.

What if he could do the *Holy Grail* from start to finish. (She could.) What then?

What might *that* be worth?

'Miranda. She's a bit moody.' And you, missus, are away with the fairies, he thought.

Jane took her hand out of his, and took a step back. 'Miranda just gets excited about certain ideas she gets into her head which have little to no basis in reality.' She moved past him, brushing up against him, because . . . well, who knew why, and went out into the hall.

Shay rubbed his belly and followed right on her heels. Was it just him, or was something going on?

He moved past Jane, who had stopped in the

doorway of the dining room, and headed straight for the open bottle of wine on the table. 'Who wants a glass?'

'Who doesn't?' Niall retorted and, making the best of his long reach, held his glass out to Shay.

'Said the actress to the bishop,' Miranda chirped.

Niall shook his head. 'You haven't quite got that one, pet,' he said, dropping a loud kiss on her forehead.

'It's not got exactly the meaning that it's meant—' Shay cut himself off at the sight of Miranda's knitted brows. 'But you're on the right track.' He'd hate to lose her spontaneous good will over something as silly as an old joke. 'Jane?' He held up the bottle. 'How about yourself?'

She stood, stock still, uncertain. Twilight fell through the windows to play with the candlelight: true to form, Miranda had placed tapers and votives all around the room. A jug of fresh flowers sat in the middle of the table, set casually but lovingly, and another fire was burning in the room's smaller grate. The smell of something comforting cooking was subtly flavouring the air, and the CD player was shuffling between Ella Fitzgerald and Norah Jones. It had all the earmarks of home, of what home might mean, could mean – but wasn't home the place to run away from? Something was warring on the edge of her senses, probably feelings, or something, pesky fucking feelings of . . . of . . . of wanting versus not wanting, bubbling up to mess with her head.

'Jane?' Miranda popped her head around the cupboards. 'It's a French Cabernet, just so you know. Bergerac.' She beamed at Shay. It took him so completely by surprise, he almost dropped the bottle. 'When we were in our early mid-twenties, Jane and I took a wine-tasting class in order to meet men. We actually learned something, in spite of that.'

'Any luck?' asked Shay, looking from the grinning Miranda to the now frowning Jane.

'None whatsoever. The course was made up entirely

of women. Even the teacher was a woman.' Jane sauntered over to the table and picked up an empty glass. 'Let's see what I remember.'

Shay splashed a small measure of the rich, red liquid into the crystal glass. Delicately nosing the bouquet, Jane then lifted the glass into the candlelight, assessing the colour and clarity before she hazarded a sip. The wine flowed silkily down her throat, and Shay was sure that it was the sexiest thing he'd ever seen in his life. She held out her glass to him, and he filled it, never taking his eyes off her.

Miranda shredded some lettuce to within an inch of its life. This was going great! She threw some pine nuts into a pan to toast them for the salad, and nudged Niall. 'I think it's going great!' she whispered as he briskly cut up an onion.

'I think you should probably leave them be,' he replied.

'Don't be such a drip,' she grumbled.

'Said the actress to the bishop,' he said, and kissed her again, lightly this time, on the mouth.

'Two can play that game,' Miranda retorted, pushing him up against the countertop. His hands full of knife and onion, he was helpless as she slid her arms around him, tucking her hands into the back pockets of his jeans.

Jane turned her back on the sight of her friend having a romantic moment with her 'partner', and sat down at the table. Shay was sneaking a look at the papers he'd brought along with him, sheepishly putting them away when he clocked Jane clocking him.

'Got any smokes?' she asked, and reached for the wine. 'Nice vintage, by the way. Miss What's-her-face would be proud.'

'She made us call her "Miss Wilson",' laughed Miranda. 'I forgot about that. We were all the same age, too, pretty much. It was weird.'

'She probably only started teaching the class so that *she* could meet somebody.'

Shay leaned forward. 'Is it as bad as all that? Aren't there, like, six million people in New York City?'

'Eight,' said Miranda.

'Nine,' corrected Jane. 'You've been gone almost a year. It's gone up.'

'All those people let in to make up for my absence,' laughed Miranda, and she set down a plate of olives, cheese and ciabatta.

'Nine million and you had to take a course to get a date?' Shay shook his head.

'Well.' Miranda sat down and refilled her glass. 'At least half that number are women.'

'And let's say that a third of that fifty per cent live out in the boroughs – a no-go zone.' Jane leaned forward as Shay held out a light.

'Speak for yourself,' Miranda snapped. 'There were perfectly good men living in the hinterlands of, say, Brooklyn.' She grinned over at Niall. 'Anyway. So what does that leave, roughly?'

'About a million and a half,' she and Jane said in unison, and laughed.

'So,' said Miranda, reaching for a cigarette. Jane's brows arched, but she said nothing, and Miranda shrugged. 'One point five million—'

'Right. And just how many of them do you suppose are gay?' Jane stubbed out her cigarette.

'Go on, guess.' Miranda urged, and both she and Jane pinned Shay with expectant gazes.

'Em . . .' Shay shrugged.

'Seventy per cent,' Jane said firmly.

'All right, so, but there are still—' said Shay, caught up in the game.

'No, no, no.' Miranda shook her head adamantly.

'Of the remaining six hundred thousand or so, three hundred and fifty thousand are men that we will never,

ever meet, unless they're fixing our boilers or putting out a fire, leaving maybe – maybe – three hundred thousand-ish.' Jane got lost in her own number crunching. 'Write off half immediately as actors, and we are left with a grand total of a hundred and fifty thousand available male types.' Jane shook her head. 'It's true.'

'It is.' Miranda nodded, and topped up everyone's glasses.

'You both sound like you know what you're talking about' – Shay handed Jane another cigarette – 'and it follows, I mean, Niall said. He'd send these emails back, he was falling over the women, like, and vice versa; he was batting them away day and night . . . er . . .'

Jane shouted with laughter as Miranda pushed Niall back into the pantry. Her muffled demands – 'What women? "Batting" them away, huh?' – were silenced rather abruptly, and Jane shook her head at Shay.

'You sure know how to say the right thing at the right time.'

He grinned. 'When you've got it, you've got it.'

Rising, he tossed his cigarette into the fire and threw another peat briquette on to it. Turning, he saw that Jane was sneaking a peek at his papers. It was her turn to do sheepish. 'I see you're working up a list of venues.'

He rejoined her and they both, without really thinking about it, huddled together at the end of the table. 'It's not going to be easy. Dublin's a big theatre town, but in the range I'm looking for, we come up a bit short.'

'I met this guy on the plane coming over here who said he had a theatre – Gerard—'

They both jumped guiltily as Miranda set down a fresh bottle of wine. 'Oh, no, go on, work away!' She pushed the bottle towards them, and turned for the kitchen. 'I've got loads to do in here. It's so exciting to see Jane involved in theatre again!'

'Oh, give it a rest,' sighed Jane, and lit up again.

'This is an improvement, believe me,' Shay muttered, and reached under the table for the actors' headshots.

They passed the time before dinner arguing over the merits of the people they – Shay, Jane corrected herself – were planning on calling back. He had good instincts, she decided, testing them out by purposely putting actors forward that she herself wouldn't touch with a ten-foot pole.

'I wouldn't touch him with a barge pole,' Shay grumbled, holding up Ronan's picture, and Jane laughed. At his perplexed look, she shook her head. 'Nothing,' she said, taking the headshot from Shay. She sighed. 'You don't have much of choice.' Unless you do it yourself! she wanted to shout at him.

'Hmmmmmm.' Shay reluctantly returned Ronan to the callback pile.

'Headshots?' Miranda asked brightly, setting down a steaming bowl of sautéed vegetables. 'You're not calling back all those, are you?' Her smile strained around the edges – as much as she wanted to see if Jane and Shay would 'take', she didn't want tons of people trampling her garden.

'No, that's Mount Blonde,' Jane sneered, dumping the tottering pile of pictures behind her on to the floor. Miranda winced and immediately went around and moved them into the hall.

'The business still full of them, hey?' she asked as she returned and collected the bowl of wild rice Niall had moved to the counter. 'Blondes are Jane's pet peeve,' she told Shay as she set down the bowl.

'They are a bit like a virus,' Shay agreed, winning another sterling smile out of Miranda. His brows knit as it began to dawn on him that maybe – he looked over at Jane, who was watching him with folded arms and a patiently expectant look.

'Finally sunk in, has it?' she murmured, pouring fresh glasses of wine all round.

'I was shooting actors' headshots for a while, just to make money, but it wasn't worth it,' said Miranda, as she bustled around with bowls of food. 'It wasn't the expense or anything, but the time! I mean, I understand the insecurity and all, but some of these people I came across, jeez.' She nudged a bowl of stuffing in between the veg and the rice, and set the salad down beside that, then sat and picked up her glass. 'And the men were worse than the women. That endless parade of blonde women.'

'Umm hmm. Shay's got a "rake" of wigs, anyhow.' Jane stared hopelessly at the spread of food before her. She'd better start hitting those hills every day, or else she'd be in the market for another new, but decidedly larger, wardrobe.

'Oh, so it wouldn't matter if the lead had, say, black hair?' Miranda queried, her voice the essence of innocence.

She was rewarded by an obvious look of disgust from Jane. 'He hasn't even got a play yet.'

'Actually, I—' Shay began.

'Please, help yourselves,' said Miranda as Niall brought over the carved chicken and sat down himself. 'So, then, the whole thing's up for grabs, isn't it?'

Jane began piling salad on to her plate. 'Not exactly.'

'It's not like it's set in stone. The "type" he needs for the lead, I mean.'

'He doesn't even have a *play*, so this entire conversation is pointless.' Jane accepted a sliver of chicken from the platter Niall held out to her.

'In fact, I—' Shay tried again. Niall laughed and passed the chicken to him as Miranda cut Shay off again.

'I remember the first time I saw you. Act, I mean.' Miranda leaned her elbows on the table and turned towards Shay. 'We're all friends from college, Jane and Darren and I – you remember Darren, don't you? He was here in December. Anyway it was an art college, very serious, dead serious, like, all of us obsessed with our course work, working really hard. I knew I wanted to be a photographer, and Darren was a born interior designer – you should have seen his dorm room – *anyway*, Jane wasn't sure what she wanted.

'In the middle of spring term she started disappearing for hours at a time, at night. Darren was convinced she was dealing drugs or something ridiculous . . . and then the posters started appearing for the spring drama society's show. We didn't even know there was a theatre on campus! And there was Jane, bigger than life – I know it's corny, but she was Jane but not Jane, the title role in . . . *A Doll's House*.'

'Hedda Gabler,' Jane corrected, her voice barely a whisper.

Miranda dropped her eyes for a split second, but not before Shay caught the flash of success. 'Of course. You didn't do Nora until the autumn.' She turned back to Shay. 'How could anybody ask an eighteen-year-old girl to play that kind of part? Who is crazy enough to believe that it wouldn't fall on its face? It didn't – and only because of Jane. It was almost . . . frightening, how good she was. I had no reference point towards my friend – she was gone. But it couldn't be anybody *but* her, do you know – I'm not making any sense—'

'I know exactly what you mean,' said Shay, his voice low. He chanced a look at Jane – her face was composed, impossible to read.

The CDs had played out, with the only sound in the room being the crackling fire and the wind beating against the darkened windows. Miranda stared down at her plate, moved by the memory, worried that maybe she'd gone too far. Niall ran a hand down her back, and Shay sat back and toyed with his rice. Jane sat still as stone.

The ringing phone screamed into the hush, making them all jump, then laugh, then burst out in a babble of chatter to make up for the uncomfortable silence.

'Leave it,' said Niall. 'Get back to that chicken.'

'Nice one, mate,' said Shay, fighting the urge to stroke Jane's hair.

'Lovely food, thank you,' Jane said smoothly, reaching for her wine. Her throat felt tight, sore almost, and her skin felt itchy all over. More fucking feelings? Ugh.

She remembered that time – better than Miranda ever could. She sighed, and looked up, directly into Shay's sympathetic eyes.

'There's always Ibsen,' she said brightly. 'Although he may run a tad too long for a first production.'

'I have a play!' Shay shouted.

'OK, OK, we're not deaf,' Jane snapped, to cover up for the leap of anticipation she unwillingly felt.

'So?' asked Niall.

'What is it?' Miranda leaned forward.

Shay cleared his throat. 'I wanted to do something Irish, but classical – not a cottage play, but not Shaw, either. It didn't necessarily need to be set in Ireland, per se, but it did have to have, as far as I was concerned, some kind of Irish pedigree –'

'You know, I never quite made the lawyer connection with you, but it's becoming abundantly clear.' Jane sat back and crossed her arms. What was her heart doing, beating like that?

'And so I've selected a period piece, or costume drama, if you will, that's a cheerful mix of mistaken identity and light romance that will, with the right cast, reveal a deeper level of identification with human nature and the need for men and women to, perhaps, mislead one another into thinking themselves better or, paradoxically, worse than they really are in order to—'

'What's the play?!' Niall, Miranda and Jane shouted simultaneously.

'*She Stoops to Conquer!*' Shay said triumphantly.

Silence greeted his announcement.

'Well, don't all leap about at once.' He sat back, stung.

'No, it's a good choice. The O'Connors are perfect for it.' Jane toyed with her wine glass, and ran their – Shay's – list of actors through her head. 'Jason is great for the brother, what's-his-face, and I suppose Ronan will have to play Young Marlow.' Even though *you* should be playing that part! she shouted at him again in her head.

'I suppose I'll ring Nuala, or was it Fionnuala, about Miss Hardcastle.' Unless of course you would be willing – if you weren't so bloody stubborn.

'Oh, yeah, Goldsmith.' Niall nodded and shrugged. 'Sounds good.'

'Didn't the Abbey do that last year?' wondered Miranda, earning a scowl from Shay. 'Well, it's not my fault, I think they did. Didn't we go?' she asked Niall.

'Maybe. Not big on the theatre myself,' he said, earning a glare from Jane.

'I don't really remember it,' Miranda mused. Then she perked up. 'That's a good sign.'

'Shite,' growled Shay. 'Shite, shite, shite.'

'No really!' Miranda backpeddled. 'I can't remember a thing about it! Tell me all about it!'

'If Miranda can't remember something she saw only last year, then there's probably nothing to worry about,' said Jane, and she went on. 'It's a comedy of errors – Marlow is the lead male, who becomes tongue-tied and awkward around his potential betrothed, Kate, who has to pretend to be somebody she's not in order to be courted by him, blah, blah, blah. In doing so they discover hidden depths in themselves, tada, and there's a happy ending.'

She poured Shay another glass of Cabernet. Sitting back, she had that look on her face, the look Darren called 'Down to business whether you like it or not'. 'You've got the perfect cast for that property. Don't blow it now. We'll go and see Gerard on Monday – I mean, I'll introduce you – I'll take you to his theatre, we can – you can – talk to him about the space—'

'Give it up, Jane!' Miranda leapt up from her seat, towering over the table. Jane and Shay reared back defensively, and Niall carried on eating. 'Just do it, just get involved, just produce this shagging show! For fuck's sake!'

Hands on hips, she stood there, waiting.

'Well, maybe I'll pitch in a bit in the beginning – OK, OK!' Jane mockingly held up her hands to ward off Miranda. She smiled, and turned to Shay.

'If you want a hand, I'll help you out.'

He sighed to himself. He wanted her to play Miss Hardcastle. He just plain wanted her.

'Fair dues,' he said blandly, extending his hand. They shook. Miranda sat down and raised her glass, the rest following suit.

'To Shay and Jane's new . . . partnership!' Miranda smirked at Jane as the crystal rang out around the table.

'Excellent.' Jane took a sip and leaned forward. It was Miranda and Niall's turn to scootch back warily. 'I think I'll get to work immediately. We need a photographer. And a carpenter. And we need you both to start before the end of next week.'

Shay grinned at his plate, and got down to the business of eating. He never wanted it said that he didn't know when to get out of his . . . partner's way.

17

A weak spring sun was doing its best to show its face amongst the low grey clouds, and the odd glimmer of light bouncing off the Liffey made Jane glad of her sunglasses, even if they spent most of their time perched on the top of her head. After a minor squabble with Shay about engaging Jackie's services as company car-and-driver, they grabbed the DART from Bray into the city centre, and made their way briskly up the quays to Gerard's theatre.

It had been a busy week, a week of phone calls and proposals, and almost constant theatre-going, leading to what, to an outsider, would sound like a non-stop, repetitive and mind-numbing post mortem of what they'd seen and where they'd seen it.

To them, it was a non-stop source of satisfaction.

'I liked that Bewley's place,' Shay said, out of nowhere, apropos of nothing – but Jane was getting accustomed to his rare but silent moments of internal wrangling. She was doing exactly the same thing herself.

'I didn't *dis*like it, but A, they've got their season in order and B, it's not like *She Stoops* is a one-woman show – it's too big for that stage.' Jane flipped her shades down as the sun made another appearance. The breeze blowing off the river smelled pleasantly of the sea, and as they walked down the street, Jane got the buzzy kind of vibe off the people and the traffic that made her think of midtown. Wild.

'But the lunch thing, the way they give you your lunch with the price of the ticket – it's bloody smart.' Shay stopped them at the next corner, his arm protectively going out to prevent Jane from crossing against the light.

'I'll have you know that I'm a world-class jaywalker,' Jane snapped.

'I don't doubt it, but I'm not going to lose you after all that effort I put into convincing you to help out.'

' "Help out"? Is that going to be my credit in the programme? "Jane Boyers: she helped out"?' She darted across the road at the first break in the traffic, and stewed as she waited for Shay.

He shook his head. 'You are such a wagon!' he shouted.

'I am not!' she shouted back. 'I'm a producer! I'm producing this show!'

Shay jogged across, only just missing getting flattened by a courier on a Vespa. 'Of course you are. We both are. Together. Co-producers. Right?'

'Right.' They resumed pace, and headed west. 'Helping out,' Jane scoffed to herself. He didn't know what he was getting for free—

'Hey, but what about that place in the middle of town? It was down the road from the other place, the blue one.' Jane cut off her own train of thought as she flipped her glasses back up on top of her head.

'Which place? By the Clarence?' Shay guided her through the traffic, a hand gently laid on the small of her back.

'I'm sure I can negotiate this rather light pedestrian traffic on my own, thank you,' she said primly, stepping up her pace to move away from that warm hand. 'Yes, that place. Why don't I know the name of the street?'

'Because you're integrating,' Shay laughed.

'Anyway, it was a studio space, but if you did a kind of non-specific staging, it seemed like it could work.'

'Non-specific? What, like that thing we saw at the Gate?' Shay shook his head. 'No thanks.'

'That wasn't so much non-specific as faux-designer. Or something. I certainly don't mean that. I mean, maybe, period but ironic. Painted flats, or even painted scrims? Very stagey-looking, but the acting wouldn't be, or maybe a little, or—'

'Will we cross?' Shay grabbed Jane's elbow, bringing her back to reality.

'But it's on this side, isn't it? Gerard said past the Four Courts and then down a lane before the church.' She flipped her shades down again.

'It is, yeah, but I'd rather not—'

'Well, this must be the Courts. Oh my God, that guy's got his wig on!' Jane grabbed Shay's elbow and tried to move him through the crowd, but he wasn't moving.

'Jane, let's—'

'Shay? So it's yourself.'

Jane felt Shay stiffen, and they both stopped short at the sound of the commanding, booming voice.

Jane considered the man before them, wig under his arm, wearing his tie and bib, his long black robe billowing in the breeze. A fraction of an inch shorter than Shay, yet with the same rangy build – for this was surely Shay's father – he nevertheless seemed to loom taller, looking down his nose at them as he was.

'So it is.' Jane had a hard time not gaping at Shay's tone, a mixture of ice and bite that she'd never thought his easy going, optimistic vocal chords could manage. His eyes lost their usual brightness and, flat and cold, they flicked warningly at Jane, and resumed the stare down he was in with his father.

'Your mother was only asking after you . . . yesterday, was it? Last week.' The older man's eyes flicked to Jane, paused, then returned to meet his son's.

Well. Jane used her shades to hold back her hair, the better to see him with. Aren't you the picture of politeness? she thought.

'Please send her my regards,' Shay said.

Wow, thought Jane. We really should be doing *Playboy.* Or *Oedipus.* Fascinated by the change in Shay, Jane gazed up at him raptly, shaking her head.

'And who might this be?' Jane found herself staring into eyes the exact hue and temperature of Shay's.

'This is my partner, Ja—'

'Certainly didn't waste any time, did you?'

Jane rushed in to explain. 'By partner he actually meant—'

'American? Oh, ho,' boomed Shay's father. 'Well, I don't suppose it will break poor Fiona's heart any less, whether she be Irish or a foreigner.'

'If what I've heard of Fiona is true, Mr Gallagher, she hadn't got much of a heart to break.' What an asshole! And who the hell was Fiona? Jane wondered, slipping her arm around Shay's back and snuggling into his side.

'Jane Boyers, Seamus Gallagher – Judge Seamus Gallagher, I mean to say.' Jane neglected to hold out her hand.

'You'll soon find that Shay can be somewhat, er, idealistic about things, miss, in a way that prevents him from fully committing to anything for the duration. Poor, dear Fiona, nursing her broken heart—'

'Over cocktails on the Croisette, if she's still running true to form.' Shay smoothly cut his father off, and draped his arm over Jane's shoulder. Hip to hip, they both smiled thinly at the older man. 'And if I've heard correctly, she's already lined herself up a few contenders for her hand, as it were. Likely lads with more ... conventional ambitions.'

'So, still playing at that theatre business?' Seamus boomed, shifting his armful of files against the now blustery wind.

'We have a saying from my hometown in the States, Mr Gallagher, that goes something like, if the bull doesn't know enough to get out of the calf's way, he'll find himself on the receiving end of mature horns. I'm paraphrasing, of course.' This really isn't my style, Jane thought – rescuing is Darren's favourite pastime.

But it seemed that where Shay was concerned, she was playing against type.

'We've an appointment, Da,' said Shay, cutting off any possible response. Jane noted the emphasis on the 'Da', nasal and drawn out, and let Shay turn her towards their destination. 'Love to Ma.'

The back of Jane's head tingled as she imagined those eagle eyes burning into her bob. *That* was an eye-opener . . . she supposed the thing to do would be to let Shay tell her what that was all about –

'So who's Fiona?'

'Here we are. Bow Lane Theatre.' All chivalry forgotten, Shay pushed his way through the front door, leaving Jane gaping as the door slammed behind him.

For all his eagerness to get into the place, Shay sat front row centre and stared broodingly at the floor. Jane looked down at him as Gerard led her out from the dressing rooms, and took an imperceptibly deep breath. No stranger to family stress herself, at least she knew when to put it aside – or rather, just to forget about it altogether. And Fiona? Who the hell was Fiona? Poor dear Fiona?

'You won't find a better equipped backstage in all of Dublin,' boomed Gerard, as he surreptitiously edged aside a bucket full of water.

'Half the light bulbs are missing in the ladies' dressing room, and the men's doesn't have a bathroom – loo.' Jane craned her head back to get a look at the rig. 'Are these all you've got?'

'We've got some out on lend to the Peacock,' Gerard

replied as he joined in her in her scrutiny of the stage's ceiling and lights.

'I'll take their phone number, ask them for a count,' Jane said equably. She hoped he didn't think she was buying *that*. Chancer, she thought fondly. She had to like that about him.

'No need for that,' Gerard said, just as equably. She's going to get her fingers burned, he sighed. That American style just doesn't wash round here. 'They've got fifteen Lowell's, and a few pin spots.'

'So that's forty altogether. Not great.' Jane moved off upstage and took a look at the ropes. 'The rig doesn't lower?'

'We've got ladders. Three.' He waited at the apron of the stage as she counted off the distance from the back wall to the downstage edge. She looked towards the back of the house, holding up a hand as she shielded her eyes from the work lights.

'Is that the booth?' She pointed up at a window in the theatre's back wall.

'Em, no, that's the office there. Pressed for space, same old story all over the world. The lighting board and sound gear gets set up back in the corner there.'

'Is the board computerised?' Jane lowered her hands to her hips. If the answer was no, she'd have some bargaining chips. As it was, she figured she had more than a few areas for negotiation, what with half the lights missing, the dressing rooms little better than broom closets and the—

'We'll take it.' Shay sprang to his feet and jumped up on to the stage.

Gerard watched Jane's eyebrows disappear into her hairline.

'Excuse us for a moment, would you, Gerard? My associate and I need to have a quick discussion.' Yanking Shay aside by the elbow, she all but threw him stage right, into the wings.

'Nice negotiating skills! Some lawyer!' Jane practically spat out the words.

'I'm not a lawyer! And I was a barrister! There's a difference!' Shay spat back.

'We can't just *take* the place! We have to haggle and nurgle and wangle a few extras out of him! Are you crazy?' Jane kicked over a bucket and sent Gerard scrambling for a mop. 'Look around you! Buckets tucked all over the stage – hmm, what could that mean? That the cleaning lady was in? Or that the roof leaks? Hmm, half of their instruments are out "on lend". Does that mean that Gerard has a heart of gold – or that he doesn't have any more lamps?'

'I want it. It's perfect. I could see it, Jane. When you were up there I could see it.' Shay looked down at her and gave her his first grin in what seemed like ages. 'It's the place.'

She huffed, but felt a weird thing like relief as the light returned to his eyes. 'Will you let me at least try to shave a few dollars – euros – whatever – off the price? I couldn't live with myself otherwise.'

He tugged her on her stubborn chin. 'Just don't put the man off – we don't do things here the way you do them in New York.'

'Bollocks!' Jane laughed, and marched back out centre stage. Gerard hastily put aside the mop.

'Bit of a problem with the . . . pipes,' he muttered.

'Umm hmm. Well, as my colleague expressed, we're interested in booking, but we need to put a few things out on the table.'

Gerard gestured to the stage manager's desk that sat crammed up between the wall and a slightly tatty futon in the stage-left wings. 'We've got a standard contract, covers all the usual bits and bobs.' He banged on the kettle and got out some mugs. Jane rolled her eyes and earned a light smack in the shoulder from Shay. He shook his head warningly and held out her chair.

'It's black with two sugars for me, and milky with no sugars for Jane,' he said, sitting down in the somewhat rickety chair provided. He looked back over his shoulder at the empty stage, and felt his equilibrium return. No time to think about auld Seamus at the minute, he thought, no time for him at all.

He turned back to see Jane frowning at the contract. She speed read through the thing in less time than it would take for Shay to take it out of her hands, and he snuck a glance at Gerard, whose grinning eyes spoke volumes. Jane's manner would go over safely enough with himself, Shay thought . . . but he didn't know how lucky they'd get elsewhere.

'It seems fine – actually, you should take a look yourself,' said Jane, handing Shay the contract. 'In his former life, Shay was a— well, never mind. Your rates are fair enough, I suppose, but seeing as there's no enclosed booth, and that you've got a significant amount of lights out "on lend", *and* the fact that there's no rehearsal space—'

'We had a cancellation for the weeks previous to the ones you've mentioned – they paid in full, cancelled fairly late in the day, so sure, you can make use of the place yourselves.' Gerard passed around the tea with a faint smile on his face.

Jane's eyebrows did their disappearing act. 'Free of charge?'

'Full use of the house, the storage, the dressing rooms. All of it.'

You're nuts, Jane thought. 'That's generous,' she said.

It's worth it to see you fighting back your absolute giddy delight, thought Gerard. 'Ah, sure, we like to support new artists around our gaff,' he said.

Shay looked up from the contract. 'It seems fine, but there are one or two—'

'Sign it,' said Jane. Gerard handed him a pen. Shay shrugged. And signed.

'There's still a thing or two we need to discuss,' said Jane.

'Plenty of time,' boomed Gerard. 'Sure we'll be in each other's pockets for the next month or two. Plenty of time.' He turned to Shay. 'She drives a hard bargain, yer one, so she does.'

Shay picked up the warning in the seemingly benign statement, but he couldn't imagine how in the world Jane could possibly be less American. Ah, well, they'd just have to cross that bridge when they came to it.

'Well, we've got tons to do before the day is done.' Jane grabbed up her handbag and tucked the contract under her arm. She nodded at Shay. He rose and they shook hands all around. 'We'll see you next Monday, Gerard. Hope those lamps are back by then. Cheers!'

The barman stood, waiting, two pints of Guinness in his hands. Bent over her reams of paperwork, Jane didn't notice; Shay helpfully moved a stack of headshots out of the way, digging out two beer mats from beneath Jane's purse.

'I'll tell you, that guy's not afraid to charge, but he's got a good space. I won't hold my breath about those lamps, though. I can't believe that he's going to let us in for almost a month before the run! He could have made double his money, no problem.' Jane lit up a cigarette and shook her head gleefully. It was bit chilly for the Brazen Head's beer garden, but there was no way she was going to keep leaping up all afternoon when she wanted a smoke. 'Well, he's crazy, we're lucky, I guess. Although we need to red flag all those buckets, and he definitely needs to get rid of that futon; there's barely room to swing a cat back there. So I suppose we should ring everyone for callbacks, have them come to the cottage. It's not ideal but they're familiar with the room, I think that kind of comfort promotes good performances. Callbacks are so tricky, we'd better hope that they come through, we don't have too many to choose from.'

Shay watched Jane talk . . . and assess . . . and project . . . and basically, he thought, enjoy herself. It was a far cry from the edgy and uptight woman who'd shown up out of nowhere only weeks ago: the passion that was evident in her voice, her face, her entire body, made him wonder about other outlets for that passion she might disclose if he—

'What?' Jane narrowed her eyes at Shay – he'd been staring at her, unblinking.

'A toast,' he proposed suddenly. 'To, em, my theatre company yet to be named.'

Jane raised her glass. 'My God, this weighs a ton. Anyway, to your show.'

'Our show.'

'Our show. You really should come with a name for the production company, we need to get some letterhead made up and—'

Jane's mobile rang (she'd got her own as Miranda had long since claimed hers back), playing 'New York, New York' in all its polyphonic glory.

'Jane Boyers. Hi, how are you? You got my message. Uh huh . . . Bow Lane Theatre . . . mmm hmmm . . . no, but we'd probably cover some expendables, I'll need to check the budget . . . oh, yeah, of course . . . profit share, yeah . . . cast of eightish, not sure yet, waiting on the director, what else is new . . . great, excellent . . . will you come to callbacks? Good, see you then. Cheers, bye.'

Jane shook back her hair, triumphant. 'That was Cathleen Doyle, our make-up artist. I bet we can get her to take care of the hair, too.' She raised her glass, and they toasted again. 'To Cathleen! This stuff isn't so bad.'

'Take it easy. If you're not used to it, it'll go straight to your—' Shay was cut off by the phone again.

'Jane Boyers. Hello, thanks for getting back to me . . . yes, we're a new theatre company. It's called something in Irish, I'm afraid I can't pronounce it,' Jane laughed along with the caller and made faces at Shay. 'Anyway, we're producing a Goldsmith play— yes, exactly, that one – yes, we know. Plenty of time since the Abbey's production – right, right. So we need some interns, basically – ah, trainees, right . . . whatever you've got, stage

management, rigging crew, running crew, all three in one
. . . exactly . . . Excellent! Have them send their résumés
– CVs – directly to Bow Lane Theatre . . . Yes, Gerard . . .
a what? . . . right, right. OK, thanks! Cheers, bye.'

'No flies on you,' murmured Shay, starting to feel
slightly overwhelmed.

'That was the Gaiety School; they're going to put
some of their students in touch with us. Slave labour, but
it'll be good experience for them.' Jane leaned back
against the banquette and smiled at Shay. 'They know
Gerard, of course – apparently he's a "decent skin".' She
laughed and reached for another cigarette. 'Things are
falling into place.'

He opened his mouth to reply but—

'Hello, Jane Boyers. Oh, hi, yeah, we're a new theatre
company producing out of Bow Lane Theatre – yeah,
Gerard – he's a decent skin – and we're starting to look at
set designers. The director is Shay Gallagher. I saw your
work in that theatre out by that mall – right, right . . .'

It appeared that all he was going to have to do was
show up and direct. That was exactly what he wanted . . .
wasn't it? Shay took a long pull from his jar, and signalled
the barman for another. He was saved from further
introspection when a lanky woman dropped into a seat at
their table.

'Are you well recovered, missus?' She cut her eyes at
Shay and waggled her eyebrows at Jane.

'Shay, this is Sinead, a friend of Cathleen, our make-
up artist. Sinead, this is Shay, he's the cousin of my
friend's partner.' Jane waggled her eyebrows right back.

'Howya. So you're the actor-lawyer fella?' Sinead
leaned back after having helped herself to one of his
cigarettes.

Shay sighed. 'I'm not a— Jesus, never mind. Close
enough.'

Sinead grinned at Jane and clocked the piles of
papers. 'So what's all this, then? Making a play?'

'That's one way of putting it.' Jane narrowed her eyes and leaned forward. 'Want to audition?' Shay frowned, and then cocked his head as he appraised Sinead.

Sinead blushed, something that Jane was convinced she didn't do too often. 'I'm no actor. I'm underemployed, but I'm no actor. I'm a . . . a teacher!'

'Have you ever been onstage before?' Jane shot back, and Shay cocked his head the other way.

They were both looking at her as if she were a monkey in the zoo. 'I was in the drama society at UCD, but—'

'Are you free on Friday afternoon?' Shay offered her another cigarette, which she took, even though she hadn't finished the first one.

'Em, yeah, but—'

Jane held up a light, and in confusion, Sinead ground out her unfinished cigarette and leaned towards the flame. 'Come along with Cathleen, then. She's working for us as well. We may have something for you to read, no pressure, of course.'

'Of course,' Sinead mumbled.

'No pressure at all,' said Shay, leaning his elbows on his knees and seeming to stare directly into her brain.

'Right, well maybe, we'll see, cheers, bye, bye.' Sinead was out the door and gone.

'Miss Neville?' Shay and Jane sat back in concert.

Jane nodded. 'I've got a feeling . . . she's so lanky and angular, I think it would be an interesting contrast with stocky Jason as Tony Lumpkin.'

Shay nodded. 'It's worth a try. Poor thing, we threw her completely off balance.'

Jane laughed, unapologetically, and Shay leaned forward, scrutinising her now, hoping to throw her off balance somehow, hoping to find the right thing to say that would touch her, make her want to touch him, too—

'Jane Boyers. Darrrrrrrren! Miranda said you rang – called – the other night! How are things?'

She had no idea how Irish she sounded, Darren thought. 'Good, good. Just thought I'd check in, see how you were. You got your own phone?' Darren stared out between the buildings opposite to admire his view – glimpse, really – of Central Park West.

'Yeah, I got roped into producing this show – theatre again, after all these years!' She crossed her legs and snuggled into the banquette. 'It's fun!'

'Well, that's great, honey. You sound really good.' She sounded like a completely different person, Darren thought as he sat down heavily on the window seat he'd made out of an old trunk. Was he going to lose another friend to stupid Ireland?

'Yeah, I'm OK, I got over the luggage thing, and the job thing, oh, and the flat – the apartment thing. Everything's fine.'

'Miranda said that you and Shay were . . . close.'

'Miranda needs to get a grip,' Jane bit out, and Darren breathed a sigh of relief. The Jane he knew and loved hadn't entirely disappeared.

'But you're working with him, aren't you?'

'Mmm hmmm. So, too bad you can't come do the set design, we could use you.' Jane smiled over at Shay and pointed to her empty glass. Shay shook his head.

'Oh, he's there with you.' For some reason, this lowered Darren's spirits even further.

'Yeah, hold on—' She held the phone away and gestured to the barman as Shay counter-gestured. 'I liked it, I want another—'

'You haven't got the tolerance for it, pet, you'll be crawling out of here on hands and knees.'

'Well, then let's eat something, peanuts or crisps or something.'

'We'll get crisps and a half of Guinness and then I'm putting my foot down, Jane.'

Oh, my God, Miranda's right, thought Darren as he listened to the byplay coming tinnily down the line.

Under any other circumstances other than attraction,
serious attraction, Jane would never play along like that.
He'd seen her flatten countless potential suitors for less
than trying to tell her what she could or couldn't drink.
He ran a hand through his hair and headed for the old
apothecary chest he'd turned into a mini bar.

'Hellllooooo, Dar! You there?'

'Yeah, honey, still here.' Still here, all alone and
feeling very, very sorry for himself.

'Listen, I think I have another call coming in. I'll ring
you later. Call you later. You know what I mean. Hey, I,
um, you know, wish you were here. You know, miss you.'

Darren stared into the receiver and then shook it,
amazed. Had Jane just expressed a feeling of her own
free will? He grabbed the Absolut Mandarin and had to
stop himself swigging straight from the bottle.

What if she didn't come back? What if she went and
fell in love with this Shay person? What if she made it as
a producer in Ireland, and got married and stayed there
and never came back?

It sounds as though you are projecting, Darren . . .
The voice of his shrink swept soothingly into his mind.

Yes, he said to himself, stop projecting. It's just a
feeling Miranda has, and although she is extremely
intuitive, she can't really know what's going on.

No, the only way to know would be to see for himself.
Crossing over to his appointment book, he flipped
through the pages for the next few weeks . . . he could
manage it, maybe in ten days or so . . . but that would be
meddling, wouldn't it? Poking his nose around? Wasn't it
absolutely, positively, none of his business?

He tucked the vodka under his arm, dug out his
credit card, and booted up his laptop.

Jane set down her phone and frowned at the tiny glass of
porter. Shay shook his head in advance of any
complaints, and started gathering up papers.

'We've done enough work for one day. Come on,' he raised his voice against Jane's protestations. 'You've worked yourself mental, we've got a venue, a make-up artist, some trainees, another actor, and, from the sound of that last call, a PR agency. Well done, let's call it a day.'

'OK. I can get behind that.' Especially as this stuff was starting to go to her head.

Not that she'd let him know.

'How's your friend? Darren?'

'OK. He sounded kind of tense . . . but he always sounds kind of tense. I think he misses Miranda a lot. And me too, maybe.'

'Why only maybe?'

'Oh . . . I was kind of a bitch to him before I left.' Jane lifted her glass, swirling the white foam into the black liquid, reluctant to admit that she felt – there she went again – relieved that Darren wasn't permanently mad at her, and felt guilty about the whole thing, too. Two feelings for the price of one. Ugh, she thought, throwing back a healthy gulp of the Guinness.

Shay moved over beside her on the banquette. At her lifted brow, he explained, 'Yer man there was knocking me in the back of the head for the past twenty minutes.'

'Wow, where'd all these people come from?' Jane realised she'd lost all track of time, and by the looks of things, space.

'It's half five on a Friday, everyone's out for the weekend.' Shay looked around, wondering how it looked in her eyes.

'God, in New York, no one would even begin to think of going out until nine, ten o'clock,' Jane said. 'Especially if you were trying to avoid working over the weekend.'

'Jesus, I'd like to see you try to get anybody in these parts to work on a Saturday.' Shay handed her a cigarette and lit them both. 'We don't live to work here.'

'I've been living to work for . . . a long time.' Jane blew out a stream of smoke, and retreated a bit. All those years, killing herself to 'make the grade', working for lunatics, and with lunatics – and going a bit crazy herself. And she had that Emmy to show for it, but what else? Not when all she'd really wanted to do her whole life was—

'Old habits die hard!' Jane chirped brightly. 'But it was worth it. You'll be able to concentrate on your directing, and I'll be available to put out all those little fires that break out, even when you think you've had it all covered.'

She raised her glass and beamed at Shay. 'This has been a really good day!'

I t had been a really bad week.
  The first flush of success faded rather rapidly: they couldn't get a set designer who would work for a profit share of the takings during the run; the trainees who had come to meet them had all universally suffered from severe cases of self-importance; the lack of a stage manager meant more work for Shay who, in Jane's opinion, really needed to get his vision together; the lighting guy they'd met and hired had almost immediately got a paying gig in London.

  And nobody returned her phone calls! If she rang at nine a.m., no one was in. By ten she was leaving messages all over town, and by one o'clock was following up, which was pretty pointless because no one was ever there. Shay patiently tried to explain to her that lunch hour was from one to two, but she couldn't get it through her head that *no one* was around at all, that everyone in Dublin took lunch *at exactly the same time*.

  At least, they both sighed to themselves as they readied Niall's studio, the cast was assembled, and were expected for the first read through any minute.

  Not, huffed Jane as she made a circle of the chairs they'd dragged in from the cottage, that that had been a piece of cake, either. She'd stopped short of knocking on people's doors when *those* phone calls had gone unanswered; the only people who'd been on top of things had been the O'Connors and Mihal O'Whatever. The younger ones had some serious work-habit issues that Jane intended to address up front.

Shay buzzed around the room, moving things around in preparation for the transfer to the theatre. He wanted the actors to feel that they were in safe hands, hands that had at least assembled all the necessaries to produce a professional performance. The costumes he'd intended for the show were hanging from the rack, and several of the pieces of furniture that Niall was meant to restore were displayed along his worktop. He had the script broken down, and ideas scribbled into the margins of his play book, and dammit if he wasn't going to make this work!

He dragged what he was beginning to consider 'his' table to the front of the room, and fell into one of the chairs that he had put behind it. He checked behind him, the fruits of his labouring over Uncle Des's gear spread out behind him in all their glory. He looked down at the table, and at his playscript, stroking his hand over the binder's red cover, determined to enjoy this moment, the moment he'd dreamed of, had worked for, had been dumped by Fiona over, had fallen out with his father about . . . Taking a deep breath, he leaned his elbows on the book and nodded his head. Yeah. He was ready.

He was as nervous as a bag of cats, Jane thought indulgently. 'Ready to go?' she piped, making him jump.

'More than ready,' Shay boomed.

'All psyched up?' Jane moved around behind him and shook him by the shoulders.

'Deffo,' Shay said, and rolled his shoulders. They seemed tense.

'Excellent!' Jane began to rub the knots in his back in earnest. 'Never let them see you sweat,' she said, digging her knuckles into his spine.

'Arrrrrrrhhhhhhhhh uuhhh, uh, never,' Shay moaned, and dropped his chin down on to his chest.

Jane kept a steady rhythm going, and felt his muscles

relax under her hands. She stroked down across his shoulders and dug into his biceps, testing the strength of the muscles she felt there – and they were certainly strong. With a half smile on her face, she ran her hands down his broad back and up again, feeling the ripple of muscles against her palms. Leaning into it, she kneaded his shoulders and neck, and smelt the freshness of his skin after his shower, imagined him sluicing warm water over his chest and down around his—

Her burgeoning fantasy stopped short as he grabbed her hands, pulling them down on to his chest so that she fell against his back. She looked down into his eyes, warmly brown and slightly drowsy, and he managed a half-smile. 'If you keep that up, I'll be of no use to anyone – but yourself.'

Jane stepped back hastily. 'Maybe that's taking good producer-director relations a bit too far,' she laughed, her voice catching in her throat.

Shay reached out and grabbed her hand. 'Let's go out to dinner.'

'That's a good idea – it'll be a nice company-bonding event.' Jane wiggled her fingers in protest of his grip.

'No, just us. Before everything goes bananas with the show.'

Jane looked down at their locked hands, looked into his smiling yet unsure eyes, and wondered why, again, she was hesitating. 'As long as it's nothing like a date,' she replied, lightly.

It was like watching the sun duck behind storm clouds. Shay scowled. 'Sorry, I'm sure I'm not as good a catch as one of those fifty eligible stockbrokers in Manhattan.'

'I didn't mean it like that, I just meant, well, we're working together *and* living together, well, sort of – isn't that enough togetherness?'

The snick and hiss of a shutter snapping down brought them back to reality. Miranda grinned at them from the doorway. 'Thought I'd get some candids of preproduction. That OK?' Unless you two want to go on holding hands, that is, she thought.

'Great idea,' said Jane, stepping over to her side of the table and opening her playscript.

'Work away,' said Shay, rising to go and straighten out some costumes that were hanging perfectly straight.

Niall came sloping in with a sketchbook and charcoal; he hoped to get some inspiration from the read through as his cousin was strangely hard to pin down about the look of the thing. 'There's a crowd coming up the drive – will I go collect them?'

'No, you're all right.' Shay left the costumes and went over to the door to welcome his actors.

'So . . . how're things?' Miranda hid her satisfied smile behind her camera, and grabbed a shot of Niall dubiously fingering a voluminous petticoat.

'What things?' Jane tried for blasé, thought about joining Shay in the doorway – and decided against it.

'You know! You! And him!' Miranda's shutter released again, catching Shay framed between the studio's enormous doors, hands on hips, silhouetted against the midday sun.

Jane knew it was probably a bad idea but – 'He asked me out on a *date*.'

'Oh?' Miranda made a note to self: fall around laughing later on. 'And?'

'And nothing! A date? Who goes on dates any more? It's ridiculous! I'm not going to date him, I gave up dating in 1991. And I don't – I mean – and we're working together—'

'Don't be so middle class!' Miranda sang.

'And living together, kind of. I mean, in the same house, or whatever, and even if I was interested, which I'm—'

Jane's babbling protestations were cut off by the explosion of chattering voices that soon filled the studio with the excited sound of actors on their first day of a new gig – hyped up, anxious, anxious to please, ready to perform, already performing.

Jane grabbed up the pile of photocopied texts and went to stand next to Shay. 'Hi, Marie, good to see you. Martin, hello, here's your playscript. Mihal, finally got your name right, here you go. Jason, come in, great. Paraic, how are you? Glad you finally got my messages. Theresa, how are you? Good to see you. Here you go, Nuala – oh, sorry, Fionnuala. Ronan.' She'd almost forgotten about him. He was cultivating that just-got-out-of-bed look big time, thought Jane – but then, he might actually have just got out of bed. He squinted at her sideways, like a member of a boy band.

'Jane, great to see you, meant to give you a bell, got a commercial,' he drawled, toying with ends of a lock of her hair.

'Take a seat, everyone,' Shay called, turning his back on Ronan and Jane, and thereby missing her swat her hair out of Ronan's hand. Jane moved towards the front of the room.

'We're just waiting on the make-up department, and one of our actors,' Jane announced, smiling around at the group, and noticing the dynamics already falling into place. The O'Connors sat side by side, of course, joined by Mihal – the old guard consolidating. Jason sat alone, with an empty chair on either side of him, comfortable but watchful, his solid belly stretching his Hugo Boss shirt. Theresa seemed to be trying to make herself invisible, and had pulled her chair a little bit behind the circle. Nuala – Fionnuala was already giggling at something Ronan had whispered in her ear, flicking her long blond hair back over her shoulders.

Here we go, Jane thought.

'This is Miranda McMahon, our photographer, and Niall O'Donnell, our carpenter. We expect to have the rest of the key personnel in place by the end of next week. While we're waiting, I'll pass around this form that

I'll need filled out before you leave today so that we can try to accommodate everyone's schedules.'

The group shrugged as one, and passed the sheets around.

'I'd also like to get your biogs as soon as possible for the programme.' Jane handed round another sheaf of papers, and reminded herself to find a graphic designer . . . did Miranda know how to do desktop design? Too bad Darren wasn't here . . .

'We'd also like to keep a record of your details on file, emergency phone numbers, et cetera, so—' And off went another sheet. The actors were beginning to send each other little looks around the circle, and Ronan leaned into Nuala – Fionnuala again, making her giggle – again. Jane silenced them with a look of her own.

'Here are the specifics of the run and the breakdown for the profit share—'

Audible groans were stifled before they could begin by the banging open of the studio's big doors.

'Sorry we're late,' Cathleen called as she rushed into the room. 'Howya Jane, howya Ro, are you Shay? How's it going? Traffic was desperate.'

Sinead lingered in the doorway, momentarily taken aback by the number of people in the room, all staring at her, at the racks of costumes, at the general air of busyness and seriousness. She considered legging it back to Dublin.

Jane was at her side before she knew it. 'Great to see you, come on in, here's your script, I highlighted your part, this is Jason, your nemesis, and Paraic, your love interest—'

'Paraic, ya eejit!' Sinead laughed. 'Since when are you an actor?'

'I could ask the same of you, Shinny.' Paraic grinned, his thin face lighting up.

'Yer one here thinks I've got presence,' Sinead replied in plummy tones.

'Well, you've certainly filled out since primary school,' he murmured.

Miranda caught them in mid-laugh, and she moved across the circle to get a similar shot of Fionnuala and Ronan. Fionnuala threw up a hand.

'Oh, Gawd, like, no one said anything about photographs,' she simpered, in the same nasal accent as Ronan's. 'I haven't got my face on, I mean.' Jane sneered at her behind her back – if Fionnuala hadn't spent an hour on her make-up, Jane would eat her own MAC lipstick.

'Yeah, like, what kind of usage are we talking about here? I really need to talk to my agent,' said Ronan, who despite his assertion, was posing, doing that head-tilting boy band squint again. Bored by the both of them, Miranda moved away, earning a pair of sharp glares behind her back.

'Right.' Shay rose. It had been easy to let Jane break the ice, but it was his turn now. She took her place at the table, and opening her play, looked at him keenly – along with everyone else.

He wasn't a stranger to being the focus of a multitude of eyes. He'd spent a fair few years at the bar, surrounded by onlookers, but this . . . this was different. In the hustle and bustle of the planning stages, the dreaming, the hoping, the actual moment of beginning had never quite crystallised in his mind. His imagination had glided over the nuts and bolts of organisation to opening night – and now he was facing the 'everything in between' part. He took a deep breath and realised that he was ready to begin.

'From what I've heard, our choice of play couldn't be better, despite the fact that there was a recent production,' he began. Good one, Jane thought. Blast those doubts away. 'Does anyone even remember it, at all?' Cosy, insider laughs all round. Miranda's shutter snicked away. Niall's charcoal scratched busily across a sheet of coarse paper. Jane let go of a breath she'd hadn't known she'd been holding, and sat back, calm.

'As you can see, our company have assembled the necessary elements to create the world of our play' – he paused as the group took in the set pieces – 'and today, we'll begin building you into the cast that we are convinced can best do this show at this point in time.'

The door opened again, quietly this time, and a small, dark, long-haired girl slipped into the room. Jane rose, indicating to Shay that she'd take care of it, and went over to meet her.

'We're dealing with language that has lofty, Shakespearean qualities, but we must remember, this is a comedy—' Easy on the theory there, pal, Jane thought as she handed the girl a script, and sat her down at the director's table.

Shay wound down. 'Right so. Let's begin.' He looked towards Jane, who smiled and said, 'Everyone, this is Naomi. She's a trainee, studying at the Gaiety School. She'll be doing, well, whatever we need her to do, and her first job will be to read the stage directions for us.'

As Naomi began speaking in the requisite flat tones that seemed absolutely necessary to the reading of stage directions (Shay hoped she wasn't on the *acting* track; at least she wasn't acting them, Jane thought), the collection of disparate strangers, who'd literally only just walked in the door, began to breathe in unison, and started that mysterious, alchemical process that, owing as much to luck as to talent, would gel them into an able cast.

Shay abandoned his text to listen, and watch, and bloody well enjoy. And Jane left off making her notes as she watched him watch them. He really did it, she thought, and a warm liquidy thing happened in her belly. She smiled faintly as she watched him acting along with the players. And right on the heels of her little session of warm fuzzies was a blast of arousal that hit her so hard she was sure it showed; a blast so strong that she immediately took refuge in her notes again.

*

At the end of Act One, Shay called for a break, and the burst of nattering that broke out was full of pleasure and relief. Jane turned to Naomi to ask her to make the tea – and saw that she was already busily warming the pot. Ronan and Fionnuala stepped out for a smoke, and Shay stretched his arms above his head, feeling much looser than he had in ages.

'An hour and ten. We've got to get that down.' He turned to Jane, all ill feelings forgotten.

'I think you need to look at cutting those songs, and maybe that pub scene.' Jane skimmed through her text. 'Hmm, take a look at the beginning of Act One, Scene Two—'

'I will. Later. What did you think about—'

Naomi stood at the end of the table, and quietly interrupted. 'Tea?'

'Milky, no sugars for me; black, two sugars for Shay. Naomi, this is Shay, our director.'

'Howya,' she said, and went back to making their cups.

'Naomi the Trainee. A woman of few words.' Shay shook his head.

'I have a strong suspicion that Naomi the Trainee will be a godsend,' Jane mused, and turned back to her script.

'Looks good,' said Cathleen as she joined them. 'So what have you got in mind, make-up wise?'

She and Jane looked at Shay. 'Em, not sure, yet.'

'Well, I've a few ideas, but once I show the cast, they'll be able to do it themselves. Definitely the older couple, and that thin fella. They know what they're about.' Cathleen looked at Shay shrewdly. 'I wouldn't mind getting more involved in other aspects of the production.'

'Such as?' Jane sat back, perturbed.

'Oh, you know, being up here with you two. Like, assisting.'

'I haven't got anyone in line for it.' Shay thought about it.

'We still need you to do the make-up,' Jane said.

'Yeah, yeah, of course, of course, no worries.' Cathleen beamed.

'Why the change of heart?' asked Shay.

'I did a few gigs in the last few weeks, just got the bug to know how it all happens, like – at the top.' Cathleen shrugged.

'You're grand, then, why not?' Shay felt a weight slip off his shoulders.

'But you still have to take care of the initial make-up,' Jane insisted.

'Honest to God, missus, no worries. She's a tough customer,' Cathleen said to Shay.

'Go on and round everybody up for Act Two, so. Your first act as Assistant Director,' said Shay.

'She's still going to have to—' Jane narrowed her eyes as Cathleen made the rounds.

'She knows, I know, I'll tell Naomi, I'll tell anyone you want. It'll be grand.'

'We'll see,' Jane muttered darkly, and grabbed up her script. 'We'll see.'

Sugary tea and nicotine lifted the second act off to a flying start, and the meshing of the group allowed for a more leisurely assessment of everyone's strengths and weaknesses. They're starting to relax, Jane thought, and they're starting to size each other up.

She could see Marie wince every time Fionnuala opened her mouth. Who could blame her? The girl had no comic timing whatsoever, except to slow things down every time she laughed apologetically at a flubbed line or a dropped cue. What was Shay thinking? Surely she couldn't be the best, even of a bad lot.

Ronan, thought Shay, was barely the best of a bad lot. Smooth as silk and twice as slippery. He began worrying in advance how he was going to guide the performance from self-conscious aerobics infomercial towards something resembling humanity. Why had he let Jane talk him into using that plonker?

Must Shay sneer every time Ronan opened his mouth? Jane shook her head at him. They'd had no choice, and he wasn't *too* too terrible. Superficial, yes, but not outrageously bad. She watched Martin flinch after a scene with Ro, and sighed inwardly. Plant a red flag in that direction.

Mihal sat still as a stone – it was impossible to tell what he was thinking. As he was playing all the second-ary men, he had to be on the ball, yet his concentration seemed to be casual at best. Jane watched him for a moment – was he? Yes. Jesus. He'd learned his lines and was already off book.

He's a star, Shay thought, also glued to Mihal's latest rendering of one of his many characters. And that Theresa was dark horse, barely there until she opened her mouth. The two of them made a funny pair; he so tall and thin, she so small and round. They'd work well together. And she was definitely giving Marie a run for her money.

She was a dark horse, Marie thought, after she finished her scene with Theresa. She wondered where she came from. She crooked a brow at her husband, who shrugged. He in turn tilted his head towards Ronan and Fionnuala, and Marie imperceptibly rolled her eyes.

Sinead was doing great. I'm always right, Jane thought, and gave herself a mental pat on the back. And she and Paraic seemed to be getting on well . . .

Too bad Paraic was too 'character' for Young Marlow, Shay thought ruefully, he'd got buckets more talent than that . . . plonker. He sighed, and barely covered his recoil as Fionnuala's D4 tones destroyed another monologue. If only Jane—

Ronan! There he went again! Too cool, too contemporary! Jane seethed. If only Shay—

Ronan wondered if Nuala had a car. He'd hate to take the shagging bus all the way back to town, like.

Nuala wondered if she should get more streaks in her hair.

Paraic watched Mihal – yer man was already off book! He decided to skip the match tonight and swot his lines.

Sinead was delighted she wasn't making a prat of herself, and wondered when Paraic had got so fanciable. This might be the craic after all.

Jason thought about his tea.

Naomi recited the closing direction, and everyone applauded themselves. As they all prepared to tell each other how wonderful they were, Jane rose and held up a hand.

'Thanks, everyone, that was lovely. Please remain seated for the moment, and fill out the scheduling form for me. Then we'll be able to set up the rehearsal schedule ASAP.' The cast dug in their pockets and handbags for pens, and threatened to burst into chatter again, when Jane's voice rose above them all.

'Everyone! Thanks. A couple of things need to be put on the table right from the start. First, please be off book by Monday.' Universal groans. 'I know, I know, but the sooner you're off the better our time together will be. Mihal appears to be the only one who has his lines down' – Ronan and Fionnuala glared at Mihal, who stared them down impassively – 'and isn't it procedure here, anyway, in this part of the world?'

'In England,' Shay said. 'But—'

'England, Ireland, whatever,' Jane said breezily. 'Another thing is punctuality; not only in terms of rehearsals, but in terms of returning phone calls. We need to hear from you in order to get things moving, and I'd rather not have to go through what I did just getting you all here today.' She smiled. 'I worked on a show in New York for which we had to institute a fining structure. I'd rather not do that here – but we were able to pay for a fabulous opening-night party at Tavern on the Green!' Jane laughed.

Nobody else did.

'Thanks Jane!' Shay jumped to his feet. 'If you've

filled out your, em, forms, then you're free to go. Naomi – oh, there ya go, right, hand them over to Naomi. So. We'll be in contact.'

The grumbling began before they got out the door.

Looked like he and his partner were going to need to take a meeting – ASAP.

'How'd we get mixed up in this, again?' Miranda huffed a lock of hair out of her eyes. She hauled another box full of . . . well, it looked like random crap to her, but hey – what did she know?

Niall grunted behind her, his arms full of the lumber that Shay had insisted they bring along. If there was one thing he knew, it was wood, and this stuff—

'C'mere, am I mad?' He turned his back to the room at large, which was buzzing with activity, and gestured to Miranda. 'Look at that.'

Miranda studied the plank. 'It's a bit . . . short?'

'No, love, look at *that*,' Niall insisted, jabbing a finger at several small holes.

'Termites?' Miranda guessed, and as her boyfriend was conveniently located right in front of her face, she couldn't resist a quick up-on-her-toes nuzzle of that boundlessly attractive place behind Niall's right ear.

'It's dry rot.' Niall shook his head, but still managed to drop a kiss on Miranda's forehead. 'It's useless. It's all useless.'

'Tell Shay.' Miranda shrugged, and went out to get another box out of Jackie's taxi.

Niall dragged the wood to the stage and, taking one look at his cousin, realised that the state Shay was in, he wouldn't hear an elephant drop down from the ceiling.

Shay stood, slightly wild-eyed, downstage centre. If one more person asked him a question, he thought, he was going to go absolutely positively fucking spare. He rubbed his eyes and thought to himself: Shay boy, it's the first day in the theatre. You've had one week, one long week of fielding calls from Gerard, from the lighting rental crowd, from the sound system crowd, from the insurers, the actor's union, Ronan's shagging agent . . . it was enough to put anyone on edge. Imagine, he thought, if you hadn't got Jane on board.

He looked over from his downstage vantage to where she was sitting behind the stage manager's desk like a queen on her throne – only instead of wielding a sceptre, she had the house phone welded to her ear. The desktop was ruthlessly organised, and Shay knew it was worth his life if he went near it. She was doing a mighty job of things . . . but . . .

At least half of all those calls he had fielded this week were from his actors (who had got his number off the contact sheet that Jane so efficiently drawn up), actors who were passive-aggressively complaining about Jane's tactics. He was going to have to talk to her about her New York-style efficiency which, in this part of the world, was tantamount to bullying.

She'd tried to hide the kettle, for Jesus' sake! Was she striving for outright rebellion?

'Cuppa?' asked Niall. Jane slammed the phone down, hard.

'How are we doing with that lumber?' she asked pointedly.

'There's a massive problem with this lumber,' Niall replied, and held out a plank to her as she crossed the stage. He pointed to it.

'Dry rot,' Jane sighed. 'I'll get on the horn, find a supplier. How much will we need, Shay?'

Both Jane and Niall looked at him expectantly. His eyes bulged. That was a question! Another bloody question! The very thing that he swore was going to send him over the edge straight into loo-la land.

'Everything's unloaded,' Miranda called from the front of the house. 'Now what?'

Shay spun away, faced upstage, and wanted, more than anything, to commence tearing tufts of hair right out of his scalp.

Jane took Niall aside. 'I think that's all the help we'll need today, thanks.'

Niall looked at his cousin. 'He's all right, yeah?'

'You tell me,' Jane murmured. 'Has he ever had a nervous breakdown?'

'Not so far,' Niall replied, grimly.

'He just needs to settle in, get the feel of the space. We'll sort out the wood by the end of next week.' Jane watched Shay begin to pace, back and forth, sidling up against the upstage wall, and she was reminded of that poor old polar bear in the Central Park Zoo, the one that had gone nuts and spent his days doing the same short lap of his pool, over and over and over.

Her polar bear looked like he was heading in the same direction.

Niall passed Cathleen on her way into the space, carrying a box. He responded to her cheerful 'Howya?' with raised eyebrows, and, grabbing Miranda, got the hell out of there.

'Howya!' Cathleen called up to the stage. 'Where do you want this?'

Niall and Miranda crossed the quay to walk by the river. Neither minded the light drizzle, and Miranda disdained to carry an umbrella – it made her feel like a native.

Linking hands, they walked alongside the low stone wall and looked down into the Liffey.

'I once thought I saw an otter floating towards the sea,' Miranda said.

'On its back – fins first?' Niall joked.

'Nope – and it only turned out to be an old football.'
They both laughed. 'I was so disappointed.'

At Grattan Bridge, they shifted over to the boardwalk
and ambled towards O'Connell Street. With the arrival
of spring came the coffee vendors who operated out of
well-fitted little stalls that sat at intervals along the way,
each the picture of optimism with their collections of
outdoor tables and chairs. Despite the rain, a few
diehards sipped their cappuccinos, and watched the
world go by with its head down against the wind.

As Miranda threw an arm around Niall's waist, he
tossed one of his over her shoulders, and they strolled
hip to hip alongside the rail. The rain stopped, but the
smell of it still hung in the cool air. The fat grey clouds
that had done their business over Dublin raced east to
give a bit of the same treatment to London.

'Things aren't looking good for a dry summer,' Niall
said ominously. 'The swallows aren't roosting under the
eaves, and the goats won't go up the mountain.'

'Our mountain?' asked Miranda, although strictly
speaking Mullin's Mound was only a hill.

'No, in Clare. I got it from Silé.'

Miranda tensed. 'Oh? Is she well?'

'She is, yeah.' Niall ran his hand down Miranda's
back, and searched for otters in the Liffey.

They ambled in silence, and Miranda could feel a
good brood coming on. What if Silé wanted the house
back? They were living rent-free – a situation for which
any New Yorker would sacrifice a kidney, cut out
singlehandedly with a rusty butter knife – but it came
with countless square feet of insecurity. *Nothing*, thought
Miranda, comes without a price tag. It's simple karmic
economics. They'd put so much work into the house,
Niall in construction and recovery, Miranda in style and
homey touches, that the place looked miles better than
when they'd first moved in. What if Silé wanted to sell it?
What if they had to find someplace else to live? What if

she never got any more work? What if—

'Darlin'? Miranda!' Niall waved a hand in front of her eyes.

'Sorry.' Miranda moved away from their embrace and leaned her elbows on the rail, staring moodily into the river. What had set this off? Niall wondered – Ah. Shite. Silé. The cottage.

'She's delighted that we're making a go of the place.' Niall ran a hand down Miranda's back again. 'It's ours for ev— for as long as we want it.'

'I never thought, ever, that I'd complain about the lack of a lease, but . . . there's some security in that.' *I'm feeling insecure about – everything.*

'It wouldn't work that way, especially as it's family. We're grand, Miranda, I promise.'

'Could we – you – uh, buy it from her, or something?' That was an idea.

Niall blew out a baffled breath. 'Well, I could, but I can't spend my grant money on a cottage. I have to buy supplies with it, live on it.' Not that he hadn't considered it . . .

'Yeah.' Miranda sighed, and they both stared into the water now, elbows on the rail, not touching. There's a step missing here, Miranda thought. What was it?

'I've been here almost a year now,' she began. 'And I got the book together, and I'm in limbo waiting for the book to come out, that poor book has a lot riding on it, it's got to get me more gigs, and I'm not really working, and I'm not sure about my visa, and we don't – it's not our – my – your – house and—' She covered her eyes with her hands. 'And I love you and—' And what? 'And I don't want to go back to New York.'

A little chill chased down from Miranda's scalp to the tips of her toes. I said it. Out loud. I mean it. It's true, she thought. She didn't want to go back. She wanted to stay.

Niall felt a tension, which he hadn't known he'd been feeling, dissolve; he felt a knot at the back of his neck, which he'd only vaguely known was there, release.

Right, he thought. She doesn't want to go back.

She wants to stay.

'I don't want you to leave,' he replied, and they swayed in concert, shoulder to shoulder, leaning into each other.

'OK,' she said.

'OK,' he murmured, and threw his arm back over her shoulders. She turned to tuck her face against his neck, and they embraced.

Shifting her head over to his shoulder, she started thinking aloud. 'I guess I'd better get off me arse and get some work. This Shay thing'll help; maybe I can send some samples around to theatre companies. It won't make me rich but – hmmm, you know, I've never seen a kind of backstage photo-j book about the gamut of Irish theatre companies. Maybe I could work on something like that, it's spec, I know, but . . . it's something.'

Niall smiled into her hair. 'There ya go. Happiest planning.'

She leaned back and looked up into his warm blue eyes. 'What about you? I saw you sketching away for the last week. Ideas?'

He nodded, and stared across at the buildings on the south side of the quays. 'This Shay thing had sparked something, a kind of sculptural-architectural yoke. I can't say yet . . . something about the missing spaces of Dublin, the way everything's been torn away with no thought to . . .' His voice trailed off promisingly, from Miranda's point-of-view. We, she thought, are back on track.

'C'mere, I'll write to Silé about the cottage, get something organised, right?' Niall stopped examining the pictures in his mind's eye, and looked down at Miranda. She smiled at him, and hugged him, and he then looked down at the river: the sun now shone brightly as if the rain had been a figment of their imaginations, and as the light bounced off the water, Niall was dazzled by its brightness, the light dancing and sparkling as clear and clean as a diam—

He gazed down at his lover – his partner – his friend, and would always swear that he felt an actual squeeze around his heart, he actually felt something physical, as though a hand had reached in and grabbed it for a split second. Miranda looked up into his eyes, quizzically smiling, and he took a deep breath. And then another one. And then he opened his mouth and—

And then a combination of panic, elation and determination shut it again. He hugged her tight, rocking them both a little, and he blew out another breath.

Miranda mentally shrugged. Whatever. They were definitely back on track, and she expelled her own breath of relief and satisfaction.

'Will we go?' she asked. 'I'm keen to hit *The Yellow – The Golden Pages*.'

Niall nodded, lost in a thought that left him both thrilled and utterly terrified.

'So this Shay . . .' – Miranda shook her head – 'he seemed pretty overwhelmed.'

'He . . . he's ambitious, right?' Niall tried to explain it properly without feeling disloyal. 'Always the man with the plan. And always, always bites off more than he can chew.'

'Lucky Jane's there, but . . .' Miranda grimaced, a mixture of worry and humour.

Niall fought back a smile. 'But she's very American.'

Miranda shivered. 'I mean, *I* was American, but I was *aware* of it, like, kind of playing it up worse but with a – a sense of humour.'

'Jane is dead serious,' Niall laughed, then frowned. 'And Shay is in over his head.'

'It's a bad combination.' Miranda shuddered. 'Can you believe she tried to hide the kettle? I mean, an Irish operation without tea?'

'Sure, it's a classic time waster,' Niall defended the

notion, 'but a tragic mistake, nonetheless.'

'If he doesn't get his act together, she's going to lose patience,' Miranda predicted.

'If she doesn't calm herself down, he's going to explode,' Niall replied.

They stopped, both imagining the result – and laughed.

'We're so mean,' Miranda giggled.

'It'll be good for him – might relieve that building sexual tension.'

Miranda jogged up and down. 'I was right, I was right, you noticed it too!'

Niall shrugged, and started them along again.

'Neither of them know it, but I know they're each exactly what the other needs.' Miranda stopped skipping next to Niall, and grinned. 'He's so spazzy, but spontaneous, and she's so thorny, but focused. It's a match made in heaven! I hope it works out for them,' she went on wistfully. 'I hope—'

Niall playfully tugged at her hair. 'Now, missus . . .'

'Now mister . . .' and she tugged her head away, 'I'm just saying.'

'Miranda . . .' Niall warned.

'I know, I know, it's none of my business, but I just want her to be as happy as I am.'

Niall slid a hand into the back pocket of her jeans. 'Let's see about spreading some of that happiness around – just between us.'

Miranda grabbed his hand and started pulling him towards Tara Street. 'I think that can be arranged,' she purred, and they ran across O'Connell Street, laughing.

Jane grudgingly admitted, but only to herself in the silence of her heart, that this cups-of-tea thing was useful. Waiting for the kettle to boil, the action of making the tea was as soothing as she hoped the actual stuff itself would be to Shay, who was now sitting on the floor, back up against the wall, behind the stage manager's desk, wedged in next to that damn futon.

She cast her eye out into the house. Cathleen and Sinead, who'd come along to help out before going off to give some grinds (whatever they were), were calmly sorting through the props and having a good old gossip. Naomi the Trainee had, of her own initiative, organised a props department, had replaced all the light bulbs in the make-up mirrors in both dressing rooms, had ironed and hung up all the costumes, brushed the wigs, and polished the shoes; now, of her own volition, she was mopping the stage floor.

'Naomi!' Jane called. The girl paused and looked up calmly. 'I'm promoting you to stage manager.'

'Cheers,' Naomi said softly, and got back to work.

The house door opened, and in walked a trio of goth dudes. Jane took one look at Shay, who was digging his fingers into his forehead, and moved to the front of the stage to handle it. Naomi joined her and said, 'That's Declan. He's a technician from my school. I thought you might let him help out on the show.'

Dec the Tech. Sounded good to her. It was a short conversation.

As Dec silently organised his mates and began the arduous job of unsnarling metres of cable, Jane turned once more to Shay. He had given up trying to prise his brain out of his skull, and now he leaned his head against the wall with his eyes half shut.

Jane stood still so as not to betray the slightest quiver of unease to the crew. Arms that looked casually folded at her waist ended in hands that clutched elbows in a white-knuckled death grip. Somehow, somewhere along the line, she'd got invested in this production; somehow she'd crossed the line dividing 'won't do' from 'do or die'. She was in, heart and soul – and she had a comatose director on her hands.

Get up! she wanted to shout. There's no time for a

breakdown! Fake it till you make it! Pull yourself together! How many times had she seen this: a first-time director coming across all hot-shot and can-do, and then folding like a house of cards?

She opened her mouth to blast him with her customary tough-love pep-talk – and stopped as Shay slowly and painfully pulled himself up to standing. He faced her, his hair a tangled nimbus framing his head, his skin pale, his jaw set.

'Has anyone any queries for me?' He choked on that a fraction, then cleared his throat on a strangled growl.

A tingle began in Jane's fingertips, an icy-hot thrill that ran up her arms, leaving goosebumps behind; it rushed up into that region of her chest that surrounded her heart. Hands that had been clenched now shook with some other unidentifiable damn emotion – all she knew was that she wasn't angry any more, that she could have respect for a guy who felt like shit but was determined to carry on, and along the way to her heart from her head, that respect got twisted up into something that felt like it kind of could be like—

Shay moved closer and Jane forgot to breathe.

Jesus, the head on her! 'Do I look that bad?' he asked, trying to smooth down his hair.

Jane turned and almost threw herself bodily on to the kettle. She felt a light sweat gathering on the nape of her neck as she poured hot water into the teapot. Saying nothing, she made him a cup.

She's furious with me. 'Jane, I – I'm grand,' he said, trying for jaunty. 'No worries, we'll get on with it.'

She handed him his tea, and went over to the desk, avoiding eye contact. Time for that lecture, she said to herself sternly, and sat back to read him the riot act.

She looked up and saw him cradling the tiny blue and white china cup in his big hands, looking sheepish while trying to look nonchalant, and she felt that damn thing in her chest again, as if her heart had blown up like a helium balloon.

'Shay . . .' she began, then stopped when she heard her own voice, breathy and, ugh, girly. She cleared her throat. 'Why not go out, have a walk, get some air? Take a mental health day, as we say in the States.' She sat back and hoped she looked authoritative. 'We don't really need you here – go on, go home and work. Break down the script. Let's get Niall busy. Take a little walk. I'll see you at – at home, later. OK?'

So she thinks she can kick me out of my own theatre? he thought to himself.

But then, a bit of stroll couldn't hurt.

Saying nothing, he put the cup down on the desk, and walked out the door.

Jane spun around in her chair and sat, staring at the wall. Shit, she thought. Dammit!

Smart girl, thought Shay, as his long legs ate up the quays to make his way up Westmoreland Street. A nice brisk walk to get the wheels turning. Excellent.

It wasn't as if he couldn't see the show in his head. He could: he *could* see it, could see Mihal in that severe black frock coat, see Marie in that wig, Sinead in that stripey silk dress. He could hear mousy little Theresa's surprising bellow, he could hear Jason's affected lisp, could hear the soundscape he kept forgetting to tell Jane she needed to organise . . . he could see and hear all this, could run the play backwards and forwards in his mind . . . and, for some reason, his sense of perspective and point-of-view was from on the stage rather than in front of it . . . he kept putting Jane up there in the lead . . .

Shay boy, get over it. She won't do it.

He jogged across the intersection underneath the DART bridge, idly clocking the Customs House to his right. I'm going to have to make do with Nuala – Fionnuala – whoever! he thought, but he knew what he wanted and Fionnuala wasn't it. Hands in pockets, lost in thought, he steamed past the flashy new buildings lining the river, unseeing but thinking, thinking, thinking . . .

So if he had it all in his head, why couldn't he say exactly what he saw? Right. He strode past the Point Depot. Start with the basics. Bright but with dark bits, like bas-relief. Walls that turn or rotate with one thing, an interior, on one side, another – like the garden – on the other. Stage hands in costume moving everything. Simple.

'It's clear as day,' he mumbled to himself as he walked away from town, past the ferry terminal, and East Wall, further out along the river to the sea.

The salt air revived him. I'll take a leaf from Jane's book and make some lists – and tell everyone that it'll all be sorted by the end of next week, she thought.

It always seemed to work for her.

And what was going on in her hard, beautiful head? He had to get her to stop that take-no-prisoners managerial style, but he was the first to admit that diplomacy wasn't remotely his strong suit. And what about that look on her face? As if she'd never seen him before? Was it a mistake that they were working together? Given a choice, now, he'd rather have a chance with her romantically, like . . . than have her look at him like he was an eejit.

He noticed, vaguely, that he was close enough to the tankers and barges to make out the faces of the men on the ships. The brisk ocean breeze was soothing, and helped to focus his mind. As the pictures in his head snapped into focus, his confidence slowly restored itself. Niall wanted direction? He'd get direction! Cathleen wanted a copy of his (non-existent) notes? She'd have 'em! Jane wanted—

Jane, Jane, Jane, clanged in his head, mimicking the clang of the metal that struck against the masts of the boats docked in the harbour. That look in her eye . . . it was kind of like . . . confused fright?

She thinks I'm a washout, Shay thought. She thinks I'm a plonker. She thinks, 'I let that asshole talk me into producing, what, nothing? A big fat zero?' In his mind, he put on a thick New York accent.

You'd better watch your step, lady. You're pissing people off left and right. You've got some serious interpersonal issues, baby. If you don't watch out, you are outta here.

He stopped, realised that the sun was sinking fast, and that his feet were killing him. He looked around, confused – that was a walk, all right. An hour? Two? He sighed, and in a daze, he turned, and woefully retraced his steps back to town.

You betcha, babe, he thought, warming to this newly honed Yank inner voice, one false move and you – are – history.

Because, said a quieter voice, the last thing I want is you watching me fall flat on my face.

21

They were, it seemed, finally ready to get down to some serious work. Not wanting to intrude, Jane sat in the last row of the house.

Dec the Tech had managed to get a decent if temporary and skeletal lighting plan set up, and Jane made a note to ring Gerard and ask him to hunt up those 'lent-out' lamps.

Niall had managed to jury-rig the flats that Shay was adamant about using into some semblance of a design.

Naomi the Trainee had worked out, by herself, the necessary structure of the backstage area: which props lived stage right as opposed to stage left, which costumes, which shoes, etc., and was keeping as clean a stage manager's book as was possible, given that Shay had decided to change the blocking *again* in Act One, Scene Five. As he physically went through each of the character's motions, Jane saw Naomi patiently erase, and Cathleen clutch her own pencil in a death grip.

Finally, the actors were able to get down to it. Martin cleared his throat, and, on Shay's cue: ' "I did not expect you so soon back. Are your mother and her charge in safety—" '

Shay jumped up from his seat and approached the stage again. 'Great, great, Martin, but the line here is more like "I did not *expect* you back *so soon*", than—' and Shay did an approximation of Martin's delivery. So involved was he in the interpretation, that he failed to notice the growing annoyance in the older man's eye. Marie laid a hand on her husband's arm comfortingly – warningly.

'Got it?' Shay asked brightly. 'Go on, so. From the top.'

As Marie, Martin and Jason began again, Shay leaned over to Cathleen. 'Where's thingie? Fionnuala?'

'I'll get Naomi to buzz her,' she whispered to Shay, and then louder, 'No, Jason, the line is "Very safe, sir, at my aunt Pedigree's", not "Sir, she is safe at my aunt's Pedigree." '

Jane crept forward a few rows. 'Jason, you were supposed to be off book last Monday. See me at the break.' She made a note in her book, and missed the ripple of rebellion that her comment inspired.

Shay cringed inwardly, and then outwardly as the house door banged open and Ronan strolled in.

'You're late,' Jane commented, and made another mark in her book. 'See me at the break.'

Ronan smirked, and slouched off to drape himself in the fourth row.

The trio onstage began again, only to have the entire room plunge into darkness. The usual alarmed hubbub broke out immediately, and Jane snapped on the mini-torch she always kept handy. She played the light around the house to find Dec trying to mask a small outburst of smoke.

'I need to re-route a couple of lines,' he said laconically, and Naomi came out with a tray full of lighted candles.

Cathleen tipped her head to the side as Naomi ranged the squat pillars across the front of the stage. 'Look at that, Shay,' she said, nudging him. 'That's an idea. Footlights.'

'Did Naomi get a hold of What's-her-name?'

Cathleen was too transfixed by the stage to reply.

Footlights! Jane crept forward a few more rows. She made a note, and saw Cathleen do the same.

Good instincts in that one, she thought.

'Right, we'll just soldier on,' Shay boomed, as if the lack of light demanded an increase in sound.

' "I did not expect you so soon back," ' projected Martin. ' "Are your mother and her charge in safety—" '

Dee DEE *dee dee DEE* dee DEEEEE—

'Mobiles off, please!' called Jane.

'Sorry, like,' came Ronan's voice. A scuffling noise, footsteps, the door opening, slamming shut.

Jane beamed her little light on her book and made another note.

' "I did not expect you so soon back," ' said Martin. ' "Are your mother and her charge in safety?" '

' "Very safe, sir," ' said Jason. ' "At my aunt's – aunt Ped—" '

The door banged open and Sinead gasped, 'Isn't that gorgeous—'

'Quiet!' Shay roared.

'Sorry!' Sinead whispered.

'Ouch!' Paraic yelped, as he tripped in the dark and banged his knee on a seat.

'You're *late*,' Jane hissed, making notes.

'Fuck's sake,' Sinead muttered, and she and Paraic groped their way backstage.

'OK, lads,' Shay addressed the onstage actors—

'I don't appreciate the use of that collective noun,' Marie intoned.

'Right, Marie, sor—'

The door crashed open again. Ronan.

'Phone OFF,' Jane said firmly, and everyone waited, in the dark, for the tell-tale beep.

'Please, lady and gents,' Shay begged.

' "I did not expect you so soon back," ' Martin declaimed. ' "Are your mother and her charge in safety?" '

' "Very safe, sir," ' Jason lisped. ' "At my aunt Pedigree's." '

' "Ah, death!" ' Marie trumpeted. ' "I find—" '

And the upstage flats came crashing down.

'BOLLOCKS!' Shay hollered, jumping up on to the stage. Niall came racing in from stage right, and with his cousin's help, he pulled one of the set pieces upright.

'It's no use,' said Niall, in a low voice. 'These are rubbished.'

'Bollocks,' Shay groaned.

Jane strode down the aisle past the last few remaining rows. 'What's wrong with those flats? Dec, what about those lights? Shay, where the hell is Fionnuala!'

'She quit.' Naomi crept out of the shadows, stage left.

'She what?' Jane demanded.

'She quit.' She got a toothpaste commercial.' With that, Naomi slid back into the dark.

'Bollllocks!' Shay whined, the whine turning into a snort, the snort turning into laughter. Cathleen, who'd been trying to hide her own giggles, joined in, and Sinead and Paraic stumbled in to find the whole room falling about laughing.

Except for Jane.

'It isn't remotely funny,' she spat as she slid into the banquette in the back room of Mulligan's. She scowled around the table: Marie was off in one corner, telling Sinead and Paraic a story that had them roaring; Mihal and Martin were deep in conversation, sitting side by side but looking off ahead of themselves, nodding and alternatively tapping each other emphatically on the forearm; Naomi and Dec were quietly drinking and holding hands; Cathleen was at the bar, waiting to collect her round, while Ronan stood beside her, posing.

Shay slid in next to Jane.

'I don't think that breaking for the day was a good idea at all—'

'Slainté!' Shay shouted, and everyone toasted.

They all looked at Jane.

'Raise your glass,' Shay shot out of the side of his mouth.

She did, and almost had her pint knocked out of her hand in the cast's enthusiasm to toast with her.

'Shay—'

'Drink.'

She drank. 'Shay—'

'Oh, cheers, cheers,' called Cathleen as she sat down, and it all went around again.

Jane sank down into her seat. Am I the only one taking this seriously? she wondered.

'Don't look so serious,' said Shay, in a low voice. 'We'll begin again tomorrow.'

Jane shook her head. 'You need to get the blocking down. Will we do that tomorrow?'

'We need to blow off some steam. You're – it'll all work out.' He took a deep pull from his jar, and added, he hoped convincingly, 'It always works out.'

'Did you appreciate the impact of the candles? I think you should think about footlights.' Jane saw Cathleen's eyes light up as she turned to them.

'It looked lovely. It's a way around the number of lamps we have to work with.'

'Maybe,' said Shay, noncommittally, and he got up to talk to Martin and Mihal.

Cathleen got up and took his vacated place. 'Em . . . I had this idea, for the make-up.'

At least someone was doing her job. 'Go on,' Jane urged.

Cathleen pulled a sketchpad out of her rucksack. 'I did some research. I – I'm not going behind himself's back . . .'

Jane flipped through the pages. 'I see where you're going – I like the stylised rouge, and the eyebrows—'

'It's period, but modern, like. But' – Cathleen looked worriedly over at Shay – 'I don't want to step on any toes.'

Jane looked over as Shay and Martin howled with laughter about something. 'Some toes could use a good stomp.' She exhaled, and took another sip of her pint. 'I like this,' she said, turning back to Cathleen. 'It's a fantastic idea. Unfortunately, we don't know if it's in our director's direction.' She paused, looked concerned. 'He's not a . . . chancer, is he?'

Cathleen shook her head. 'Not at all.' She absentmindedly took a cigarette from Jane's pack. 'But . . . he's really an actor, isn't he? I mean, he keeps leaping up on to the stage, like. And he's good. Very good.'

Marie cut off Jane's reply. 'All right, girls?' she asked as she shifted over a stool.

'I object to the use of that collective noun,' Jane replied coolly.

'Got me there, missus.' Marie raised her glass and Jane followed suit. 'It's ingrained in our culture, I reckon. We do things differently over here. In general.'

'I think I'm catching on,' Jane said, rising. 'Where's the loo?'

Marie exchanged a meaningful look with Cathleen, who rose to make room for Shay.

'All right, Marie?' he asked cheerfully. This castbonding thing was going down a treat.

'Not too bad,' she replied, and continued equably, 'it'll all work out – it always does.'

'It does indeed.' Shay sighed inwardly with relief. This was an excellent idea –

'Yer one is coming on a wee bit strong,' Marie went on, in the same peaceable tone. They watched Jane join Ronan at the bar.

Shay fidgeted. 'She's great at what she does—'

'She is indeed,' Marie soothed. 'And if there were only more like her. But', she went on, meaningfully, 'she's bruising some toes.'

Shay took her meaning and nodded. Then he scowled when Ronan started, as seemed to be his habit, to play with Jane's hair.

'I thought she was an actress,' Marie mused. 'She read so well with us at the audition. We thought we'd be playing opposite her. She's exceptional.' Rising, she went to the loo, feeling she had done what she had intended to do, and sent the smallest of nods to her husband.

Sinead and Paraic took up the vacated seats next to Shay, and began nattering, never noticing that Shay's attention was fixed on the byplay at the bar.

I cannot believe I 'snogged' this eejit, Jane thought. And why am I standing here, on the receiving end of an endless line of shite and irritating little touches? She guessed it was either that or she would start yelling at Shay again. Either deal with someone with whom she didn't care to deal at all, or deal with Shay, whom she thought she might like to—

She knew it came together! She knew it would work out! But they had left a theatre full of overloaded circuits, a broken-down set, and the absence of a female lead!

Her belly did a little tango at that last. No female lead. Her work on *She Stoops*, apart from the no-light, no-set, no-blocking, no-design problems, was almost concluded. She'd fulfilled her part of the contract, so . . . What if? NO. She'd given up acting for good . . . and had gone on to be a leader in her field . . . except she certainly wasn't in her field any more . . . There was no reason she couldn't – no, no, no; a producer's work was never done, she mustn't kid herself . . . but . . .

Her train of thought crashed due to the intrusive and damp application by Ronan of his tongue into her ear. Rearing back in disgust, she ploughed backwards into Shay's chest.

'We'll go over those notes now, will we?' Shay grabbed Jane's elbow and led her over to her bag and coat. 'All right, lads – everyone. We're off. Work to do.' A bemused but gratified Jane said her goodbyes, and left the pub.

Heads crashed together around the table, and whispering ensued as the pair made their exit. Ronan, who didn't notice, busily began posing once more.

Shay flagged down a taxi, and opened the back door for Jane. She rolled her eyes, and got in.

'I don't know why you wouldn't let me ring Jackie,' she groused as he shut his own door behind him. He instructed the driver and sat back as Jane started loudly flipping through her notes.

She was busily counting the day's demerits, and he watched her rapidly scan the pages. Far from worrying about the conversation they needed to have, he wondered about Ronan. What does she see in that guy? He grunted in disgust.

She looked up. 'Yes?' In the filtered light, his face half in shadow, he looked dangerous, dangerously sexy. She was just about able to ignore that annoying flutter she still felt in her chest, and she was barely able to resist sliding over, closer, taking a meeting perched on his lap. The thought of it made her smile, a blinding and adorable smile that had Shay thinking impure thoughts.

'Hated to break up yourself and Ronan,' he said smoothly, trying to gauge her reaction. In the reflected light of the street lamps, with half her face thrown in shadow, she looked like a femme fatale from a Humphrey Bogart film. God, he wanted—

'You've been pretty grumpy about him from the start,' Jane said, narrowing her eyes smugly.

'I don't think it's good idea to—' Em, wrong thing to say . . .

'Date someone with whom you are working?' she went on primly. Busted, pal. 'Believe me, I agree.'

Ambiguous, that, but ever optimistic, Shay decided it meant she wasn't keen on that wanker.

Now on to the next order of business.

'Jane, we need to have a chat. About the running of the show.'

She sighed loudly, an explosion of relief. It was about time. 'I'm so glad you brought that up,' she said, spinning it immediately towards the positive. 'It's vital that we keep the lines of communication open, Shay.'

'Right.' He allowed himself to be distracted by a hen party, making its way tipsily down Leeson Street. 'Em. So. The thing with the – the marks for lateness . . . and for leaving the mobiles on, and' – he gulped – 'the bit about the "too many cups of tea" . . . it's not working.'

Jane beamed. 'I couldn't agree more.' Shay grinned back – now, how hard was that?

'I really think we need to start instituting fines.' Jane ran her finger down a column of figures, and Shay groaned.

'I hate to do it,' she mused, taking his response for agreement, and she watched South County Dublin blur by her window. 'But it's the only way to get the team to toe the line.' She turned, and saw Shay's consternation. 'What?' She patted his arm. That was a mistake; she wanted to run her hand up his arm to his shoulder to the back of his neck. 'We'll keep them low, fifty cents at the most.'

'No!' Shay roared, scaring the taxi man into grinding his gears. 'NO – not – working – cast – mutiny – No. More. Lists. No. Fines.' Breathing heavily he glared out the window. So much for diplomacy.

'They need to know who's boss,' Jane said quietly after a few moments. And right now, my friend, it ain't you.

Shay wriggled in his seat. If he was no diplomat, he did even worse at interpersonal confrontation. Give him the distance and pomp of the courtroom any day . . . 'I'm the boss. Me. I'm the boss.'

The quiet statement had the effect of dropping a bomb in the back seat. The taxi man leaned on the gas and flew towards Foxrock.

'I thought we were partners.' She almost choked on the word.

'We were – we are. We'll talk about this later.'

Jane turned in her seat and faced him. Even in that

low, low light, he could see the hurt in her eyes. 'I have considered, from the beginning, that my job was to make your job easier.' She swallowed back a weird lump in her throat. 'And I imagine it's easier for you to direct when your cast is actually physically in the same room with you, when they are off the phone, and when they know their lines!' Her voice rose, and she caught herself before she gave in to the impulse to screech.

She *never* raised her voice. It was the cornerstone of her professional reputation – she *never* lost her temper. She never, *ever* shouted. She shook back her hair, and Shay saw that the hurt was still there, but she'd rallied, and her eyes were cold as ice.

'Perhaps you're annoyed that I'm getting this credit—'

'Jane—'

'Without having stumped up any cash. I can probably come up with about—'

'I – this is – I'm paying for it! Don't be ridiculous!' As if he would allow anyone else to gamble their funds on this chance!

'Chill out, Tarzan, I'm just trying to establish the parameters.'

Shay reached over and took her hand. At the immediate tension he felt in her fingers, he thought: She doesn't care for me at all, does she? 'I'm taking a chance and I won't gamble your funds. You haven't got an income, for God's sake!' As to that, how was she managing?

'I'm getting along fine. I've always been good with money.' She smiled thinly. 'I got a very healthy exit package.'

'I'm grateful for your help. I need it.' Shay looked down at her hand, so slim and lovely in his own.

'I –' The wind was blowing in her eyes, that was it, that was why they felt runny. 'I have to have some authority on the set. I'm not going to be some figurehead.'

'We're co-producers,' Shay said firmly.

'I just want to do my job.' She rolled up the window

against the breeze that was surely making her eyes sting.

'It'll work out, Jane.'

'I know!' It almost happened again, she almost started to shout. She pitched her voice low, through sheer force of will. *What is going on with me?* 'Do you agree that we have equal power, equal responsibility?'

'Yeah, sure, all right—'

'Then we have to be responsible to each other, and for each other. And if we decide that the cast need more . . . leeway, then you're going to have to tighten up your work habits.' She watched him fight a scowl. 'It's got to start at the top.'

'It's all coming together,' he grumbled, and stopped the imminent sulk at the sight of her impassive face. 'Give me to the end of the week.'

Jane nodded. 'We have to do whatever we need to do, for the good of the show.'

'Then, let's say, you just mind what I'm doing, and you leave the cast to me.'

Jane thought about it. 'So you're saying that you're answerable to me.'

Shay nodded vociferously. 'And you leave the cast to me.'

'Naomi, and Cathleen—'

Shay gestured magnanimously with his hands. 'You get Naomi, I get Cathleen.'

'And, just to get this clear, you essentially have to report to me.'

'Exactly.' Exactly? Exactly what? Shay's brows knit as he tried to work out what he was agreeing to.

'I can live with that.' Jane sat back, satisfied.

Shay looked out the window, confused. He wasn't entirely sure he'd solved the problem – in fact, he had a sneaking suspicion that a bigger one was looming somewhere on the horizon.

22

Sinead struggled with the row of small buttons that ran up the back of her dress. 'Jesus wept,' she muttered, twisting and turning, trying to get a better angle on her reflection in the dressing-room mirror.

'C'mere to me,' said Marie, and turned Sinead's back towards herself.

'I haven't got the proper bra for this yoke,' Sinead whinged, trying to get her breasts to sit nicely in the bodice.

'Well, it's only a dress rehearsal,' Cathleen said, dropping into the room with some wigs she'd just curled.

'Seems a bit previous, as we all don't know our lines,' Marie groused, turning back to her own costume, missing the face Sinead made at her in the mirror.

'I need to sit you both down and go over the make-up plan—'

'Cathleen! Cazza!' Shay shouted down the hall. 'I need you in the house.'

'I'm in with the girls, getting their make-up organised!' Cathleen's shout was a shaky mix of anxiety and frustration, and she hurriedly set out her brushes and her cotton wool.

'Where's Jane?' hissed Sinead, as she sat down next to Cathleen and tugged a wig on to her head. It itched.

'She's out there, but she's not handing out demerits any more.' Marie held her own wig up in front of her face, and then sniffed it suspiciously.

Cathleen taped some drawings up to the mirror. 'I'd take a few black marks if she'd only get this shop organised again. Right. Here you are . . .'

Onstage, Niall was desperately trying to patch together the shaky flats. Shay came up and clapped him on the back.

'Niall boy, what's the story with the flats, mate?' Shay felt he'd succeeded in sounding genial but firm.

Oh, very nice, Niall thought. I'm doing you a favour and you take that tone with me? He menacingly hefted the hammer in his hand, but Shay got distracted by Cathleen's furtive cross in front of the upstage wall.

'Cathleen,' he called. 'I need—'

'I've to show the lads how to do their make-up,' she bit out, and kept going.

'I need that scenery up in five, mate,' Shay said, and turned to see Declan hovering behind him.

'We need more lights,' he said.

Shay ran agitated fingers through his hair. 'Right, I'll—'

'Em, like, these trousers are so not my size,' Ronan called from upstage, holding the waistband of the tweed jodhpurs a good twelve inches from his belly.

'Caz!' Shay shouted, as she made her way across the stage again. 'Ronan's trousers—' He got an intimidating glare in reply. For fuck's sake, he thought, why wasn't anything getting done? He waved a dismissive hand in Ronan's direction. 'Just – put on a belt for chrissakes, we'll have it sorted by the end of the week.'

'It is the end of the week,' Ronan sneered, and beat a hasty retreat back to the dressing room.

'We need—' reiterated Declan patiently.

'More lights, more lights,' Shay said. 'I'll get Gerard on the phone.'

'I can take care of that, Shay,' Jane called serenely, looking up from the blocking plan he'd hastily drawn up last night. Very late last night.

'Not to worry, not your job; leave it with me,' he called back, and he flinched at his desperate tone. He watched as Naomi quietly, competently and, with no fuss at all, did whatever Jane had just asked her to do. No shouting. No begging. Sitting there, the two of them, an oasis of calm in a wildly rampaging storm.

The fact that all that calm existed solely to keep its eye on him didn't help his composure much.

Mihal glided on to the stage, dragging his feet in great sweeping strides as he paced the width of it. He flung his arms in tandem, in great sweeping arcs, and began to vocalise. 'Maaaaaaooooooeeeeeeeeeeeoooooooooh!' he bellowed, and Niall dropped the flats as he nearly jumped out of his skin. Upon impact, they broke on the seams he had so painstakingly patched up, and in more places besides.

Martin chose this moment to begin his warm up as well, a kind of t'ai chi, though as if executed by a stuttering bunny. He hopped from posture to posture, letting out yelps of sound as his feet hit the ground, and humming loudly as he swayed through the gentler movements.

Theresa, usually always on the verge of invisibility, began to let out little, shrieking, ear-splitting whoops, and was soon joined by Marie and Sinead, who started to trill from low to high register in chattering tones while they thumped their chests.

Shay, trying to ring Gerard about the bloody lights, exploded. 'Do you have to do that now?'

'They have to warm up, Shay,' Jane said quietly.

The actors all looked at her, then back at Shay, nodding. 'We have to warm up,' said Marie, and Shay's shoulders dropped in defeat.

'Fine, fine – Gerard? Howya. Shay here—'

Jane watched him pace around the audience. She sat back, and under the desk her fingers were drumming madly on her knees. She had stayed out of the way for the last three days, gently pushing Shay to lock down the look, feel and sound of the show. She sat there every day, at the desk, watching things alternately gel and fall apart. She said very little, did nothing to interfere, and kept herself to herself.

She thought she was going to go completely insane.

Shay made his way to the front of the house, and turned, as if he'd almost forgotten that he had a room full of people waiting on him. 'Take five,' he barked, and went out into the lobby.

'Cup of tea, anyone?' Jane rose and graciously went over to the kettle.

The cast froze, uncertain. It had been a peculiar week, as the usual chaos of their personal experiences of 'the rehearsal process' had instituted itself, the kind of chaos that was familiar to them all . . . but it had felt strange, somehow. The order that they had all rebelled against had, in retrospect, been comforting, and had, in a way, given some structure to the meetings. Now that it was gone, well, it was a wee bit . . . frightening. They approached Jane the way they might approach a wild animal that was supposedly housebroken; with extreme caution and a potentially dangerous amount of curiosity.

Sinead was the first to beard the lion, and Cathleen soon followed suit. Seeing that the way was clear, the rest followed, but for Ronan, who quickly powered up his mobile and started an urgent, mumbled conversation.

Jane impressed them by remembering how each of them took their brew, and passed around a plate of biscuits. She made small talk, and the cast began to relax, sitting around listening to Martin and Marie tell a story about the very first time they'd ever worked in the Gate, their comfortable laughter cut off short by the slamming of the theatre door.

'Where's yer one, the new girl? The new Nuala?' Shay demanded as he strode down the aisle.

Cathleen looked at Naomi, who did her best

impression of Jane, and raised her eyebrows in response.

'I think she rang and Naomi took the call,' supplied Jane helpfully.

Shay ground his teeth in frustration. 'I wonder if Naomi would be good enough to tell us what happened,' he said, overly solicitous.

Jane nodded at Naomi, who said, 'She'll be here in an hour, but she can't stay for the whole afternoon.'

'Fuck's sake,' Shay breathed. He sat down at the table heavily, and slammed his binder down on it. He looked up, and the cast were looking at him with the kind of blankness they had assumed with Jane.

He clocked the teacups, and Jane, holding the pot, and his eyes narrowed. What was she playing at? Standing there, all innocent, with the cast ranging behind her as if they'd gone over to her side?

'Tea break's over,' Shay said, and returned to his seat. At Declan's expectant look, he mumbled, 'Talk to you later', and then turned to Naomi. 'I wonder, would it be all right with Jane if you read the part of Miss Hardcastle until, em, yer one shows up?'

Jane felt a sharp jolt of disappointment. She had been sure he was going to . . . 'Anything to help out, Shay.' She just stopped herself from snarling. 'As we said the other day, the most important thing is the show.'

Naomi took a seat onstage, and Jane joined Shay and Cathleen at the table. Cathleen was manning a small boom box, trying to approximate the sound cues. He'd had good ideas there, Jane conceded, as the atmospheric yet pertinent sound effects underscored the action.

He hadn't quite figured out his staging, though, and Jane, shaking her head, began to make notes . . . which Shay saw out of the corner of his eye.

Every time her pencil lightly scratched across the paper, he twitched. She was writing with such focus – was she even watching the run through?

Apart from Ronan, and the fact that everyone hates

him, thought Jane, they're a great cast. When Shay wasn't giving them line readings – she must talk to him about that, that's a no-no in Directing 101 – he had guided them into relationships that went deeper than the text might belie on the surface. But the movement was awful and as Jason collided once more with Martin, Jane scribbled in her book—

The house phone rang.

Bollocks! Shay pounded his temples with his fists. Would they never get up a good head of steam? He looked at Naomi expectantly – who looked at Jane, who nodded.

Naomi rose and answered the phone. A brief, hushed conversation followed, and Naomi returned to her stool, and picked up her script.

'Yer one isn't coming at all – she got a part on *Fair City*.'

The cast looked at Shay who dropped his head in his hands.

The silence was deafening. Nobody moved. Jane's pencil snapped in half.

Shay looked at his shoes. Jane looked at him, and wanted, suddenly, more than anything, to—

'Oh, gosh, I'll just get up there, will I?' She sprang to her feet, the broken pieces of her pencil falling to the floor, rolling around on the floor, sounding like a rock slide in the silence.

'All right,' Shay said, baffled. 'Work away.'

She calmly made her way up the steps and on to the stage. The cast moved back, apprehensively, hopefully. Naomi got up, taking the stool, and held out the performance copy of the text. Jane smiled.

'I've got the lines,' she said lightly. 'Will we take it from the top?'

At the break that would stand in for the interval, Shay finally let himself breathe once more. Cathleen's eyes were shining and Mihal solemnly shook Jane's hand. Martin winked at her, and rubbed his hands together, and Marie gifted Jane with a rare smile. Jason nodded at her and went off to have a snack, and Sinead strolled up to her, arms akimbo.

'You were blazing!' she crowed, and punched Jane on the shoulder. 'Nice one!'

Jane hugged her arms to herself. 'Thanks,' she said simply.

'Now if we could only get rid of himself,' Sinead said darkly, glaring at Ronan, 'We'd have a hell of a show on our hands.'

Jane narrowed her eyes, and wondered if she could fire Ronan. As if feeling her gaze upon him, he strolled over, in his Westlife fashion, forgetting that his trousers were bunched around his waist like a laundry bag.

'Not bad,' he drawled. 'I can give you a few pointers; there's that bit where—'

'Keep your pointers to yourself, Ro,' Jane said, and walked away.

That, she thought, had felt great.

Amazing.

Wonderful.

Familiar. It was like coming home and finding the place hadn't changed, but had got larger somehow, more comfortable – safer. She appreciated the kudos from the cast – her fellow players – but she didn't really need them. She saw how they had all responded to her, to each other, loosened up, lifted her as much as she lifted them. She smiled to herself and wondered if Shay was ever going to say anything to her—

'Thanks for helping out,' came his voice, and she looked down at him, confused. He stood in front of the table and missed the incredulous look that Cathleen shot him.

'Helping out?' Jane cleared her throat. 'Excuse me?'

Shay consulted the list of actresses he had in his

hand. 'I should be able to get Naomi – sorry, she's "yours", isn't she? I'll get Cathleen to ring around, see if we can get one of these third alternates in.'

'In for what?' There was a sensation shooting around Jane's nerve endings, a threatening cocktail of anger, mortification, hurt, and sheer and utter disbelief. The cast and crew seemed to sense this, and edged away from the playing area, Marie going as far to collect her coat and bag.

'I know that you're not an actress—'

'How dare you! After what I – you plonker! Wanker! Eejit! Chancer! How dare – as if you could find – what kind of a director are you?'

'What? I'm the—' What in the name of God was she on about?

'A director who has no sense of . . . of direction! Are you even watching what's *happening* up here? We're all falling over each other – no one ever ends up where they need to be next – Mihal has to sneak across upstage after nearly every one of his scenes—' Jane took a calming breath, and had no way of knowing that she looked like she was going to explode. 'We need to meet. We agreed it was my job to shadow you and—'

'Shadow me? Stalk me! You've been following around after me for days, writing, always writing in that bloody book, scratching away with that bloody pencil—'

'It's my job, as we agreed! I let you have the entire rest of the production and my one and only concern was you, and the way you were doing your job—'

Shay looked apoplectic, and Naomi quickly gathered the props, locked them away and, picking up her rucksack, nipped out the back door with Dec.

'I'm doing my job just fine, missus!'

'You are not!' Jane shrieked. 'You're fired!'

'YOU CAN'T FIRE ME!'
    'I'M YOUR BOSS!'
  'THE HELL YOU ARE, MISSUS!'

As Shay and Jane went at it hammer and tongs at the top of their lungs, Cathleen gathered everyone together and led them out of the theatre. She turned off the house lights, and closed the door gently behind her.

Neither of them noticed.

'I got up there, off book, and lifted this damn show up to the level it needs to be at! How dare you insult me by looking around at some goddamn "third alternate"!' Jane threw up her hands. 'Third alternate, my arse!'

'You want the part?' Shay bellowed. 'After all that "I'm not an actress, I'm a producer" carry on? You want the part? You want the part? After all that "I work with bankable talent on high-budget" blah blah? You want the part? You want the part?'

'YES! I WANT THE PART!' Jane screamed, her voice bouncing off the rafters like a gunshot.

'FINE!' Shay roared, and they both fell silent, heaving in great gulps of air, standing practically nose-to-nose, chest to chest, eye to eye.

Later, Jane would swear that it was she who—

Shay would, someday, congratulate himself for finally—

In any event, one of them grabbed the other and they fell on each other.

Jane had always scoffed at the idea that people 'didn't know what came over them', or that 'it was the heat of the moment', positive that it was some sort of foggy romantic rationalisation, the province of fiction, of sitcoms and romance novels. But sure enough, in the heat of the moment, not knowing what came over her, not caring, she grabbed Shay by the shoulders as surely as his arms – those long, strong arms – caught her to him in a velvety vise, lifting her on to her toes as they ravaged each other's mouths.

Yes, yes, yes, yes! – it was all Shay's brain was good for, the blood having left his head entirely, the feel of her strongly soft body pressing against his, her sweet mouth tantalising his neck as she nipped and licked his throat, her fingers digging into his hair as she kissed him on the lips once again, oh yeah, oh yeah, oh God, finally, finally, finally . . .

I'm sure I had my reasons for deferring this so long, Jane thought . . . and then rational thought went out the window as Shay lifted her fully off the floor, stumbled stage left and, turning, fell back on to the futon, breaking her fall, and enabling himself at long last to run his hands all over her body, slipping long fingers beneath her top to stroke her spine, to skate lightly over her ribs—

'Ayyyyyyeeeeeeee!' Jane squealed, nearly kneeing Shay in the groin. 'Don't!'

'What?'

'Ticklish!'

Making sure that her thighs were firmly sandwiched between his own, he experimented with wiggling his fingers at the nip of her waist, and he wasn't disappointed when she struggled in hysterical agony.

'Stop it!' she wailed, and he grabbed her chin.

'Do you want me to?' he asked, and tensed, waiting for her answer.

They fully looked into each other's eyes for the first time.

Shay was barely breathing. Jane licked her lips nervously.

'No,' she whispered. 'No. Touch me somewhere else.'

'Anywhere else?'

'Anywhere.'

She fell on him, and their tongues met, hot and sweet, their lips battling to taste more, taste deeper, and Shay unzipped Jane's hip-hugging trousers, ripped open the zipper and slid his hands down over her delicious flesh, stroking, squeezing, feeling her thighs melt against his, feeling the heat of her arousal and he slid a finger down, and forward and—

'Ah!' he yelped as Jane set her teeth on his neck, then kissed him, hard, on the spot where she'd bitten him in reaction to his touch. Her fingers quickly and efficiently unbuttoned his shirt, and then, baring his chest, began planting little kisses and long licks all the way down to his belly, which began to twitch as her hair tickled his skin along with her tongue.

He ran his hands up her back and beneath her top, expertly unhooked her bra with three fingers. Smirking, she rose up on her knees and took off her top, shrugging aside her bra, and perched on his lap, guided his hands up on to her breasts.

Her lovely, beautiful breasts. Shay's throat went dry. He sat up as she leaned forward and added his shirt to the growing pile of clothes on the floor. She linked her arms around his neck as he rubbed his face against her nipples, teasing them with little kisses until neither of them could take any more. He took one into his mouth. He stroked down her back, pushing off her trousers, and flipped her over on to her back, never breaking contact, never stopping his hands as they stroked her.

He leaned up on his elbows, brushed the hair out of her eyes, and had a momentary pang that this wasn't the way he wanted it to be, it wasn't the way he'd hoped they would – well, he'd thought—

As Jane's hand slipped into his fly, which she'd so silently and cleverly undone, he realised that, sometimes, he thought too much.

And then it was all reaching limbs and straining bodies and the last of their clothes were discarded as they tried to taste and feel every inch of the flesh of the other and Shay thought, *This is too fast*, and Jane thought, *Faster!*, and Shay groaned as he entered her and Jane sighed then rose to meet him again and again and again until they both felt the tension build and build and build until they both reached the release that they'd been searching for.

The sound of their hearts pounded in their ears as they lay tangled together on the cramped couch. Shay slowly lifted his head and saw Jane's eyes glittering from underneath very satisfied lids.

'Again,' she whispered.

'Oh, yes,' he replied.

They lay, spooned, on the narrow futon, Jane curled into Shay's body, with his jumper pulled over them for warmth. The intimacy of the posture belied the internal upheaval that was slowly building after their spontaneity found time to second guess itself, and in the cold light of the stage manager's lamp – the only light burning, they both noticed, now – with their passion spent, they had plenty of time for recriminations.

Keep it light, Janie, she thought to herself, get up and get out . . . but she couldn't make herself move. Shay's chest rose and fell, calmly now, against her back, and she tucked her face into the bicep that curled so gently around her shoulder.

What was she thinking? thought Shay, and he was about to ask her, but then thought twice. What if she turned all shy – which, in fairness, he couldn't imagine. Worse, maybe, if she went all casual on him, like nothing had happened? But what had happened, exactly, anyway, at the end of the day? They had blown off some steam, taken care of the tension that had been building for days – weeks . . .

Feeling strangely shy, Jane wanted to, to, to chat or something, make small talk, and wondered why Shay, who probably talked in his sleep, was so silent. All he wants, I bet, she thought, is to jump into his jeans and run out the door. All he's thinking about, I'm sure of it, is how to make sure he lets me down easy or something, before he makes a mad dash for freedom. Isn't that the way these things always go? Didn't she know perfectly well how to play this game?

She was tensing up, Shay could feel it in her legs and back; she wanted to get out of there, she wanted to forget this ever happened, she wanted to forget about it and move on and she thought he was crap and he knew he was not crap, sure he wasn't . . . but what if she thought so, what if she just couldn't wait to be off? There must be some sort of New York time-frame, how long you lay around with someone you'd just shagged on impulse, ten minutes or less, then 'Taxi!' Shite, shite, he thought – we lost the run of ourselves.

I know how to do one-night – er, afternoon stands, Jane assured herself. There's no reason why we can't continue to work together, why we can't continue to cohabitate, in a manner of speaking, without any messiness . . . maybe he thinks I suck, which I so do not . . . but what if that's what he . . . and why he isn't . . . say something!

Say something, Shay boy, go on, a bit of humour, a bit of a joke, go on –

'So that was the auld casting couch, hey?' he quipped.

Jane felt her entire body go cold. 'What?' she hissed.

'Wanted the part that much did ya— arrrrrrghhhhh!'

Jane retracted her elbow, and rolled off the futon on to the floor. In a flash, she had pulled on her knickers, pulled on her trousers, and was now wiggling into her bra.

'Jane, Jesus, I'm only joking—'

'Let me tell you something, pal, your sense of humour leaves a lot to be desired. You spent weeks trying to talk me into this damn play, and into playing that part—' Jane swiftly pulled on her top.

'Weeks? In fairness—'

'Almost as often as you were trying to get me to go on a *date* with you.'

'That is out of order, mis—'

'And then we finally have a nice little romp and—'

'A nice little—'

'And you just had to ruin it, ruin all that spontaneity and . . . and sexiness and shit. You just had to put those size thirteens right between your teeth, didn't you? Didn't you!'

Shay draped his jumper over his hips. 'It was sexy, you are so – Jane, c'mere –'

'Too late, cowboy, how *dare* you imply that I need to fuck my way to the top—'

'Hello?' A voice came out of the darkened house.

'Jane, I wasn't! I'm . . . I'm an eejit, right, surely there's some statute of limitations—'

'Hello?' The voice called, louder.

'Don't try that lawyer crap with me!'

'I am NOT a—'

'HELLO!!!'

Jane clutched her jacket to her chest, and Shay dove behind the couch. Grabbing her handbag off the desk, she stuck her head out of the wings.

And saw Darren picking his way down the aisle in the dark.

'Dar! Darren!' Jane ran down the stage, down the steps, and into his arms. What timing!

'Why are you alone in the—'

'Jane!' Shay called.

'Who's *that*?' Darren gasped.

'Let's get out of here. I've got to get – let's go.'

Linking her arm forcibly through his, she yanked him up the aisle and out the door.

'Jane!' And the door slammed shut.

Shay threw himself down on the couch, and allowed the full wave of his eejitness to flow over him, allowed himself to realise what shite he'd talked, and allowed himself to wonder if he'd ever make it up to her.

Ah sure, he thought, sure you will. But . . . he sat up and dropped his head into his hands. How?

Leaning back, he dragged on his pants and then his jeans. Disconsolately, he found one sock, and discarded it when he couldn't locate the other. Pulling on his shirt, he shook his head. Haven't a clue, he thought.

Flowers? A note? An apology via skywriter? The front page of *The Irish Times*?

Come on, it was kind of funny; there they were, she'd just demanded the lead role in his first production, and then boom, down on the couch. You had to laugh.

But then, you mightn't.

He rose, and shoved his feet into his shoes, and wandered out to the darkened stage. I've done it – in more ways than one – but here we are. On this stage. In two and a half weeks' time we'll be opening and I made it happen.

I did, and Jane did.

And he'd got what he wanted, achieved what he'd set out to do. It had seemed bleak, at times, more often than not, and he'd muscled through it all, the auditions, the leaky roof, the blown-out lamps, the falling-down set, that plonker Ronan, the grief he'd got from his family, all of it, got through with flying fucking colours, mate – and there was no way a little misunderstanding was going to come between him and this gorgeous, sexy, talented woman whom he wanted to be with.

If she didn't care, he wouldn't have hurt her feelings. Right? Right! Excellent. So now, time to take this to the next level, one that was mature, well thought out, was

216

still spontaneous, and made up for the slightly unnerving impulsiveness of this afternoon.

There was nothing for it. They had to go out on a proper date – even if he had to trick her into it.

24

Naomi, with great tact, laid a pair of folded-up socks on the stage manager's desk.

Jane, who was helping out with a few phone calls, chasing down those damn lights and setting up a meeting with the PR woman, set down the phone as casually as she could. She resisted a foolish impulse to stuff them into her handbag – for God's sake, they were only a pair of socks.

'So what do you think went on here after we left?' Sinead whispered. Marie leaned in closer, and Martin and Paraic pretended to be above it all, to no avail.

'Sure Naomi's been gathering up clothes for the last twenty minutes,' Marie hissed back, and they all stifled their laughter.

'Nothing like a bit of a roll to break the tension.' Martin pinched Marie on the bum.

'Well, I didn't know they were an item,' insisted Sinead, and Cathleen slipped up behind them.

'We're ready to go in ten, please do your make-up, will you, and stop nattering about those two,' she said quietly. 'And if they weren't an item before, they should be now. The futon's broken.'

Snorts of laughter were cut short by Jane rising from the desk chair. 'Caz, I need to know what you want my make-up to look like.'

'Ready when you are, Jane,' she replied, swiping a dangling blond lock off her forehead.

'Thanks, um, for doing double duty here—' Jane began her first ever sincere professional apology.

'Sure, you're doing the same yourself, we're all caught up in it now, aren't we?' In a manner of speaking, Jane thought.

Darren, who was not known for his timing, had transcended himself, and his faltering rationalisations about being in Europe for research didn't fool Jane – she knew he had always hated being left out.

She had practically dragged him by the hair to the Brazen Head, and the beer garden where, despite his protests as to the earliness of the hour, she sat and smoked and nursed a pint while he tried, with no luck, to get her to tell him what was *happening*. From there, Jackie collected them and brought them back to Wicklow, where Niall, Miranda and Darren had a lovely meal of roasted, curried lamb, and Jane sat, nursed a glass of wine, and jumped every time the wind blew against the letterbox. She pleaded fatigue – busy day, back acting again – and fled to her room, where she chain smoked some more and tried to figure out whether she was edgy because Shay could come in at any moment or because he hadn't at all.

As Cathleen now briskly set about doing Jane's face, Jane closed her eyes, and decided that, for once in her life, she was going to purposely figure out what she was feeling—

'All right, gir— ladies?' Shay's voice went through her and she kept her eyes closed.

Look at me, he begged her silently, while keeping up a grand natter with Marie.

'Shay?' called Declan. 'I've got those lighting cues . . . cued.'

'Right, so,' he called back, and went out to the stage.

'Relax, there, love,' murmured Cathleen, and swept some peony pink lipstick on Jane lips.

'It's been a while since I had anyone do my face,' she replied, and swore she heard a choked giggle.

'It'll be all yours again after this. I just want to get it set so you can see . . .' and Cathleen brushed and painted and finally powdered.

Jane opened her eyes and smiled. The pale foundation set off rosily coloured cheeks, and her lips stood out like a flower ready to unfurl. The arch of her eyebrows were exaggerated, little bird's wings above the heavily outlined eyelids, with her lashes looking impossibly long, making her eyes the entire focus of her face, a face she barely recognised – which couldn't hurt. Not today.

Cathleen bustled out as her name was shouted from the house, and Marie tossed a long matted object into Jane's lap.

'What is that?' Jane recoiled from the heavy lump as it hit her lap.

'It's yer wig,' said Sinead, as she tugged her own on to her head. It still itched.

'It's the best of a bad lot,' said Marie as she tugged a length of stocking over her head and wiggled her own wig on top of it.

'Has it had its flea shots?' Jane quipped as she picked up a brush.

'I wouldn't do that,' warned Sinead.

'You'll have nothing left but the scalp,' added Marie.

'Has anyone told Shay?' Jane congratulated herself on her businesslike tone.

'We were going to bring it up yesterday,' said Marie, 'but—'

'Places, everyone, please,' came Naomi's soft voice over the dressing-room speaker.

Marie and Sinead hurried out of the room, and as they passed, Jane noticed a few clumsy stitches holding

Sinead's bodice to her skirt, and that Marie's train was moth-eaten.

She held up her own frock suspiciously, and pulled it on. 'Jane,' came Naomi's voice again. 'Places.'

'Coming, coming,' she called and, despite the questionable wig and the dubious dress, forgot as best she could that she had a lot on her mind, and went to get lost in the play.

Darren sat in the back row. There were vibes quivering all over the place, and, while the cast went admirably through their paces – he had to say, this show looked like it was going to get up on its feet and run like the wind – there was definitely an undercurrent. Darren was an expert when it came to undercurrents, and he could feel them a mile away.

Thank God I'm here, he thought, ready and waiting to interpret any and all feelings. He sighed as he watched as Jane and that stuck-up guy went through their scene again. Wasn't she wonderful? He draped himself over the row in front of him and watched her go. Isn't this great? he thought, and decided to take full credit for her transformation – a kind of inverse transformation, actually, back to where she was happiest.

Miranda snapped a few more photos and went back to join him. 'I think something's up with Jane,' she whispered.

Darren angled his head towards her archly. 'That sounds familiar. Hmm . . . where have I heard that before?'

'Yeah, yeah, OK, but—'

Cathleen glanced back and shushed them with a look.

'She was having a fight with someone in here yesterday. I think it was *him*.' They both regarded Shay as, once again, he got up on the stage to show Ronan what he was meant to do. Ronan scowled at him and said nothing. Jane stood still as a statue. Shay spoke to her, and touched her on the arm as he passed.

The entire room held its breath.

The scene began again.

'Did you see that?' Darren murmured. 'When he touched her? Her pupils kind of contracted.'

Miranda nodded. Anybody could see it, even from where they were sitting. 'The futon is broken.'

'What?' yelped Darren.

'Quiet!' Cathleen called.

'Sorry!' said Miranda, and she and Darren began whispering furiously.

Jane patiently worked out a crick in her neck while Shay once more tried to get Ronan to do the thing he wanted. She'd have to talk to him – well, she'd have to talk to him, maybe, she guessed, someday, even if he seemed to be avoiding her like the plague, but *anyway*, she was going to have to tell him to—

'Like, stop showing me, all right? Can you not just explain what you want?' It was a mark of how deeply the cast loathed Ronan that they all turned away at his remark. They all had the same complaint, to be sure, but Shay won out in the indiscernible cast-preference-sweepstakes every time.

'Shay,' said Jane, and she felt that thing again, that thing of everybody watching her. They should be watching her, but not like this, like they were waiting for something other than Goldsmith's drama to unfold.

'Yes, Jane?' He turned to her, smiling; a blazing, beaming smile that made her face feel hot.

'I hope I'm not out of line—' she dared, diplomatically.

'No, of course not, go on,' he encouraged enthusiastically.

'But Ronan may have a point. Could you give him a verb to enact, maybe? I don't know if that advice is too American—' and the cast laughed warmly at her self-effacement, and she rewarded them with a modest smile. 'You know, instead of asking him to copy your interpretation, or to play an adjective, which is passive, you could provide him with an action, a verb . . .' She racked her brain. 'Something like—'

'Lure,' Cathleen said, feeling bold, her voice breaking slightly. They all turned to look at her and she blushed. 'I don't mean to talk out of turn—'

'No, that's a good one,' Shay said. 'Cheers, Cazza. Lure. Right. So that's your action, isn't it, to lure Jane, em, Kate into not just providing you with, em, romantic sport, em, but to convince her that you're someone you're not, to seduce, to entrap, to—'

'Right, yeah, whatever,' Ronan cut him off, and Jane stepped in again.

'That's very helpful, Shay – that will help my performance in the scene, too,' Jane added graciously.

'You're wonderful,' Shay said, and the two of them paused for a heartbeat.

Marie and Martin exchanged one of their almost invisible looks, and Sinead nudged Jason, who was clueless, and Paraic doubled over in the wings.

Darren and Miranda snuck up a few rows.

'I knew it,' said Miranda.

'Holy cow,' breathed Darren.

'Wonderful,' Shay repeated.

'Thank you,' Jane exhaled.

'Will we continue?' asked Cathleen.

' "If you keep me at this distance",' drawled Ronan, ' "how is it possible you and I can ever be acquainted?" ' And, as he embraced Jane, she replied, ' "And who wants to be acquainted with you—?" ' but then stepped back, annoyed.

'Not alluring enough for you?' Ronan sneered.

'Is that a mobile phone on vibrate in your pocket, or are you just happy to see me?' she sniped.

'Fifty cents!' Shay roared, and everyone looked at him as if he'd gone mental. 'No mobiles during work! Turn it off! And you've got a fifty-cent fine!'

Jane cast her eyes down to the floor and realised, in that moment, that she had finally identified that unfamiliar feeling.

She was crazy about him.

Irrevocably, undeniably mad about him.

She chanced a glance up at Shay as he stood, holding his hand out, waiting for Ronan to dig deep, and smiled to herself, the tiniest, barely discernible of smiles.

A volley of knowing looks shot around the stage and into the house and Darren and Miranda moved into the front row, gaping. Jane noticed them, made a face, and the scene began again.

This time, they made it past the sticking point, and as Jane and Ronan exited, the next scene began to play. Sinead was doing her best not to scratch her head but—

'Shinny, would you ever stop that?' Shay whined.

'It's bloody infested!' she hollered.

'It's perfectly fine—'

'Shay?' Jane stuck her head in from the wings.

'Jane, yes?' he said, smiling again.

'The wigs need some work. I'll ring around at the break, find a place that might give them the once over.'

'I couldn't ask you to—'

'No, no, we're all doing double duty around here.' She smiled and faded back into the dark.

'Right. Caz, make a— right, got it. Naom— ah, *Golden Pages*, good woman yourself.'

The scene picked up steam, and as Marie turned to leave, a combination of the muddled blocking and the fragility of her frock resulted in Jason treading on the train of her dress and entirely tearing it away.

'Shite,' said Jason, one of the rare times anyone had heard him say anything other than a line.

As Sinead moved to help Marie, Martin backed into her, trod on her hem, and Sinead's skirt fell down.

'Whoops!' she laughed and fled for the dressing room.

'Where'd you get those lacy hold-ups, Shinny?' called Cathleen, and Paraic edged around to follow Sinead backstage. A whoop of laughter cascaded out of the back, and everyone applauded.

Except Shay. *Am I the only one taking this seriously?* he wondered.

'Shay?' Jane bit back her own laughter. 'I don't know about anybody else, but I could use a break.'

He nodded, and everyone made for the kettle.

Jane stood centre stage, and felt at a loss. *So, OK, she was into this guy, all of a sudden. Now what?*

'Uh—' she began, only to be cut off by Ronan.

'Will I be charged for making a phone call?' he asked snidely. Shay responded with a glare, and Ronan left the building, dialling as he went.

'What a plonker.' Shay sat back in his chair and looked up at Jane.

'Yeah,' she said, and then stood there.

Darren and Miranda slipped out of the front row and went up to join the scrum of whisperers who had gathered around the kettle.

'I—' Jane began again, and was interrupted by the entrance of Mihal and Theresa. That took some doing, as they were as catlike as Naomi.

'You – I—' said Shay, and stopped as Naomi brought them each a cuppa.

'The wigs – the costumes—' *Better stick to business right now.*

Shay opened his mouth and thought, *not now. Stick with the work to hand.* 'I'll have to find somebody, I don't know, I—' The dejection on his face made Jane's heart tremble. *Man, I've got it bad!* she thought. *What a nightmare! I don't want a boyfriend, I don't want a partner, I don't want—*

'I – don't worry, it'll all work out,' she said.

Cathleen handed Shay his phone, saying, 'It's Gerard about the guys coming to fix the roof.'

Shay took the phone, smiling apologetically at Jane. She smiled back and caught Cathleen grinning at her.

'Nice verb,' she said acerbically, and Cathleen only laughed and went to get her brew before she called an end to the break.

The group reconvened placidly, and stood idly in place. Shay returned scowling and slammed his phone on the table. 'Where's Ronan?' he asked, and everyone shrugged. 'Great,' he growled. 'Naom— right, thanks, OK. Naomi's going to track him down. Please stay in your places, we'll begin sharpish.'

It's a physical impossibility for actors to stand on a stage quietly for any length of time. Thirty seconds is an eternity when they're out under those lights, and as the seconds stretched into minutes, each in their own way began to fidget performatively. Sinead and Paraic continued whatever they had begun in the dressing room, pulling faces and communicating in a kind of cod sign language; Marie and Martin began recounting a story about when they had played on the mainstage at the Edinburgh Theatre Festival, and reenacted the best bits, for no one's benefit but their own; Jason rocked back and forth on his heels and declaimed a monologue under his breath; even Mihal and Theresa, the most stoic of players, started to play 'mirrors', an improvisational theatre game. Jane paced and looked out into the dark house for Naomi, who returned, shook her head, and went back to the desk. Jane mimed 'phone call', and Naomi lifted the handset of the house phone.

Shay was staring up at the ceiling. Thanks a million, Uncle Des, he thought bitterly, and shut his eyes. We're so close, he thought, almost out of the woods, and now the wigs have fleas, and the costumes are falling apart, and Gerard's got his builders in for the next four days and—

'Sorry?' he said. Naomi had crept downstage centre, and Jane hovered worriedly at her back. The rest of the cast had moved forward, and everyone was staring at him in horror. 'What?'

Naomi looked scandalised, and Jane put a comforting hand on her shoulder. He tried again. 'I didn't hear you, what?'

'Ronan.'

Shay threw up his hands. 'Has he lost his way?' he cracked.

'No.' Naomi gulped, and Jane squeezed her shoulder. 'He. He got a shampoo commercial. He. Quit.'

The silence continued, deafening. No one moved. No one breathed. Everyone waited.

If anyone deserved to raise an absolute barney, it was Shay. He duly rose, and almost delicately shut his play book.

'That's it,' he said quietly. 'It's over.'

25

Shocked, they all watched Shay pull on his jacket and make his way down the aisle.

Everyone looked at Jane.

'DON'T YOU DARE LEAVE THIS BUILDING!' she shouted, and Shay stopped, but didn't turn.

'Don't you dare move,' she continued, more softly, but still projecting. Darren and Miranda ran in from the wings, and Sinead hurriedly filled them in. Miranda couldn't help herself: she started taking pictures.

Jane considered her options. She could go for the 'we need you, you can't go' tone, or the more forceful 'it's not just about you any more' or 'winners never quit, quitters never win' . . .

'Shay.' She felt the goodwill of the group rushing in waves against her back. 'It's not over. It's only begun! So the wigs need a little work, so the costumes need a tweak! So what? I haven't participated in a single production that hasn't had its problems. I'm sure that Marie and Martin can tell you – they've got more experience than any of us in this room – that it's not easy; it's hard. This is hard work we're doing here. The crowds come in, leave entertained, and think, "Oh, well, what kind of job is that?"

'It's not a job, Shay,' she said passionately, her voice threatening to break. 'It's not *just* a job. None of us are here to make a million dollars – euros – whatever. We're

228

here because we have to be, we don't want to do anything else, we *are* this. This is "us". And we're here because of you. You got this all together. You had the guts and the vision to get us all in the same room, and we need you. We need you.'

'It's a fucking mess, is what it is,' Shay replied, still with his back to the stage.

'Well, godammit, it's *our* mess. All of ours. As much as we need you, it's not just about you any more. Every one of us has invested in this production, and you can't call it off. We're too close.' She took a deep breath. 'We all need this show.'

'Thanks, Jane, but—'

Theresa, of all people, came forward. Nonplussed, Jane moved aside and the rest of the group gaped.

'Excuse me, but I have something to say.' Shay finally turned around. 'You've got a lot to learn as a director, but you're an excellent actor, and I see no reason in the world why you can't play young Marlow.' With that, she retreated upstage once more.

Jane cocked her head, and grinned down at Shay. 'I think it's about time I made an executive decision. You're hired.'

Shay began to shake his head. 'But—'

'No buts.' Jane waved his reply away. 'I am co-producer of this show, and whether you like it or not, you've got the part.'

The collective breath exploded into whoops and applause as Shay smiled, and throwing off his jacket, jumped up on to the stage. They increased in volume as Shay bowed before Jane, snatched up her hand, and kissed it. Flustered, she pulled it out of his grasp and joined in the applause.

'We'll need a director,' he shouted over the noise, and Jane gestured towards Cathleen, who blushed and stuttered.

'I couldn't, I – I don't know—'

'Co-director, then,' said Jane. 'And you're officially off make-up duty.'

'All right, so,' she laughed, and another round of boisterous clapping filled the theatre.

'The show must go on,' quipped Shay.

'It always does,' said Jane.

If things didn't go entirely smoothly, they were definitely less rocky as the home stretch to opening night began.

Cathleen stood with her hands on her hips, and stared at the floor. Shay, Martin and Paraic stood waiting on the stage.

'It's always been a problem, this,' said Martin, and they all nodded.

'Let's try to— the thing is, Shay has to stay behind for that last bit, right?' Cathleen looked up and her eyes darted around the stage. 'And Martin and Paraic need to leave . . . but there's no passage behind the upstage wall.'

'Right.' Shay moved around a bit to loosen up his brain.

'And the thing is, I have to be left to enter in my next scene,' Martin added.

'And I have to be right,' said Paraic.

'Lads, it isn't rocket science, but we won't figure it out by talking about it, I'm guessing,' said Cathleen. 'So, Shay, you need to end up in the middle there, and Martin, what if – well, you and Paraic don't need to leave together, do you?' Excited, she grabbed up Shay's binder, which she had inherited with the job, and consulted the script.

'Paraic, you need to be on this side of me, but what if you both cross down from me on your lines and exit?' Shay could see things much better from where he was – a world of difference from what he was now considering as being trapped down there behind that table.

'Eureka!' intoned Martin, and Paraic quickly went through the movement to see.

They all nodded, feeling something akin, they were sure, to what that caveman must have felt when he banged out the first wheel. Elated, they ran through the adjustments three more times, and there was much backslapping when the action became second nature.

Jane watched, in full make-up, from behind the desk. Leaning her elbows on the top, she shoved aside her list of things that Shay needed to do, and relished the moment. The inexplicable had happened, and they were entering into the most enjoyable part of the process, when they could still make discoveries, but felt fully confident. Closer to show time, fears often got in the way, and it took a good five days of the run before they'd get back to the comfort level they were experiencing now. She smiled to herself, and caught Darren's eye. He grimaced at her goodnaturedly from the makeshift wardrobe department, as he sorted through the costumes. What had looked like a group of promising frocks and trousers, had, after a few outings on the boards, shown their weaknesses, and Darren was busily sorting the wheat from the chaff, with the majority unfortunately falling on the side of the latter.

'You're a star, Dar,' she said. 'Let us know if there's any way to salvage this stuff.'

'I've got a few ideas,' he said. 'Low-budget ideas, of course.'

'But high-quality product, I'm sure.' She smiled, and opened her mouth to continue, but became utterly distracted by the action onstage.

She, thought Darren, has got it bad. He swallowed past a lump in his throat, his feelings warring between happiness, smugness, and jealousy. Happy that she'd found someone that she really seemed to be falling for, smug because he'd known it would always happen to her despite her protestations to the contrary, and jealous . . . as jealous as he'd been of Miranda's happiness earlier that spring.

It had been fertile ground for his sessions with his therapist, this jealousy thing, and it had brought Darren almost to the brink of admitting that his celibacy was starting to wear thin. When he said he couldn't even remember why he'd chosen to abstain, well, the eyes of the normally sphinx-like Dr Spitz glittered with something that Darren hazarded to guess was excitement, and the man had actually re-crossed his legs. To Darren, this signalled that he himself was on the verge of a breakthough, and it made him nervous. He thought that springing this trip on the good doctor might encourage him to revert to his usual inscrutable ways, but last week's announcement actually inspired Dr Spitz to cough and lean forward.

It was as close to open approval as Darren had ever experienced. Oh, sure, they subsequently went on the usual journey through the standard therapeutic hoops, from gentle probity on the part of Dr Spitz ('What might your real reasons be for taking such an impulsive journey?') through to Darren's rationalisation ('I've been working like crazy and I need a vacation! I deserve a vacation!') and ended, as it always did, in honesty ('I don't know what's going on with my friends and it's driving me crazy. They may need my help and I don't care if it's rescuing behaviour, I feel left out and abandoned!') Whew.

He did what he could with the clothes that might make it through the coming run, and took the rest out to the alleyway to put in the garbage before Shay saw what he was doing. Shay was a bit crazy when it came to this stuff, some kind of inheritance, he remembered Miranda told him, and had an attachment that went outside the bounds of sense, if you asked Darren. It was better to just spirit the stuff away and let Jane handle him.

He clutched the tattered remains of what might once have been adequate outfits for a repertory company, and sighed. Yes, definitely feeling left out, he thought, and was in the middle of processing this information when he walked into Jason.

'Whoops,' said Darren, backing up against the wall to let him pass . . . and was surprised when Jason stopped and leaned a hand on the wall, casually.

'All right?' Jason asked, flicking his eyes over Darren's face, and smiling.

'Uh . . . huh,' said Darren, thinking, Well, my gaydar went on the blink the minute I came through customs. Who knew?

'First time in Dublin?' he went on, adjusting his posture and bringing himself a shade closer to Darren's chest.

'Third time, actually,' Darren replied, and swung away from Jason's encroaching belly.

'Been out and about, I reckon?'

'Not really. I've spent a lot of time with Miranda, and we travelled around—'

'We've got some decent clubs in town,' Jason said, shifting his hips forward a tad. 'We'll go get a jar sometime.'

'Maybe,' Darren said, and fled down the hall.

That, as Dr Spitz would say, had been instructive. It seemed pointless to be envious of his friend's good romantic fortune if he wasn't even ready for his own.

He's so not your type, he said to himself, but that was what he always said. He had his standards, however, and, based on past experience, he knew that actors didn't necessarily make the best long-term bedfellows—

His internal debate was stopped short by the sight of Niall having a psychotic episode in the alleyway.

He'd liked Niall pretty much from the start. Miranda had duly arranged for them to meet before she and Niall had flown off to Ireland, and had gained Darren's wholehearted approval. He thought Niall to be talented and considerate, level-headed, and wonderfully affectionate with Miranda. Luckily, he hadn't met him for the first time at this very moment.

Niall was pacing up and down the narrow space like a caged panther, his black hair sticking up wildly in all directions, and he was muttering to himself in a kind of angrily pleading tone. Wild-eyed, he looked up at Darren, and gestured at the flats that he had propped up against the theatre's outside wall.

'You're a designer, you tell him. You tell him!' And Niall set about pacing again, shaking his head and mumbling.

Darren dumped the ratty costumes in the big black garbage can on wheels, and went over to inspect the flats. They had so many patches on them, they looked like Frankenstein's monster. The plywood was flimsy and the frames had—

'Dry rot,' Darren said firmly. 'It's not only pointless to use them, but dangerous.'

'He won't hear of changing – bloody uncle and legacy and some shite about the symbolism of putting on his first show, having something of the family around him—'

'Is he attached to his family?' Darren couldn't imagine Jane coping with that. Look at how Miranda was taking the whole extended-Irish-family thing!

'Jesus, no, they practically disowned him when he quit the bar to do this.' Hmm, OK, but, as Darren well knew, family issues always will out.

'And on top of it he doesn't even know if this is the way he wants the bloody feckin' show to look!' Exhausted, Niall leaned heavily against the opposite wall and glared at the offending wood.

Darren held up a finger, and went back into the theatre. In moments, he returned with a can of what he guessed, from the smell, was something like turpentine – the label read 'white spirits' – and removed the discarded costumes from the bin. With a meaningful look at the now-grinning Niall, he sprinkled the liquid over the fabric. Niall quickly and efficiently piled up the flats, and they stuffed the sodden clothes beneath them. Darren solemnly handed Niall a lighter, and, with glee, he touched the flame to a particularly bedraggled petticoat.

'I don't give a shite about the consequences,' Niall said fervently. 'I'll donate some boards out of my own stock, I don't care. I never want to see these bloody things again.'

They watched the flames flicker and grow, and Niall felt an impulse to dance wildly around the inferno that he had to put down to his most assuredly pagan ancestors.

'I haven't been officially asked,' Darren began, 'but I have some simple but elegant ideas for a setting. We'd need some two-by-fours and some dyeable fabric, muslin maybe.' His eyes focused inward and he imagined his scenery, and Jane in front of it, Jane and Shay. He nodded, and Niall clapped him on the shoulder.

'I've got a cousin out in Cabra who can fix us up. As much as you want.'

They shook hands, Niall quite zealously, and Darren left him to enjoy the ensuing glow.

Making his way backstage, he had to cut across the playing area as Jane and Shay ran one of their scenes. Cathleen indicated that he should go, for they were so lost in the work that he could have paraded by with a herd of water buffalo, and they wouldn't have heard them.

' "Suppose I should call for a taste of the nectar of your lips",' whispered Shay as he snaked an arm around Jane's waist. ' "Perhaps I might be disappointed in that too." ' Perhaps not, he thought, oh, definitely not.

' "Nectar! Nectar!" ' laughed Jane, gracefully disentangling herself from his embrace and, swaying flirtatiously, made him follow. ' "That's a liquor there's no call for in these parts." ' But to have one more, even only more taste of his lips—

' "How old are you?" ' teased Shay.

' "O! Sir, I must not tell my age. They say women and music should never be dated," ' Jane scolded coquettishly. But I guess that depends upon your interpretation of dating—

' "Pray, sir, keep your distance",' she continued, her voice quavering with just the right amount of curiosity and fear ... which didn't seem to her to be emotions manufactured only for the scene.

' "I protest, child, you use me extremely ill",' Shay murmured, running his fingers delicately, tantalisingly, up Jane's arms. He gathered her close, closer – closest. ' "If you keep me at this distance, how is it possible you and I can ever be acquainted?" '

And he leaned forward, bending her slightly back, wrapping an arm around her waist once more.

Jane's hand came up to push at his chest, then turned into a searching caress, her fingers hovering at his cheek.

Their mouths stopped – a hair's breadth away ...

The moment hung like a bird in the air, caught on an invisible current. Jane's lashes fluttered down in surrender. Shay breathed and slowly closed his eyes as well, and Cathleen leaned forward, and Sinead sighed, and Darren swallowed against that recurring lump in his throat, and Marie and Martin reached for one another's hands.

They were breathing in unison, their lips poised and expectant, and even though it was a handful of seconds, it felt like hours, and fiction blurred with fact and Jane wanted it and Shay wanted it and the spectators wanted it and—

BANG. In came Miranda, rushing up the aisle. 'I just got three assignments from *The Irish Times*! The money is crap but—' Everyone was glaring at her. 'What?'

'Nothing, nothing,' Shay grumbled.

'Just having a moment up here.' Jane tried to laugh it off and realised she was short of breath. Miranda shrugged, and went off in search of Niall.

'Take five, everyone,' Cathleen called, and was immediately surrounded by people with queries. Jesus, no one warned you about the endless questions and demands, did they? she thought to herself.

'When are we going to get more lights?' asked Declan.

'Is something burning?' asked Jane.

'Cathleen, can you talk about the costumes at some point?' called Darren before he headed off to take a look at the condition of the props.

'I got a quote from the wig people, can we look at that now?' said Jane, and she and Shay crossed down to Cathleen.

'I'll take that,' said Shay, and as she handed it over, their fingers brushed and Jane got a tingle and she thought, enough! It's only his . . . feckin' . . . fingers!

He sniffed at the air. 'You know, it does smell like fire.'

'I need more lights. I can't do the footlight yoke without more lights.' Dec never raised his voice, but they could hear that he was at the end of his rope.

'I'll ring Gerard,' sighed Jane.

'No, I will,' said Cathleen.

'No, let me,' Shay insisted.

'Let's all ring him; maybe that's the tactic we haven't tried yet,' Jane muttered.

'I need to go out.' They looked at Naomi, aghast. She never made any requests, much less what, coming from her, sounded like a demand.

'Right, so,' Cathleen said, at sea. 'Em, will you be long?'

'No. I need Dec.' And they left.

'Jesus, she's not leaving us, is she?' Shay looked stricken.

'I don't know what we'd do without her.' Cathleen's voice broke.

'She's coming back,' said Jane. 'I'm sure of it. Shay, there's a problem with the costumes. We three need to put our heads together . . .'

As they sat around the director's table, the little annoyances and huge problems of producing a show took over, and Jane was able to cope with Shay's eyes on her, his voice in her ear, his general presence. As they argued about the setting (which none of them knew was now reduced to ashes in the back), it felt like they had got back on an even keel, and she didn't even mind that Shay's mind wasn't quite on the subject.

Shay had, in the last few days, become obsessed with the notion of taking her out for a meal. It was superseding everything else in his mind, and in some strange way, had actually helped him get his lines down; he was so fixated on figuring out how to get her alone, without making her think he was getting her alone, that it allowed him to relax while memorising his part. Directness, despite Jane's own tendency towards that in the personality department, wasn't going to work. Neither was a hearts-and-flowers approach . . . or would it? No, he couldn't chance it, he'd have to go for underhanded and sneaky. He nodded to himself, but then noticed that Jane and Cathleen were staring at him, perplexed.

'Sorry, lost the plot,' he apologised, and tried to concentrate on the hair repair quotes.

'Will we call it a day?' asked Jane, wanting nothing more than a little time away from her feelings.

'I wanted to go through the last bit, one more time. I'm still not happy with the tableau,' Cathleen said briskly.

'You're a quick study,' Jane said admiringly, and made her way back up the stage. 'Slave driver. Better watch that cast morale.'

'Caz, I need to speak to you about a few things, before you leave,' Shay said, the light bulb finally going on.

She looked at him, worried, but he shook his head and smiled. 'You're grand, it's about . . . the morale of certain members of the cast.'

As the group gathered for a run-though of the closing

moments of the show, the house doors opened slowly, creaking, drawing their attention. It was Naomi and Declan, their arms full of lamps.

'Jackie's out front, we've got about twenty more in the boot,' Naomi puffed as she hefted the lamps on to the stage.

Shay whooped, jumped down, kissed her on the head, and ran up the aisle to fetch the rest. Jane looked down at the furiously blushing girl.

'Naomi, I'm promoting you to associate producer.'

'Cheers,' said Naomi, and she, too, went out to help gather up the last round of lights.

26

Cathleen locked the door behind them, and they all assembled outside the theatre.

'In this country,' Jane whispered to Darren, 'it takes about twenty minutes to say goodbye.'

As the chat went around the small group, and the time for leaving seemed to come and go, Jane finally proposed, 'Let's all go have a drink.'

'Good idea!' said Miranda, feeling that her news hadn't received the attention it deserved.

'Em, can't pet, gotta go see a horse about a man,' Niall said, and kissing her quickly, headed off west towards Stoneybatter. Miranda frowned, and then decided against acting like a clingy girlfriend ... even though it took all her strength not to pester him about the 'horse'.

Shay glanced at Cathleen. 'Gotta go meself, em, see you all tomorrow, right?'

'Oh, I'm heading in that direction,' Cathleen said, and they both nipped up the lane and into Smithfield.

Jane frowned at their backs as they left, and felt especially annoyed when Shay's hand set lightly on the small of Cathleen's back as they crossed the road.

'I'm sure they have tons to talk about,' assured Miranda.

'I'm sure they do,' Jane said coolly.

'I'm sure it's business,' Darren added, looking worried.

'I'm sure I couldn't care less,' Jane grumbled, and Miranda and Darren exchanged a furtive glance. 'Will we go out or what?'

'How about the Morrison?' Miranda suggested, allowing for the need for 'cool'.

'No,' said Jane, having since found out that was where she had been when she was snogging Ronan. 'I have bad memories of that place.'

'You haven't wasted any time, have you?' Darren joked, and got treated to a cold stare.

'Mulligan's?' Miranda offered.

'I'm sick of it,' Jane said, and headed down the quays.

Miranda glared at her back. 'The Front Lounge.'

'Darren will hate that, it's such a gay meat market,' Jane called back.

'Actually, I—' Darren tried to interrupt.

'OK,' Miranda ground out, 'how about Doyle's?'

'Too collegiate.'

'The Long Hall?'

'Too crowded.'

'The Czech Inn?'

'Too empty.'

'Fuck's sake!' Miranda cursed.

'You really haven't wasted any time.' Darren had to hand it to Jane – when she put her mind to something, even if it was integrating into a place she hadn't even wanted to visit, she did it.

'Grogan's!' Miranda said firmly, moving fast to get in front of Jane.

'They have tables outside?' Jane demanded.

'It's freezing!' Darren dug into his pockets for his gloves.

'You get used to it,' Jane said. 'I've never been to Grogan's . . .'

'That's it then,' Miranda said, heading for the Millennium Bridge.

'Is it pubby or is it like some New York rip-off?' Jane

asked, and she and Miranda argued up the quays, with Darren in their wake.

Miranda led them in through the back door, and rushed to her favourite table, tucked against the wall that divided the small pub into two smaller rooms. Darren had fought strenuously to sit indoors, and, for once, had won.

'This works,' said Jane, duly nothing that there was the requisite number of old fellas at the bar to speak of the place's authenticity.

'What'll you have?' Miranda asked, pulling her wallet out of her photo bag.

'Pint of Guinness,' said Jane, as she settled herself in the corner. Darren shook his head in disbelief. There were probably more calories in that one pint than she'd consumed in all of last year. 'Same,' he said, and pulled off his suede coat.

'It's nice to be back,' he offered, when Miranda had returned with three pints of the porter.

'It's even nicer to have you back,' Miranda replied, as she held up her pint.

'This is another thing, we all have to toast or else, I don't know, the island will fall into the sea,' Jane said to Darren, and they all clinked glasses.

'I do detect a small, winsome note of fondness in your voice?' Darren chided, and he started to sip.

'Wait, you have to wait until it settles!' Jane grabbed his arm, and he set his drink back down, and they all watched their pints morph from brown to black, in reverent silence.

'Jane's picked up quite a few mannerisms in her time here,' Miranda murmured, her eyes dancing.

'And a teeny little accent, just like you did, Miranda,' Darren added.

'Well, you know – and I explained this to you before, Dar – you have to pick up the lingo or sure you'll never be after getting anything organised.'

'You're absolutely right, and it's part of the fun, too, don't you think? Part of the whole point of living, even if it's only for a short time, in a foreign culture, is to acquire some of the traditions of one's host country—'

'All right, all right!' Jane cut off their arch dialogue. 'So, what, I'm supposed to admit that I was a self-absorbed bitch and a rotten friend? Is that what you want?'

'You've already apologised to *me*,' said Miranda pointedly. She and Darren looked expectantly at Jane, who huddled defensively against the slightly seedy banquette.

'Darren, I already said sorry over the phone, remember, when I got here and rang – called you on Miranda's cell – mobile – argh!' She threw back her head and laughed, and Darren reached out and stroked her arm.

'I sound like one of an old married couple, but it's been a long time since I heard you laugh.'

'I had a shitty year, guys,' Jane admitted. 'And I . . . I didn't think that I deserved to complain about it, I guess.' Darren was about to charge in with some sort of psychological bon mot, but Jane held up a hand. 'I had everything going for me, except for the stupid Bob thing, and I didn't realise that it was all starting to go against me. I didn't realise . . .' and she trailed off, shook her head.

'Go on,' Darren urged soothingly.

Jane glared at him. 'No shrinking, Dar. I don't know what I didn't realise, OK? Give me a break.'

'Anyway,' Miranda cut in briskly, 'you've had an excellent holiday—'

'I knew it was the best thing for you,' Darren cut in complacently.

'And you're in a show, which is fabulous,' Miranda continued.

'*You* are so fabulous, do you think you'll go back to acting again?' Darren gushed.

'– And,' Miranda cut across him, 'you're, em, getting to know Shay . . .' She let that hang, meaningfully, and she and Darren edged forward a little.

'So what's this about *The Irish Times*?' Jane asked coolly, reverting to form.

Miranda knew a brick wall when she ran up against one. 'Yer one, who's doing your PR, got me another gig, and the pictures got printed in *The Ticket*, the entertainment thingie, and the photo desk called me to see my book.' Miranda grinned triumphantly. 'I need to stay busy until my book launch, which has now been bumped back to September, I'll go crazy waiting, otherwise.'

'So you'll be staying until then?' Darren asked.

'Em, yeah,' Miranda replied uncomfortably, and reached for her pint.

'Oh.' Darren sat back, and rubbed his stomach. He felt a little afraid, for some reason.

'I, um . . .' Miranda took a breath, and looked up at her friends. 'I – I'm staying. Here. I'm not moving back.'

They sat in silence, digested the news. Darren sighed, and nodded, and reached out to squeeze Miranda's hand. He couldn't say he wasn't surprised, nor that he wasn't happy for his friend but he felt—

'I feel sad,' Jane said, staring down at her pint.

Darren gasped and grabbed her up in a bear hug. 'Jane, Jane, good for you! Oh my goodness, you identified a feeling, all by yourself!'

Jane sighed into his shoulder, and shook her head. 'Sure, I don't know meself,' she said, liltingly, and they all laughed.

'I'll have to sort out my post – mail, Darren. Thanks for letting me have it sent to you,' Miranda said, choking up.

'Anything you need, any time,' Darren replied, breathing through an intense need to howl. 'Do they have vodka?'

'Don't ever change, Dar,' Jane laughed, with a lump in her own throat. She turned to Miranda, and smiled. 'So I guess things are good with himself.'

'Yeah,' Miranda laughed, then frowned. 'Although he's been a little weird lately, a little secretive. I don't know what's up with that.'

Jane shrugged. 'I've never claimed to understand the male mind.' She looked down at her hands. That sadness thing was still hanging around. 'Well, we'll hold your place in Manhattan, in any case. If you ever want to come back.'

'Fair enough,' said Miranda, blinking back a few tears. 'It's a little bit scary. I wish you guys could be here too.'

'We'll come visit,' Jane said. 'Probably not for such an extended time, but—'

'Oh, I keep forgetting!' Darren reached back and dug into the deep pocket of his jacket, and handed a packet to Jane. 'Here's *your* post. Seriously, can I get a Martini?'

As Miranda led him to the bar to help him order a vodka-based drink, or five, Jane flipped through the handful of letters; Darren had judiciously edited out any junk mail, and most were bills. She came to an envelope bearing a familiar logo, gold-embossed searchlights elegantly dropped in the upper right-hand corner of the thick cream-coloured missive, and her palms started to sweat.

When she opened it, and read it, her heart lurched, and looking furtively at her friends, she shoved the letter deep into the bottom of her handbag.

The theatre was as hushed as a cathedral as the cast, in full costume and make-up, gathered in the darkened house to watch Declan run through the lighting cues. They ranged around behind Cathleen and Shay as the brightly coloured lighting plan struck Darren's simple but highly effective setting: Niall had built frames with the wood he'd got off his Cabra cousin, and using muslin and some of the lengths of fabric that Shay had that weren't mildewed, Darren had created large, vibrantly coloured flats of different textures, which turned elegantly and soundlessly on some poles Niall had rigged up. On the sides of some, there was the indication of the Marlow house; on the opposite, the pub that played a part early in the play; some were covered in *trompe l'oeil* foliage that slid back slightly to be framed by potted topiary plants, placed at intervals upstage, to fill out the garden that was needed for the end of the show. At certain stages, the flats would be backlit, to allow a shadow play to unfold to enhance the main action, to allow Jane to eavesdrop, in silhouette.

And all across the apron of the stage ranged thirty footlights that ran the gamut from bright white to a deep cobalt-blue.

'We'll do a cue to cue,' said Cathleen quietly. 'If the cast would take their places, please.'

The women floated up the steps to the stage, swathed in lengths of cunningly dyed muslin – well, I got that right, thought Shay. Darren had run up bits of detail to fill out the outfits, with a striped bustle running down Sinead's emerald-green skirt, and a dull gold full-length jacket for Marie to wear on top of her flowing scarlet gown.

Jane delicately lifted her skirt, a bright robin's-egg blue, and pressed a hand to her silver velvet bodice. Her wig, freshly cleaned and lavishly curled, sat securely on her perfectly balanced head as she made her way to the wings. Naomi smiled at her, and fussed a bit with her maid's costume: she and the stagehand she had miraculously found would be in charge of changing the aspects of the flats, and were in full rig-out themselves.

The run through, without lines, went off without a hitch, and the silence that met the last fade out said everything, as far as Shay was concerned.

It was going to work after all.

'Thank you, everyone,' Shay said, at the end of the dry run of the curtain call. 'But thanks especially to Darren, who, for lack of a better term, really saved our bacon.' The ensuing applause made Darren blush scarlet. 'It was a bit of a busman's holiday,' Shay continued, 'but I hope it wasn't too taxing.' He leaned down and the men shook hands, Cathleen leaning over to plant a smacking kiss on Darren's cheek, and Jason winked at him from beneath his top hat.

Declan brought up the work lights, and the spell was broken. The usual chatter broke out, and Darren went onstage to help Naomi with the few props that were used throughout the show.

'Shame we couldn't have used more of Uncle Des's gear,' Shay said to Darren, as Darren passed him with a slightly careworn urn.

'I've been meaning to talk to you about that stuff,' Darren replied. 'There are several pieces that—'

'Sure we'll talk about it over the cast meal tonight,' Shay boomed, and nodded to Darren, having given him his cue.

Darren glanced over at Jane, who was back behind the stage manager's desk, reading a fax from the PR agency.

'Oh, Shay, I'm afraid I can't make it tonight. I, uh, have some work to do on, uh, the chaise for Scene Ten.' God, what a lame excuse, but it was the best he could come up with.

'Oh, Dar, come on, don't work so hard,' Jane called, setting aside the fax. 'This is your holiday – vacation.'

'Oh, well, jet lag, uh, want to finish, uh . . .' He fled into the wings.

Sinead and Paraic came out in their street clothes. 'What's our call for tomorrow?' asked Paraic, hitching his rucksack over his shoulder.

'You're a slave driver, Cathleen,' said Sinead, winking

at Shay. 'Working us till seven at night, working us on a Saturday; you're like a feckin' American. No offence, Jane.'

'Aren't you coming along to the Mermaid?' Jane asked, coming out on to the stage.

'Can't, barely got me lines, gotta get to work,' Sinead said, and she and Paraic left the theatre.

'Looks like we'll have to ring the restaurant, change our numbers.' Shay looked dejected and, smiling gamely at Jane, he went off to change.

Jane moved down to Cathleen, who was mumbling to herself.

'Good work, Caz,' she said.

'Hey? Ah, thanks a million,' Cathleen replied absently, her brow furrowed.

'You certainly deserve a nice dinner out,' Jane said.

'Em, can't make it. I've got this idea ... I need to work something out before tomorrow. I hope Shay won't be too disappointed. This outing means a lot to him.'

'Hmph,' said Jane, who saw the O'Connors creeping up the side aisle of the house. 'Aren't you coming along?' she called.

'Have a lovely time,' said Marie, who grabbed Martin's arm and dragged him to the door.

Jason came out and patted his belly. 'Are we off?'

Jane beamed at him. 'Any minute now!' and she ran off to the dressing room.

Cathleen crooked her finger at Jason, and started whispering furiously in his ear.

When Jane returned, it was to find Shay waiting. Alone.

'Where's Jason?' she asked, confused.

'He had another, em, engagement,' Shay sighed.

'What about Mihal? And Theresa? Where'd they go?'

Shay laughed. 'Disappeared into the ether, as usual. Looks like it's just you and me.'

Jane's brow furrowed. She took in Shay's suit and his

freshly shined Oxfords. 'How strange,' she murmured. I think I've been had, she thought to herself.

'You won't back out on me, will you?'

Jane shook back her hair, and buttoned up the tightly fitting Louise Kennedy coat she'd picked up . . . just for the hell of it. 'Of course not. We can go over a few things while we eat.'

Shay shook his head, and offered her his arm. 'No business tonight. Deal?'

Jane hesitated, slipped her arm through his, and felt her pulse leap. 'I'm not going to make a promise I can't keep,' she replied, and they walked down the aisle, and locked the door behind them.

27

'And I don't want to know. Thirty lamps! When I
... saw Naomi walk in – and yer man Jackie, he's a
star. We should work out some sort of company car deal
with him, give him an ad in the programme. I'd say it'd
save us a few bob—'

Jane rolled her eyes at that one as they made their
way through Temple Bar and up that street, whatever it
was called, the one that had that Chinese food place on
the corner. So much for not talking about business . . .

And she'd proposed the very thing about Jackie ages
ago . . .

Her thin-edged heels slipped and slid between the
cobblestones, and when Shay's hand grasped her arm, it
only served to further skitter her balance; when his arm
came around her waist, accompanied by a stern look to
stem any protests, she wondered what he'd do if she
leapt up into his arms.

Dame Street was teeming with punters on touristy
pub crawls; hen and stag parties in for the weekend from
Manchester; intimidated-looking clusters of Americans
wearing shorts and sandals and clutching maps; lazily
strolling Italians who always seemed to be strolling
lazily, and never actually going in anywhere and sitting
down. Rushing past all these were actual Dubliners of all
shapes, sizes and postal codes: slightly orange-tinted
gaggles of bottle blondes shrieking their way towards the

Clarence; track-suited twenty-somethings dodging the pedestrian traffic and heading for the quays; goth kids descending upon the Central Bank; older couples done up to the nines for a night out at the theatre.

They were all on display through the broad plate-glass windows of the Mermaid Café, and Jane shook her head, cutting off Shay's monologue about what a chancer Gerard was.

'Of course he's a chancer – all theatre owners are chancers, or they'd never make any money.' She changed the subject. 'Look at all these people! It's like everybody's out. I can't decide if it's because Dublin is so small, or because it's so sociable.'

Shay tossed a glance over his shoulder. 'A bit of both, I reckon. But Dublin's not *that* small.' He turned back to Jane who looked astonishing in the candlelight. The flickering flames picked out the vibrant green in her eyes, her red lipstick glistened. He leaned his elbows on the table, leaned towards her, wanting to say something – the right thing, for once – wanting to touch her face, stroke her cheek, make her laugh.

Jane sat back and picked up her menu.

'Too bad about the rest of the group,' she murmured.

'What's wrong with them?' asked Shay as he perused the list of the restaurant's attractive offerings.

'Too bad they couldn't make it. Seems strange, with all that planning, that they all ended up with something else to do.'

'Ah well, the Irish . . .' Shay looked at her sorrowfully. 'And, well . . .'

Jane frowned. 'What?'

Shay shook his head, and played with his fork, avoiding Jane's gaze. 'I was afraid that – I thought – I thought they'd finally warmed to you.'

Jane gasped, and it rang out over the loudly boisterous room. 'They *love* me! I can't believe you think that, after—' The combination of the horror at the sound of her own screeching voice and the twinkle in Shay's eyes made her narrow her own.

'You're a real joker, aren't you?' She slapped her menu down on to the table. 'I think I'll have the monkfish.'

'Once a fella knows the way, you're easily riled,' Shay smirked.

Jane jerked up her chin, and refused to be drawn. 'I may even have the goat's cheese salad for an appetiser.'

'All that urban savvy and you take the hook every time,' he sighed.

'I'd suggest the Northern Italian Chardonnay. It's a lovely vintage.'

He grinned at her and flagged down a waiter. As Jane joshed with the lad, Shay revelled in the changes in her, changes that had been wrought in such a short time – and decided that he deserved more credit than might be conceivably due him.

As the waiter left to fetch the wine, Shay leaned forward again. 'An appetiser and a main course . . . and to think you wouldn't even touch a butty on your first day here.'

'A salad and fish is a long way from bread, butter, and pure fat.' Jane sipped at her sparkling water.

'Well, you look fit, anyway. Filled out. Glowing, like.'

'Is this your idea of flirting? It's generally a bad idea to point out that a girl's put on a few pounds.'

'What if I was flirting with you?' The question rattled around Jane's brain. What if he was? So what? What's stopping me? she wondered. What's been stopping me ever since I clapped eyes on this guy? We've already *done it*, what difference does it make?

'Did you hear me speed-running lines with Jason? He's got them down, he just doesn't think he does.'

'Sorry, we're not supposed to be talking about work,' Shay said. I want to talk about how sexy you look, now, he thought, and when you're onstage opposite me. I want to talk about what had just been running through that lightning fast mind of yours before you . . .

But what will we talk about? Jane thought, and she was off again. She shifted uneasily in her chair. Far too many dangerous things were on the agenda now, and what was that tingly feeling all along her nerve endings?

She looked a little panicked, he thought.

In desperation, she snatched up a piece of bread, dipped it in the olive oil. 'Who can blame us? Really, it's exciting, we've worked hard—'

'No,' Shay said with finality. 'No shop talk.'

'You might find me boring without work to talk about.' Where had that come from?

'Never.' Shay toyed with his empty wine glass, and she noticed his look changed, the kind of look that came over someone's face when he was thinking about kissing you . . .

The tingling increased as he held her with that unwavering stare. 'We'll see,' she replied, trying for lightness. 'I bet we can't avoid the subject for more than twenty minutes.'

'What'll the forfeit be?'

That damn tingling turned into a roaring in her head. Where was the bloody wine? 'Fifty cents?' she rejoined lightly.

Shay laughed, and leaned forward, shaking his head. The candles lit up his golden-brown eyes, they looked like honey caught in a jar, and the shadows that fell across his face carved out a rugged charm. 'I think we can do better than that.'

A burst of noise exploded out of the stairwell as the restaurant's private room emptied. Grateful for the distraction, Jane turned to see a group of pink-cheeked, soberly dressed older fellas spill out into the main room and head for the door. Comprised mostly of business men, you could, thought Jane, smell the smugness from where she was sitting. She turned back to Shay and saw that his face had gone blank, the way it had the day they'd met his—

'Da,' said Shay laconically, rising, and brushing down the front of his suit jacket. 'Slumming?'

'Shay.' Seamus nodded, his eyes glancing off Jane.

Shay, directing his comments to Jane, but never taking his eyes off the older man, said, 'My father's crowd usually prefers L'Ecrivain or Roly's Bistro.'

This meant nothing to Jane, but she got his drift. She sipped from her glass and sat back. Just don't get me mixed up in this, pal.

'We're off to the Olympia, some entertainment of some sort going on.' The scorn with which he invested the word *entertainment* had Jane sitting up stiffly in her chair.

'You'll be pleased to know, Mr Gallagher, that Shay's production is well on its way to a successful run.' She smiled thinly. 'It's one of the most professional debuts I've ever seen.' If I do say so myself, she thought.

Seamus ignored her.

It was a mistake.

'I don't think I saw you on the opening-night invitation list – must have been an oversight,' she purred, and saw Shay jerk at his jacket.

A slight blush added to the wine-and-brandy ruddiness of Seamus's face.

'I'd hate to think that you wouldn't be coming out in support of your –' she almost said 'only son', but she didn't know that much about Shay, did she? '– of your son's new career.'

'It's all right, Jane, I suppose me da will wait until *The Irish Times* weighs in.'

'Oh, Shay, I forgot to mention, we've gotten the RSVPs from the press – they'll all be there. *The Irish Times*, the *Independent*, *HQ*, the *Sunday Tribune*, the *Sunday Times* . . .' Jane let her voice trail off.

'You've done excellent work – not to mention your

starring role, as well,' Shay replied smoothly, his heart skipping a beat. Critics?

'So you're an actress,' said Seamus, giving that last word a bit of a sneer.

'Jane's one of New York's finest. It took some finessing to get her, em, on board.' Shay grinned at Jane, enjoying himself now.

'As I said before, Shay, when I practically begged you for the part—' Well, let's not go there.

'It was I who begged you,' Shay insisted. And rather persuasively, at the end of the day. In a manner of speaking.

Jane turned to the older man. 'Will we put you down for two for opening night, Seamus? Surely you wouldn't want to miss Shay's acting debut!' Jane smirked and sat back again.

It was like watching Mount Vesuvius struggle to avoid erupting in such a public place. 'You're *acting*?' Seamus sputtered, and Shay bowed slightly in response.

'He's wonderful, Seamus, you'd be—'

'I'll thank you to stay out of family business, young lady,' Seamus hissed.

'Ah sure, Da, she's practically family herself,' Shay said elliptically, and Jane gulped down a mouthful of her water. This was starting to get out of hand.

One of Seamus's party stuck his head back through the door and called to him. Saying nothing, he stalked to the door, which he shut forcefully behind him.

The waiter arrived with their wine, and they sat in silence while he filled their glasses.

'Should we put him on the guest list?' Jane asked.

Shay shrugged, his good humour gone. 'He's stubborn,' Shay said.

Jane arched a brow and chose not to say anything.

'And the apple didn't fall far from the tree, you're thinking,' he said.

'So, are you like the only son, or something?' Their appetisers arrived, and Jane cast an imperceptible,

255

longing glance at Shay's deep-fried crab cakes.

Cutting one of them in half, Shay dropped a piece of the fish on to her salad. 'I am the eldest and only son of a man who pulled himself up by his bootstraps and brought the last remaining branch of the Gallaghers kicking and screaming out of the bog.'

'I haven't got a clue what that means.' Jane forked up a sliver of the crab cake and let it melt on her tongue. When she got back to New York, no more of this . . .

She looked over at Shay pushing his food around his plate.

New York seemed very, very far away at that moment.

'Don't let him put you off your food, because then I'll have to eat it, and I'll get fat, and that'll just be another thing on your father's long list of crimes against humanity.'

She loved it when he smiled. 'I have two younger sisters, the little one is brilliant, finishing her masters in Trinity, and well able – and willing – to take over my place in the family firm.' He decided to eat, because good food was more important than bad blood.

'I grew up being told what I was going to do, and when, and was kept separate from the rest of the Gallagher riff raff, who were supposedly lunatic arty types, living hand to mouth and all that carry on. Every summer', and his eyes lit up at the memory, 'I would run away to my granny's in Clare – that's Niall's gran as well, he was always there, that's why we're good mates – and throw myself on her mercy. My father was nothing in the face of his mother, but I would get an annual bollocking, come autumn. It made the rest of the year all the worse for it, but . . . I couldn't help it.'

'I used to run away from home all the time,' Jane replied. 'To my crazy Auntie Margie, who had lived on a commune most of her life and then moved home to raise goats and make pottery. She was a hippie, and she used to grow pot in the shed.'

'Have you any sisters or brothers?' This was turning out to be a real date.

Ick, this was like some kind of first date or something. 'Two older brothers. They stayed on the – they're still at home.'

'Stayed on the . . .?' Shay left the phrase blank, but Jane shook her head. 'On the range? On the homestead? On the farm?'

Jane looked up at him, her eyes slightly guarded. Oh, what the hell. 'Cattle. Big money, when the market would bear . . . when it didn't, when the winters were bad, or when there was a virus, then . . . then very little money.'

'And you went off to the big bad city.' Shay nodded. It made sense to him. He couldn't imagine why she seemed so tetchy all of a sudden. 'I can't picture you out on a farm, rustling cattle.'

'I've worked hard to ensure that.' She sighed, and looked down at her clean plate. 'It wasn't *Little House on the Prairie*, but it wasn't what I wanted, at all. I thought I might like – Aunt Margie put it into my head to go to art school, but that wasn't even what I – well, I got in to an art college in Brooklyn, and I never went back.'

'Ever?' Shay couldn't believe that. 'Holidays? Summer break?'

'Miranda and Darren took care of me . . .' She tilted her head, thought about that. It was true. She'd always taken it for granted. 'I worked my way through school and stayed in the dorms in the summer, and worked in the city, and discovered, well, "the stage",' she said ironically, wanting to end this stupid trip down memory lane, 'and knew . . .' And knew that I wanted more than anything to act.

'That you wanted to be an actress.'

'As with your father, *actress* was a dirty word in my house, exactly the kind of thing I wanted to get away from.' The waiter cleared their dishes, and Jane tilted back her wine glass.

'But did you not—'

'So what does your mother think of all this?' she cut across him.

Right, so. Back to me. 'Aoife is the perfect sort of Dublin Four matron, always off at a high tea given in aid of some charity. She is the perfect judge's wife. But she's a good mum, she always had my back.' Shay drained his glass as well.

'And Fiona? You never explained—'

Shay topped up their wine. 'Fiona. The perfect judge's wife-in-training. We'd— this is ridiculous, it sounds like a sitcom – no offence – we'd been through school together, our families knew each other, if you take my meaning . . .' Shay shook his head. 'I don't even remember asking her to marry me. She cooled off when I began to make noises about quitting the profession, and posted me back the engagement ring – which I don't even remember buying – when I did call it quits.'

Jane swallowed. 'You must have been in love with her.'

'Must I?' Shay asked, and the waiter set down their main course.

They ate in silence. Jane found that she was starving.

Shay raised his glass. 'I'd like to propose a toast.'

'Just as long as the whole room's not in on it,' Jane joked.

Shay smiled, and then turned serious. 'To *She Stoops*. To opening night. To . . . the future.' He paused and stroked his wine glass down hers. 'To us.'

Jane licked her lips. 'To . . . us.'

Jane had dessert.

Jackie drove them back to the cottage, casting an ominous eye over Shay as he paid the fare. That's nice of him, thought Shay, looking out for Jane. He hoped that Jackie'd actually have something to worry over.

'Will you have a whiskey with me?' Shay whispered

as they let themselves in to the house. Jane nodded, and went into the front room.

She didn't care if it was practically May – she wanted a fire. She went over to the hearth and, lighting a few candles on the mantelpiece, set about starting a fire.

May! How did that happen? Her return ticket was dated for next Friday, opening night; she'd have to change it, but to when? She thought about that letter she'd received, the letter from Fox, and decided not to think about it.

What has happened to you, Janie? she thought as she set the firelighter to flame. You should have rung them – called them! – by now. She watched the turf begin to smoulder and fiddled with the tongs, adding another briquette to the drawing fire.

I have a commitment, and I always see my commitments through, she snapped. I haven't completely lost the run of myself.

Shay came in to see her laughing, kneeling in front of the roaring blaze.

Fire.

Candles.

Whiskey.

Yes!

'What're you laughing about?' he asked, and dropped down to sit on the floor, leaning up against one of the sofas.

'I'm even thinking in Irish slang, now. I was kind of a bitch to Miranda about it.' She took her glass of Jameson's and stared moodily into the amber liquid. 'I thought she was being pretentious. And after having moved to a little outpost on the Atlantic Ocean! I just couldn't believe that anyone in their right mind would want to leave New York.'

'I've never been there.'

'Go 'way!' Jane exploded, and they both laughed, and then shushed each other.

'I've been to China, and Australia, and all over

Europe, and Africa, and Jesus knows where else, but never to New York.'

'You'll have to—' Come visit me, she was going to say, but the words got trapped in her throat.

'I will, someday. I have those dreams of Broadway, remember?' He smiled at her, and shifted over, making room for her next to him.

She hesitated. She remembered, all right, remembered being bitchy to him, too, afraid he was drawing out her own most desperate dreams, remembered feeling hopeless and angry and frightened and disoriented and—

She sat down next to him, hard, and said, simply, 'I remember.'

They listened to the kindling crackle. 'Will you invite your father?' she asked.

Shay shrugged. 'For form's sake, I suppose.'

'Cathleen has invited everyone she's ever met.'

'She's a decent skin, is Cathleen. Naomi asked me for a few comps herself.'

'Aren't she and Dec adorable? They must communicate psychically, or something.' Jane took the cigarette Shay passed her, let him light it. Their eyes met in the flame of the match, and Jane looked away.

Well, will I or won't I? I'd rather not think about it too much . . . Aren't you crazy about him after all, kind of? I'd rather not think about that too much, either . . .

'I knew she was going to be a godsend. And you were dead right about Sinead. She's bloody terrific.'

Jane nodded smugly. 'I'm always right.'

'She and Paraic seem to be . . . getting on well.'

'They're old news.' Jane exhaled. 'Saw that one from the first read through. I think Mihal and Theresa are, um, an item.' Was this conversation a good idea?

Jane stilled as Shay passed a hand down her hair, once, twice, three times.

Maybe . . . maybe not. Maybe?

'I can't let my imagination go there, frankly,' Shay said softly.

'No,' said Jane, shifting ever so slightly towards him. 'No.'

'I don't want to talk about them. Jane.'

No, the last thing she needed right now was talk. 'Let's not talk at all.'

The turf fell apart in the grate, and flames licked up into the chimney, bronzing Jane's skin as she turned fully towards Shay. He opened his mouth – they had to talk, he had to tell her, he had to say, Jane I'm mad about you, I really fancy you, I more than fancy you, I might even lo— he gulped, stopped himself, let her touch his face, let her brush the hair off his forehead, let her put a finger gently, teasingly to his lips.

She shook her head again, threw their cigarettes into the fire, turned and slid her hip up against his so that she was facing him, let him snake a hand around the back of her neck, let him look at her like that, the way someone looks at you when he wants to kiss you –

This time, it started out slowly, building as the fire built, a spark here, a struggling flame there, as they gently explored one another's mouths. Lips touched lightly, searchingly, and tongues dipped in and out, again and again, the sweetness of their breath intermingling, and little kisses dropped along jawlines and necks, hands grew increasingly demanding as the fire stoked, a fire that had been banked by nerves and uncertainty and now, given the slightest stir, was soon burning out of control.

They never made it to the couch.

Clothes were dispensed of with the same kind of mindless abandon that had visited them at the theatre, but this time they were aware of dancing light upon their bodies as they tormented each other with their mouths. Jane trailed her fingers up and down Shay's chest, running her hands down over his back and over his thighs, revelling in his fitness and strength.

Shay tickled her once, just to let her know he hadn't forgotten, and she smiled at him, a smile that tore at his heart as he caressed her belly, ran his hands down the side of her body, caressed her breasts and nuzzled her neck, breathing in that smoky scent she'd worn the very first day he'd met her, the scent that had tortured him from the start.

Their mouths met again, hotter, wetter, wanting, wanting, and as they stretched out in front of the fire, Shay desperately wanted a stronger connection, one that went beyond the mere yearnings of their bodies, one that would give him something to go on, one that would let him know that she wanted him, too, much more than this moment, maybe, maybe for a much longer time.

'Jane, I have to tell you, Jane, we have to talk –'

'We do not,' she whispered, and slithered her hands down his body and touched him, stroked him, until language escaped him, and she laughed gently into his mouth as she kissed him again.

The fire flashed higher as he petted and stroked her in return, finding her own heat, and for her, language became inarticulate moans as he led her higher and higher. She wrapped her thighs around his hips, and as he slid into her warmth, they both sighed and clutched and moved, moved, moved until the last lick of flames consumed them, leaving them spent and tangled on the hearth rug in front of the cheerily dancing flames.

The turf smoked, and the candles threatened to burn out. Jane wanted to cuddle, hated herself for wanting to. It couldn't be that way. It wasn't that way. She was leaving soon – but couldn't begin to tell him.

I could hold her, he thought, for ever, here on the hearth rug. He could touch her for ever, but already he felt her withdrawing, could feel her leaving him, somehow.

I'm not a complete eejit – the last time notwith-standing. I know how to – to court a woman, he thought, although they'd seemed to have skipped over that part rather handily. He rubbed his face in her hair even though he could sense she was ready to jump up and leave the room. He felt like he was missing something, some crucial piece of information that would let him know what he should doing next.

'Come to bed. My bed. You liked it well enough, that first day.' That seemed harmless enough –

Jane struggled to get up, and grabbed one of the blankets that were folded on the couch. 'No. Busy day tomorrow. Busy days ahead. Full run throughs and all.'

It was impossible for a man not to get a bit of an ego bruise off that. 'What's the story? Don't you—' *Like* me? Jesus, that was pathetic.

'I don't – well, it's too late, I suppose, but I, I don't want to get involved. We're working together, and . . . I don't want to get involved. In that way.' Jane ran her fingers through her hair, and dropped her head into her hands.

'Too bloody late, missus,' Shay said, and laughed shortly. 'Too bloody late for that.'

'Of course it's not,' Jane retorted, gathering up her things. 'Look, it happens all the time, look at the rest of the cast, passions run high, you're working for this common thing, hormones start raging, and boom. We both get what we're after.'

'You're dead right,' said Shay equably, and got a little thrill of spiteful triumph when he saw Jane blanch. 'Just a one-off – well, two-off. An occupational hazard, we could even go so far as to say?'

'We could.' Wasn't this what she wanted? Wasn't this the best way to handle this? Wasn't this the thing to do, because if she didn't, she was afraid she'd—

'Well, I won't.' Keep those tables turning, Shay boy. 'I don't say. That's not what this is for me. And I'll make sure that you understand that. I'll make sure you know exactly what it is I'm after.' Kissing her gently, lightly on the mouth, he slapped her on the bum and sauntered out of the room.

Jane stamped her foot. Then looked down at it in disbelief.

He made me stamp my foot! Understand what? she wondered. The eejit bollocks of a—

She sank down on to the floor and stared at the glowing embers. She felt something, in her chest, a little squeeze, and then a lightness, a feeling of – of wanting and hope and confusion. I can't go there again, she thought. 'I can't go there again, ever,' she said aloud, desperately. She wrapped her arms around her legs, chin on her knees, as if by curling herself up as tightly as she could, physically, she could protect herself emotionally as well. 'I can't, I can't, I can't . . .' she whispered. *Can I?*

As the fire burned down to ash, Jane sat there, in the semi-dark, and started to wonder, with a little jump of trepidation mixed with hope, exactly what he was after – and how he'd show her.

'It's like bloody Massey's in here,' Sinead quipped, and eyed Jane in the dressing-room mirror.

'I don't know what that is.' Jane busily began applying foundation.

'It's the funeral home,' Marie replied, and she and Sinead had a fine old laugh.

The women had each staked out their own areas in the narrow space, and commandeered their own personal chairs and stretches of the make-up table, the boundaries of which were strenuously guarded. Woe unto anyone who should transgress these boundaries, and mess about with another's things.

Jane's things were currently fighting for space with enormous bunches of flowers.

Roses. Sunflowers. Tulips. Lilies. Gerbera daisies and snapdragons. It was impossible to ignore them, and she couldn't bring them back to the cottage, because then Shay would think—

Who knows what Shay would think? thought Jane, but of course, that wasn't true at all.

Everyone knew what Shay was thinking. And no one was bothering to whisper about it any more.

'Would you ever lay off on the flowers, mate?' grumbled Paraic as he suited up for the day's work.

'You're making life miserable for the rest of us,'

groused Martin, as he brushed down his costume. 'Forty years of marriage, toddling along well enough, and now it's all, "Sure, when's the last time you bought me an auld posey?" and "The romance is gone, all gone."' He glared at Shay in the men's dressing-room mirror.

'Sorry, lads, but I'm a man on a mission,' he said airily as he knotted his cravat.

'Some mission,' said Paraic, as he buttoned up his waistcoat. 'Not doing too well in the wooing department, far as I can see.'

Shay scowled as the slippery cravat slid through his fingers. 'It's just a matter of time.'

'Time is relative, of course,' said Martin, sitting down in his chair and starting to lace up his shoes. 'When's she off for home, anyway?'

'Home?' Shay felt confused, and then realised that Martin meant New York, not the farm. A farm girl, he grinned to himself. Never in a million years would he have guessed.

He looked up and saw both men staring at his reflection. 'Em . . .' New York. Home. Bollocks. He'd forgotten about that.

'When are you going to put that poor fella out of his misery?' demanded Marie as she buttoned up Jane's frock. 'It's throwing my own marriage into turmoil.'

'Marie,' said Jane as the woman jerked a bit too briskly at the dress. 'In fairness, it's only a bunch of flowers.'

'Don't be such a thicko,' Sinead sniped. 'It's obvious the man is daft for ya.'

'What if I don't know how I feel about him?' Jane retorted, and the question was greeted with snorts of derision.

'If I broke a futon with a fella, I don't think I'd have to think too hard about what I thought of him,' Sinead laughed.

'What's the point of thinking what I think of him, if I

am thinking anything about him like *you* think I should be thinking, when I'm leaving after the run?' There, she'd said it.

'You'd better step up the pace, mate,' said Paraic, turning to look down the back of Shay's frock coat, checking his tails weren't crushed.

'It's the fast pace I'm trying to counteract,' moaned Shay.

'You young people,' Martin began, before he was shouted down by the other two. He tried again. 'You never get the balance right. A little heat here. A little cool there. A flower or two. Or *two*, mind. Nowadays, it's all legovers and then scrambling to get back to the courting part. It's a disgrace.'

'So is she leaving or isn't she?' Paraic asked, and Shay looked at him blankly.

Marie sat down heavily in her chair and Sinead reached over to grip Jane's hands. 'Sure you can't stay for ever, can you?' she cried.

'I didn't think of that,' Marie sighed. They both looked at her with empathy shining in their eyes. 'There's no chance of an extension on your visa?'

'It's a terrible thing, trying to get work permission here,' Sinead added.

'Even if you got a theatre to sponsor you, it's not easy, I know; my sister's husband's cousin is Australian, and it was no end of bother.' Marie shook her head.

'I can't stay here!' Jane as good as wailed. 'I – I have to work, I have to go back to work –'

'Ah, well, greater range of parts on offer, to be sure, to be sure.' Marie allowed herself a twinge of envy. 'I remember when Martin and I were in the Lincoln Centre with a Synge Festival back in—'

'I work in television,' Jane cut in rather desperately. 'I work in TV.'

'She lost her job, and her flat, and her luggage,' Shay explained. 'She could just as well stay here.'

Martin shook his head. 'It's a huge gamble. And for someone of her skill, we've not got enough to go round, over here. Marie and I are only getting our hands back in after years in the wilderness.' He stared down at his feet, and Paraic clapped him on the back.

'I can't imagine that she'd go back to producing, not after—' Of course he could imagine it, and Shay's heart sank.

'I can't be an actress, not now, not at my age!' Jane stared at her reflection, and picturing it, shuddered.

Marie frowned and rose. 'Jane, you're a lovely woman at the end of the day, and a hardy article altogether – but I wouldn't have taken you for a fool.'

'Nice,' Jane hissed as the woman swept out of the room.

'She's right.' A voice came from the back corner, and for the second time, Theresa spoke her mind. 'It's bad enough you can't see a lovely fella throwing himself at you, but if you throw away your talent, then you've no more sense than a donkey.' And she slipped out of the room quietly.

Jane appealed silently to Sinead, who shook her head. 'You won't get any sympathy from me,' she said, eyeing the profuse arrangements that clogged the make-up table. 'And in fact,' she went on darkly, 'it wouldn't hurt any of the lads around here to step up to the mark.' She stomped out of the room in search of Paraic.

'Ah, Jesus, she's going to start bollocking me about flowers again,' said Paraic, responding to Sinead's demand he meet her in the wings. 'You want to get this sorted, mate, before the run, or it's all banjaxed.' He hurried out of the room.

'At least ask her what her plans are.' Martin shot his reflection one last look, and went out to the stage.

'You're all eejits,' offered Jason, who hefted himself out of his chair. 'Ask Darren what to do. For fuck's sake.' And he left as well.

Darren. Of course.

'I've never seen so many flowers,' sighed Darren, fidgeting.

'Stop fidgeting,' Miranda ordered. 'Lift up your head.' She snapped another portrait of Darren in front of one of the parlour flats.

'I don't see the point of taking my photograph on the stage,' he began.

'You need a new picture, those last ones I took are too old. And', Miranda went on tantalisingly, 'this may open up a whole new range for your work.'

'I'm not interested in set design,' Darren muttered, then smiled blindingly.

'You never know,' Miranda teased. 'Think of La Scala.' And she caught an intensely attractive and focused look on Darren's face.

'Hmph,' he said, and dreamed of Italy. 'Anyway, what's going on with them?'

'I promised Niall I'd butt out,' Miranda explained. 'And what's up with him? He's been shut up in his studio all day, every day.'

'Working?' Darren offered.

'I guess,' Miranda said, and she fussed unnecessarily with the settings on her Nikon.

'You've got nothing to worry about, you know.' Darren tugged on a long red curl.

'I know, but it's kind of a hobby.' And their laughter was cut off by a furtive-looking Shay.

'Darren, mate, can I have a word?' Miranda moved off and went to download her images.

'I need to talk to you, too; some of the things you were going to use for props are—'

Shay cut him off. 'Sure, sure, but not now. C'mere, I

need your help with something.' He led him off down the stage and towards the back of the house. When Jane came out onstage and began to warm up, Shay dragged Darren deeper into the shadows.

'What am I doing wrong?' he demanded, and Darren looked confused.

'I think you're doing great, really well. Jane usually blows her leading men off the stage, but you're more than a match for her—'

'That's not what I— well, that means something, but I mean in real life, not in fiction.'

'Ah.' He arched a brow. 'So you come running to the gay male best friend, hmmm?'

Shay wriggled uncomfortably, but nodded, shame-facedly.

Darren literally bit his tongue. This is so not my business, he thought and far be it from me to betray a friend's secrets, but he was being asked directly, sort of, wasn't he? And he wanted to *help*. And poor Shay, he's mortified . . .

'In all the years I've known her, Jane was only in love once, and she'd never admit to it, even now. She was young, impressionable, aching to find someone that fit into her new life . . .' Darren got lost in the memory.

Shay cleared his throat impatiently as he saw Jane shade her eyes with her hand, looking out into the house.

Darren shook his head. 'Got lost there. She dated this guy all through college, which, I might point out, was the exact antithesis of what she set out to do when she moved to New York, and he dumped her the day after graduation. He didn't want to stay, you see. He had other plans all along, and never told her he was heading back to Missoula or wherever. An architect, if I remember correctly.

'It must sound extreme, but she never dated anyone again, not for any length of time. She spent years cultivating her hard-nosed, thick-skinned, high-powered producer image. She doesn't want to fall in love again.'

Shay hung his head.

'Or so she *says*.' Darren gripped Shay's arm, noticing that Jane had noticed them. 'Frankly, I don't believe her. And you could change her mind.'

'How, mate? That's what I'm asking you!' Shay's voice cracked with the strain. 'Do you know if she's— she's going to leave, isn't she?'

Darren took pity on him. 'I'd be surprised if she didn't, Shay,' he said gently. 'But does that mean you couldn't follow?' With that delightfully loaded question, Darren hurried back to the stage. 'We have to talk about those so-called props!' he sang, and brushing by the curious and glowering Jane, he disappeared backstage.

'What was that about?' she challenged Shay as he joined her on the stage.

'Business,' he replied. Personal business . . . and he began his own vocal warm-up.

Cathleen clapped her hands and the various squeaks, shrieks and bellows wound down. 'Let's take it from the top.'

Half an hour later, Cathleen clapped her hands again, in aggravation.

'Will the company come out onstage, please?' She stood, and raked her hands through her hair. Surely they couldn't be losing it this close to show time? The timing was off, the energy was not so much low as subterranean, and there was an air of tension hanging over the proceedings that hadn't been there four days ago –

Ah, right. She bored holes into Shay as he moved downstage.

'It's a bit ropey today, hey?' he commented.

'That's one way of putting it,' Cathleen replied, and hopped up onstage.

She was five foot nothing, but she was bristling. Jane might have enjoyed it immensely if she hadn't become inexplicably nervous throughout the afternoon. She was off, they were all off, but it was the kind of thing that could snowball out of control, resulting in an avalanche of stage fright. Jane was terrified of stage fright.

But Cathleen's stern voice pulled her out of her internal soap opera. 'Lads – and ladies – I know we've been working hard, and I know that we all could use a bit of a break, and I intend to propose that we take the rest of the afternoon off –' She looked at Shay and he nodded. 'And by "off" I mean no going to the pub, no shopping, no messages in town, but off, home; you and your scripts. We've only four days left to opening and we can't start flagging now; it'll only make us more nervous on the day.

'Now, is there anything going on that I need to know about?'

That was very American, Jane thought, impressed.

Cathleen cast her eye around the group. Marie and Martin were at opposite ends of the stage, highly unusual for them. Sinead was scowling down at her feet and Paraic's face was a study in hang-doggedness. Mihal and Theresa seemed to have gone off one another as well, and only Jason was his usual, detached self.

'Anything going on backstage, perhaps? Any little niggling wants that we haven't seen to, anything at all?' She looked at Marie encouragingly, tossing a look in Jane and Shay's direction for good measure.

'If there's anything we can do, Cathleen or Jane or I, you've got to let us know, lads – everyone.' Shay turned to the group, arms opened expansively. 'It is, as Jane said, not too long ago, all of us in this together. It's our show.'

Looks volleyed around the stage, as Sinead widened her eyes meaningfully at Marie, and Marie jerked her chin at Martin, who shrugged, and looked over at Paraic, who hunched his shoulders and looked pleadingly at Sinead.

Mihal stepped forward. 'There seems to be something

of a drama unfolding backstage as regards a certain lady receiving certain items from a certain gentleman.' His bald head gleamed under the lights, and as his voice filled the room, the others got the impression that he was still speaking as his character. 'While it is, most certainly, the business of only the parties involved, it seems to be impacting adversely upon the general morale. It's nothing that a few well-purchased and thoughtful roses mightn't solve. I imagine.'

Jane blushed a deep and painful scarlet, and Shay gritted his teeth. 'Looks like I'll have to cancel the skywriter.' Everyone chuckled, except for Jane, who was rapidly resembling a radish having a heart attack. 'And that full page ad in *Variety*.' The chuckles turned to giggles. 'And the RTÉ Orchestra, that was meant to come by for a spot of serenading—'

Jane spoke over the laughter. 'Shay! I need to talk to you. Now.'

She stomped off towards the dressing room, realising when she crossed the threshold that it was not the best place to have this conversation; when she turned to leave, she bumped fully into Shay.

His hands came up and rubbed at her shoulders. 'Sorry, pet, I didn't mean—'

'You never do,' she bit out, mortified. She cast a look over her shoulder at the hothouse that the room had become, and moving past him, led the way to the alley.

'Let's scarper, lads,' Marie cried, and they all fled to change and go.

The brisk air of the late-afternoon cooled Jane's cheeks somewhat, and she began to pace up and down the narrow passage. Shay nudged at a pile of burnt – was that wood? And fabric?

'You know, I think bloody Niall torched all that lumber!' He bent down to get a closer look.

'Shay.' He looked up at her and rose at the look on her face. There was anger there, to be sure, and discomfort, but something else he couldn't quite figure out, something beyond the momentary embarrassment, something beyond confusion.

'This has to stop.' Jane took a deep breath, and massaged her tightening belly.

'I didn't mean to embarrass ya, Jane,' Shay said, contritely. 'I went a bit far, you know me—'

'I don't know you! I hardly know you! We just met, by chance, and I was at a loose end, and I got involved in this show, and that's it!' She clenched her fists against a slow, sad feeling creeping into her chest. 'That's all it can be!'

'Why?' It's not that plonker from university, is it? he wondered.

'I – I made the mistake of – of having an affair with my boss, where I used to work, the television station – you know where I worked.' Why was she going into this? 'I thought I could handle it. I did handle it, I handled it just fine, but it blew up in my face, and now the same thing is happening and I—' Shay came towards her and she moved quickly out of his way. 'This can't go on.'

'What can't go on?' Shay folded his arms. I'm not going down without a fight, he determined.

'This! The flowers, and the notes in the flowers, which they –' she gestured madly towards the theatre – 'don't know about, thank God. The – the poems, and the sentiments, and the – the—'

'Courtship.' Shay smiled at her irate expression. 'We call it courtship over here, Janie.'

'It has to stop! What's the point?'

Shay tilted his head. 'What do you mean, point?'

'I'm leaving. After the run. The next day, in fact.'

'OK.' He tilted his head the other way as she looked at him incredulously.

'OK? Just "OK"? That's it?'

He shrugged. 'I'm glad you let me know. Thank you.'

' "Thank you"?!' she gasped. 'So that's all this was to

you, it was just a show-time fling, just a – just a—'

He walked towards her, slowly, backing her close to the wall but not up against it – he'd never hear the end of it if the frock got spoiled. 'I didn't say that. I said "thank you". Now I know that I'm running out of time.' He tweaked her nose and she batted his hand away.

'You're as thick as two short planks!' Jane started jabbing him in the chest. 'No more flowers. No more notes. No more making me cups of coffee in the mornings. No more packing my goddamn lunch! No more looks at me, like – like you're going to kiss me any minute. No more of any of it!' Chest heaving, she glared at him.

He merely smiled.

'Ah, Jane,' he murmured, leaning in and stealing the lightest, quickest of kisses. 'I'm not going to be making promises I can't keep.'

On his way out, he passed the florist's deliveryman, carrying a huge arrangement of deep red cabbagehead roses.

'They said I'd find Jane Boyers out here?'

Shay laughed as her strangled scream followed him down the hall.

'... And apparently, some of that gear of Des's is worth money,' Shay finished, as the food got passed around the cottage's dining-room table.

'More than money,' corrected Darren. 'A small fortune.'

'Go 'way,' scoffed Niall. 'He and Auntie May lived out of a caravan.'

'Nevertheless, they had exquisite, if eclectic, taste,' Darren insisted.

'You know that nasty-looking tea set, the one that looks like cabbages?' Shay asked.

'It is utterly one-of-a-kind,' Darren breathed. 'I've never seen a full set, and in mint condition. Down to the teaspoons with the ceramic handles. It's almost priceless.'

Shay gestured with his fork. 'There you go.'

'Do you know any antiques dealers? Reputable antiques dealers?' Darren served himself up a heaping portion of lasagna.

'Who's that cousin, on your mother's side?' Shay turned to Niall.

'Alastair. You met him, Darren, the times you were here, before.' And Darren's heart skipped a beat.

'Oh, Alastair. Yes, I seem to remember him,' he said, nonchalantly, refusing to meet Miranda's smirking glance.

'He's in Italy, I think.' Niall shook his head. 'I'll ask the mother to ask the aunt.'

'Wonderful lasagna, Jane,' said Darren, hurriedly changing the subject. 'What's the occasion?'

Oh, nothing special, except that stupid Shay is 'courting' me, and I feel guilty that I haven't even bought him so much as a pint. 'Nothing special – comfort food before the big day.'

'Two days to go!' Miranda chimed in brightly. 'Let's have a toast.'

Shay stood, and they all followed suit, albeit Jane reluctantly. It just kept getting more and more complicated, this toasting thing.

'I'd like to propose a toast to Niall and Miranda, for taking me in when I had nowhere else to go, for putting up with me and my auditions and callbacks and my dyeing things in the tub, and for helping out when I needed it most. To Niall and Miranda!'

'To Niall and Miranda!' cried Darren enthusiastically, and Jane grudgingly.

'To Darren! Who stepped off his plane and literally walked into the theatre, ready to work, doing things without our even having to ask –'

'Typical,' muttered Jane.

'– and for creating the kind of setting I didn't even know how to describe. To Darren!'

'To Darren!' And the glasses rang together once more.

Jane braced herself. Shay cleared his throat. 'And to Jane!'

And that was it. To cover up the brevity, Miranda whooped, 'To Jaaaaane!', and Darren almost shattered his glass in his attempt to paper over the awkward moment.

'And to Shay,' Niall said. 'Who pulled it off.'

'Even if we weren't sure he knew what he was getting into,' added Miranda.

'And even though he had a truly bizarre attachment to

some of the junk he was trying so desperately to make work,' supplied Darren.

'Did you burn my wood?' Shay demanded of Niall.

Niall quickly jumped in. 'And at the end of the day, and in all fairness, to Shay, who is a bloody decent actor.'

Then he turned to Jane, who shook her head once, and smiled thinly.

'To Shay!' they shouted, and Jane sat down the minute her glass was in no danger of setting off some sort of cataclysm.

Jane watched Shay dish himself up more lasagna, listened to him joke and tease and tell outlandish stories about all their production woes, and couldn't have been more irritated.

He'd roped them all in, hook, line and sinker – and Jane was too pissed off to worry about mixed metaphors at the moment. He'd hooked her worst of all, swept her up in the dream, and now she was sure he was trying to trick her into something. There he was, coming across all humble and lovable, one minute telling her he was going to make sure that she knew that he wasn't going to be taken lightly, and then embarrassing her with all that affection and flowers and whatever, and *now*, there he was, not caring less that she was leaving!

Her glass slammed down on the table.

'Jane, apologies,' Shay said, concerned. 'I've let your glass go empty.'

She sneered at him, but held out her glass.

'Ah, Jane,' he said, 'I'm sure you'll be missing these kind of meals and such, when you're back in the Big Apple.' He nodded over at Niall and Miranda. 'I'm sure we'll all think of you fondly, when we're gathered all around the table here, having the craic. I know I'd miss it. I'm sure I would.'

Miranda's eyes narrowed as she passed Darren the garlic bread, but he put a calming hand on hers. He thought he had a pretty good idea what Shay was up to.

It was devious.

It was underhanded.

Reverse psychology.

It was brilliant.

'I'm sure,' Jane agreed, and shoved her serving of salad and pasta around her plate.

'But you'll be back in the swing of things in no time, no doubt,' Shay shook his head ruefully. 'It'll be like your time in Ireland never even happened.'

Yikes. That was going an inch too far. Darren swept into the breach, a breach that, from Jane's sputtering and fondling of her butterknife, threatened to loom large.

'I understand that opening night is sold out,' he offered, scooping up another wedge of lasagna.

'And Cathleen said that all the critics will be there, too!' Miranda helped herself to some wine, and topped up Niall's glass.

'Who'd have guessed it,' Niall put in his two pence. 'It just goes to show you what a theatre town Dublin is, if a young company can come out with their debut production and get the kind of attention— ow!' Miranda's elbow retracted, and he twigged what she'd copped on to.

Both Jane and Shay had stilled, and in the low light, looked as if they'd both turned an unbecoming shade of green.

Darren mouthed 'stage fright' to Niall, and grimaced. He'd forgotten about that. Jane was breathing deeply and slowly, and her fingers were scrabbling at the tabletop. Shay simply looked mummified.

'Uncle Des also blessed Shay with a Louis Quinze, if you can believe it, *chaise de soleil* – a sixteenth-century French beach chair!' He and Miranda laughed far too loudly. 'It's seen slightly too much "loving", if you know what I mean, but it should clean up rather nicely.'

'What's that sort of thing worth?' asked Niall, and Darren was off and running.

Jane jumped up and started to clear. The breath had begun to re-enter her body, and she figured that some light aerobic activity – walking to and from the dining room – would get her back on track.

God! She'd forgotten about that feeling, that feeling of weightlessness that had nothing to do with relaxation, and everything to do with terror. The feeling that her mind was wiped clean of everything that had to do with the play, with her ability to put one foot in front of the other. She leaned over the sink – she'd never forget the time she was doing *The Cherry Orchard* and she had stood stock still, in the wings, for two hours before the curtain rose.

Shay exploded into the kitchen behind her, shoved her away from the sink, and stuck his face under the running water. When he was gasping for breath, he knew he'd be all right.

Dripping, he groped for a tea towel. As he rubbed his face dry, his voice came through, muffled, but full of agony. 'Once, when I was in *The Plough*, I was so terrified I fell asleep. They had to throw me onstage. I didn't wake up until I hit the floor.'

'We'll be fine, it happens to everyone, it happens to the best of us, I had an acting teacher once who always said, "Darling, even Olivier was crippled by it". We'll be fine, we'll be fine . . .' Jane's voice trailed off to a whisper, and Shay reached over to give her a hug –

She stepped back smartly, and as she left the kitchen, said, 'I know what you're up to.' She turned in the doorway. 'And it isn't working.'

Isn't it? he thought, and followed on behind.

Miranda was patting Niall's hand, who was too polite to ask Darren to stop carrying on about the perils of restoring Victorian claw-foot bathtubs.

'Oh, Dar, are you still kvetching about that job? Honestly!' Jane tempered it with a smile, and pinched his cheek.

'You've already one foot across the water, to be sure,' Shay said. ' "Kvetching". Next thing we know, you'll be shouting for "coffee to go" and "a bagel and schmear".'

'Not bad, considering you've never been to New York,' Jane retorted.

'Ah, well, life is long, you never know. Hey.' He put on a thick Noo Yawk accent. 'Yoo nevuhhhh knoooow!'

Miranda snuck a little look at Niall – this was turning out to be one strange dinner party. She looked to Darren for a clue, but he was smiling into his wine glass.

Her mobile sang from the front room. 'Oh, sorry, let me get that.'

Miranda's voice went from confusion to realisation to uncertainty, and she walked into the room, still on the call. 'Fine, that's great, she'll be delighted . . . of course, of course . . . no, here is fine . . . What time? . . . Right, right, OK, cheers, bye, bye, bye.'

She rang off and stood, clutching her mobile. 'That was Dublin Airport. They have your bags.'

'You've got to be kidding me.' Jane stared at her in disbelief.

'Nope. Apparently they made it all the way to Auckland and back.' Miranda knew how much her things meant to Jane, and figured she was too stunned to demonstrate her ecstasy. 'They're going to drop them down here tomorrow morning.'

'Just in time! Isn't that great,' Shay said brightly.

'Do you have a minute?' Jane asked acidly, and rising, led the way to the pantry.

Shay waggled his eyebrows at the rest of them, and jogged along behind her.

Jane jerked the chain of the light that so helpfully dangled from the ceiling, and closed the door.

'You are a wanker,' she said.

'All right,' Shay replied.

'And a plonker and a bollocks.'

'Don't forget eejit.'

'And if you think my feelings are hurt because you obviously can't wait to see the back of me—'

'You're amazing. Listen to you, and to think you didn't know what a "yoke" was—'

'So you can just cut it out, right? Just lay off the "nice knowing you, keep in touch" routine.' Satisfied, Jane made to move past him out the door.

He put out a hand, held the door shut. 'If your feelings weren't hurt, sure you wouldn't be lecturing me amongst the bags of flour.'

She faced the door, refused to turn around. 'They aren't.'

'I haven't figured how you can be such a superb actress and not know a thing about your own motivations, your own "verbs".' He slid his fingers into her silky hair –

'Ouch!' Shay jumped up and down on one foot, trying to soothe the toe she'd just stomped on. He knocked down several boxes of cereal.

'I save it all for the stage,' she said loftily, pleased by his muttered cursing.

'Not all of it, Jane,' he said when the feeling had returned to his foot. 'Not all of it.'

Jane snuck a look over her shoulder. Even in the unflattering overhead light, he looked infinitely sexy. 'Look, so we had a thing, you bought me a bunch of flowers, I never thanked you properly, so thanks, and stop – stop rejoicing in my departure.'

Shay moved a step closer. Either she would walk out now or she wouldn't. 'I may be laughing through my tears, you know.'

'You are so corny.'

'You are so prickly.'

'Stop . . . whatever it is you're doing.'

Shay leaned forward and rubbed his cheek against her hair. 'We've got three more weeks together. I want to be with you.'

Jane's eyes widened – luckily, he couldn't see. 'That's direct.'

'Yeah, I've been hanging around this American girl – woman,' he corrected himself hastily. 'She's not one for mincing words.'

If he only knew that she'd been mincing them into a fine powder. 'This has gone too far already.'

'Don't take it so seriously,' he murmured, dropping a hand lightly to her waist.

'I'm not.' Oh please, what? 'That kind of girl'? Since when? she thought.

Since him. If it was going to be anything, which it couldn't be, then it definitely wasn't going to be some hit-and-run holiday thing.

So why couldn't she just *tell* him?

'Jane.' He turned her tenderly, giving her every opportunity to rush out the door, or stamp on his toe again. 'Jane, let me kiss you.'

'Whaddaya mean, "Don't take it too seriously"? You're the one with the shagging courtship carry on and the—'

He laughed and leaned down to her, his mouth hovering over hers. 'You have done a bang-up job, learning the lingo,' he said, and kissed her softly, searchingly, and she held off as long as she could before she kissed him back. She looped her arms around his neck, and he leaned her against the shelf that held the washing powder and kissed her, slowly, kissed her for its own sake, not as the forerunner of seduction, but as the seduction itself, the end result, and she kissed him the way she hadn't kissed anyone in years, with the awareness that this was Shay, he was himself, and she kissed him for the joy of it, and the joy of him.

Niall looked at his watch. 'Cuppa, anyone?'

'That strudel was lovely, Niall,' Darren said, licking his fork clean.

'I'll have a cup of chamomile,' said Miranda, straining to see the pantry door.

'I'll make a pot, will I?' Niall rose and tiptoed into the kitchen.

'What are they up to?' Miranda said, shaking her head.

Darren rose to give Niall a hand, and called back to her. 'You have to ask? Or is it because you're practically a married woman?' Darren joked, and they heard Niall drop the kettle.

'Don't worry, honey, no pressure,' Miranda laughed. 'Thanks, Dar. Don't you know that heterosexual men get all wiggly when they hear the "M" word?'

'Not all,' Niall muttered and when he rose, came face to face with Darren.

Who smiled quizzically ... then beamed ... then pokered up at Niall's warning glance.

'Here's me running for the hills, love,' he called back, and thrust the teacups into Darren's hands.

'We should go back out there,' Jane breathed.

'We should,' Shay agreed, and they fell on each other once more.

'We shouldn't do this,' she moaned.

'Oh, we should,' he begged to differ.

She tightened her hold on his neck, and he hugged her, running his hands up and down her back. He ran his tongue teasingly over her lips, and she groaned, and he groaned, and they took it from the top.

'I think I'll turn in,' Darren yawned, and started collecting the tea things.

'Leave it, leave it.' Niall waved him away.

'We've got it,' Miranda said. 'Sweet dreams. Oh, and we'll track down Alastair for you.' She laughed as Darren primly left the room with no comment.

Miranda turned to Niall. 'I have a feeling, about

Darren and Alastair. They got on really, really well those times they met—'

'You're a hopeless romantic.' Niall framed her face in his hands. 'I love you, you know.'

It never failed to make her heart leap. 'I know.' She smiled. 'I love you, too.'

'Good.' They heard another something fall off a shelf in the pantry.

Miranda smothered a giggle. 'Will they ever come out of there?'

'Let's go find our own closed door to get behind,' Niall murmured.

'Kiss me again. You owe me one for every rose, tulip, daisy, and God knows what else.' Shay nibbled at Jane's neck.

'I'm not going to sleep with you again,' she said definitively.

'OK.'

'You're awfully agreeable—'

'Sshhhh, come here to me, and bring that mouth with you.'

Jane pulled back, looked up in his face, those golden eyes heavy with passion, and then burrowed her face in his chest. If she was going to get sad about leaving, not that she was going to, but she might – this kind of thing wasn't going to help –

'Janie, you're not going to cry, are you?' Shay asked hopefully.

'No. I never cry.' And she pulled his face down to her once more, and decided to forget about it all until tomorrow.

Thank God for opening night, thought Jane. It served to take the pressure off her celibacy.

I held out, she thought proudly. I've done more innocent snogging than I have since I was sixteen – but I held on. Ha! Take that, Mr Courtship, Mr Flower Man. Sure they'd had the odd grope backstage in between cues, a few heated sessions in the front room of the cottage, a couple of tussles in the back of taxis (never Jackie's; Jane had her boundaries), but they hadn't got naked again, and Jane felt virtuous. Sexy and randy and aching, most of the time, but virtuous that she hadn't bent to the pressure.

And the pressure of their first performance soon superseded everything.

She started doing some deep-breathing exercises that Miranda had tortured her into trying, to help mitigate the nerves. Breathing in for four, and out for four, she fingered the crystals Miranda had also given to her, and to the rest of the cast, little chunks of lapis lazuli and hematite to . . . to do something. She'd seen Miranda and Mihal standing in the hallway, having an intense conversation about the benefits of sodalite. She didn't know if they were going to work, but she figured a new superstition wasn't going to kill her.

All her old ways of fending off disaster had come rushing back, as if they'd never left. Among her rituals to ensure a good performance were: leaving the house at exactly two and a half hours before show time; striding around the stage three times before entering the dressing room; and arranging her make-up and brushes according to size in descending order from left to right.

She'd watch Marie go through her own paces, as the older woman laid out her costume in layers on her chair in dressing order, and brushed her hair with her eyes closed in what appeared to be a set number of strokes on each side while she wordlessly mouthed her lines.

The room was full of the scent of flowers, as Marie, Sinead and Theresa had been the recipients of abundant bouquets. Jane fingered Shay's latest offering: a little pot of forget-me-nots.

She started the next part of her regime, a thorough massage of her hands and feet. She was going to be fine. Just fine. And if she didn't let herself think past this night, and the handful of days before she went back to the States . . . well, that was fine, too.

Shay slid past Niall, who was busily making last-minute repairs to one of the bits of furniture in the hallway. Amazing, how the minute the front of house was off-limits, the place seemed busier than it should have been, how the numbers of the cast seemed to have trebled, how little room there was to manoeuvre.

He palmed the little stones Miranda had pressed on him. Everyone was grateful for a boost, from anything, and even Jason, who had sneered a bit, was rolling them around in his left hand. Shay laughed: since he'd arrived, Jason had done everything, from opening the dressing room door to applying his make-up, with his left hand.

Superstition. Ridiculous. Shay made for the dressing room himself, and backed out again when he realised he'd stepped over the threshold on his left foot.

He re-entered on his right. It couldn't hurt . . .

Darren stuck his head into the ladies' dressing room. 'Break a leg, everyone! See you after!'

'What time is it?' Sinead demanded in a strangled whisper. As Darren started to consult his watch, she cut off his reply. 'Don't tell me! I don't want to know!'

Marie gently set down her brush and rose to dress in silence, each item of clothing receiving the same number of pats to smooth them into place.

Theresa sat, eyes closed, still as a statue, in her corner.

'What time is it?' Sinead pleaded again.

They knew to ignore her by now.

'Break a leg!' Darren called cheerily into the men's dressing room, and getting no response but for a wave of Jason's left hand, he bustled out into the house.

Miranda moved down the hall, and grabbed some candid shots of Mihal holding his crystals to his chest and doing some deep breathing, of Martin resolutely keeping his back to the room and avoiding his own reflection until the exact moment he had to begin putting on his greasepaint, and of Shay trying to give himself a neck and shoulder massage.

'Ten minutes!' came Naomi's voice over the tannoy. It was soon followed by Naomi herself, and the excitement of the evening seemed to be having the greatest effect on her. So unflappable, so imperturbable, she was beside herself with nerves and restlessness.

'Ten minutes!' she sang from the doorway, and Sinead put her hands over her ears. 'The house is full! We've got a sold-out house!' She scampered off to spread the news to the men.

Full house. When Sinead started to hyperventilate, Theresa shoved her head down between her knees. Marie started making little whooping sounds, and Jane felt her entire body seize up, go cold.

She walked right into Shay as she blindly stumbled out of the dressing room.

'Sold out,' he croaked. 'Full house.'

'Ssshhh, ssshhh,' Jane urged hoarsely. 'It's all a lie;

there's no one out there, there's no one there at all.'

A great surge of noise rumbled out from the theatre, laughter and chitchat that seemed to grow and grow in volume and energy until it sounded like Romans waiting for the first Christian. Jane involuntarily clutched at Shay's top coat.

'You're a star, Jane, you're wonderful, you've got nothing to worry about—'

'No!' she hissed. 'We can't tempt the fates. I'm terrible, I don't know my lines, I don't even know the name of the play.' She begged him with her eyes to play along.

'Right, so, em, I'm going to lose my voice, and trip over my own feet, and fall off the stage into the audience.' Shay could see the merit of this exercise.

'OK, OK, OK, OK,' Jane mumbled, and Shay joined her until they became a chorus of nerves.

'Places, please!' came Naomi's tremulous voice over the speakers, and Jane and Shay froze as the rest of the cast moved into their positions in the wings.

Miranda saw the two of them huddled in a corner, and motioned to Niall. They stood helplessly as Shay and Jane seemed to be lost in a vortex of fear.

'Five minutes, you two,' said Niall ... which was exactly the wrong thing to say. They gaped at him, and then recommenced their inarticulate muttering.

'Do you have those crystals I gave you?' asked Miranda helplessly, and got no reply.

'Are they going to be all right?' Niall asked, starting to feel rather unnerved himself.

'Jane will be, she always is. If we could only get their minds off—' and the opening music began to play.

Shay and Jane froze further, and stared sightlessly at the floor.

'We have to get their minds off this,' Miranda said. 'We have to do something . . .'

Niall took a deep breath. He directed Shay and Jane's

attention towards himself and Miranda, going so far as to take Jane by the chin until she made eye contact.

He turned to Miranda, and framed her face in his hands. 'I wanted to wait, to uh, take you back to Brooklyn, and do this, but since we're staying here, together, uh . . .' He hadn't thought he'd be so tongue-tied, and decided to let the wee box do the talking.

Miranda's heart leapt, then fell, then seemed to stop beating as Niall held out a small, beautifully carved box.

'I know I've been keeping myself to myself the past while. I wanted this to be a surprise.'

'It's a lovely box,' Miranda whispered, and couldn't reach out to take it.

Jane and Shay came out of themselves and started to breathe again, a dawning smile on Shay's face, a stinging starting to needle Jane's eyes.

'I – I was – when you said you wanted to stay, well, I always wanted you to stay with me, Miranda. Whether it's here or anywhere else in the world. I want to be wherever you are. For always.' He gently lifted the lid.

Miranda covered her mouth with her hands, and tears started flowing down her face. Nestled in the glowing wood on a velvet pillow was a glittering ring of three round diamonds, in an old-fashioned setting.

'That's Gran's,' said Shay, choking up.

'It's lovely.' Jane wrapped her arms around her waist.

Miranda looked up at Niall, and he smiled at her.

'Take it,' he said.

'Ask me properly!' Miranda laughed.

'Will you marry me?'

And she took the ring, only to give it back to him to slip on her finger. They started to embrace, but Jane stepped between them.

'There's my cue!' She kissed Miranda, and hugged Niall, and stepped lightly, resolutely, and with great presence, on to the stage. Her voice floated back into the wings, full of life and playfulness. ' "You know our agreement, Sir. You allow me in the morning to pay and receive visits . . ." '

'Hello, cuz,' Shay murmured as he embraced Miranda, and stuck out a hand to shake Niall's heartily. 'Well done, mate. Well done – Jesus, it's almost my cue—' and he rushed off to get into position.

'I love you,' Miranda said, her eyes shining into his.

'I know,' he replied, and they moved back into the depths of the wings for a world-class snog.

On the first Monday of the run, Jane spread the newspapers across the stage manager's desk. As she leafed briskly through each one to get to the arts pages, she thought, so far so good – on Thursday, in a new supplement to the *Evening Herald*, the theatre editor had been particularly eloquent in her praise. That's a well-written review, Jane had thought admiringly, and she cut it out carefully.

The opening-night party had been a real 'hoolie', as Sinead called it, and Jane had been unusually abstemious. She'd seen Shay lurking, all night, out of the corner of her eye, and had busied herself by working the room, meeting friends and relations of the cast and accepting the praise that flowed unstintingly her way. It was a nice change from New York, where everyone was too damn cool to be kind, and she'd had an exceptionally hard time getting away from Naomi's mum, who talked a mile a minute. That explained Naomi's reticence, and Jane chuckled to herself.

Then she sighed, and gazed around the darkened theatre, the set pieces hanging in the half-light like ghosts, the wings littered with props that would need to be organised later that day. The empty house was full of little noises, creaks and groans that might have been frightening had Jane not felt so . . . at home.

Not in Ireland, although she was having a lovely time, and she'd surely be back, and would love to keep up her new friendships . . . but in the theatre. I, she thought, have badly missed this, the thrill of live performance, the strength of the bonding between the players, the myriad tragedies that always worked themselves out, the victories that no one would understand but themselves. Even the stage fright . . .

The feeling of standing there, her hand in Shay's, as they took their fifth – fifth – curtain call! The glare of the lights, the exhilaration vibrating off every one of her fellow cast members, the steady beat of approbation coming from the house, oh God! She stroked her hands down her face, and rubbed at her throat, a bit sore after yet another night of shouting and smoking . . . and, if she was being honest, a bit choked up with emotion.

It had been some 'holiday'. Jane shoved the papers off the desk and into the rubbish, carefully putting aside the reviews. She'd have to get them blown up and laminated and posted somewhere outside the theatre, maybe they could take out an ad with some of the quotes. They still had a full two weeks of houses to fill, and despite the fact that the company would certainly be able to get family and friends to get their butts in seats for the duration of the run, Jane didn't want to take any chances. And there were a few producerly things she'd need to take care of, may as well get back into the swing for, when she went over to the Fox Network.

She sighed and dropped her chin in her hands. Who knew that her disappearance would have worked in her favour? Despite that fact that it had been weeks since they'd sent that letter, when she finally did ring, the powers-that-be couldn't have made her feel like a hotter commodity. It seemed that the industry had glossed over her departure from WCTV as a 'firing' and had dubbed it 'creative differences'. Fox were offering her exactly the kind of package she'd felt she deserved from her old network: three shows a season that would be all her own, of her own conception, and an Executive Vice President of Production plaque on the door to her corner office.

So why did she feel so blah?

She closed her eyes and relived some of the high points of the last few performances: her hilarious banter with Sinead had reached a level of finesse that was incredible when you took into account that this was Sinead's first show; the joy of playing opposite Jason, whose own personality came to life when he was playing someone else; watching Marie and Martin from the wings, their presence and professionalism lighting up every scene; Mihal and Theresa and Paraic . . . and Shay.

She licked her lips, and tried to ignore the lump in her throat. She loved watching his transition from the unsure bumbling Marlow, when she played her scenes with him as Kate, to the cocky assurance he assumed when he thought she was a chambermaid. She allowed herself a sigh, a longing sort of sigh, and remembered his eyes as they drank her in every time he saw her enter the playing space.

Too bad I don't do relationships, she thought briskly. That's what it's been about all this time, me trying to keep away from him. I know his kind, she thought darkly, it's a hop, skip and jump into gooey loverland, holding hands and reading the Sunday papers over bagels and coffee, with a dog not too far behind.

But if I did do relationships—

'I thought I'd find you here.' Shay stepped up on to the stage, a bag under his arm. 'Did you read the one from the *Indo*?'

'Hmmm, a bit lacklustre, but we can pull out a few quotes.' Jane handed him the collection of reviews.

'I have a set of my own,' he laughed, embarrassed. 'They loved you.'

'You, too,' she said, shifting things around the desk meaninglessly.

'Did you eat?' She shook her head. 'I knew it,' he scolded. 'You take terrible care of yourself.'

'I do *not*,' Jane said firmly.

He loved making her shout. 'Here you go. For old times' sake.' He passed her a cup of takeaway coffee, and unwrapped a wadge of aluminium foil.

'Butties,' Jane groaned, and grabbed one up – for old times' sake.

She made short work of it. 'I saw you talking to that agent on Friday.'

Shay nodded, and swallowed. 'I didn't like him, he reminded me of Ronan, all grown up.'

Jane laughed, and scooped up another butty. 'Don't get too picky, now. You ought to sign with someone right away, based on the strength of this show.'

'Ummm,' Shay replied, getting his mouth around another bacon sandwich. 'I think I might like to do a bit of study.'

Jane's brow furrowed as she picked up her third delectable slice of white bread and butter and rasher. 'You're not procrastinating, are you? You've got a problem with that.'

'You know, Jane, I'd appreciate it if you wouldn't beat around the bush.' Right, just one more . . . 'No, I was gassing with Martin about it – yer man's got miles of experience – and he thought I might benefit from some time in drama school.' He shrugged. 'I meant to go, anyway, may as well be a mature student.'

'It's a big commitment.' Jane's heart sank. She'd hoped he might – might come and visit . . . 'But you'll be great.'

'Cheers.' A gentleman, he left her the last one.

'Will you go back to Trinity?' she asked, staring woefully at the butty before she gave up the ghost.

'Don't know,' he said blithely. 'But I'd best get me arse in gear if I want to start study in the autumn. And I'll sell whatever gear Darren tells me to, give myself a bit of a funding grant.'

Jane nodded. 'Great. Great.'

'May even look to producing another show. Gerard – ah, he's a decent skin, at the end of the day – he said he'd give me a preferential rate.'

'Don't forget to count the lamps,' Jane joked, and looked away.

Shay shot her a look from beneath his eyelids. 'It won't be the same without you.'

'Of course it won't,' Jane said blithely, crushing the aluminium foil.

'I couldn't have done this without you,' he murmured.

'Of course you couldn't,' she countered.

'It's been nice having you around the gaff, too. Well, Niall's gaff.'

'And Miranda's. Will you be moving out?' Jane poured three sugars into her latte.

Sugar? Shay took that as a promising sign. 'I've got a cousin who owns a place in town and might rent me out a room. Yeah, looking forward to following through on this acting gig – it's down to you that I even got up there at all.'

'Ah, sure,' Jane croaked, and mangled her coffee cup. 'Have you made your reservation?'

'Yes. The day after the load out – get out.' She really could use a cigarette.

'When do you start work?' Keeping it carefree was killing him.

Jane shook her head. 'No, *negotiations* start, a few days after I get back. There's haggling and nurgling and wangling to do. Don't want to look too eager. It may take weeks.'

'Jesus. Different world altogether.' They smiled, and Jane looked away.

'Jane.' He waited until she looked up at him defiantly. 'I'll miss you.'

'Of course you will,' she said gruffly, and then smiled. 'You'll never meet another producer like me.'

He smiled too. 'I'll never forget that cab journey, when you started going on about the fifty cents—'

'I'll never forget you roaring "Fifty cents!" at Ronan that day,' Jane retorted.

'We've got some lovely memories,' he said, looking at her.

'Yes,' she said, looking at her hands.

'Can you not be with me, just for the time we've left?' he asked.

She shook her head. 'I can't.'

Shay sat back, and clapped his hands on his knees. 'Ah, well. Can't blame a man for trying.'

Jane squeezed his coffee cup into a tight little ball and pitched it into the bin.

'Ah, well, that's the actor's life, I reckon; ships passing in the night, the passionate romps, the glamour of the brief encounter—'

'Shay!' Jane said firmly. 'Quit while you're ahead.'

He grinned, and rose. 'So we'll keep it just mates, till the end of the run?'

Unable to speak, Jane simply nodded, and Shay strolled off backstage to organise the props.

Someday, when she was safely back in New York, she'd figure out why, at this moment, everything hurt.

Someday, he'd get past that last defence. Shay smiled to himself and thought: and much, much sooner than she thinks.

Sinead threw her arms around Jane once more. Any time Jane was an arm's length away, Sinead couldn't resist another hug.

'I can't thank ya enough, Jane,' she cried. 'I had the time of my life.'

'You're a star, Shinny,' Jane said, patting her on the back.

'I got my name in *The Irish Times*! She stepped back, winked at Jane as she picked up the box she'd dropped, and moved away. 'And I fell in love to boot!'

Jane watched her carry the box out to the waiting van as the company loaded out of the theatre. Was it as easy as that? 'Sinead and Paraic fell in love' – could it be that simple?

Whatever inconveniences they'd suffered in Gerard's house, one of them was not the get out. Everything packed up quick as a wink, and they didn't need to break down the lighting plan or take anything back to a rental house, or even sweep up after themselves – Gerard had a crew coming in the next day. It just about made up for the lighting debacle, thought Jane, and she smiled again over the memory of Naomi struggling up the centre aisle, arms full of lamps.

The costumes were folded away, and the wigs sealed into hermetic boxes. Since Niall had burnt all of the unwieldy flats, they didn't have to worry about them, and

Darren was painstakingly removing his handiwork from the frames, which Niall would eventually break apart.

Jane dusted down the desk and surreptitiously tucked a copy of the performance's programme into her playscript. She snuck a look around to see if anyone was watching, and also slid in the sugar packets she'd used the Sunday she and Shay had the butties together. It was the last time they'd had a private moment; even with their days off, he seemed to have been disappearing earlier and earlier, and their only contact was during the show. She allowed herself that fraction of sentiment, along with the pot of forget-me-nots he'd given her, the last of the flowers . . .

She briskly set about checking the drawers for anything they might have left behind and, satisfied, rose to help carry out some boxes. She stopped short of ploughing right over Naomi.

'Naomi, you're so quiet!' she exclaimed. 'I didn't see you there at all.'

'I wanted to thank you for giving me a chance,' Naomi said softly, and handed Jane a card and a small, flat, wrapped package.

'I don't know what we would have done without you,' Jane said, and gave the girl a hug. 'You've got a great career ahead of you, you know.'

'I got a gig working in the Gate over the summer,' Naomi burst out, and beamed proudly.

'That's fantastic! Don't let them take advantage of you,' Jane warned. 'But I imagine you'll be in charge of production in a matter of weeks.' They hugged again, and Jane felt a prickle in her eyes.

Get outs always kicked up a lot of dust.

Tucking the gift into her handbag, Jane lifted the box again, only to have to put it down once more to shake Mihal's hand.

'A pleasure working with you,' he intoned, and Theresa came over to say her goodbyes as well.

'Good luck to you, and I expect we'll be reading all about you in the New York papers.' It almost sounded like a warning, but before Jane could respond, the pair of them left by the stage door, hand in hand.

Jane grabbed up the box, and got as far as centre stage, where she found Martin comforting a weeping Marie.

'Happens every time,' he grinned, while he patted Marie's back soothingly. 'She's a tough auld boot until it's all over.'

'Auld boot, my eye, you auld bollocks,' Marie sobbed, and then hugged Jane, box and all. 'You're only a dote, you are, and the best of luck to you, all the best.' She sniffled, and Martin handed her a handkerchief. 'And I pray to God you'll take my advice and not waste that talent sitting behind a desk the rest of your life. I want to see you – see you back here – to work together again – oh, Martin!' she wailed, and fled the building.

Martin planted a kiss on Jane's cheek, and then patted it. 'You're a wonderful actress, Jane. But you know that. Take the risk.' He looked over to where Shay was whispering with Darren. 'Every risk that comes your way. You know,' he mused, as he turned to her again, and picked up his carryall and umbrella, 'The two of yees remind me of Marie and I. But that's a story for another time.' He winked and went off to comfort his wife.

Cathleen came up to her and took the box. 'Never mind that, let the lads see to it,' and she unceremoniously thrust it into the arms of one of Declan's goth friends, commandeered to help out for the afternoon. 'C'mere to me. Isn't life grand? What if you hadn't come into BT and saved me that day? I might still be stuck behind that counter!' They laughed, and hugged. I have had more hugs today than I have had in ten years, thought Jane.

'So what's next for you, Caz?'

'I've applied for this assistant director's yoke at the

Abbey. The pay is crap, but the connections, the networking . . .'

Jane laughed. 'You have become positively American.'

'Ah sure, you may find me on your doorstep one day, begging for a job in your fancy television station.'

'Please come visit. Any time. Once I have a place to live in, that is.' Jane's gut cringed at the thought, but she pasted on a bright smile.

'Jesus, you'll be all right, won't ya?' Cathleen stroked Jane's arm.

'Darren's going off to London to take care of Shay's valuables, so I'll be at his for about a week. Don't worry,' she said. 'I'll be grand.'

Another quick hug, and Cathleen was down the aisle ordering the boys around.

She stood and looked around the space one last time. She breathed steadily through her nose, willing her heart to stop racing, and turned to smile at Darren and Shay.

'Will we go for a few jars?' she proposed.

'I've to prepare for my new digs, I'm afraid,' said Shay, slipping the little piece of paper Darren had given him into his pocket. 'So I'll say my goodbyes now.'

'We were going to have a meal at the cottage—' Jane offered.

'Bad night for me; can't do it,' Shay shrugged.

'Well, give us a bell, maybe, my flight's at two.' She could have bitten off her own tongue at the sound of her plaintive voice.

'Give us a hug!' Shay boomed, and he embraced her in a crushing bear hug which left her breathless.

He allowed himself one touch of his cheek to her hair, and then stepped back, lifting the last box. 'Have a safe journey.'

'Good luck,' she called to his back, bereft. 'Don't look at me like that,' she snapped at Darren.

He rearranged his sympathetic gaze into something more neutral. 'OK, honey. Will we go? How about that jar?'

Jane took a deep breath and nodded. 'I'll be right behind you,' she said, her face blank, and soon she was alone on the stage.

It's time to go, Janie. Once final look, then ... onward. Through sheer force of will, she blinked away the dampness in her eyes.

'What's up with yer one?' Niall asked as he, Miranda, and Darren watched her say her goodbyes to Jackie outside the Departures terminal at Dublin Airport.

'That', said Darren, 'has been this year's burning question.'

'You mind yerself, now, and have a safe journey back to New York,' Jackie admonished. 'And when you come back, ring me the day before, and I'll come to collect ya.'

'Thanks, Jackie.' Jane impulsively hugged him.

'Now, now, you'll be back, so you will, sure you've got himself wrapped around yer little finger.'

Jane smiled, patted Jackie once on the arm, and slung her carry-on bag over her shoulder.

Himself hadn't even bothered to ring to say goodbye.

It just goes to show me I was right, Jane thought, and she joined her friends.

The plonker.

She swept by her three friends and pushed her luggage cart into the building with a vengeance.

'Do you see what I mean? She's all prickly, like,' Niall said, and Darren nodded knowingly.

'When she's this upset, she gets very ... brusque,' Darren offered, as they cautiously made their way into the airport in her wake.

'Can she not have a bit of a cry and let it out?' Niall wondered, and Miranda shook her head.

'Jane doesn't cry,' she explained, and they waited while she checked in at Aer Lingus, and Darren at British Airways.

Miranda admired the sparkling ring on her left hand,

and smiled up at Niall. 'People are going to start pestering us about a date,' she said.

'Already?' Niall exclaimed, and it took a few seconds for Miranda to see that he wasn't joking.

'Oh, just wait,' she said.

'Shay bought me a first-class ticket!' Darren loved first class. 'They put me on an earlier flight, I've only got half an hour. Will we get one last cuppa?'

Jane joined them, her ticket clutched in her hand. 'If I never see a cup of tea again, it'll be too soon.' Nevertheless, she marched off for the escalators that led to the food court.

Niall rolled his eyes. 'C'mere, I'll leave you to say your goodbyes. I'll go out to the car, all right?' He kissed Miranda, shook Darren's hand, and called 'Safe journey!' to Jane's ascending back.

'I can't wait to hear all about the wedding plans,' Darren called to him, and Miranda saw his wince from across the departures hall. She laughed, slipped her arm through Darren's, and headed for the escalator.

Jane defiantly drank a cup of coffee and stared at the monitor, watching her flight creep up the list, and vaguely listened to Darren quiz Miranda about her wedding plans.

'We don't even have a date yet, Dar,' Miranda said, nodding meaningfully in Jane's direction. 'I hope you have a good time in London.'

'I hope I pick up a client or two. Alastair' – he felt his heart skip a beat, again – 'seems very well connected. I'll write the whole thing off, regardless.'

Miranda smiled into her tea. 'Alastair seems to be a lot of things. One of them was, hmm, how will I describe it, "delighted" that he wouldn't miss seeing you.'

She turned to Jane. 'Alastair is one of Niall's cousins.'

'Imagine that.'

'And he's lovely and tall and he has black hair like Niall, and . . . blue eyes? No . . .'

'Grey,' said Darren, against his better judgement.

'Beautiful grey eyes, and tons of lashes.' Miranda stared off, casual-like. 'He and Darren got on so well . . .'

Jane's eyes scanned the monitor, and she shrugged dismissively.

They sat in silence, and Jane twisted the plastic stirrer in her hands until it snapped.

'Want to talk?' Darren asked.

'About?' Jane looked over at him coolly.

Miranda sighed gustily. 'She's back on form, Dar. No point in asking her if she's "OK", she'll just snap your head off.'

'I am "OK",' Jane snapped. 'I'm "fine". I'm "wonder-ful". I'm . . .' She stilled, and rubbed a hand against her throat, felt her breath catch, and catch again, and again, blinked once, twice, and burst out, 'He didn't even ring me! He couldn't even make time in his suddenly busy schedule to see me off! Couldn't even come for a jar! Men! What are they like? Eejit! Wanker! Begging me to come on board, and I come on board, and I work my tail off, and I *save* his entire production, and he wouldn't be doing some acting degree if it wasn't for me, and one minute it's all roses and shagging tulips and the next it's "Afraid I can't, must move into me flat" rubbishy bullshit!'

Darren and Miranda exchanged a glance – 'How dare he, how dare he court me and then – and then act like it was nothing, like I don't have *feelings*, like my feelings can't be *hurt*! I have feelings! I have feelings! And it's all his fault, making me get up there and want to act again, the bollocks, it's all his fault, and what, he can't even lift the bloody *phone*!' She shook her head in disbelief, and snapped the handle off her mug. Darren reached over and gently took it from her hand.

'We didn't realise that you felt this way, honey,' he said gently, and Miranda was grateful for his soothing presence.

'I can't believe he didn't come to see me off,' Jane muttered, taking a cigarette out of her pack and shredding it.

Miranda looked helplessly at Darren, and he shook his head. 'It's all going to be OK, Janie,' he said, taking what was left of the cigarette out of her hand.

'I – I was starting to – he was – I thought this might be different.' She looked up at her friends, who, for the first time in years, saw sheer vulnerability in her eyes. Darren looked stunned, and Miranda took over.

'Well, he's certainly different,' Miranda joked softly, and brushed Jane's hair out of her eyes. 'And he's crazy about you.'

Jane shrugged. 'Some guy. Just some guy. I only slept with twice, for God's sake. Snogged him. So what?' She decimated another cigarette.

Miranda sighed. 'He meant a lot to you, didn't he, at the end of the day?'

Jane shook her head violently, and the 'no' turned into a 'yes', a faltering 'yes'.

'It doesn't have to be this hard, does it?' she begged Miranda.

'Yes and no,' she replied. 'And that's what makes it so special.'

A generic female voice called Darren's flight. He cleared his throat. 'Uh, time to go. Walk me to the x-ray?'

Jane rose, nodded, and stopped as her friends made to move on.

'I –' she gulped, and went on. 'I could have fallen in love with him, you know.'

Miranda nodded. 'I know.'

They linked arms, and headed downstairs.

Jane wandered aimlessly through duty free. She gazed fondly upon all the touristy tat that was for sale, and unable to look without buying, she ended up with a box of Butler's chocolates and a shamrock-covered teapot.

Clutching her plastic bag, she staggered past the displays of salmon and sausages and Aran jumpers and found her way to her gate.

In a haze, she boarded, the cheerful Irish flight attendants pointing her to her seat. The flight was empty, and Jane had two seats to herself by a window. She gazed out at the Dublin mountains, misty in the distance, and watched as they began to blur . . .

'No!' she told herself sternly, and decided to open the package that Naomi had given her.

The entire company had signed the card, and Jane stopped herself before a sniffle could start. She unwrapped the package – it was a photograph. Of herself and Shay. The final moment of the play, their final moment, together, the smile they had exchanged nightly just before their crowd-pleasing kiss. She saw her face, alight with joy, his smile glowing with promise . . .

When the first tear dropped into her lap, she wiped at her face, incredulous. The second and third soon followed, encouraging their usually reticent kin to follow and pour down her cheeks. The first sob took Jane completely by surprise, and she looked around, panicked, not wanting to make a fool of herself . . . and when the next sob escaped, she couldn't have cared less. Her entire body heaved with the tears, and she pulled her in-flight blanket over her head, and leaned against the body of the plane.

She pulled it down again as the jet began to taxi, to pick up speed, became airborne, and she strained to see out the window, wiping the seemingly endless flood of tears out of her eyes, to get a last look at Ireland, at a place where she'd never wanted to be, a place that had allowed her to be . . . herself.

The plane banked, and turned its back on Dublin, the tears rolled down, and Jane gave up.

If this was going to be a crying jag, she'd make it a good one.

'I might have fallen in love with you . . . you bollocks!'
she wept, and pulled the blanket back over her head.

She cried.

And cried.

All the way home.

32

June, and midtown Manhattan was burning in an early summer heat wave, the blue sky outside the plate-glass windows of Fox's head office as bright as if it had been a stage set.

Jane stood with her back to the receptionist's desk, her briefcase held firmly in her hand, her manicure flawless, her suit the height of fashion. An Irish designer, she'd say, if asked – picked it up while I was over there, producing a show. Theatre, yes, she'd nod, and smile, ignoring the indulgent looks of Fox's bigwigs. Slumming? they'd imply, and Jane would smile enigmatically and sign her contract.

They'd been in negotiations for weeks, her agent increasingly annoyed with Jane's provisos and require-ments. She shook her head, and eyed the receptionist beadily again. Making her wait, were they?

Assholes.

She refused to pace. She refused to sit. She just wanted to get this over with and get on with her life.

She'd been back for three weeks and two days. She'd received emails from all her new friends – well, most of them, and Jane refused to let the thought of Shay tumble around in her brainpan.

Eejit.

The contract was loaded with perks, and privileges,

and had plenty of room for growth. It was exactly what she'd always wanted.

Wasn't it?

Marie and Martin had got starring roles in *Juno and the Paycock*, and following its Dublin run, the production would tour the world – she'd be seeing them in September at Lincoln Center. Naomi was doing well at the Gate, and Cathleen had got into her assistant director's programme.

Jane was delighted for them all.

Wasn't she? So why did she feel this longing, this slight envy? She had everything she wanted, just the way she wanted it. Hadn't she?

'Mr Phillips will see you now,' the receptionist called, and Jane turned and made her way to the boardroom.

Five minutes later, she punched the 'down' button on the elevator. What had she just *done*? A bell dinged and blindly she turned to the opening doors – and walked straight into Shay. She stared at him, stunned.

'Howya,' he said.

'You're dressed as a pirate.' She stared up at his grinning face.

'Niall didn't get his hands on this to burn it.'

She shook her head, blinked. Nope, he was still there . . . complete with feathered friend.

'What are you doing here?' she demanded, and let her heart flip and flop to its own content.

'I came to save you,' he exclaimed mellifluously. The receptionist considered calling security.

'Pirates *kidnap* people,' Jane corrected. Are we really having this conversation? she thought.

The bell dinged, and the 'down' light winked.

'And anyway, I saved myself.' With that, she strode into the elevator.

*

They stood on the pavement, and crowds of people flowed by them, not sparing Shay a second glance. *Gas!* he thought, and decided not to remove his eye patch. Jane did it for him.

They studied each other, and Jane didn't know whether to laugh or kill him.

'So . . . didja miss me?' he asked cheekily.

'You—'

'Plonker, eejit, bollocks, yeah, yeah, are you not going to kiss me?'

'No.' Jane headed off downtown. And was beginning to feel like she needn't doubt he'd be right behind her.

'I missed you,' he offered, jogging along. Had she always walked this fast? He tore after her as she crossed against the light, and narrowly avoided getting flattened by a feral pack of bicycle messengers.

'Jesus, Jane, I missed you every— would you ever slow down, Jane!' He grabbed her arm, and pulled her out of what he was beginning to perceive as an ocean of humanity, endlessly rolling forward.

'What?'

'What? Are you joking me? Here I am, big as life, after we've been apart for ages, after I've upped stakes to be here with you—'

'*What?*' Jane stood, and finally understood what it meant to be 'gobsmacked'.

Shay spread his arms as if to embrace her and all of Forty-eighth Street. 'I've moved to New York. To be with you.'

'And I was supposed to what, intuit that? As if every Irishman who emigrates comes in costume?' Her heart was pounding enough to break a rib.

'I'm telling you now, aren't I?' This wasn't going according to plan.

'I am so pissed off at you!' she shouted, inspiring a round of supportive applause from a group of women out smoking in front of their building. Shay laughed, and bowed to them, which inspired a hearty round of booing.

'I'm going to like it here – everyone's mad!'

'You let me go without a word,' Jane said hoarsely. 'You let me leave thinking that I'd imagined the whole thing—' Her voice broke, and *dammit*—

'Ah, Jane, don't cry, please. I'm an eejit, but I didn't want to say anything, in case I had to have an alternative plan.'

'Do you have any plan at all?' Jane demanded, and quickly slammed on her sunglasses.

'I've applied to Juilliard, and Columbia, and NYU, and the Actors' Studio,' he said proudly. 'I've got auditions all next week.'

'Oh.' Jane felt oddly disappointed.

'But that's just a sideline, a bit of a nixer, like,' he went on, 'as the only reason that I'm here is to continue courting you.'

She'd give him a break soon, but not right away. 'Oh?'

He nodded. 'Got it all mapped out. Darren – sound man, if it wasn't for him, I would never have found you – Dar gave me a list of all your favourite restaurants, and movie theatres, and what not, so I've only to consult the list for ideas.' He stroked her cheek. 'I reckon we'll be about halfway through it, and you'll give up and agree to be my girlfriend.'

'Girlfriend,' Jane sneered.

'Partner?' he murmured, and Jane blushed. 'Will you ever give me a kiss, I'm standing here and dying, Jane.'

'I'm still mad at you.' And she headed downtown again.

He'd have to lay off the cigarettes if he wanted to keep pace with her. 'Tell me what to do.'

She stopped again. This was a moment that had potential. She tipped her shades back, and Shay quailed at the look in her eye.

She was going to make him pay. It would be worth it.

'I'm afraid I'll have to get back to you on that, I'm

extremely busy, so give me a number I can reach you at, and we'll talk.'

'Em . . .' He grimaced. 'I reckon you're busy with your flash new job.'

Jane scuffed the pavement with the toe of her Manolos. 'I, uh, didn't sign the contract.' She huffed out a breath. 'I didn't take the job. I couldn't.'

Shay swept her up in his arms and spun her around and around, to the tune of catcalls from nearby construction workers. 'Hey, hey!' Shay called to them, and they gave him the thumbs up. Jane wriggled out of his embrace.

'And . . .' he asked.

'And?' She shrugged.

'You didn't sign the contract because . . .?'

'BecauseIgotanactingagent,' she mumbled.

'Excuse me? Didn't quite catch that –'

'I got an agent, an acting agent; William Morris, OK?' She struggled not to beam at him – and lost.

'Jesus, no flies on you,' he whistled admiringly. 'I'd better get into a course, you'll leave me in the dust.'

'I doubt it. Something tells me you're going to integrate just fine.'

They stood in silence – or rather, they stood, not talking. New York is never silent. A swirl of noise surrounded them as taxis honked and women laughed and men shouted into their cell phones. Surrounded by activity, they found a still point to stand and just be.

'I was so mad at you,' Jane whispered.

'I wanted to surprise you,' he said lamely.

'I hate surprises,' she shot back.

'I'll keep that in mind.'

'Youhurtmyfeelings,' she mumbled in a rush.

'Hmmm?' Shay urged.

'You. Hurt. My. Feelings.' There, she'd said it. And it looked like he was sorry for it. That was good enough.

'Will you let me kiss ya now, Jane?'

She started walking again, heading west. 'So where are you staying?'

He consulted the paper, covered in the notes he'd taken down from Darren. 'Em, Hell's Kitchen? You know it?'

She nodded. 'Very well.' She'd lucked into a one-bedroom – a one-bedroom! – on Forty-fifth and Ninth.

'In the mid-Forties, is that what you say? And the Ninth Road.'

'Avenue. It's avenue, not—' She stopped dead in her tracks in the middle of Broadway. 'You chancer.'

He smiled winningly at her as he led her to the kerb. 'It's a grand idea altogether – we can make up for lost time.'

'You are determined to – whaddyacallit – wind me up, aren't you?'

'Please kiss me, Jane, I'm dying.'

'Take off that damn parrot.'

Under the bland stare of the latest Calvin Klein underwear model, under the rush of neon that blinked continuously day and night, on the traffic island in the middle of Broadway, Jane kissed him. And he kissed her back.

'You'll need to get some kind of job, under the table, or something, get out there, meet people, keep busy.' She started to jog across Seventh Avenue, and reached back to grab his hand.

They walked hand in hand past the Belasco Theatre. She spared a glance at their intertwined fingers. It really wasn't that tiresome after all.

'I might, but I don't need to work, not for a while. Darren got me a fortune for that cabbagey stuff and some of the other bits.' He stopped her again. 'So I'm all yours – for as long as you want me.'

Jane took a deep breath. 'OK,' she said simply, and their second New York kiss took place under the marquee of the Music Box Theatre.

Shay tilted back his head and admired the larger-than-life photographs of the actors who were starring in the current show. 'That'll be us someday.'

Jane nodded. 'Yes. It will be.'

They walked on.

'So are you legal, or what?' It had only just occurred to her.

Shay cringed. 'I will be when I get a place on one of these courses.'

'And what if you don't?' She was already getting used to having him around.

'Ah, well, you can always marry me,' Shay said casually.

'*What?*' Jane exploded. 'Don't be ridiculous.'

'It's just an idea. Don't get your knickers in a twist.' He paused. 'So will we?'

'No,' said Jane, a small smile on her lips.

Shay slid her sunglasses down to the tip of her nose, and smiled into her eyes. 'I've heard that before,' he said.

'What are you like?' She laughed, and they ran across the avenue, hand in hand, towards home.